THE PRISONER IN THE MASK

DENNIS WHEATLEY

DENNIS WHEATLEY

THE PRISONER
IN THE MASK

Frontispiece Portrait by
MARK GERSON

Original Illustrations by
TONY BENYON

Distributed by
HERON BOOKS

Published by arrangement with
Hutchinson and Co. (Publishers) Ltd.

© 1957, Brook-Richleau Ltd.
© 1972, Illustrations, Edito-Service S.A., Geneva

3933

CONTENTS

FIRST GLIMPSE OF THE FUTURE DUKE DE RICHLEAU

UTSIDE the snow lay a foot deep on the ground and to all appearances the great house was fast in the grip of the Russian winter. But tomorrow a score of moujiks would again sweep clean the paths about it and clear the fallen branches from the sleigh track that led through the larch woods to the little town of Jvanets.

A full moon in a cloudless sky made the frozen scene almost as bright as day. To the east the plain stretched unbroken towards the limitless grain-fields of the Ukraine, to the north sprawled two acres or more of stables and farm buildings, to the south there were dark forests, and to the west a succession of terraces dropped down to the broad ice-bound waters of the Pruth.

In those days—the early 1890's—the river formed the south-western frontier of the Czar Alexander III's vast dominions. Across it lay the Burkovina, then part of Rumania, and the Carpathian mountains, beyond which stretched the plains of Hungary, while farther away to the north there jutted out the bulge of Austrian Poland. Kiev, Bucharest, Warsaw, Odessa and Budapest all lay within a radius of 400 miles; so although the house stood on Russian soil it was in the very heart of Central Europe.

It was a rambling fifty-room mansion, and had been built over a hundred years earlier by a brave and handsome Hetman Plackoff, whose forebears had ruled as autocrats in those parts for many genera-tions. Catherine the Great in enlarging her Empire had annexed his territories, but he had served the beautiful and amorous Empress well in more ways than one; so she had restored his lands, used her good taste to help him to plan and furnish this fine country seat, and had made his sons pages at her glittering court.

But for a generation past there had no longer been a Prince Plackoff in the service of the Czars. The last had left only a daughter and she had married a French nobleman of equally illustrious lineage, the ninth Duc de Richleau. Although his family had long since regained the fortune they lost during the Revolution, the present Duke preferred life in Russia, as he could live there still in feudal state. In consequence, for many years they had made their home at Jvanets, leaving it only now and then for a few months to plunge again into the social whirl of the great capitals.

The loss of his wife in '88 had been a great blow to him, but after a while he had resumed his normal activities, and among them was lavish entertaining. At Jvanets he could offer his guests some of the best shooting in South Russia, and friends of many nationalities willingly travelled great distances to participate in the famous winter drives organized by his Chief Verderer for the hunting of bear, wolf and boar. But on this January night of 1894 his house-party was a small one and, purely by chance, almost entirely French.

In the main rooms of the house there was no hint of the bitter cold outside. Heavy curtains of rich brocade were drawn across the tall double windows and liveried footmen kept well supplied with logs the blazing fires on the big open hearths.

Dinner had run its usual eight courses and when the ladies had left the room the men lingered for a while over their Tokay and Madeira. Now gathered at one end of the table they made a more picturesque group than would have such a party at the present day, for it was an age in which individuality of attire was still permitted.

De Richleau, now in his forty-sixth year, was wearing a traditional Russian costume; a high-necked, short-skirted blouse of figured black brocade, tightly belted at the waist and trimmed with sable. He was of medium height, broad-shouldered and carried himself very upright. His cheeks were rosy, his nose aquiline and his dark hair was turning grey. In the same fashion as the Russian Grand Dukes he had a square beard neatly parted in the centre and brushed outward, beneath an upturned moustache.

His son, Armand, who carried his second title, Count de Quesnoy, was wearing what would now be called a smoking jacket, of deep blue velvet with arabesques of braid on its satin lapels. Young Prince Igor Préobajenskoi, the only Russian present, was in the white and gold uniform of the Imperial Guard and one of the three French guests,

2

General the Marquis de Galliffet, had on a semi-military mess-jacket designed by himself. The other two wore the loose-fitting fore-runners of modern tails with stiff, bulging white shirt-fronts and wide open collars, the points of which stuck up almost to their ears. The seventh member of the party, and the oldest, was the silver-haired Abbé Nodier. He acted as chaplain to the household but was also a valued friend of the family, for he had once been the Duke's tutor and was now tutor to the eighteen-year-old Count.

Next in age to him was the General, then sixty-two and France's most distinguished soldier. He was clean-shaven except for a sweeping cavalry moustache and wore his white hair *en brosse*, like a Prussian. He had served at the siege of Sevastopol, in Italy, Algeria and Mexico. Above all he had won imperishable glory in the Franco-Prussian war at the disastrous battle of Sedan. As Brigadier commanding the 3rd Chasseurs d'Afrique he had led them in the charge again and again, and towards the end, when his Divisional Commander had asked if he could help protect the flying infantry from massacre, he had replied: '*Mon Général*, we shall continue to charge until either there are none of us left or we have no horses left upon which to charge.'

Beside him sat Gabriel Syveton, a heavy-faced man in his early forties. His sensual mouth was partly hidden by a drooping fair moustache, but he had a broad forehead and his pale blue eyes held a hard intelligence. He had been a Professor at the Sorbonne until a few years back when his father died and left him a considerable fortune, amassed at an iron foundry in Lens. He had then devoted himself to politics and was immensely ambitious both to become in time a Minister, and also socially. His first wife had died in giving birth to an only son, and he had since married again a young girl whose family were of the English aristocracy. Until recently his bourgeois extraction had debarred him from such company as he was enjoying at present, and he had been unknown to the Duke until the third French guest had asked if he might bring him and his wife to Jvanets.

His sponsor was the Vicomte de Camargue, who was in his middle thirties but looked considerably more as, although his mutton-chop whiskers flourished, he had become prematurely bald. He was very tall, stooped slightly and spoke with a marked lisp.

The party was completed by Prince Igor and the Duke's son. The

Prince was a nephew of de Richleau's and there only because, having recently married, he had been asked to bring his wife on a formal visit. He was twenty-two, had a mop of dark curls and was handsome in a slightly Tartar way; but few women would have given him a second look once their glance had fallen on his cousin.

Although the Count de Quesnoy was barely eighteen he was already within an inch of the five feet eleven that he was finally to attain and he showed no trace of the gaucherie frequently associated with his age. His hair was dark and slightly wavy, his forehead broad, his face oval, with a rather thin but well-modelled mouth, and a pointed chin that showed great determination. He had inherited his father's aquiline nose, but his eyes came from his mother. They were grey, flecked with tiny spots of yellow. At times they could flash with piercing brilliance and, although he was not yet fully conscious of it, they held hypnotic power. Above them a pair of "devil's eyebrows" tapered up towards his temples.

When the men had finished their wine they made a dutiful appearance in the drawing-room of the Countess Olga Plackoff, a widowed cousin by marriage of the Duke's who, since his wife's death, had kept house for him.

There was a little music, of a quite high standard for amateurs, mild clapping and well-turned compliments. The Duke enjoyed a game of backgammon with the Vicomtesse de Camargue, and his son manœuvred Angela Syveton into the adjacent conservatory for half an hour's tête-à-tête, while the rest of the party held a *conversazione* round the blazing fire.

As the French clock on the marble mantelpiece chimed eleven, the Countess Olga caught the eye of the Marquise de Galliffet. Rising, the ladies lifted their voluminous skirts a trifle with their left hands, extended their right hands for the gentlemen to kiss in turn, then with rustling trains and gently swaying bustles swept from the room on their way to bed.

Following them out, de Richleau bowed them away up the wide staircase, then led the men across the hall to his smoking-room. Such sanctums, where in polite society the male addiction to the pestiferous herb was then alone permitted, were usually gloomy, sunless parlours in the region of the gun-room and back stairs; but the Duke was a great lover of fine cigars and smoked half a dozen daily, so he had overruled his wife's objections and used for the purpose the fine apartment in which he dealt with his correspondence.

It was broad and lofty so that the oil lamps on the writing table and on two fluted columns made a pool of warm light only in its centre. The pictures on the walls were shrouded in deep shadow and the ornately-scrolled and gilded ceiling could be glimpsed only when a log thrown on the fire made it burst into a sudden blaze.

The men settled themselves on the long sofas and in deep arm-chairs. As Armand poured drinks for them at a side table he knew that they would soon be immersed in French politics, as had been the case every night during the stay of the three French guests. Politics bored him at any time and tonight he meant to make an excuse as soon as he decently could to slip away—but not to his own bed. His thoughts were already busy with the delights he would experience if he could succeed in seducing Syveton's lovely young wife.

CHAPTER II

BEDROOM SCENE

NGELA SYVETON lay wide awake in the broad four-poster bed. The big room was not quite in darkness, but the gentle glow of a night-light on the bedside table did little more than show the outline of her profile.

It was a good one; forehead not too deep, straight nose, full lips and slightly jutting chin. Seen full face her forehead was broad, her eyebrows well arched and her jaw-line square almost to the point of truculence, but the suggestion of obstinacy was offset by a generous mouth and a pair of big pansy-brown eyes which, given even the smallest reason, became gay with laughter.

Yet Angela had not much to laugh about these days. She was English by birth, only nineteen years old, and had been married for six months to a Frenchman more than twice her age whom she already detested.

From the worldly point of view her marriage had been considered extremely satisfactory. Her father was the sixth son of a not particularly wealthy Earl and he had married the youngest daughter of a naval Captain; so although he had done quite well in the Diplomatic Service, and two years earlier become Councillor at the British Embassy in Paris, they were far from rich.

Angela was the eldest of three sisters, so when Gabriel Syveton had shown an interest in her he had met with no discouragement from her parents. On the contrary, it had been tactfully pointed out to her that, although Syveton was a middle-aged widower with a son of eleven, and came from a family of provincial industrialists, he was very rich and spent his money lavishly; that she could, if she chose, become the mistress of his fine house overlooking the Parc Monceau; that he could give her an equipage which would rival the best for driving in the Bois, and that instead of having her clothes made by a "little woman" she would be able to buy the most lovely creations of Worth and Paquin. It should be added that, while no pressure whatever had been used,

6

she had been given clearly to understand that the sooner she was "happily settled" the better the chances would be of her sisters, who were plainer than herself, attracting suitable husbands.

In accordance with the conventions of the day, Angela had never been left alone with her wealthy suitor for more than a few minutes at a time; so she had had little chance to form an accurate estimate of his character. His conversation, although given rather over-much to French politics, was often amusing, he treated her with the greatest politeness, and showered her with expensive flowers, huge boxes of chocolates and such other gifts as etiquette permitted. The parties he gave, ostensibly for her family but, as she knew, for her, were enough to turn any young girl's head, and while she was not in the least attracted to him, she could not help feeling flattered and well disposed towards him on account of all these attentions.

Like many another well-bred maiden of the nineties, she had at length been persuaded to put aside dreams of handsome young officers, with their way still to make, for a husband as old as her father who could give her a fine establishment. She had got her mansion, her retinue of servants, her carriage with the spanking greys, jewels, furs and furbelows; but she had also got Gabriel Syveton. And she knew now that her mother had taken advantage of her ignorance about what really mattered in life to betray her wickedly and shamefully.

Angela had believed that marriage consisted of a loyal partnership in which husband and wife placed one another's interests before anyone else's in either sickness or health, and that as affection grew between the partners kisses were exchanged with the same spontaneous enthusiasm as was customary between well-loved members of one's own family. When she arrived on the night of her wedding at a small château that had been lent to them for the honeymoon she had not the faintest conception of what was about to happen to her.

How she had managed to survive that first fortnight she could not now imagine. Night after night Syveton had forced her to submit to what she could think of only as the most abominable and humiliating degradation. She had at first believed him mad, then disgust had led her to making a fierce resistance; but that had seemed to excite him all the more. His awkward attempts to soothe and persuade her had been succeeded by an animal glare in his pale blue eyes and time and again, with his great strength, he easily overcame her.

7

On her return to Paris, shyly and in hesitant phrases she had questioned her mother; only to be told quite casually, 'Men are like that, my dear; but it is nothing to make a fuss about, and it is your duty as a wife to submit. Some women, I am told, even come in time to derive pleasure from it.' Her mother had then gone on to enlighten her about babies not really being brought by doctors in little black bags, but arriving in the same way as kittens.

This information had in no way decreased the loathing with which Angela had come to regard her husband and, as she was a perfectly healthy young woman, it was her mental attitude which continued to make her frigid during his embraces. Resentful but unable to alter matters he had, after a couple of months, installed a pretty little thing who worked in a flower shop as the successor of numerous other girls under twenty, in an apartment which he had long rented for that purpose. But from time to time, goaded by the belief that he might yet bring his beautiful young wife to warm and pulsing life, he sat up drinking till a late hour, then made brutal attempts to do so.

Never knowing when one of these assaults might occur, Angela often lay awake for hours sick with apprehension, but now, for once, as she gazed up into the deep shadows of the four-poster's canopy she was not thinking of Gabriel Syveton.

Instead Armand de Quesnoy filled her thoughts and, as the house-party was breaking up next day, tears welled into her brown eyes at the realization that she might never see him again after she left Jvanets the following morning. From the day of her arrival he had constituted himself her cavalier, and they had spent many happy hours together: the only happy hours she had known since her wedding.

Convention permitted far more liberty to young wives than to unmarried girls; in fact it was fully accepted as a part of social life that the former should openly carry on flirtations and, although Angela had not yet realized it, in loveless unions like her own it was not at all unusual for girls of her class to begin taking lovers within a few months of their marriage. Most husbands had their mistresses, and by tacit understanding turned a blind eye to their wives' affaires; but even those who were possessive would have been thought churlish had they shown resentment at their wives receiving the most gallant attentions from other men who were socially their equals.

In consequence no member of the house-party had thought it in the least reprehensible that Armand should seek Angela out at every opportunity and frequently take her off on his own. Had the Count been an older man Syveton, still being a prey to his unrequited physical passion, might have privately forbidden her to receive Armand's attentions except in public, but regarding it only as a boy and girl affair, he had done no more than embarrass her a few times by chaffing her about her conquest.

As far as Angela was concerned, he was quite right. She had been too young to do more than dream of knights-errant before leaving her home in Gloucestershire, too carefully chaperoned while living in Paris with her parents to get further than having a preference for some dancing partners over others, and, since her marriage, much too miserable to take notice of the attentions paid her by various men who came to lunch or dine at her house; so this was the first time that she had fallen in love, and her emotions were similar to those of a schoolgirl who has become hopelessly enamoured of a married man.

The way Armand carried his handsome head, the sight of him on a mettlesome horse, the sound of his voice when he lowered it a little to pay her some compliment, all made her pulses quicken alarmingly; and each time, morning and night, that he formally kissed her hand she felt a tremor run through the very depths of her being. Yet, with every ounce of will-power that she could muster she strove to conceal her feelings because, to her, the fact that she hated her husband did not make them any the less guilty ones, and she knew only too well that no happiness could come to either herself or Armand should she encourage him.

Nevertheless her will had not proved strong enough to resist the temptation of enjoying his company. With gay nonchalance he always swept aside such flimsy excuses as "letters to write" and insisted on taking her for a sleigh drive into Jvanets, visits to the hot-houses or down to the frozen river. A wide space there was kept swept clear of snow so that the house party could skate, and the ladies be pushed round in small sleighs upon it. One sleigh was fashioned like a swan, and nearly every afternoon Angela, wrapped in warm furs, had nestled in it, her heart beating furiously as Armand thrust it before him across the ice as swiftly as a galloping horse, slowing down only to bend forward and whisper sweet nonsense in her ear.

9

That he returned her unspoken love she had no doubt at all, and each night she had become more bitterly conscious of her own tragedy. De Quesnoy was a great "parti"—far greater than a man like Syveton could ever be; so had she only met the Count seven months ago her parents would have been overjoyed when he had asked for her hand, as she was confident he would have done. Since he was still so young they might have been made to wait a few years, but what greater bliss could there be than that of being engaged to him?

Then marriage. He would want an heir, of course, to succeed to his ancient titles, and she, too, would like children—if they were his; so she would have put as cheerful a face as possible on those humiliating preliminaries. Perhaps with a man whom one loved it would not prove humiliating at all. In any case it was unthinkable that Armand would ever regard her as did Syveton—to be taken in the dark like an animal for his brutal selfish pleasure. Armand was so gentle and so unspoiled. Although he looked a man he was, in years, still hardly more than a boy. He was, of course, more worldly-wise than herself, but, she supposed, as physically innocent as she had been six months ago. For the first few months of marriage he would have asked no more than she could give willingly—to sit for hours embraced, cheek pressed to cheek, with now and then a sweet lingering kiss.

But such bliss was not for her. He had come into her life half a year too late. She had not even the hope that this brief idyll might be repeated. Perhaps, though, that was just as well. She recalled her concession that he might call her by her Christian name when they were alone together, the tremulous half-avowals that she had made him, and the promise he had wrung from her that on her return to Paris she would send him a photograph of herself; and how he had vowed that he would have it framed in a jewelled shrine with doors of beaten gold that locked, so that only he could gaze upon it.

Should they be thrown together for any length of time, there would be the awful risk that she might be carried away, admit that she loved him, and let him kiss her. That she did not love her husband would be no excuse for being disloyal to him. Even though she had not fully understood what she was doing when she took her marriage vows she must keep them. They had been made before God, so were between Him and her, and to dishonour them would be to rob herself of the last thing she could call her own. It was better by far that this sweet and lovely interlude should be over now and, unmarred by any sense of guilt, could long be held as her most treasured memory.

Suddenly her thoughts of Armand were cut off as sharply as if a shutter had been pulled down between her and a lighted window. She had caught the sound of a door opening at the far end of the room. The yard-wide draught curtains at the head of the bed hid the door from her view; but she knew that it could only be her husband coming to bed, and she had not expected him for a long time yet.

It was some while now since he had made any demands of her, so each night it became more likely that he would again do so. Her throat went dry with apprehension and the nausea she always felt at his approach rose in her. Swiftly she closed her eyes, feigned sleep, and prayed silently that he would refrain from rousing her, as had proved the case for the past week.

His footsteps sounded softer than usual, and as he passed round the end of the bed she missed the light from his candle, seen on other nights as a red glow through her closed eyelids. She guessed that the flame had been blown out by the sudden draught as he opened the door, for the room was kept almost too warm by a big porcelain stove, whereas the passage was always chilly. He would relight it from the night-light, then go into his dressing-room, which would at least mean another ten minutes' respite.

He did not do as she expected. She had not had time to turn over and pull the bed-clothes up over her chin before the rustle of the sheets would have told him that she was awake; so she was still lying on her back, and she knew instinctively that he was now standing beside the bed staring down into her face.

'Angela.' The word was only breathed and next second a pair of lips were pressed firmly on her own.

For a moment she lay absolutely still, doubting the evidence of her senses. That whisper had been in Armand's voice and the kiss was unlike any her husband had ever given her. Yet Armand would never have come to her in her bedroom at night, He would not dare. But . . . but he might! Those grey eyes of his that sent tremors through her had told her a dozen times that, young as he was, he was the type of man who would dare anything.

Another heart-beat and her last doubts were dissipated. Thrusting one hand under her back and sliding the other beneath her head he lifted her a little into his embrace. His voice came again. 'Angela, my sweet! Oh Angela, how I have longed for this moment.' Then once more his lips closed on hers.

Wrenching her mouth away she gasped: 'Armand! Oh, Armand; you must have gone mad to behave like this.'

'I am no madder, darling, than Romeo was for Juliet.'

Angela's mind was reeling. At those whispered words she could have swooned with joy; yet, somehow, she found the resolution to cry: 'Let me go! Let me go!' and to attempt to thrust him from her.

'Softly, beloved, softly,' he cautioned her in a firmer voice. 'It might prove awkward if someone heard us talking.' But he relaxed his hold and sat back from her, perched on the side of the bed.

'Awkward!' she repeated breathlessly. 'It would be terrible. If my husband found you here he would kill you.'

De Quesnoy shook his head. 'Don't worry your sweet self on that score. He could do no more than challenge me, and I am a better shot than he is. I proved that on Thursday in the shooting gallery. My only regret would be that duelling weapons have now degenerated into little more than toys; so I could hardly hope to kill him for you.'

'Armand!' she gasped. 'How can you say such a wicked thing?'

'I see nothing wicked about it. You hate and fear him, don't you? I know that to be so from the way I've caught you looking at him.'

'No, no! That is not true. And he is my husband.'

'You mean, poor little one, that you are his slave, bought by him in the marriage market. In my eyes he is no better than a Barbary pirate who has captured a beautiful Princess, and dragged her into his sleeping quarters against her will. I only wish that we lived in an earlier century; so that I might come to your rescue and rid you of him.'

'You must not speak to me like that. And you must go—go at once. Only think how utterly shamed I should be if anyone learned that you had come to my bedroom.'

'They will not, Madonna. The servants have all gone to bed. Igor is now making love to his young wife, and the older men are still talking French politics downstairs. They will be arguing such trivialities for at least another hour, just as they have done on previous nights.'

'All the same, you must go.' Angela's breath was still coming fast. 'You . . . you have no right here.'

'To the devil with rights!' He gave a low laugh. 'All that matters is

that I love you. I hinted to you more than once in the past few days that before you left Jvanets I'd find a chance to show my real feelings for you; and how else could I do so but by coming to you like this?'

'But it is wrong, Armand, and wicked. I am another man's wife. Whether I love him or not makes no difference. I belong to him; and you have come here like a thief in the night. You have acted like a thief already, before I had a chance to prevent you.'

'What, by kissing you? Oh come; then in that case every man who's not a fool is a thief; for it is said with good reason that stolen kisses are the sweetest.'

'Armand, you must go. I cannot let you stay here.'

'Nonsense, my sweet. We have ample time, and soon we will use it to some purpose.'

'I do not understand you.'

She was sitting bolt upright. When she had jerked her head aside after he had kissed her one of her dark gold curls had fallen across her cheek. As she lifted her hand to sweep it back the thought flashed into her mind what a mercy it was that, as she was leaving Jvanets in the morning, she had told her maid that for tonight she would not bother to have her hair done up in curlers. It would have been hateful to leave Armand with a memory of her looking like a scarecrow. All the same she must get rid of him, and quickly.

With an amused twinkle in his grey eyes, he remarked. 'What extraordinary creatures you women are. You come down to dinner with bare arms and back and with a good part of your bosoms exposed to every man's glance; yet you go to bed in a thing like a tent.'

It was true enough that apart from Angela's face and hands not an inch of her showed. A pink ribbon drew the neck of her thick nightdress into tight pleats below her chin, and its voluminous sleeves were also drawn tight by ribbons round her wrists. Giving him a surprised look, she asked:

'What else would you expect me to wear?'

He smiled. 'If you were mine I would have you sleep in gossamer silks edged with the finest lace.'

'But ... but it is only *cocottes* who expose themselves in such a shameless fashion. And this is no time to talk of such things. You must go, Armand. Leave me I beg.'

Ignoring her plea he replied: 'Your ideas about night attire are out

13

of date, my sweet—at least for young and pretty women. And where can a lovely girl display her charms for her lover's pleasure more suitably than in her bedroom? Anyway, I have known two of excellent social standing who did so.'

'Armand! Do you really mean that you have already had two . . . two mistresses?'

'Why should that surprise you. I am not a child.'

'No; but in England many young men of your age have not yet left their Public Schools; and for one to enter on an affaire of that kind would be considered terrible.'

'Then I am sorry for the English.' De Quesnoy gave a low laugh. 'Here in Russia, from the age of sixteen, it is customary for the son of the house to explore the possibilities of all his mother's prettiest maids. But it was my good fortune that my father did not approve of my having to do with peasants. He brought from Vienna a charming young widow whom he had engaged ostensibly to teach me dancing, but in fact to educate me in the arts of love. Before she left last summer she paid me the compliment of telling me that she could not have hoped for a better pupil; so, you see, you need have no fears that I shall prove inept at playing Adonis to so lovely a Venus as yourself.'

Angela blushed to the roots of her golden-brown hair. Could she really have understood aright? Was he suggesting . . . ? No, surely not. Her brown eyes round and her mouth a little open, she stared at him as he sat smiling nonchalantly on the edge of her bed. She noticed now a thing that the dim glow from the night-light had not previously revealed to her. He was no longer wearing his evening clothes, but a robe of crimson silk tied with a broad sash at the waist. His neck was bare and as he moved slightly she caught a glimpse of his chest. Was it possible that under his robe he had nothing on? That he had deliberately undressed before coming to her room? If so his intentions . . .

'I don't know what you mean,' she gulped. 'And I . . . I don't wish to. You are to go! To go at once. I order you to!'

Instead of obeying he leaned towards her, took one of her hands, and said in that low voice of his which she felt could have charmed a bird off a tree: 'Dearest Angela. Why pretend not to understand when my heart is an open book to you. Had we all night to talk in it would still not be long enough for me to tell you how much this past fortnight has meant to me. You have brought a poetry and sweetness into my

14

life that it lacked before. I have come to adore the very ground you walk on, and you—you love me in return. I am certain of it.'

'No, no!' she broke in hurriedly. 'You assume too much. I have never said so.'

He bent his face nearer to hers. 'Not in so many words, perhaps; but I have seen it in your eyes a dozen times. Angela, we love one another. That is the truth. You cannot escape it. Why be so cruel to us both as to try? To give is more blessed than to receive. Give me the joy of hearing you whisper "Armand, I love you".'

'If . . . if I do, will you promise to go at once?'

'I will go the moment you have given me your love.'

'Very well, then.' Her words suddenly came with a rush. 'Armand, I love you. I know it's wicked of me but I can't help my feelings. You are the only man I've ever loved or ever shall love.'

'Oh, Angela, my sweet! How happy you make me!' Throwing his free arm round her shoulders he drew her to him and kissed her on the mouth.

'No, Armand, no!' She struggled away from him. 'I can't let you do that. And you must go now. You promised.'

'Indeed I did. But I had not then realized how deeply you cared for me. By your sweet confession you have placed us on an equal footing. You have given me the right to claim what before I would only have begged. The laws of man are made only to be broken, because they are stupid and unjust. Before God we are united by our love. Angela, I need you desperately; and you need me. We cannot now part like this.'

Her pansy-brown eyes again grew as round as saucers, and she gasped: 'Are you . . . are you suggesting that we should run away together?'

Fortunately for de Quesnoy the light was dim, so she did not see the enthusiasm suddenly drain from his face leaving it like a mask. He found Angela enchanting. Like most upper-class English girls of her day, her governesses had given her a far better education than she could possibly have received in a modern school, and compared to her most continental young women were ignoramuses. Never had he come across such a fascinating combination of female loveliness in which sensible conversation was combined with alluring innocence. He was as much in love with her as he had ever yet been with anyone.

But to link his life with hers? That was a very different matter. Worldly-wise beyond his years, he realized that she would, almost at once, become a millstone round his neck. He already had an income of his own; so he could take her on a tour of the Italian cities where society was notoriously lax and did not bother overmuch if a foreign nobleman's fair companion was his wife or not. But what then? In honour bound he would have to do his utmost to persuade the Vatican to grant her an annulment of her marriage to Syveton. And if they did he would have to marry her himself.

That would mean the abandonment of his most cherished plans. His secret ambition now was to become a soldier and rise to high command in the French Army. Before he could even take the initial step of joining it, he anticipated meeting with the most violent opposition from his father, and if he saddled himself with Angela that would be the end of the matter. How could he possibly expect to rise in an army largely controlled by staunch Catholics, with the scandal of having enticed away another man's wife blackening the very beginning of his career?

While these disquieting thoughts had been racing through his mind, Angela's thoughts had run on with equal swiftness. For a few seconds her earlier visions of life with Armand had again entranced her; but she was quick to realize the many obstacles to its achievement. Without waiting for him to reply, she answered her own question.

'No, no; it is wonderful to dream of but quite impossible. There would be the most terrible scandal. It would break my poor papa's heart. Besides, think how awful it would be if I failed to secure an annulment. I'd have to live in sin with you for the rest of my life. Then you'd never be able to have a legitimate heir; unless . . . unless I gave you up to another woman, and I'd rather die than do that.'

Relieved as de Quesnoy was, it was contrary to his nature to play the hypocrite in such a matter, and he said quickly. 'Bless you for your sound common sense, my love. I was not proposing that we should elope, and had you suggested our doing so I should have done my best to dissuade you. It could end only in ruin for us both.'

'Then there is no more to be said.'

'Oh but there is.'

'No, nothing. And you must go now. You really must. You have been here for at least twenty minutes, and every moment you remain we run a greater risk of discovery.'

'My father likes staying up talking and never lets his guests go up to bed till after one; so we are safe for another half-hour at least.'

'But Armand, you promised.'

'I promised that I would go when you had given me your love.'

'I have already confessed that I love you.'

'That was to speak of it; not to give it.'

She shook her head, but he hurried on: 'The sight of you, the subtle perfume of your hair, and hearing you speak those words carried me to heights sublime, but love can only be given through the sense of touch. Have mercy on me, Angela, and carry me with you to the seventh heaven.'

There could be no mistaking his meaning now. Angela's heart was pounding heavily; her mind in a whirl. Armand's approach was so different from her husband's, but his intention was the same and his words did not stir in her any answering thrill of physical passion. She was not angry with him but greatly distressed. Under his dark "devil's" eyebrows his grey eyes glittered as they were caught for a second in the flame of the night-light. He looked so boyish, so beautiful, yet now so wicked, that he recalled to her mind a picture she had once seen portraying a fallen angel.

'Armand,' she gulped suddenly. 'Tell me the truth. Did you come here hoping that I would . . . would let you get into bed with me?'

'Why, yes, my sweet," he replied with a smile. 'For what other reason does a man come to the bedroom of the woman he loves, in the middle of the night?'

Angela winced. 'It . . . it might be just to tell her that he loved her.'

'There must be a first course to every feast; but words are not enough to still the hunger of love. Had you been staying here longer, or if we lived in the same city, I'd be content tonight with a promise—or even half a one. But this may be the only chance we will ever have to show how much we love one another.'

'I've said I love you. I can do no more. You seem to forget that I am married.'

'Forget!' he exclaimed in surprise. 'What an extraordinary thing to say! Were you not, and I had forgotten myself so far as to come to your room, I would be too ashamed to look at myself in the mirror tomorrow

17

morning. It is the very fact that you are married that entitles me to ask you to give me a richer memory of you to treasure than your just saying that you love me.'

'I cannot! Armand, I implore you to leave me! Please go—please!'

'Angela, have pity. You are going away tomorrow. We have only tonight left. Don't let's throw away this last precious half-hour. Let's crown our love; so that even if we never meet again we'll always be able to look back with undiluted joy on it.'

'What you ask is impossible.'

'In God's name, why? If you loved your husband your refusal would be understandable. Or if you had already taken a lover, and were obsessed with the thought of getting back to Paris to him; but from a dozen things you have said to me it's quite clear that you have not.'

'No!' she burst out with sudden firmness. "And I never will.'

'Oh come, Angela, be sensible,' he protested. 'It's absurd to talk like that. Except in rare cases where a marriage is truly made in heaven, every woman does. And yours most certainly was not. What happiness can you expect to get out of life unless you do take lovers? That you will do so is as inevitable as that tomorrow's sun will rise. Why, then, put it off for another few months and leave me miserable? Please, please, my beautiful Angela, let me be your lover now.'

Tears started to her eyes. As he sought to put his arm about her again she pushed him roughly away. Her voice bitter with disillusion she half-sobbed: 'The sense in which you use the word is the very antithesis of what love means to me. It makes men no different from animals.'

De Quesnoy released her and stepped back. A new light of understanding dawned in his eyes. 'You poor darling,' he murmured. 'So that brute Syveton has been misusing you.'

Next moment he caught his breath. Every muscle in his body tensed. A muffled sound, and a streak of light on the ceiling, had gripped his attention to the exclusion of all else. He knew then that either he had talked too much or his father too little. Syveton had come up to bed and was now entering the room.

18

CHAPTER III

THE GERM OF A CONSPIRACY

LTHOUGH Gabriel Syveton's snobbish instincts were greatly gratified by staying with a Duke, personal scheming had played no part in his being invited to Jvanets. He was a prominent official of the *Ligue de la Patrie Française* and, with de Camargue, a member of the powerful secret Committee whose object was to restore the Monarchy in France. The Vicomte was an old friend of de Richleau's, and had been chosen to approach him on a certain matter; but he was afflicted with a lisp, so by no means a fluent speaker, and it was with the idea that Syveton, who was, should act as advocate that he had asked permission to bring him.

During the first week of their stay they had felt that it would be premature to broach their mission until they had satisfied themselves that de Richleau was capable of playing the role they had in mind for him; and in the past few evenings, although there had been much discussion of French politics, no really suitable opening had presented itself.

In consequence, on this last night as soon as the ladies had retired to bed, and the men were congregated in the Duke's sanctum, Syveton had at once turned the conversation to the sad state of affairs in France. And, indeed, there was ample cause for all the Frenchmen present to be concerned for the future of their country; for over a hundred years she had been declining generation by generation from her great estate and afflicted by a steady draining of her power, prestige and population.

Since 1789 France had been twice a Limited Monarchy, twice an Empire, twice ruled by absolutist Bourbon Kings, twice dominated for a few years by Dictators, once by a Directorate of Five, and had three times been a Republic. She had twice been invaded, conquered and compelled to support an enemy army of occupation, and twice been the victim of civil wars leaving her people bitter and divided. Eighteen years was the longest period for which she had enjoyed any one form of government, and all of them had had to contend with constant conspiracies aimed at their overthrow, strikes, riots and savage street fighting.

The first Revolution had cost France, in massacres and conflicts, two million lives, the ruin of her industry and the loss of her most valuable colonies. During the twenty-one years of foreign wars that followed a third—and physically the best third—of France's manpower had perished in Napoleon's campaigns, and the British had swept her commerce from the seas. In the middle years of the century wars in North Africa, the Crimea, Italy and Mexico had further drained her resources; then in 1870 she had been overtaken by a major disaster.

By graft, glamour and chicanery the Second Empire had managed to maintain itself against growing opposition until the dissipated and ailing Emperor's government had, against his will, deliberately picked a quarrel with Prussia over her support of a candidate to the vacant Spanish throne. Mentally drunk on memories of their grandfathers' victories, and physically drunk from too much liquor, France's levies had marched to war shouting '*À Berlin*'. At the hands of that terribly efficient triumvirate Chancellor Bismarck, War Minister von Roon and General Count von Moltke, they had been utterly overwhelmed. Three months of appalling slaughter had culminated in Napoleon III being taken prisoner and the Third Republic being proclaimed.

There had followed the siege of Paris, an ignominious armistice, the payment of a huge indemnity and the loss of Alsace-Lorraine. Then in the spring of '71 the mobs of Paris had defied the Provisional Government at Versailles and striven to force Communism on the nation.

The President-Elect, M. Thiers, had shown great resolution and sent the army in to restore order. De Galliffet, barely recovered from his wounds, had been one of the senior commanders charged with this unhappy task, and it was still held against him that, having forced the barricades, they had, within twenty-four hours, shot ten thousand workers.

This ruthless suppression of Anarchism, Marxism and Syndicalism had ensured the Conservatives ascendancy in the Chamber of Deputies for several years but, unhappily, they were divided among themselves. The Legitimists wanted to put the Count de Chambord on the throne as Henry V of France, the Orleanists wanted the Count de Paris as "King of the French" and the Bonapartists wanted to make the young Prince Imperial Emperor.

Their divergent aims enabled the Liberal M. Thiess to defeat the machinations of all three parties and when that shrewd old statesman retired none of them fared any better. His successor, Marshal Macmahon, had been a Legitimist by birth and a Bonapartist by circumstances, but with each successive election the Right was losing seats to the Left Centre and by the later seventies Socialism was again becoming a force with which to reckon. A demand by the Chamber that the President should surrender his right to make senior military appointments had so enraged the Marshal that he had given up his office in disgust.

Henceforth the qualities of integrity, proved statesmanship and even the ability to represent France worthily in a social sense were to play no part in the election of her Presidents. Candidates whose honesty and strength of character might have guided the country to better times were jockeyed from the lists, and mediocre men who could easily be manipulated or coerced were put into the Elysée Palace by groups of unscrupulous politicians.

Jules Grévy, who followed Macmahon, was just such a man. Long versed in the shadier forms of political intrigue, spineless but subtle, and exceptionally mean, he used his office to amass a huge personal fortune. After nine years he was forced to relinquish the Presidency owing to a first-class scandal. A quarrel between two of Paris's most glamorous prostitutes led to the disclosure of a widespread organization for the sale of honours, the controlling brain of which was the President's son-in-law, who actually lived with him in the Palace.

It was the Radical journalist Clemenceau who secured the election of his successor by urging his fellow politicians to "vote for the stupidest candidate". Sadi Carnot, whose abilities were confined to engineering, was their choice, and they got him in on the fame of his grandfather, the great Carnot, known for his brilliant direction of the wars of the Revolution as "The Organizer of Victories".

In consequence it was the Prime Ministers and leading politicians, rather than her Presidents, who had been the arbiters of France's destinies for the past fifteen years. The result had been a bitter and unceasing cold war waged between the factions for personal ends, instead of a united effort to bring the country back to its once dominant position in Europe.

The death of the Count de Chambord had merged the Legitimist and Orleanist succession in the person of the Count de Paris, who for a while had lived in the capital with all the state becoming a monarch, except for a crown; but by '86 the rising power of the Socialists had enabled them to get a law passed expelling him, and all other claimants to the throne, from the country.

Bonapartist hopes had received a sad blow in the death of the young Prince Imperial while fighting as a volunteer with the British forces in the Zulu war; and the next Napoleonic heir had, unhappily for his cause, left his wife, the daughter of the King of Italy, to live openly with a pretty mistress and, worse, was both a declared radical and a free-thinker.

This last deplorable lapse caused many Bonapartists to go over to the Monarchists, for the nation had now become divided by a bitter struggle between the Church and atheism. The attack on religion was led by Jules Ferry, as Minister of Public Instruction in the Freycinet Government of 1879. And later, as Premier himself, Ferry had, with the backing of the now powerful Socialist party, led by the anarchist Jules Guesde, put through many anti-clerical measures.

A bill making education compulsory had been followed by others establishing state schools and forbidding the teaching of religion in them, a compulsory secularization of the Universities, and one rescinding the concordat which had existed with Rome; so that in future only radical divines who would prove subservient to the government had any prospect of being made Bishops. In addition, first the Jesuits then other teaching Orders had been expelled from France, and those that remained were allowed to do so only on permits which could be revoked at any time.

As the greater part of the upper and middle classes were still deeply religious these measures had met with fanatical opposition, and the unity of the country had then been further disrupted by the appointment in '86 of General Boulanger as Minister of War.

His blue eyes, red hair and fair beard made him a striking figure and he soon became the idol of the masses. As a member of a radical ministry he went whole-heartedly to work to socialize the Army. Many of his reforms were excellent, but he set the men against their officers and greatly weakened its effectiveness by dismissing from their posts several of its best commanders simply because they were practising

Catholics. In spite of that the ignorant began to regard this flamboyant and vigorous adventurer as another Napoleon, and Paul Déroulède's League of Patriots, which had been built up to many thousands strong, with the object of launching a war of revenge against Germany, gave him their enthusiastic support.

A change of government forced his retirement from office and his political associates had by then come to regard him as such a danger to peace that no group of them would include him in a new Ministry. Thereupon, behind the backs of his Socialist allies, he started intrigues with both the Bonapartists and Monarchists. His lying promises to his backers of all parties led them to stage violent riots on his behalf and, had he had the courage to give the word, he could probably have made himself Dictator. Instead, he proved a man of straw, fled to Brussels with his consumptive mistress and, two years later, theatrical to the last, shot himself on her grave.

All these dissensions had been aggravated by nation-wide financial catastrophes. From '78 onward the dreaded Phylloxera had destroyed vineyard after vineyard, bringing ruin to thousands of wine-growers during the years that followed. In '81 the shares of the great Catholic Bank, the Union Générale, were changing hands at six times their nominal value; in '82, owing, it was said, to the machinations of its Jewish and Protestant-controlled rivals, it went bankrupt, bringing scores of smaller banks down with it and swallowing up the savings of innumerable people. Most disastrous of all, in '86 the Panama Company collapsed. As usual, numerous venal politicians were involved and it was found that M. Baihaut, the Minister of Works, had accepted a bribe of £15,000 to help to keep it going long after he knew it to be insolvent. The investors lost sixty million pounds, and there was hardly a family in France that was not affected.

As de Richleau's guests had been at Jvanets for close on a fortnight they had already discussed many of these matters, but they had reached no conclusions; and Syveton, acutely conscious that this was his last opportunity to approach the Duke, had been waiting impatiently for a chance to do so. At last, after half an hour or so, it came. He gave a quick glance at de Camargue, and announced with conviction:

'Many if not all the ills that France has suffered during the past twenty years might have been spared her had she but had a King.'

De Richleau nodded. 'I think you are right. It was a tragedy that the chance was lost in '71. If only the Count de Chambord had not insisted that the white banner with the *fleur-de-lis* should again be accepted as the flag of France he could have been crowned at Rheims as Henry V.'

'Was there ever such childish folly!' snorted de Galliffet angrily. 'To throw away a kingdom for such a quibble! And who in their senses could suppose that an Army that had marched to Moscow, Vienna, Naples and Madrid under the tricolor would ever give it up?'

'There speaks the Bonapartist,' de Camargue lisped. 'It wath under the *fleur-de-lis* that France gwew up into the foremost power in Europe. But I'll agwee that His Highness wath straining at a gnat.'

'I am no Bonapartist,' the General retorted. 'I had my first commission from Louis Philippe; and although the figure of that bourgeois monarch, carrying an ill-rolled umbrella as he pottered unattended through the streets of Paris, was not one to inspire a soldier's devotion, I served the Orleanist government faithfully. To Napoleon III, President Thiers and Marshal Macmahon I gave an equal loyalty. By conviction I have always been a Liberal. Those, too, are the sentiments of the greater part of the French people. Again and again the elections have shown it by the return of majorities to the Left Centre.'

'Can that be taken as a true criterion?' asked the old Abbé Nodier mildly. 'As each outgoing government has either confirmed the Prefects of the Departments in their appointments, or nominated new ones, the bias must always be in favour of candidates having the same political complexion.'

'Well said, Father! Well said!' exclaimed Syveton. 'The powers of Prefects to aid or hinder candidates are immense. One of their favourite tricks is to send a few rowdies to the meetings of their political opponents, then use the police to break up the meetings on the excuse they are riotous assemblies. By such methods many an election has been rigged in favour of the Left.'

The Abbé shook the silvery locks that framed his round wrinkled face. 'Such tactics are deplorable. I recall, too, that in the election of '85 the Minister of Public Instruction issued a circular letter to the staffs of all the National Schools. It took the form of a veiled warning that if they did not work for the Government candidate they might lose their posts. As no schoolmaster is ever appointed unless he is a declared atheist they needed little urging. But the unfair thing was that an official notification was sent to all priests at the same time, informing them that if they did not remain strictly impartial they would be expelled from their parishes.'

'It is all the more wemarkable,' observed de Camargue, 'that in the election you speak of the Conservative vote wath more than doubled. But when the Chamber met the Wadicals and Socialists united to wob us of our gains. By using their majowity they succeeded in unseating no less than twenty-two of our Deputies on twumped-up charges of having committed election offences.'

The General gave a vigorous nod. 'You are right, of course, about the use of such unscrupulous measures. But I greatly doubt if even clean elections would give the Monarchists a majority in the Chamber. It can I think be said, though, that a great part of our Liberals would rather accept a King again than continue to see themselves represented, and the nation disgraced, by such a pack of scoundrels. That, as I was about to say, is my own feeling.'

'*Mon Général*, you have there the crux of the matter.' Syveton leaned forward eagerly. 'The only hope for our poor country lies in a new Head of State; a man whom everyone can respect and who has no axe to grind.'

'Only a King will fill that bill,' de Richleau remarked, 'and although the Count de Paris is a most excellent man I do not see the French people accepting him as their monarch. Like de Chambourd, he missed his chance. After their pact at Frohsdorf, Marshal Macmahon could have ensured his succession to the throne, but like only too many of the Bourbon Princes he dilly-dallied until it was too late. In '86 his prospects again looked good, but he so mishandled matters that he got himself expelled from the country. Still worse, by becoming involved with that rogue Boulanger he compromised the whole Royalist party. No, no! I would sooner expect to wake up one morning wearing the crown of St. Louis myself.'

It was the very opening that Syveton had been waiting for. He said quickly: 'There are many people, Monseigneur, who hope that you will.'

'Eh! What's that!' laughed the Duke, his eyebrows shooting up and wrinkling his broad forehead. 'You jest, Monsieur. My remark was intended only to convey the extreme unlikelihood of the Count de Paris

25

ever becoming King of France. But His Highness is the legitimate heir and while he lives it would ill become us to discuss any other.'

'Monseigneur, permit me to disagree. You have already admitted that as far as our cause is concerned His Highness is a broken reed. We all know him to be relieved that the call to a high destiny should have passed him by. He is now happily engaged in writing a history of the American Civil War, in which he fought so gallantly as a young man. But must France be sacrificed on that account? Surely it is our duty to ignore the claim which he no longer presses, and select some other great noble of Bourbon descent under whose banner we can throw out the "Money changers in the Temple".'

'Yes, yes, I see your point,' the Duke admitted, still hardly recovered from his surprise. 'But why should you, and it seems certain friends of yours, consider me to be worthy beyond others of this great distinction? Admittedly I have Bourbon blood on the wrong side of the blanket, but there are three others at least who are more nearly related to the royal house.'

'That is true, Monseigneur; but if we are to abandon the principle of strict legitimacy it would be absurd to allow our choice to be governed by degrees of consanguinity. Among the few who on that count would rank before you, one has become a Protestant and another is a chronic invalid; while among those who are also of the blood, but more distantly, there are none with better qualifications for Kingship than yourself.'

De Richleau shook his head. 'I thank you for the compliment, Monsieur, but I cannot take your suggestion seriously.'

'I was never more serious in my life.' Syveton spread wide his powerful hands. 'It was for this that de Camargue asked you to receive me here as a guest. I had hoped to broach the matter earlier, but I felt it essential that in a series of conversations we should first impress upon you the depths to which French politics have sunk, and that the only means of lifting the country out of this hideous morass is by another Restoration.'

'I needed little impressing about the state of things in France,' replied the Duke. 'That for years past it has become common parlance among decent people to refer to the Republic as "The Slut" is evidence enough of that. In fact it was mainly from shame and disgust at the behaviour of her so-called statesmen that I decided to make my home here in voluntary exile. I think you right, too, that the best hope for those who are still compelled to live in France is to select a nobleman of good character having Bourbon blood, then attempt to place him on the throne. But I am not your man. There are others better fitted than myself to play this great role.'

'Indeed, Monseigneur, there are not. Of that I am convinced, and I am far from being alone in my opinion. This question has been long and earnestly debated by the Monarchist Council, of which both de Camargue and myself are members. After the most thorough discussion of the personalities of all the nobles having the Blood, it was unanimously agreed that you were in every way the most suitable. The Council have empowered us formally to offer you the headship of the Royalist party and will pledge themselves to do their utmost to seat you on the throne of France.'

Up to a few moments earlier young Armand de Quesnoy had not been listening to his elders. His thoughts had been engaged with his chances of seducing Angela. To make the attempt he had to get away from the others while it was still comparatively early, and when guests were present it was not for the son of the house to be the first to go to bed. But he had already thought of a way over that, and had been just about to put it into execution, when exciting thoughts about her were thrust from his mind on hearing her husband express the extraordinary hope that his father would one day wear the crown of St. Louis.

From that point Armand absorbed every word that was spoken with the most eager interest, and his swift mind grasped in a moment what such an amazing development would mean for himself.

By nature he was that unusual combination; a student and a man of action. From every book he read sprang the desire to read others, but he was also a huntsman of no small prowess and his ambitions in that direction did not stop short at game. Young as he was he had already tasted the thrill of hunting women and bringing them to happy submission by a blend of audacity, gaiety and apparent devotion, of which he possessed the secret. But above all he craved to hunt men. Not as individuals, but in the mass. Soldiering was in his blood, and he had studied the campaigns of all the great Captains of the past. He knew that it must be many years before he could hope to direct a battle but in the meantime he could imagine no exultation equal to leading a cavalry charge against the massed formations of an enemy. In short, he was a young man that the gods had endowed with an inquiring mind, good brains, excellent health and all the natural instincts.

At the thought of his father as King of France, tremendous visions danced before his eyes. He would be Dauphin, the Son of France. Everything he asked of life would be his for the taking. The wonderful libraries of Versailles, Compiégne and Fontainebleau would be his in which to browse. The loveliest women in a whole nation would be flattered to receive his attentions. The Royal game preserves would be his to hunt in at will. Overnight he would be able to choose his own regiment and become it's Colonel. At twenty-one he would automatically be made General of Division. Within ten years he would have routed out the not-so-goods in the High Command and remade the Army of France upon a better plan.

Yet within another few moments he knew that such dreams were moonshine. His father was a placid unambitious man, and far more interested in country pursuits than international problems. He had never, even when young, worn a uniform; and he was far too set in his routine as a *grand seigneur* with ample money but no responsibilities ever to abandon it for the uncertain seas of adventure.

All too soon Armand's expectations proved correct. Having passed a hand over his curly beard, de Richleau replied to Syveton with hardly a suggestion of hesitation.

'Monsieur, I pray you convey to your Council my sensibility of the great honour they have done me by their proposal. I thank you too for having come so considerable a distance to convey it to me. But I cannot accept. I am a simple man and not cut out for Kingship. Even did you and your friends succeed in making me your monarch I should disappoint you. Not only the Senate and the Chamber, but every Ministry and even the High Command of France is riddled with unprincipled self-seekers. To dismiss them all would create chaos. Yet I could not tolerate them and they would not tolerate me. Within a month they would have united to send me packing, and you would have had all your trouble for nothing. For men of my mind the true France died in 1789. It is now a different nation. From afar I watch its decadence with regret; but years ago when I first settled here I decided henceforth to regard myself as an international, so I no longer think of France even as my country. There, Monsieur, you have the truth, so you will appreciate that no good purpose can be served by pursuing this discussion further.'

The young Count's sudden interest in the conversation having almost as swiftly been dissipated, he proceeded to put into operation the stratagem he had thought up for getting away without apparent rudeness. Speaking in Russian he said in a low voice to Prince Igor:

'I do hope that Katerina's indisposition is nothing serious, and that she will be quite all right again by tomorrow morning.'

The Prince stared at him in surprise. 'Whatever do you mean? When she went up to bed she said nothing to me of feeling ill.'

De Quesnoy shrugged. 'Perhaps she did not wish to alarm you; but she told me at dinner that she had pains in her inside.'

Igor's marriage to Katerina had been a love match and they were still in the blissful state of honeymooners. At the thought of his darling alone upstairs, and perhaps suffering, he went quite white. Armand could not help being a little amused, but he meant to relieve his cousin of his fears as soon as they were out of the room, and tell him it had been only a ruse to enable them to escape from the boring conversation of their elders.

Next moment the Prince was on his feet, and as the Duke glanced up at him he said: 'Please forgive me, Uncle, if I leave you now; but Katerina was not feeling well at dinner, and I am a little worried about her.'

'Of course, dear boy. I trust it is nothing serious,' de Richleau replied at once. 'By all means leave us.'

De Quesnoy had also risen to his feet, and said. 'I will go up with Igor, Father. Just in case anything is wanted from the medicine cupboard.'

'Do, Armand, do. Had I known I would have suggested that Igor should have gone up to her earlier.' The Duke made a gesture towards the side table. 'But before you go, please replenish our guests' glasses with a little more brandy.'

Smiling at the success of his ruse, Armand carried round the decanter, giving Syveton an extra large ration. He felt certain that, as on previous nights, the party would remain talking there for at least another hour and a half, and that should be ample for the alluring project he had in mind.

The conversation was already well under away again and it was de Galliffet who said to Syveton, 'Since our host is so definite in his refusal I believe you would do best to pin your hopes upon the Duc de Vendôme.'

Syveton replied a little doubtfully, 'But he is still only a boy.'

'At all events,' de Richleau remarked, 'he is a healthy and promising one, and his lineage is impeccable. The fact that he is descended from our greatest King, Henry IV of glorious memory, would do much to influence the people in his favour.'

'Besides,' added de Galliffet sagely, 'such great undertakings need time and much skilful preparation if they are to be crowned with success. The very fact that you must wait a few years would enable you to build him up gradually in the public estimation. He is a handsome youngster and as his Bourbon blood is illegitimate the prohibition against living in France does not apply to him. Properly handled, by the turn of the century he could be the most popular young man in Paris. Far better to exercise patience and make a good bet than rush in and make a bad one.'

'There is much in what you say,' Syveton agreed, glancing at de Camargue. 'On our return to Paris we must discuss the matter with the Council.'

While pouring the brandy Armand had caught the Duc de Vendôme's name, but given little heed to it. His mind was already racing with thoughts of how he could best make his bid to induce the beautiful Angela to surrender. Yet, three-quarters of an hour before her husband surprised him in her room, there had emerged in his hearing the germ of a conspiracy which was later to involve both of them in most desperate hazards and change the whole course of his life.

CHAPTER IV

THE TAUNT THAT RANKLED

THE reason why Syveton had come up to bed much earlier than de Quesnoy expected was one of those unforseeable minor accidents against which even the most painstaking planners cannot guard. In passing the brandy decanter the Duke and General de Galliffet had fumbled it between them, with the result that the former had received the remaining contents of the decanter in his lap. As it was then about twenty minutes to one it had been decided that it was not worth while for the Duke to go upstairs, change his trousers and come down again; so the party had broken up half an hour earlier than it would normally have done.

As Syveton entered the room he was holding his candlestick in his right hand and shielding its flame from the draught with his left. The cold air from the corridor rushing in behind him caused the flame to flicker wildly and, his gaze being riveted upon it, he did not immediately see de Quesnoy.

The Count was standing up against the far side of the bed and leaning inwards across it towards Angela. The curtains at its head hid her entirely and him partially; so in that moment of grace he might have side-stepped and slipped unseen through a door beside the bedhead which led into the dressing-room. If the dressing-room had had another door giving on to the corridor that is what he would have done; but he knew that it had not. Moreover, young as he was, he had already learned from the wild animals he had hunted that they more often succeeded in driving off the dogs when they stood and fought on chosen ground than if they allowed themselves to be run to earth.

He needed no telling that he had landed Angela and himself in a very nasty situation, but, as he had not been caught actually in bed with her, he still had a hope that he might get them out of it; so, for the moment, all he did was to take one quick step backwards, away from the bedside.

31

Angela was still sitting upright. At the slight noise and de Quesnoy's swift movement her backbone stiffened with awful apprehension. In spite of Armand's assurances, the very thing she had been dreading for the past half-hour had happened. There was now no escape from a most terrible scene. It might lead to a duel, but she doubted if her husband would challenge a man whom he must look on as hardly more than a boy. She thought it more likely that as soon as he could get his hands on a horse-whip he would set about Armand with it.

She had hardly recovered from the shock of learning that her cavalier, instead of being as chaste as Galahad, was a cynical roué, and she felt that she would never be able to forgive him for destroying the illusions she might otherwise have carried away with her. All the same, the thought of his handsome face cut and bleeding from the strokes of a whip made her heart contract. If she could have saved him by taking the blame upon herself she would have done so willingly, but she could think of no possible story which, in her husband's eyes, would excuse his presence there.

As Syveton closed the door behind him and advanced into the room with heavy steps, it was all she could do to keep herself from fainting. At any moment now the explosion must come, to be followed most probably by a horrible fracas at the foot of her bed, in which her husband, being by far the more powerful of the two, was certain to get the best of it; but not before the sound of the conflict had brought several other men running to the room, to be witnesses of her eternal shame.

It was de Quesnoy who spoke first. Only a few seconds had elapsed between Syveton opening the door and shutting it. He still had his eyes on the candle flame and had taken only a couple of paces when, in a cheerful welcoming voice, the Count exclaimed:

'Ah, Madame! Here is your natural protector.'

Syveton stopped dead in his tracks. Most of his body was invisible, but the candle he was carrying lit up his broad pale face, across which his drooping moustache now threw a grotesque shadow. Taken entirely by surprise, he exclaimed:

'Who's that?'

'Armand de Quesnoy,' came the prompt reply from out of the dimness beyond the bed.

There was a moment's awful silence. As Angela waited for her husband's reaction she clenched her hands until her finger-nails dug

32

into her palms. Yet when he spoke the restraint he was exercising on himself was hardly perceptible. In a flat but courteous tone he inquired:

'May I ask Monsieur le Comte what he is doing here?'

'Why, deputizing for you, Monsieur,' the gay voice declared without a quiver.

Angela closed her eyes. This was the end. Why could the dear, handsome, wicked fool not at least have made a pretence that he had got into her room by a mistake? After abject apologies Syveton might have accepted such an excuse rather than become involved in a quarrel which would make him *non persona grata* with the young man's father. But to dot the I's and cross the T's . . . ! It was true enough that had it not been for her repulse of Armand they might actually have been found between the sheets together. Yet nothing of the kind had happened; so why in Heaven imply that it had, or was about to. Such a spark, deliberately applied, could not fail to send up the powder barrel. It did.

'You young jackanapes!' Syveton roared. 'How dare you! Ever since we arrived here you've hung round my wife's skirts like a nosing spaniel. But I thought you harmless. It seems that after all you have ideas beyond your years. Very well, then! Since you are so anxious to learn, I'll give you a lesson. Just let me find my hunting crop and I'll flay the hide off you.'

De Quesnoy was terribly tempted to let matters take their course. Like Louis XIV who, at the same age, was a better horseman, a better swordsman and a better shot than any other man at his court, so the Count excelled in these martial accomplishments. In addition he was no mean amateur at the Russian national sport of wrestling and had even learned, from an English groom, the rudiments of boxing. In consequence, as he stood there, slender, straight and supple, but in appearance far from powerful, he felt complete confidence in his ability to make Angela's far more weighty husband grovel. But he had her to think of. Nevertheless his voice held a quiet dignity as he said:

'Were you not, Monsieur, a guest in my father's house I should feel compelled to call upon you to explain yourself. As it is I must admit that my words, intended only as a jest, might have led you to misunderstand me. By deputizing for you, I meant only that in your absence I had the honour to protect Madame, your wife, from a dragon.'

Syveton was fuming with rage. He felt certain that the younger man was making a mockery of him; yet short of slapping his face there was nothing he could do about it. Endeavouring to swallow his anger he blurted out: 'Dragon! How can you expect me to believe such nonsense?'

'There is no nonsense about it,' de Quesnoy assured him blandly. 'As I was walking along the corridor I heard Madame cry out for help. Naturally I rushed to her assistance. I burst open the door. And what did I see?' He paused dramatically.

Angela gazed at him spellbound. Syveton stared at him for a moment almost equally fascinated, then he demanded: 'Well, what did you see?'

'A mouse,' the Count replied, his lean young face not displaying even a vestige of humour. 'A mouse; and it was running along the end of Madame's bed.'

Slowly, half-hidden by the drooping moustache, Syveton's mouth gaped open. Astonishment fought with incredulity in his mind. Could it possibly be true? Surely not. This satanic-looking youth had been endeavouring to make him a cuckold, and being caught out had shown the presence of mind to play the buffoon as his best hope of appearing innocent.

As though to confirm that impression de Quesnoy struck an attitude and cried: 'It was a terrible moment! There was Madame cowering away in terror. At any second the monster might have leapt upon her. At this instant of crisis, what did I do?'

With an impatient shake of his head, Syveton retorted: 'Enough of this play-acting. I will afford you an opportunity to explain matters in the morning.'

Angela's heart sank. She had allowed herself to believe too soon that Armand had succeeded in fooling her husband. It was something that by his resource he had cushioned the first moments of their encounter, and so prevented a violent altercation leading to an immediate scandal. But he had gained only a postponement; and she still had the night to get through with the dreadful prospect of being bombarded by her husband's jealous questioning.

Deliberately misunderstanding, de Quesnoy answered with a smile: 'It would ill become me, Monsieur, to boast of my own gallantry; so if the ladies are to be regaled with this exploit tomorrow I must leave the explaining to you. But you have not yet heard the dénouement yourself. As I was about to say, rushing into the room I leapt upon the monster. And here he is!'

Withdrawing his right hand from the pocket of his robe, the Count opened it wide, displaying in his palm a dead mouse.

It had been procured for him by his valet that afternoon, and he had brought it with him to Angela's room as a precaution against just such an emergency as had arisen. Had he produced it at once the truth might have been suspected, but his skilful build-up had disguised the thinness of the story.

Angela suddenly began to titter, but by a great effort checked herself, as she knew that she was bordering on hysteria and to have let it get the better of her might have given the game away. Her husband hesitated only a second, then fully convinced by this visual evidence of de Quesnoy's innocence he held out his hand and cried:

'Monsieur le Comte, I apologize. I am greatly obliged to you for having come to the rescue of my wife.'

'Monsieur, it is a happiness to have been of service,' de Quesnoy replied. Then, maintaining a perfectly straight face, instead of taking the outstretched hand he laid the dead mouse in it, and added: 'Since you wish to dispose of the corpse of your wife's attacker, I will not deprive you of that pleasure.'

This macabre courtesy instantly rearoused Syveton's suspicions that he was being made a fool of. Surely no one could really have supposed that he had held out his hand for the dead mouse? Yet throughout de Quesnoy had behaved with perfect *sang-froid*. Had he been there with guilty intentions it was unnatural, being so young, that he should have shown no trace of fear, or at least awkwardness. Perhaps in some ways he was a simpleton. Yes, that must be it. For all his elegance and prowess with horse and gun, he was only an overgrown boy, and it was that which accounted for the occasional slowness of his mind.

As though to confirm the impression that he was mentally still half a child, the Count, having taken a few steps towards the door, turned, made a bow which included Angela, and said to her: 'I do wish you were not going tomorrow, Madame. I have had no chance yet to show you my doll's house. It was my mother's when she was a little girl, and I am sure you would love it.' Then bidding them a cheerful good night, he left the room.

Syveton, now completely satisfied, gave a tolerant chuckle and walked through to his dressing-room. Angela, who for the past few moments had been hard put to it to fight down her bubbling laughter, felt it ebb from her as though it were gas and she a suddenly pricked balloon. Armand's last shaft had been aimed at her as well as at her husband. It was as though he had slapped her face and said: "You little fool! Take that for misleading me into believing you to be a grown woman, when you are fit only to play nursery games!"

Miserably she wondered if her inability to respond to physical love meant that there was something wrong with her. Yet if there was, that was not her fault; and, in any case, she had not given Armand the least right to expect anything from her. That he should have done so revealed the unsuspected baseness of his nature; and that on leaving he should have been so unfair as to fling such a taunt at her made her seethe with anger and self-pity. Then and there she determined that should they ever be thrown together again she would do her utmost to inflict upon him a similar humiliation.

De Quesnoy meanwhile was walking back to his own room with a buoyant stride. In his light and springy step there was something faintly reminiscent of a panther: an awareness that if he chose to exert himself he could dominate most other creatures that might cross his path. He had enormously enjoyed fooling Syveton and still believed that, given another half-hour, he could have got his way with Angela.

That he had failed with her annoyed him. She was much more lovely than the Viennese widow his father had procured to give him an amatory education, more intelligent than little Vera Osakapinsky, more fun than the Countess Hilda von Kramm, and in an altogether different class from the ladies of the ballet whom he had paid lavishly to amuse him for a few nights during his last visits to Budapest and Odessa.

What a tragedy, the Count's thoughts ran on, that she should have married an oaf like Syveton. Not that he was a fool. Far from it; but he had all the heaviness in manner of a typical wealthy French bourgeois. No doubt for the past twenty years he had been so engrossed in his professorship and then politics that he had had no time to fall in love and had made do with a succession of kept women. That was no training on which to base the handling of an innocent young bride. No wonder the poor child was as she was.

That he might have shocked her profoundly himself did not even occur to de Quesnoy; and, while he was aware that his last shaft had been a little unkind, he felt that, in the circumstances, he had been quite justified in launching it. Unless she was to waste her life she must grow up, and the sooner she was brought to realize it the better. That such a fund of natural gaiety should remain suppressed, and such radiant loveliness be allowed to go to waste, seemed to him a cardinal sin. But his charming Viennese mentor had told him that in such cases a few months often worked wonders. Secretly, he hoped to be in Paris himself by the spring. Perhaps his might yet be the magic wand that would bring Angela to life.

Yet by the time he had got into his own four-poster bed he had ceased to think of her. With him, as with most men of strong personality, love was a thing apart: a delicious and intoxicating nectar to be quaffed once in a while in great draughts, but certainly not a thing to befuddle the wits by being lingered over when there were so many important matters awaiting attention out in the fresh air.

The matter uppermost in de Quesnoy's mind at the moment was certain conversations he had had with General de Galliffet. The distinguished soldier had talked at length with infectious enthusiasm about the glories of the French Army in the past and how it might yet become the means of resuscitating France's greatness.

Before 1870 recruitment for the Army had been based on an annual ballot by which only a minor percentage of the available males had been conscripted, but these were compelled to serve for a long term of years. Moreover, the better-off among the unlucky ones had been allowed to strike bargains with poorer lads to act as substitutes for them. This filling of the ranks almost entirely from the lowest classes had resulted in the wealthy and the bourgeois taking little interest in the lot of the common soldier. But after the Franco-Prussian war the situation was revolutionized by laws reducing the period of service to a short one while making it universal. Henceforth the Army became the concern of every family; its prowess in the Colonial wars of North Africa and Indo-China was followed with anxiety, and many reforms were introduced to better the conscripts' conditions of service.

This general improvement in the quality and morale of the troops, which had taken place in the past twenty years, had been paralleled by one among the officers; but mainly for a very different reason. Under the later Bourbon Monarchies and the Second Empire, promising careers had been open to young men of good family in all Government Departments. But by 1879, when Marshal Macmahon resigned from the Presidency, and the Socialist reaction gathered force, this had ceased to be the case. With men like Ferry, Jules Guesde, Juarés, Boulanger, Clemenceau and Millerand either in the Cabinet, or exercising great influence in the Chamber, it soon became apparent that the possession of an ancient name meant quite definitely that discrimination would be used against its bearer in the allocation of posts and that his prospects of promotion would be blocked from above. In consequence, since the early eighties the Army had become the only career left open to the youth of the nobility, and it had absorbed all the most promising brains among them.

It was on these grounds that de Galliffet believed that the Army was the only really stable factor in French national life. As its officers embodied a high percentage of the most truly patriotic men in France, and its inclusion, past and present, of conscripts of all classes in its ranks made it truly representative of the whole people, he felt that in a major crisis it might be relied upon to save the country from the abyss of insolvency and anarchy to which the gangs of self-seeking politicians were every day leading it nearer.

In his talks with de Quesnoy he had hinted very clearly that France could not have too many young officers of noble family, independent means and good education; and that it was just such men, should they show keeness and ability, who were certain to be favoured with rapid promotion. He had added that there was no necessity for such youngsters to submit to the unpleasantness of first serving in the ranks. The present practice of giving promising N.C.O.s one-third of the commissions granted was an excellent one, as it encouraged initiative and still made plausible to recruits the great Napoleon's lure, that in every Private's knapsack might lie a Marshal's baton; but experience had shown that as far as the *jeunesse doré* were concerned far more useful military knowledge could be inculcated into them during two years at an officers' school, so, if they proved equal to passing the tests they received their commissions direct.

Such matters were again occupying de Quesnoy's thoughts when he said good-bye to his father's guests on the following morning. A troika had been provided for each of the three couples who were leaving and two more for their baggage; and while the latter was being loaded the company stood about in the hall sipping hot spiced wine.

Angela's face was pale and there were dark shadows under her eyes. She had hardly slept a wink as she relived the scenes which had taken place in her bedroom the previous night. Every word Armand had said to her now seemed etched on her brain, and she felt she hated him for having destroyed her girlish illusions about himself.

On coming downstairs she had dreaded that he would manage to draw her out of ear-shot of the others for a few moments in order to murmur again that he loved her. Anything of that kind would now have embarrassed her terribly, or perhaps even driven her to retort that he did not know what love was. Yet the realization proved still worse. Having kissed her hand and made her a conventional compliment he deliberately winked at her, then left her to go and speak to de Galliffet. Had he slapped her face she could not have been more furious, and it was only by a great effort that she succeeded in hiding her anger from Madame de Camargue, who was standing nearby.

De Quesnoy knew that his father would strongly oppose his entry into the French army, so he had not yet committed himself with de Galliffet; but he wanted to make quite certain where he stood, and he said in a low voice:

'*Mon Général:* should I decide to come to Paris against my father's wishes, would everything still be all right?'

'Certainly.' De Galliffet gave a sharp nod of his grey close-cropped head. 'Monsieur le Duc has no influence whatever in French Government circles, so he could not prevent your nomination. Besides, I should sponsor your candidature myself, and that would ensure its going through automatically.'

As de Quesnoy murmured his thanks, the General went on: 'But you must make up your mind soon now. The year's intake at St. Cyr will be assembling at the end of this month and even for me it might prove difficult to push you in after work at the college has started.'

'I shall have decided one way or another within twenty-four hours,' replied the young Count. 'I have been waiting only until you left, as to have raised the matter with my father while you were still here might have embroiled you in a quarrel with him.'

De Galliffet smiled his approval. 'That was considerate of you, and shows a spirit that I like. Most young men would have tried to get me to win their father's consent for them, or anyhow counted on my backing. Send me a telegram, then, and if it fulfils my hopes I will put in an application for you at once.'

'*Merci, mon Général.* St. Cyr is quite near to Paris, is it not?'

'Yes. The college is at the west end of the great park at Versailles. But the students there are kept hard at work, so they are not often able to go into Paris.'

The Count shrugged, as though indifferent, but silently he said to himself: "No matter, there will be the week-ends," and he threw a quick glance in Angela's direction.

At that moment the Duke's major-domo informed him that the sleigh convoy was ready, so he came up and offered his arm to the Marquise de Galliffet. Among a chorus of good-byes the other guests moved towards the door. As the son of the house it was for the Count to give his arm to the Vicomtess de Camargue, the second senior of the ladies who were leaving,; so it was Prince Igor who escorted Angela to the third troika in the line. As she sank back under the great folding hood, which had been put up for protection against the bitter wind, her husband climbed in after her, temporarily cutting off her view of the group in the doorway.

The drivers cracked their whips, the servants shouted, then the troikas slid forward over the crisp snow, and poor Angela was carried away without obtaining the last surreptitious glance she had tried to catch of the young man who in the past ten days had wrought such havoc with her heart.

De Quesnoy had not deliberately been either offhand or unkind. It was simply that he was very much aware how narrow had been their escape the night before; and, having succeeded in dissipating Syveton's suspicions, he was anxious not to re-arouse them by exchanging even a few words in private with Angela. He had taken the strong stare with which she met his wink quite wrongly, as expressing disappointment that he had not managed to make possible a last tête-à-tête with her. But, in the circumstances, he considered it much more important that he should continue on good terms with her husband than that they should indulge, more or less openly, in any form of sentimental leave-taking.

His discretion was based on the hope that he would soon be able to get to Paris and there renew his affaire with her. But that depended on how much resolution he could summon up to overcome the opposition which he would have to face on this, for him now, most critical of days.

CHAPTER V

THE ROAD TO GLORY

O sooner were the troikas out of sight round the corner of the house than Armand ceased to think of Angela and, going up to the aged Abbé Nodier, who was among those who had been seeing the guests off, he said:

'Father, I would like to talk to you for a while. Can you spare me half an hour?'

The old man nodded his silvery head. 'Of course, my son. Come with me to my room.'

Together they walked down the wide corridor to the north-west corner of the house, where the Abbé had his sanctum. Its walls were covered with old books, many of them tattered and of little monetary value, but esteemed by their owner on account of their contents. Among them were many which might have been stigmatized as either heretical or Rabelaisian by narrow-minded priests of the present era, but Nodier still lived in the tradition of the eighteenth century, when priests were the leading scholars and made up their own minds what was, and what was not, suitable reading for themselves and their educated acquaintances.

As soon as de Quesnoy entered the room, the Chaplain asked, a shade huffily: 'Is your mind so burdened with fresh sin that you cannot wait until Friday to make your confession?'

'No, Father, no,' replied de Quesnoy blandly, as they sat down opposite one another in two worn arm-chairs. 'I've not a thing on my conscience.'

'I find that difficult to believe. I know you far too well not to have seen through that trick of yours for going early to bed last night. Can you put your hand on the cross and tell me that you did not commit adultery with that young Englishwoman, Madame Syveton?'

'I can, Father.' The Count smiled suddenly. 'My luck was out.'

'There!' exclaimed the Abbé. 'Being aware of the evil habits into which you have fallen this past year, I felt certain you had designs upon her. And I'd have you know that the intention is near as grave a sin as the act.'

'That seems to me most unreasonable; but Friday will be time enough for you to inflict me with a few Hail Marys to be said as penance for what never came to more than an enchanting day-dream.'

'You are a reprobate of the first order. I am now utterly ashamed to have had a hand in your upbringing.'

'Then, Father, you should not be. Had you failed to win both my heart and mind I certainly would not come, as I do now, to consult you on a matter which must have far-reaching effects on my future.'

The Abbé sat forward and, dropping his joking manner, said: 'Tell me, my son? Knowing my fondness for you the good God could never be so unkind as to permit me to advise you wrongly. I am all attention.'

With equal seriousness the young Count replied: 'Life at Jvanets has nothing further to offer me. I wish to go to France and become an officer in the French army.'

'Hey! Hey!' the priest exclaimed, holding up his hands. 'But what of your father?'

De Quesnoy nodded. 'That is the difficulty. Do you consider that morally I am under an obligation to submit to Monsieur le Duc's restraint should he lay it upon me?'

'Honour thy father and thy mother ...' quoted the Abbé. 'No man can ignore the fourth Commandment with impunity.'

'One can honour without necessarily obeying,' remarked the Count.

'You split straws!' came the sharp retort.

'Well, perhaps,' de Quesnoy admitted. 'But this is a case of divided loyalties. I have a duty to my country as well as to my father.'

'If you regard serving in the French Army as a duty it is one which you might well be excused, seeing that you have been brought up in exile.'

'It is not the fact of serving, Father, but the possible results of doing so—that it might enable me to play a part in saving France from anarchy and restoring her to greatness.'

The Abbé gave him a shrewd look. 'You have been talking to General de Galliffet on these matters, have you not?'

'Yes. He holds the view that the Army is the only organized body having any real patriotism and integrity now left in France. He therefore maintains that it is the duty of every young man like myself to join and strengthen it.'

'There is much in what he says; but I find it regrettable that he should make no mention of the Church.'

'Father, even you could not persuade me that I have a vocation.'

The old man smiled. 'No, my son; if you ever become a saint it will be as a St. George, not as a St. Francis of Assisi. It was to the part which the Church has played during these past twenty years in the national life of France, that I was referring.'

'About that I know only what I have picked up in casual conversation.'

'There I am in part to blame; but it was Monsieur le Duc's wish that I should exclude all matters connected with the development of modern France from your courses of instruction. It seems now, though, that I ought to give you at least an outline of Ultramontane endeavours to prevent the French people from falling entirely into the clutches of the devil.'

'Ultramontane means "from beyond the mountains"; or, in other words, "guidance from Rome", does it not?' de Quesnoy remarked. 'And I have heard it said that by subscribing to it the French Royalists have done themselves more harm than good.'

'That will not prove so in the long run.'

'I had in mind the military support given by Napoleon III to Pope Pius IX, with the object of maintaining His Holiness's temporal claims against the new Italian Monarchy, and pressure by the Church on France after the fall of the Second Empire to continue that costly policy.'

The Abbé gave a slight shrug. 'Admittedly the crusade of which you speak proved highly unpopular; but that was a quarter of a century ago. When His Holiness Leo XIII succeeded to the Tiara he initiated the *Railliement*, and so more than regained the ground lost by the Church.'

'I have often heard the *Railliement* spoken of, Father; but I know little about it.'

'Then I will inform you. Whilst it is true that the Monarchist cause suffered to some extent because an army had been sent to Italy in response to Pope Pius's appeal for help, the cause of the Church in France suffered even more from its affiliation with the Monarchists, owing to French Catholics constantly being called on to support measures in the interests of the Pretender. Moreover, it was clear that the chances of a Restoration were growing ever more remote. In consequence, Pope Leo decided that, for a while at least, the connection must be severed, so that French Catholics would no longer be regarded as enemies by their Government, and he issued . . .'

'This betrayal . . .' de Quesnoy cut in. 'Yes, why should one not call a spade a spade—this betrayal by His Holiness of his allies does not appear to have done the Church much good. It did not prevent Jules Ferry and his gang of unbelievers from driving into exile the Jesuits, the Eudists, the Assumptionists, and a score of other Orders; or of enforcing a secular education on the masses.'

'The new diplomacy came too late to prevent the persecutions of the eighties, but it put a check upon them when they might have been carried much further. The French Government could not fail to be impressed by the series of Encyclicals issued by the Holy Father, calling upon all Catholics to abandon further attempts at political domination, accept democracy and recognize Republican institutions.'

The young Count raised his "devil's" eyebrows. 'I wonder that the bones of the martyrs did not rattle in their crystal pyxes on the Church ordering her faithful servants to prostrate themselves before the "Slut".'

With a reproving shake of his dangling silver curls, the Abbé replied: 'It ill becomes one of your age to criticize the policy of the Holy See; and, although its results may not appear obvious, they are in fact highly satisfactory. After eight years of consistent wooing His Holiness has succeeded in convincing the French Republicans that he has no designs against them. In consequence their enmity has evaporated and an armistice come into existence. So, you see, much has been saved, and even achieved, for the faithful. Their position is now stronger than it has been for many years, and they are once again at liberty to carry on a peaceful penetration into all spheres of French official life.'

'If that is so, Father, I must admit that you have made your case. But you were saying just now that the chances of a restoration were becoming ever more remote. Surely if that is so the withdrawal of the Church's support from the principle of Monarchy must be largely responsible?'

'My son, I was speaking of the eighties. Matters are now very different. Today Socialism, Communism, and even Anarchy menace

France; and few people have any faith in the ability of the Republican politicians to behead these monsters. If the affair were handled with skill and resolution I believe the bulk of the nation would willingly accept a Monarchy, as in so doing lies the only hope of securing a government which will prove both strong and lasting.'

'Would the Church continue to stand aside or would she lend her help in an attempt to overthrow the Republic?'

The Abbé shrugged. 'The Holy Father could not be expected to go back on his public pronouncements as long as France remained officially a Republic; but French Catholics would be free to espouse the Royalist cause if they wished, and who can doubt that the great majority of them would do so? And that brings me, my son, to the point I wish to make. Should you decide to go to France and enter into the designs to place the Duc de Vendôme on the Throne . . .'

'What!' exclaimed the Count. 'Is it settled, then, that this youngster should be groomed for King?'

'Not definitely; but last night, after you had gone up to bed, there was further talk of it, and all agreed that no more promising candidate could be found. Should the Monarchist Committee endorse that view, it is quite possible that in a few years' time you will become involved in a Royalist conspiracy. During it you may become exasperated by the refusal of prominent Catholics to give you their active help. That is why I have explained Ultramontaneism to you.'

De Quesnoy smiled. 'It seems, Father, that you are taking it for granted that I shall decide to go to France.'

'My son, I know you better than you know yourself. Directly you spoke to me of this I realized that you had already made up your mind to do so; but I fear Monsieur le Duc will stop you if he can.'

'I may defy him. If so, can I still count upon your blessing?'

The old man nodded. 'Since your conscience urges you to exchange an easy life for a hard one, how could I deny it to you.'

Prince Igor and his wife were still staying in the house, which meant that the household would follow the same routine as on previous nights; so Armand decided that the best time to tackle his father was before they went up to change for dinner.

The Duke, not being accustomed to having his privacy disturbed at this hour, raised his grey eyebrows slightly as Armand came into his room, and inquired:

'What is it, my boy?'

Perching himself on an arm of the settee, the Count smiled a trifle nervously. 'It is, Sir, that I wish to discuss my future with you.'

'Indeed!' De Richleau looked slightly surprised. 'I thought you were quite happy here, and would be as long as the hunting lasts. But we spoke vaguely some time ago of your doing a tour of Greece and Italy in the spring. If you feel restless I am quite agreeable to your advancing the date of your departure.'

'It is not that, Sir. I wish to become a soldier.'

The Duke stared at him. 'A soldier! In God's name why? If you had to make your way in the world the career of arms is, for a gentleman, as good as any. But you have not. Your name and the one you will inherit from me are career enough. Why give the best years of your life to a dreary routine in barracks and camp, when you might spend them travelling the world, and enjoying the companionship of the most distinguished men and most beautiful women wherever you may go?'

'It is an urge that I have which will not be denied.'

'Very well, then,' de Richleau said, after a moment. 'If you are really set on this, I will write to the Czar. I am sure His Imperial Majesty would be happy to give you a commission as an Ensign in one of his regiments of Guards; and it should be easy enough to get you out again when a year or two of marching up and down has brought you to your senses.'

De Quesnoy drew a deep breath. 'I thank you, Sir; but you seem to forget that I am not a Russian.'

'What the devil do you mean?'

'Why, that even my dear mother was only half a Russian; so I am three-quarters French by blood, and wholly so by inclination.'

'That makes no difference. Officers of foreign extraction are still favourably received into the service of most European Courts, and that is certainly the case in St. Petersburg.'

'True, Sir; but it is with the French Army that I wish to serve. Now that I am eighteen, I am, as a French national, liable to be called up for military service in it. I have no wish to lose my French citizenship, or to serve in the ranks; but both can be avoided by my volunteering for a commission. And that is my intention.'

'Your intention!' The Duke jumped to his feet. His rosy cheeks had gone redder above his carefully parted beard, and his blue eyes flashed angrily. 'How dare you talk to me of your intentions! You know well enough my views on France. Is it likely that I would allow you to take a commission in the French Army?'

The young Count shrugged. 'I feared that you might take this view, Sir; but permit me to say that I find it unreasonable. I am a Frenchman, so it is in the French Army that I should serve.'

'Nonsense! There is no earthly reason why you should serve with any army. There is something behind this, I've not a doubt. Yes, I have it! That little English witch, Madame Syveton. Anyone could see that you had gone quite mad about her. This is nothing more nor less than a moon-struck youngster's clumsily-thought-up excuse for following her to Paris.'

'Were it that, Sir, I would have gone without bothering you; but I assure you it is not.'

'Then de Galliffet has been getting at you, and inflaming your mind with tales of cavalry charges.'

'No; he said only that the Army of France could not have too many young men like myself.'

'Then, since he knows my views, his behaviour as a guest was despicable!'

'Surely that is unfair. He believes France to be in peril of internal collapse, and that the only thing which can save her is a strong Army officered by honest, patriotic men.'

De Richleau had been pacing up and down. Suddenly he stopped and swung round upon his son. 'What is it to me what happens to France? When we have French guests here, as a matter of courtesy I discuss the latest news from Paris with them. But you know my views about France well enough. For half a century after she murdered her rightful King, all that was best in France drained from her. She was left like an orange that has been sucked dry. She is like a carcass that has become the prey of jackals, vultures and worms. Last night you heard Syveton make his extraordinary proposal that I should let him and his friends endeavour to put me on the Throne. Only politeness restrained me from laughing. If I had to choose I would sooner become King of some country in which the inhabitants were naked blackamoors. I would then, at least, have some hope of inculcating decency and honesty into such simple subjects. But the French are now a race without honour, principles or any of the higher aspirations. Apart from a few eccentrics like de Galliffet and de Camargue, the nation now consists of a greedy, treacherous, self-seeking bourgeoisie, and workers who have become ever more irresponsible and brutalized by a succession of bloody revolutions. Yet you, my son, the future Duc de Richleau, calmly propose that I should allow you to become an officer in an army which takes its orders from the criminals these people now elect to represent them.'

'Father, you exaggerate,' de Quesnoy protested. 'Because a part of a nation has gone rotten that is no justification for condemning the whole. There must still be many millions of good, honest men and women in France, and it is them whom I hope to serve.'

'Then the sooner you turn your hopes in some other direction the better. I will not permit you to wear the uniform of any Republic, least of all that of France.'

'My heart is set upon it, Sir; and you cannot stop me.'

'Can I not? You seem to forget that you are as yet only eighteen. For the past year I have allowed you to enjoy the private income which will be yours when you are twenty-one. But there are three years to go before you become of age, and until then I can cut off your money by the stroke of a pen. I hardly think that your enthusiasm for becoming a *sous-lieutenant* will survive the idea of supporting yourself solely on the miserable pittance paid to officers of that rank.'

De Quesnoy sighed. 'The prospect is a most unpleasant one, and I must confess, Father, that I foresaw that you might confront me with it. In consequence, I felt bound to take certain precautions against any such distressing eventuality.'

'What the devil are you talking about?'

'About your Star of the Order of St. Louis, Sir.'

'My, my . . . ?'

'The one with the pigeon-blood ruby in its centre, which is said to be worth a million francs.'

'Yes, yes! What of it?'

'When you were showing the family jewels to our friends the other day I slipped the Star into my pocket and put the empty case back in the safe. Yesterday I did the Star up in a sealed packet and without disclosing what the packet contained gave it to one of our guests who left this morning with the request that it should be banked in Paris in my name.'

De Richleau's eyes bulged and his beard was bristling. He looked as if at any moment he was likely to have a fit. 'A thief!' he gasped. 'My son, a thief!'

'No, Sir. For the time being it cannot be said that I have done more than borrow this family jewel. And I was driven to resort to that stratagem owing only to my knowledge of your fanatical hatred of modern France. You alone can make me a thief by compelling me to sell the jewel. Since I prize it as greatly as yourself only dire necessity would drive me to do so. But necessity knows no law and sell it I shall have to if you carry out your threat to deprive me of my income.'

For a moment the Duke stared at his son, then he said: 'You are old beyond your years, Armand; and there are times when I think you have a devil in you. Only possession could make a young man of such promise so determined to throw himself away. You will rue this day before you are finished, for France is as rotten as a putrefying corpse. I see though that there is no persuading you of the truth. Go then, but remember this. As long as you remain in the service of the French Republic I will not receive you in my house.'

CHAPTER VI

PARIS IN THE NINETIES

PARIS in the Nineties—what pictures those words conjure up. *La Ville Lumière*, the Mecca of the pleasure-loving from all over the world, the Queen city of fashion and the Patroness of all that was new in literature and art.

Every night hundreds of *fiacres* drove visitors from all nations up the hill to Montmartre, to watch the girls dance the can-can or to sup with a charmer of their own choice in a private room. In the Moulin Rouge, Abbaye de Télème, Bal Tabarin, Café d'Enfer, and scores of less famous haunts round the Place Pigalle, corks popped without ceasing, violinists played catchy tunes and kisses were snatched openly at the tables between jokes, crazy bets and hilarious laughter.

France was cashing in handsomely on the craving of the better-off males in more sober countries to have a place to go to in which they could let off steam; and while the "wages of sin" at length overtook a proportion of its female denizens many a hard-boiled little French girl retired with enough cash to settle down happily as the wife of a minor official, or a small farmer in the part of the country from which she had originally come. Vice had yet to be driven underground by well-meaning moralists, so this nightly Saturnalia continued from year's end to year's end, and even most of the wives of the male revellers accepted it as quite natural that when in Paris their husbands should go on the spree.

But the wives had their way of making the husbands pay. For them Paris meant dresses, furs, jewels, hats, shoes, lingerie. And if a bewhiskered spouse did not return till dawn from trips to "see the sights" with some of his men friends, he could not complain overmuch at the size of the bills that came in from the famous shops in the Rue de la Paix and the Rue St. Honoré; or at another huge round-lidded trunk in which to carry these female delights back to the United States, Russia, the Balkans, England or the Argentine.

There were, too, the Museums, the Opera, the Churches and the Galleries; the races at Longchamps and Auteuil; afternoon tea at the Ritz, the Crillion or the Meurice; and dinners at those world-renowned restaurants Larue, Tour d'Argent, Voisins and Maxims, all then at the height of their fame.

On the Left Bank there was another equally stimulating, if less plutocratic, world. There Henri Murger's "Vie de Bohême" was still being lived by thousands of students of all nationalities. From dusk to dawn the gas jets flared in their cafés while they debated the merits of the arts through all the centuries and, more eagerly than all the rest, those of tomorrow. Only six years earlier the Impressionists, infuriated at the refusal of the committee of the Salon to hang their pictures, had started an annual exhibition of their own, known as the Salon of the Rejected. Degas, Renoir and Monet could often be seen in the neighbourhood of the Luxembourg. In the cafés vitriolic leader-writers like Rochefort, Clemenceau and Drumont could be heard declaiming, and admiring circles of young people gathered round writers of such diverse talents as Alphonse Daudet, Emile Zola and Anatole France.

Such, as seen by foreigners, was the Paris to which Armand de Quesnoy came towards the end of January 1894. But it was not until very much later that he got to know, even superficially, either Montmartre or the Latin Quarter. For him Parisian life centred in the sedate Faubourg St. Germain where, behind high walls and private courtyards, stood the mansions of the great families of the *ancien régime*.

For the past half-century most of these families had lived in dignified retirement. They had ignored the Second Empire as though it had never occurred, and they despised the Republic as much as did de Richleau, but they preferred to remain in Paris rather than go into voluntary exile. Their great wealth enabled them to continue as an elegant and rigidly exclusive society that toiled not, neither did it spin. They kept chefs who were as much maestros as those in the best restaurants and their table talk was often wittier than anything which could have been heard in Montparnasse. Many of the men had taken up learned pursuits, and nearly all derived their principal amusement from a succession of affaires with the wives of their friends. The women gave considerable time to religious observances and frequently debated the merits of their respective Father Confessors; but their favourite reading was typified by Beaudelaire and Housmans, and at six o'clock each evening, when their husbands were theoretically at the Club, their maids brought to their boudoirs by way of the back stairs their lovers of the moment.

Yet even into this little world apart de Quesnoy was slow to penetrate. That was not from lack of introductions, as he was related to several of the leading families, but because he was much more tied by the curriculum at St. Cyr than he had anticipated. He arrived in Paris only a week before the term was due to start, and much of that was taken up by interviews, buying his military equipment and badgering a tailor into hurrying with his uniforms.

The Syvetons, he found, lived in the wealthiest quarter of Paris. They had a house in the Rue de Lisbonne which stood in its own grounds and backed on to the Parc Monceau. His first call was on Angela, but to his annoyance he learned that she and her husband were on holiday in the South of France. On his presenting himself to his cousins, the de Grammonts, the de Brissacs and the de Polignacs—they all received him most kindly, as too did the Marquise de Galliffet, who was one of the leaders of this exclusive society, and he was soon showered with cards of invitation; but at the end of the week he found himself swallowed up in the military machine, so had to refuse all those for the future that he had hoped to accept.

The little town of St. Cyr had a population of about three thousand and was some eighteen miles from central Paris. The train service was poor, slow and indescribably dirty, and the only alternative a carriage drive of at least two hours, so the capital was not readily accessible; but the real bar which prevented de Quesnoy going there was that for first-term students it was out of bounds.

The French Army took itself very seriously and, as de Galliffet had warned his young protégé, the officer cadets at St. Cyr were worked extremely hard. The college was housed in a seventeenth-century convent from which its religious inmates had been ejected at the time of the Revolution and, apart from equipping it with beds and desks, very little had since been done to it; so it was far from comfortable. But young men who were roused for their first parade at five-thirty, did not get away from their last lecture till six, and were expected to spend the rest of the evening reading up their notes, had little time left to worry about the niceties of existence.

On Sundays, after Church Parade, they were allowed to go into

Versailles, but they had to be back in mess for dinner; so illicit trips for the sake only of a few afternoon hours in Paris were hardly worth the risk, particularly as their uniforms made them easily liable to be noticed and reported.

This life of hardship and restraint was so different from any that de Quesnoy had ever led that he might have been expected soon to become bored and resentful; but, on the contrary, now that he was actually learning about the trade of arms he found so much in it to interest him that he thought of nothing else. All but a few of his ancestors had been soldiers and through his mother's mother he was descended from the Great Condé, so his enthusiasm was understandable; and this, together with his quick mind and agile body, early led his instructors to regard him as a young officer of great promise.

Had he been conceited or priggish, this might have led to cold-shouldering by his less gifted colleagues, but he told them airily that he owed his swift progress only to two pieces of luck—having been made to read history so extensively before coming to St. Cyr, so that he was already conversant with the development of many outstanding campaigns, and having hunted from his infancy, as there was nothing like it to prepare a man for the physical side of military life. Moreover he was decidedly open-handed. Money played little part in their lives, but wine did, and he was always calling on others to share with him bottles of the choicer vintages that he ordered both to drink with his dinner and afterwards. So, although he displayed little interest in anything but his work, they put him down as an amiable eccentric.

In the circumstances it was natural that he should have had only a vague idea how events in France were shaping, but general conversation in the mess kept him informed of the main features of the situation.

There had been fifteen cabinets in nine years and in the previous autumn the elections had shortly been followed by another change of government. Charles Dupuy, the previous Premier, had come back, but only to fall after a few weeks and to be replaced by Jean Casimir-Périer. It was, as usual, a government formed from a combination of the Centre parties, but as a result of the elections the Socialists had secured fifty seats, and the Anarchists were active. In December they had actually thrown a bomb into the Chamber, but their outrages were now turning public sentiment against them and the other parties of the Left.

From '88 to '93 Charles de Freycinet, a former Premier, had been War Minister. Although the first civilian in the history of the Republic to hold the post, he had done better for his country than the soldiers, as he had both helped to modernize the army and initiated a military alliance with Russia. In '91 a provisional understanding had been entered into and now, in the new year of '94, the Czar Alexander III had formally signed a military pact with France.

A few weeks later the Czar died, to be succeeded by Nicholas II, but the validity of the pact was not affected and the Casimir-Périer government reaped a brief popularity from having concluded this treaty which would give France greater security from the ever-growing power of Germany. But such services to the country were nothing to the venal politicians who made their disreputable living by bartering their allegiance with a different would-be leader every few months; so, in May, Casimir-Périer's government fell and Charles Dupuy again became Premier.

Dupuy was a burly, bearded man; he had spent his early life as a teacher, was devoid of imagination, and resembled in both physique and cunning a Balkan peasant. His new ministry included several promising political tight-rope-walkers of the future: Louis Barthou for Public Works, Théophile Delcassé for Colonies and Félix Faure for Marine. To the Foreign Office he appointed a permanent Civil Servant, Gabriel Hanotaux, and at the War Office he retained the only survivor of the last government, General Mercier, a reserved, courteous, courageous professional soldier.

But less than a month later this new combination was upset owing to an Italian anarchist stabbing President Carnot to death while he was carrying out a public ceremony in Lyons. Casimir-Périer was persuaded to stand for the Presidency and elected. He was the son of one of the conservative founders of the Republic and a director of the Anzin coal-mine syndicate, so a man with both traditions and wealth behind him.

Between him and Dupuy, who was a scholarship boy, there existed a natural antipathy and when, in accordance with convention, on the death of a President, Dupuy resigned office Casimir-Périer asked his friend Burdeau to form a government. Burdeau, on account of ill-health, refused, so Dupuy had to be recalled. More bitter now than ever against the President he resolved that he should be allowed no say whatever in the conduct of affairs, and Dupuy's henchman Hanotaux even went to the length of refusing to allow the President to see the Foreign Office telegrams.

Of more interest to de Quesnoy, and most of his fellow students, were the fortunes of French arms overseas. Algeria had long been ruled by France, although only in '81 had the final rebellions of its people been suppressed and the country reduced to an orderly colony. In the same year, by the Treaty of Bardo, the French had annexed Tunisia and soon afterwards subdued its much less war-like inhabitants. But the war in North Africa was never-ending. The blue-veiled Tuaregs of the Atlas could be kept in check only by establishing outposts ever farther south into the Sahara, and the trade routes to Morocco and the Sudan were in constant need of protection.

In the past ten years France had also made great conquests in Indo-China. Saigon had been occupied in the sixties, but it was another twenty years before any extensive area had been brought under French rule. When the Chinese, who claimed an ancient overlordship of these territories, became hostile, Admiral Courbet had been ordered to force the Emperor of Annam to acknowledge a French Protectorate and later to annex Tonkin. Severe fighting had in '85 led the Chinese to sue for peace, and as a bonus for these operations the French had also acquired a protectorate over the Indo-Chinese kingdom of Cambodia.

In West Africa, from the seventeenth century, the French had had trading posts on the coast of Senegal, but it was not until the sixties that General Faidherbe had penetrated its hinterland to any depth and still later that the great explorer Savorgnan de Brazza had pushed his way deep into the interior. Now, in the nineties, French expeditions were busily annexing Dahomey, the Ivory Coast, great areas of Nigeria and the Congo and one, this very year, under an engineer officer named Joffre, had occupied Timbuktu.

But it was Madagascar above all which now held the imagination of the young officers. That great island was dominated by the Hovas, who were the descendants of a warrior Polynesian race which had arrived there many centuries earlier from the South Pacific. They had accepted French Protection during the Second Empire, but they had failed to honour their agreements and, it was said, exercised a brutal tyranny over the negroid tribes which constituted a considerable proportion of the population of the island. Rumours had it that measures were already on foot to despatch an expedition under General Duchesne to reduce the Hovas to obedience, and as the General had shown great initiative in the Indo-China campaigns all the most ambitious officers would have given much to accompany him.

Soon after the election of the new President, the college broke up for its summer vacation. De Quesnoy had intended to spend it in Paris but found that nearly all the big houses in the St. Germain district were closed. Many of the old nobility still adhered to the custom of pretending to enjoy family life in the country during the height of summer and, having no flair for it, more or less picnicked in considerable discomfort at their châteaux; while others, less hide-bound by convention, took villas at Biarritz or Deauville. In consequence after a few days the Count once more put on civilian clothes, and took the night express for Vienna.

He knew the Imperial city well as he had often stayed there with his father, who when in Austria was known as Count Königstein, a title he derived from a Castle that he owned on the Danube. In Vienna, Frau Sacher was delighted to welcome the young man again at her hotel and after a day spent looking up old friends he was at once plunged into a round of gaieties.

Most of his contemporaries had now become junior officers in crack cavalry regiments, and if many of them were not overburdened with brains nobody could accuse them of lacking high spirits. Attendance at formal dinners, balls and concerts at the houses of their parents were interspersed with noisy drinking parties, mad moonlight rides across country and, one night, the kidnapping by a party of them of the whole chorus after the performance of a musical comedy at the Stadttheater.

Early in August, having worked five months' pent-up exuberance out of his system, de Quesnoy returned to St. Cyr, resigned once more to accepting its discipline as the price of acquiring the sort of military knowledge in which he had found his Austrian friends sadly lacking. But now, as a student in his second half-year, he found life there much more pleasant. Not only was less time spent on the barrack square and —for the cavalry side to which he had naturally had himself posted— in stables; but, providing their work was satisfactory, officer cadets were allowed Paris leave from midday Saturday to Sunday night every other week-end.

This at least enabled the Count to enlarge the circle of his Parisian acquaintances, and during the autumn he became on friendly terms with many families whose doors his cousins were able to open for him. A second call he had made on the Syvetons before leaving for Vienna had proved as fruitless as the first, as they were then staying with friends at the newly fashionable seaside resort of Le Touquet. He had left cards on both occasions, but this had drawn no response from Angela which puzzled him considerably.

Although he would not have admitted to being passionately in love with her, he had come nearer to that state than he had with any other girl, and even after all these months he still could not get her out of his mind. So now that it was easier for him to get into Paris he decided to try to reopen their affaire. But he did not mean to make a third call that might prove unlucky again.

Ordinarily a wealthy bourgeois like Gabriel Syveton would not have been received in the aristocratic St. Germain circle, but being a member of the committee of the Royalist *Ligue de la Patrie Française* had given him a tenuous footing in it; and that had been strengthened by his marriage to Angela, as she was the granddaughter of an English Earl—an asset that he had by no means overlooked when tempted by her youthful beauty into asking for her hand. So de Quesnoy, by tactful inquiries among his friends, was able to find out when he would be certain of finding Angela at home, and it transpired that she habitually received between three and six on the first and third Thursdays, and at ten o'clock in the evening on the first Tuesday, of every month.

To attend an evening reception in the middle of the week was more than the Count could hope to manage, but he at once took certain steps. First he mentioned to one of the senior instructors that migraine was interfering with his work, then he consulted the college doctor. A week later he told the instructor that the pills the doctor had given him were doing no good, and asked permission to make an appointment to see a specialist in Paris. His request was granted, and at half-past three on the third Thursday in September he presented himself at the house backing on to the Parc Monceau.

Such afternoon "at homes" were a regular feature of social life and mainly attended by women, who often called at several of them on the same afternoon; but quite a number of men of leisure made a practice of going to those of hostesses whom they found attractive or amusing.

57

Usually they were confined to *conversaziones* at which the latest scandals were discussed, but sometimes there was also music or diversions such as the presence of a professional fortune teller whom the visitors could consult gratis. Having a large garden Angela held hers out in it, whenever the weather was suitable, and, as she detested scandal, sought to amuse her guests with croquet, badminton and lawn tennis.

Somewhat to de Quesnoy's surprise, therefore, he was taken straight through the house and a conservatory at its back, but on emerging again into the sunlight he saw the reason. With laughter and excited little cries several young people were playing pat-ball on the two courts, and some older ones were standing about among the croquet hoops, while in front of an ornate two-storeyed garden pavilion at the far end of the lawn a number of small tables were set for tea.

Near the tables about a dozen people were chatting and among them Angela; so de Quesnoy made his way towards her. As she was talking to a couple she did not notice his approach until he was quite near her, and it was only when they politely broke off the conversation so that she could greet the new arrival that she turned and recognized him.

The blood mounted to her face and the automatic hostess's smile she had given froze upon it. With an effort she held out her hand and, having kissed it, he murmured: 'Please forgive me for taking you by surprise. Perhaps I should have sent a note asking permission to call; but as an old friend I thought . . .'

'No . . . Yes . . . But of course,' she stammered. 'You left cards before, I think. You are at the Military College at St. Cyr, are you not?'

As he made an appropriate reply he suddenly realized that although her lips were parted in a smile her brown eyes were regarding him with barely-concealed hostility. Having no idea of the effect that his attempt at seduction had had upon her, or of her belief that on leaving her room he had deliberately insulted her, he was so taken aback that, for once, he found himself at a loss for words. Recovering after a moment he made the banal remark:

'It is unusual at an "at home" to find people engaged in sport.'

'I am aware that it is considered eccentric,' she replied defensively, 'but I am excused that because I am English, and many people seem to enjoy such games. Do you play any of them?'

58

'Well, no,' he admitted. 'I fear I was brought up only to indulge in pursuits of a more manly nature.'

De Quesnoy spoke with no *double entendre* in mind but she took it that he had and, with an angry flash of her brown eyes, rapped out: 'Then you will find little to interest you here!'

'What are you saying, my dear? Surely I cannot have heard you rightly!' It was Syveton who had just come up behind them and caught their last exchange of sentences. Shaking de Quesnoy eagerly by the hand he said how pleased he was to see him; then turned to his wife and went on:

'You must not be surprised Angèle, if everyone does not care for these English pastimes. In fact I am amazed that so many of our friends should have taken to them so readily. But to imply that we are incapable of entertaining Monsieur le Count in any other way is really silly.'

Angela blushed again and said quickly: 'I did not mean anything of that kind. You misunderstood me.'

'I felt sure that I must have,' Syveton smiled, 'although your French is now so greatly improved that you rarely any longer convey a meaning you do not intend.' Turning again to de Quesnoy, he asked after his father and how he was finding life at St. Cyr, then requested him to name a day when it would suit him to come to lunch or dinner.

The Count hesitated only a second. Angela, unseen by her husband, was still frowning at him, but he thought her more alluring than ever. The sunshine brought out the lights in her dark gold curls and upon them at a rakish angle was perched an absurd little straw boater. She was wearing a striped blouse with full sleeves and a high neck, the whalebone supports of which caused her to tilt her chin up provocatively. In the past nine months she had fined down, losing the last of her girlish puppy-fat, and was now an exceptionally beautiful young woman. Both attracted afresh and determined to find out the reason for her unexpected coldness towards him, he explained to Syveton that it was only possible for him to lunch or dine in Paris during weekends, then he accepted an invitation to luncheon the coming Sunday.

Soon afterwards the arrival of more callers put an end to the conversation. De Quesnoy spent an hour chatting to several guests with whom he had a slight acquaintance, and amusing himself by challenging Angela's step-son, Henri Syveton, to a competition in drinking Café Viennoise. Fond as the Count was of that form of refreshment, the fair-haired, fresh-faced youngster of twelve won easily. But de Quesnoy had established good relations with him, which he felt might prove useful in the future. He then took leave of his hostess, whose expression he now found inscrutable.

Being much too shrewd to take any unnecessary risk of getting into trouble for having gone into Paris under false pretences, he presented himself at five o'clock at the apartment of a specialist with whom he had made an appointment. An entirely pointless interview ensued and the Count clocked into mess at St. Cyr that evening still greatly puzzled by Angela's attitude towards him.

The following Sunday brought him no enlightenment. There were a dozen people at the luncheon party and he managed to get Angela alone only for a few minutes when they were all strolling in the garden afterwards. On his taxing her with her changed manner she said that he must have imagined it; and when he asked her permission to attend her afternoon "at homes" regularly, she granted it readily.

For him to do so required further special measures, as he found it a bore to feign illness, and he would have had to continue to do so in order to keep up for any length of time the fiction that he required treatment for migraine. Fortunately, the greater part of Thursday afternoons was devoted to equine matters and as there was very little about horse management that de Quesnoy did not already know, he was able to put it to his instructors that he was really wasting his time, and could employ it to much better advantage if he were allowed to go into Paris every Thursday and spend his afternoons in the great military library at the Bibliothéque de l'Arsenal ferreting out the obscurer details of certain classical campaigns. A similar latitude was at times allowed to second-year students and having already become a star pupil now stood him in good stead. Wishing to encourage his keenness his chief instructor backed his request and it was granted by the Commandant.

From then on he read with considerable profit once a week at the Bibliothéque and on every other Thursday put in an hour or so at Angela's "at home". He soon found that Syveton usually looked in on these parties only between four and five o'clock, so by making a practice of arriving on the dot of three he generally succeeded in getting a short tête-à-tête with Angela before any other guests appeared. Her attitude was now quite friendly and he soon became fascinated again by her; so, although she gave him no encouragement, he persevered, and at their fourth meeting began once more to lay siege to her in earnest.

She admitted that it was her husband's treatment of her which made her regard physical love as revolting, that her women friends had assured her that a man one liked could make it delightful, and that she now realized that nearly every wife in her position took a lover, but added that she was still loath to risk disappointment and further unhappiness by so doing.

Having got so far de Quesnoy felt convinced that to win her now called only for patience and persuasion; so he began to reinforce his pleadings at their brief talks with a series of letters in which amusing episodes of his life at St. Cyr were skilfully blended with passionate devotion. Her replies were at first stilted but gradually became warmer and in the first week of December she at last agreed to give him the rendez-vous for which he had pleaded so long.

CHAPTER VII

THE RENDEZ-VOUS

YVETON was going to attend a rally of the *Ligue de la Patrie Française* that was to be held at Orleans on the coming Sunday, and was to stay for it over the week-end with friends in a nearby Château; so Angela was free to do what she liked on the Saturday evening.

Diner à deux in a private room was the accepted formula for such stolen meetings, and de Quesnoy decided on the Ambassadeurs as the temple which should be the scene of his eagerly anticipated bliss. He chose it because it could be approached more discreetly than most other places of its kind and was at this time of year little frequented; for it was situated among the trees on the north side of the Champs Élysées, and, although during the summer its kitchen served a large open-air restaurant, in winter only a small staff was retained to look after the couples who hired the eight or ten private rooms on its upper floor.

To such *maisons de rendez-vous* it was customary for women of good social standing to come alone in a hired carriage and heavily veiled. They left in the same manner; so no one except the waiter ever saw their faces or saw them in the company of their lovers, and the waiters in such places made a handsome living from lavish tips to ensure their discretion.

On the Thursday de Quesnoy explained all this to Angela and gave her the most detailed instructions, then he returned to St. Cyr to get through the next forty-eight hours with as much patience as he could muster.

On the Friday evening, Syveton having already left for Orleans, Angela had the Marquise de Frontignac to dine with her. The Marquise was two years older than Angela and like her had fine brown eyes; but she was a brunette with a high-coloured complexion and alluring red lips. She had been married at seventeen to an elderly nobleman whose principal interest in life was gambling and he had soon made it clear that provided she conducted her affaires with discretion he would raise no objection to her having lovers. Being a passionate young creature by nature she had lost no time in accepting the hint, and, as she was extremely vivacious as well as good-looking, there was great competition for her favours.

The two girls had met during the previous spring and mutual attraction had soon led to their becoming fast friends; but they had not seen one another for the past two months because the Marquise had been absent with her husband in Algeria, and had returned to Paris only during the preceding week. Naturally they had a hundred things to talk about, and Madeleine de Frontignac being a most amusing chatterbox her accounts of handsome sheiks and visits to harems kept them occupied all through dinner.

It was not until they had retired afterwards to Angela's boudoir that her guest asked: 'And you, my pet? What have you been doing with yourself while I have been away? Tell me, I beg, that you are no longer living the stupid life of a nun, but have by now accepted my advice and taken a lover.'

'Not yet,' Angela replied with a smile. 'But I have a rendez-vous for tomorrow night.'

Springing up, Madeleine ran to her and embraced her. 'Darling! How wonderful! Is he charming? He must be! Oh, how I shall think of you having this first lovely experience.'

Angela shook her head. 'Don't, my dear. You would be wasting your time. I am not going to it.'

'Not going to it!' repeated the Marquise aghast. 'But why not? You should have given that horrid husband of yours a pair of horns months ago. And for you to waste these best years of your life is a sin against nature. Is it that you lack courage, *cherie*? Yes, that must be it. But if this man loves you your fears are groundless. I give you my word that you will find it so.'

'Oh, he is mad enough about me,' Angela shrugged. 'But he does not love me in the true sense. All he really wants is to satisfy his male conceit that he can overcome the scruples of any woman if he tries hard enough. You see, nearly a year ago I was in love with him and he knows that. But I wouldn't give way to him. It is only that which has made him return to the attack with such determination.'

63

'How can you know that for certain?' Madeleine argued. 'You have no experience in such affairs to go on, my pet. For all you know he may have been desperately in love with you all this time.'

'No. He has a horrid cynicism about such matters which I find quite revolting.'

'Why, then, did you not show him plainly that his attentions were unwelcome before matters got so far?'

'That was owing to Gabriel. When this beau of mine first called on me here in September I was deliberately rude to him. Gabriel overheard me and was furious. He promptly asked him to lunch; then later ordered me to make him welcome whenever he called and to do my utmost to cultivate his friendship.'

'Oh delicious, delicious!' Madeleine sat back, clapped her hands and burbled with laughter. 'Although it is as old as the hills there is always something inexpressibly comic about the husband smoothing the path for the lover. Gabriel being such a climber, though, what you tell me makes it clear that your beau must be a man of consequence.'

'Yes, he is a member of one of the best families.'

'Providing he is sound in wind and limb so much the better. But why, oh why, my pet, if you have become disillusioned about him should you have allowed him to persuade you into giving him a rendez-vous?'

Angela thrust out her square jaw a little as she replied: 'Because instead of making allowances for my youth and innocence a year ago he went out of his way to humiliate me, and I swore to myself then that sooner or later I would get my own back on him.'

Madeleine's eyes widened. 'I see that there is a story here. You know Angèle that you can trust me. Will you not tell me what took place between you, when you first knew this man.'

'Why not,' Angela agreed after a moment. 'My greatest joy in having a friend like yourself is that we can safely confide our most secret thoughts to one another.' Suppressing names and places she related all that had occurred during her visit to Jvanets the previous winter, ending up with de Quesnoy's implication that she would have found a suitable amusement in playing with his mother's doll's house.

Before her friend could comment she stood up, went to her bureau and took from it a square mahogany box about eight inches deep. Sliding back the lid, she displayed its contents. Gummed to its bottom,

and arranged like a miniature stage setting, were the complete furnishings for a doll's bedroom, and propped up in the bed sat a naked
celluloid female doll with golden hair. A slip of paper was pinned to
the counterpane. Upon it Angela had written "Here is an addition to
your mother's doll's house. I feel sure it will afford you more amusement
than I could do."

Staring at her in amazement, Madeleine asked: 'What ... what do
you intend to do with this?'

'I mean to send it to him to morrow night by my maid Lucille.
Heavily veiled and dressed in my clothes and furs he will not realize
that she is not me until she has handed him the package upstairs in
the Ambassadeurs, where we are supposed to meet.'

The Marquise de Frontignac pursed up her red lips and gave a
vulgar little whistle; then she began to laugh. When she had recovered
somewhat she said: 'My pet, I would give anything to see his face when
he realizes how he has been fooled.'

'So would I,' Angela agreed with a hard little smile. 'But unfortunately that is a pleasure I must deny myself.'

'How about Lucille? Is this not rather much to require of one's
maid? He may become extremely angry and behave most unpleasantly
towards her.'

'I think that unlikely. In any case I shall reward her very generously
for impersonating me; and I can hardly wait to hear from her how he
takes it. If you are free tomorrow night why not come round here
about nine o'clock and listen to the report she gives me on her
return?'

For a moment Madeleine was silent, then she said: 'I would like
to do that; and I can easily get out of the party to which I was going.
But I have an even better idea. I am nearer to your height than Lucille
and in your furs could impersonate you better. Why should I not keep
this rendez-vous. It would be enormous fun actually to witness the
dénouement of your little plot, and afterwards I could give you a more
graphic account of it than Lucille could ever manage.'

'But ...' Angela hesitated. 'But surely you would find it terribly
embarrassing. I mean, to be alone with him in a room ... and in that
sort of place.'

Madeleine laughed. 'My sweet innocent, I have often been alone
with men before, and there is nothing frightening about such rooms.

They are generally furnished with taste—often in the Louis Seize style. The only thing unusual about them as dining-rooms is that they have an alcove at one end half hidden by drapes, and in it provision for one to lie down should, er . . . sleepiness, or some other feeling incline one to wish to do so after the meal.'

'Really, Madeleine!' Angela coloured slightly. 'You are quite shameless! Still, I suppose it is all right if you are there with a man that you love. This would be quite different, though, for you have not even met him.'

'It might prove still more amusing if I had. And I may have if he is *persona grata* in the Faubourg St. Germain.'

'I doubt if you could have done so, as he is a student at St. Cyr and was unable to get into Paris much until this autumn.'

'Perhaps, after all, that is just as well. I would back my modest talents as an amateur actress to fool most men that I was only a maid for ten minutes or so; but if he did know me and recognize me by my voice he would be in a situation to make things very awkward for me. In any case I would like to know a little more about him; and you must tell me his name, otherwise I won't be able to ask for him when I arrive at the Ambassadeurs.'

'Well, he is very handsome, but younger even than myself. In some ways, though, he is strangely mature and one would never think that he is still only a student. His name is Armand de Quesnoy.'

Madeleine's brown eyes grew round, 'Not the Count de Quesnoy?'

'Yes. You do know him then?'

'No, but I saw him one Sunday just before I left for Algeria. It was at the christening of Sophie de Lazun's new baby. I was so intrigued by his face that I asked who he was.'

Angela nodded. 'He is certainly very striking looking; and he was there. That was the Sunday in September that he lunched here. I remember his telling us that he had just come on from the Lazun christening.'

Suddenly Madeleine took Angela's hand, and said to her earnestly: 'Listen, little one. If this man wishes to become your lover you are crazy to reject him. He is young, handsome, wealthy, debonair, and as the future Duc de Richleau one of the greatest nobles in all France. What more could any woman wish for?'

'For a kind heart and generous understanding.'

66

'Oh, be sensible, I beg!' Madeleine protested. 'In this stupid business about dolls' houses you have imagined an insult where none was intended. At worst it was an ill-timed jest. Forget it, my pet. Most women would give their eyes to have a rendez-vous with such a Prince Charming. Keep it yourself. Have no fears about letting him make love to you. Give yourself to him willingly and whole-heartedly. You are so lovely that if you do that he will want you again and again and become your faithful slave. Do as I advise, *chérie*, and I swear to you that you will never regret it.'

'I once thought him a Prince Charming, but I was wrong,' Angela said with a shake of her head. 'He is a conceited, cynical young rake, and he badly needs a lesson.'

'Very well then.' Madeleine shrugged. 'Since you are determined upon it I will call for your furs and the box tomorrow evening; then later I'll return and let you know how he receives your present.'

The rendez-vous was for eight o'clock. At seven-thirty Madeleine arrived at the Rue de Lisbonne in a plain carriage. She was already heavily veiled, and having collected Angela's sables she set off again with the doll's bedroom under her arm. Angela expected her back about eight-thirty, or soon afterwards, and had ordered a light meal for them both at nine. The hour came but Madeleine had not yet returned. After waiting another half-hour Angela had her dinner. She was now becoming seriously perturbed. It seemed hardly likely that de Quesnoy would have used violence against her supposed maid, but it was possible that his anger had led him forcibly to detain her as a means of getting his own back, knowing that by doing so he would cause her mistress to worry about her. But soon after ten Angela's fears were allayed. A footman brought her a note that had just arrived by hand. On opening it she saw scrawled in Madeleine's hand on a single sheet of flimsy:

I do hope that you have not been too anxious about me, darling. I am quite all right but could not get away at once. As it is getting late now I won't come round to you tonight; but I'll call after Church tomorrow and tell you everything.

Much relieved, Angela went to bed. Next morning she could hardly contain her impatience to hear if de Quesnoy had really forced her friend to stay with him for a couple of hours, or if there was some other explanation. As soon as Madeleine was closeted with her in her boudoir, she exclaimed:

'I can't wait another moment to hear what happened. Was he terribly angry?'

'No; more surprised than angry, I think,' Madeleine replied slowly. 'Anyhow, things did not go at all as I expected.'

'Go on! Tell me, do,' Angela urged.

'Well, he took me for you to start with. Immediately I was shown into the room he gave an exclamation of delight and came forward to kiss my hand. I held out the box to him and said in a low voice, imitating your English accent as well as I could: "I have brought you a present. Please open it while I warm my hands at the fire."

'He looked a little taken aback, but took the box and began to tear off its wrappings. As I expected, the room was a very pleasant one, and over the marble mantelpiece there was a big gilt-framed mirror. As I held my hands to the fire I had my back turned to him but was able to watch his face in the glass.

'When he opened the box he said: "What a charming thought. But why this strange message when you have brought me your sweet self?"

'I threw the bomb then by saying: "Monsieur, I am Madame Syveton's maid Lucille. My mistress ordered me to bring you that box as a reminder of something you said to her when she was staying in your father's house."

'At that moment there was a knock on the door. He called "*Entrez*" and the waiter came in to ask how soon we wished to begin dinner. To the man he said: "Jules, have you any young children?"

' "No, Monsieur le Comte," replied the waiter. "But I have two little grand-daughters aged seven and nine."

'At that de Quesnoy gave rather a bitter laugh and exclaimed: "The very thing. Here; catch!" Then he threw the box at him and added: "There are some toys that may amuse them. Go now, I will ring for you about dinner later."

'When the waiter had backed out, stammering his thanks, the Count turned back to me and said in a hard voice: "And now, Mademoiselle, I hope you appreciate that by having undertaken to play this shabby trick for your mistress you have placed yourself in a very unenviable position?"

'Those upslanting eyebrows of his make him look quite terrifying when he frowns, and before I could pluck up the courage to reply he went on: "You have come here under false pretences. Why should I not take advantage of that fact to teach you and your mistress that I am not the sort of man who can be made a fool of with impunity. I have a mind to call in the police, say you are a girl that I picked up this afternoon and made an assignation with here this evening, and that I now identify those fine furs you are wearing as Madame Syveton's. You would then spend the night in jail, and your perfidious mistress would find herself landed with a pretty scandal before she could get you out again." '

'Oh, the brute!' Angela exclaimed. 'How awful for you! It never entered my mind that I might place you in such a frightful situation.'

Madeleine made a grimace. 'I suppose if I had given the police my right name and sworn that I had borrowed the furs to play a joke upon him without your knowledge they might have believed me. But they wouldn't have accepted that from Lucille; and I warned you that if he proved vindictive he might make things unpleasant for her. I never thought for a moment, though, that he would think up such a devilish scheme for being revenged upon you both.'

'I must have been mad to ever have thought of sending Lucille. But you, my poor Madeleine! What . . . whatever did you do?'

'I faltered out: "Oh please, please, Monsieur le Comte, don't do that. I can understand how disappointed you must be, but surely a great gentleman like yourself will not make a servant pay for having obeyed her mistress's orders?"

'At that, to my immense relief, his whole face changed, and he burst out laughing. "Of course not," he said, giving me a smack on the behind. "I would never dream of such a thing. By frightening you for a moment I have punished you enough. As for your mistress, tell her how by having you arrested I could easily have made her the laughing stock of Paris. It should prove a lesson to her. But I am not one to make war on women."

'While he had been threatening me those grey eyes of his had been hard as agates, and had it not been for my thick veil I really think I should have fainted; but as I stammered my thanks they became quite kind and for some reason he seemed rather amused. After a moment, he said to me:

' "And now Lucille, because your mistress has disappointed me,

I have no intention of spending a miserable evening on my own. Since you deliberately impersonated her on your arrival here you cannot reasonably object to continuing to deputize for her." '

'He didn't!' Angela's well-marked eyebrows shot up. 'Oh, the wretch! Fancy his making such a suggestion to a girl he thought to be my maid. Did I not tell you that he was a heartless, cynical roué?'

Madeleine nodded. 'I jumped to the conclusion that he meant that too; but I was wrong. As soon as I began to protest that I was a good girl and wished to go to my husband with a clear conscience when I married, he checked me with a gesture of his hand and cried:

' "Please! Please! I had no intention of making an assault on your virtue. My idea was only that over a meal we should entertain one another; you by telling me of your life as a lady's-maid, and I by telling you about mine as a soldier." '

'What an extraordinary suggestion.'

'Perhaps; although, after all, there is no reason why two people of different stations in life should not find interest in exchanging ideas. But, of course, having thanked him, I refused. I said that I must get back to you, and begged his leave to set off there and then. He wouldn't let me though. He said very firmly:

' "No, Lucille, Madame Syveton can look after herself tonight for once. You are going to spend the evening with me. But since you are a respectable girl this is no place in which to give you dinner. We will go out and dine in public. And I would like this to be a treat for you that you will remember. I will take you to one of the best restaurants. Come now, make your choice. Which shall it be? Lapérouse, Maxims, the Café de Paris?" '

'He said that! He wanted to take a lady's-maid to one of those places. He must be crazy.'

'A little eccentric, perhaps, and very self-willed; no more. But you see how embarrassing I found his invitation.'

'Of course. You could not have eaten without removing your veil. It is certain someone would have recognized you; and it would have been all over Paris by this morning.'

'Exactly. So I did my best to appear grateful, then tried to put him off by saying: "Alas, I am much too plain to do Monsieur le Comte any credit; and even if I were better looking I would not like to take advantage of his kindness. Some friend of Madame's might recognize me and for a gentleman to be seen dining with a servant would do him great discredit."

'At that he looked down his beak of a nose at me and said sharply: "A man in my position does not have to pay regard to the opinion of others upon whom he chooses to take out to dinner. As for your looks I do not care a button, as I wish only to talk to you." '

Madeleine spread out her hands in a little helpless gesture. 'What was I to do? To dine with a man in a private room is one thing. All of us, except you my pet, do so now and then, and our husbands know it. But to dine alone with a man in a public restaurant is a very different matter. Socially it would have been the end of me. The only thing I could do was to say: "Since you insist on giving me dinner and your intentions are honourable, let us stay here. It is warm and comfortable, and I would prefer it to going out." '

'And then?' asked Angela a little breathlessly.

'Why then, of course, he helped me out of your furs and I had to take off my veil.' Madeleine laughed suddenly. 'When I turned round and faced him he got quite a surprise.'

'So I imagine.'

'After one look at me, he cried: "But you are enchanting! What in the world led you to tell me that your looks would do me no credit? Any man would be proud to be seen with you anywhere." Then as his glance ran over me again he went on: "Wait though, there is another mystery here! No lady's-maid has her hair tended with the care that has been given to yours; and your hands are not those of a servant. Damn it, I have seen you somewhere before too! Where can it have been? Ah yes! I have it. I saw you in September, at the christening of Madame de Lazun's infant." '

'Oh, my dear! So he found you out after all.'

'Yes.' Madeleine nodded. 'After that there would have been no sense in my trying to pretend any longer. I told him my name and the whole story; then begged him to forgive me for the part I had played, and that he would not put either of us to shame by telling his friends about it. He gave me his solemn promise and rang for the waiter. By then he was in marvellous spirits. When the man came he slapped him on the back and cried: "Get the hot spoons for the paté, Jules! Open the champagne! This is Mademoiselle Lucille, the loveliest lady's-maid in Paris, and we are going to have a jolly evening." '

Just a shade sourly, Angela said: 'I see; so that is why you couldn't get back right away. Still, ten o'clock is not very late, so you might have come round to see me then before going home.'

'My pet, I do not want to lose your friendship;' Madeleine said with sudden seriousness, 'and I can only hope to keep it by telling you the truth now; for you would find out later if I didn't. Knowing you would be worried about me I wrote that note after dinner and sent it to you from the Ambassadeurs.'

Angela's mouth fell slightly open. 'You ... you don't mean that you stayed on there with him?'

Madeleine nodded and her eyes were shining. 'You made it clear that you didn't want him; so you can't blame me. Oh, *chérie*, what you have missed I cannot tell you! He is so strong and yet so gentle. So gay, so passionate, so tender. A man that any woman could die for. I did not get home till five o'clock this morning. And he is mine now. Mine! Mine! Mine!'

CHAPTER VIII

THE SPY ?

IVE weeks before the Marquise de Frontignac became de Quesnoy's mistress he first heard the name of Alfred Dreyfus—a name that was to ring round the world, provoke for over ten years the most bitter controversy in every strata of French society and, in the not very distant future, have a most unexpected effect on the young Count's own career.

On November 1st, 1894 the *Libre Parole* had carried a headline:"*High Treason, Arrest of Jewish Officer*", and it was from this that the officer cadets—and all but four members of Premier Depuy's Cabinet—heard that War Office secrets had been betrayed, although Captain Dreyfus had been under arrest in the Cherche-Midi prison for a fortnight.

From the welter of lies, contradictions and honest misunderstandings which for years befuddled the minds of all but the very few who knew the inside story, there at last emerged the following facts about the origins of the case.

After 1870 the War Office had been reorganized into four Bureaux. First, Administration; Second, Intelligence; Third, Operations and Training; Fourth, Movements and Railways; and before qualifying for the General Staff candidates had to do six months as a learner with each branch.

Dreyfus was an Artillery officer. He had passed well out of the *École Supérieur de Guerre* and in January '93 been seconded as a staff learner to the War Office. He had already done his six months with the First, Fourth and Second Bureaux, and was attached to the Third when fate overtook him.

At this period new weapons and methods of waging war were being developed far more rapidly than had ever before been the case; so in '76 it had been decided to establish a special department to deal with espionage and counter-espionage. This department was given the cover name of the Statistical Section. It was not affiliated to any of the Bureaux, its officers were unidentifiable on the War Office list and communicated only with the Chief of Staff or Assistant Chief. These, at the time of Dreyfus's arrest, were General de Boisdeffre and General Gonse.

The Statistical Section consisted of five officers and a filing clerk. Colonel Sandherr was its chief, and the only one of his assistants who played a leading part in the affair was a Major Henry. The latter had been promoted from the ranks for having shown great bravery and resource in the North African and Tonkinese wars. As he came from a peasant family his education was limited, but he had the cunning of his caste coupled with a fanatical devotion to the Army, which had been the means of raising him above it.

Both the German Military attaché, Colonel von Schwartzkoppen, and the Italian, Colonel Panizzardi, were believed to be operating spy rings under the diplomatic immunity of their Embassies. To keep a check on their activities, Sandherr was paying certain of their servants, among them a charwoman who worked in the German Embassy, and her contribution was to empty the contents of Colonel Schwartzkoppen's waste-paper basket into a sack which she periodically passed on to Major Henry.

By piecing these torn papers together Henry had, as far back as December '92, established the fact that someone was selling Schwartzkoppen plans of France's fortifications on both her Eastern and Alpine frontiers. The latter were being passed on by him to his Italian colleague, and one intercepted letter contained the phrase "Here are twelve large-scale plans of Nice, which that scum D. has handed to me for you."

A little over a year later another torn paper revealed that Schwartzkoppen had got into touch with someone more important than "*ce canialle de D.*", and an attaché at the Spanish Embassy dropped a hint that an officer actually in the War Office was selling information to a foreign power. But it was not until September '94 that the Statistical Section succeeded in getting hold of anything which might lead to the identification of the traitor.

When it did turn up this further torn document—always afterwards referred to as the "*bordereau*"—consisted of a list of five documents which the writer said he was leaving at the German Embassy for Colonel Schwartzkoppen's perusal. The morning after Henry had

74

pasted the bits together he showed it to his colleagues, and to his chief, who took it to General Gonse, via whom it was taken to the Minister for War, General Mercier. All who saw it were definitely of the opinion that it must have emanated from an officer employed in the War Office "because it used the language of the house".

The documents listed in the *bordereau* implied that it had been compiled by a gunner; so after it had been circulated to all chiefs of the Bureaux, and all of them had failed to recognize the writing, the artillery officers attached to the War Office came under special scrutiny. On October 6th Lt. Colonel d'Aboville of the Fourth Bureau helped his chief, Colonel Fabre, to re-examine the writing of five Gunner Captains and they decided that Dreyfus might have written it. On this being suggested to Sandherr, he slapped his forehead and exclaimed: 'I ought to have thought of that.'

The Chief-of-Staff, de Boisdeffre, who had just returned from leave, was now brought into the picture. On the 8th he laid the case before Mercier and the War Minister said that more certain identification of the writing must be secured before action could be taken. De Boisdeffre referred the matter back to his Assistant, General Gonse, who sent for Major the Marquis du Paty de Clem of the Operations branch, to which Dreyfus was then attached. Du Paty and Major Picquart, who was Dreyfus's immediate chief, then compared numerous papers in his writing with that of the *bordereau*. Picquart was dubious but du Paty completely satisfied that they were the same, and his report was so positive that it convinced both de Boisdeffre and Mercier.

Both were pressed for time as they had shortly to be present at the Army manœuvres at Limoges; but before leaving Mercier made a full report to the Prime Minister at a meeting at which the Minister of Justice, Guérin, and the Minister of Foreign Affairs, Hanotaux, were also present. Hanotaux, foreseeing the diplomatic complications which were certain to arise if a French officer were accused of selling secrets to the German Military Attaché, urged most strongly that no action should be taken, or at least until much more conclusive evidence could be produced. Mercier then asked Guérin to put a civilian hand-writing expert in touch with Gonse, who was being left in charge of the case.

Gonse was a man of mediocre intelligence and hasty judgments who concealed his inefficiency behind a high-handed manner. Having made up his own mind that Dreyfus was the guilty party, he refused the police expert full information but bullied him for a quick decision, and when it was given against his own convictions he promptly ignored it. He told du Paty to order Dreyfus to come to the War Office in civilian clothes, and to arrange to put him through a writing test.

Mercier got back on the 14th and held a conference with all the senior officers concerned. General Saussier, the Military Governor of Paris and the senior officer in the French Army, had privately advised him: "No good can come of publicity. Send the fellow off to the Colonies and see he does not come back." But in spite of this, and Hanotaux's warning that a trial would mean trouble with the German government, Mercier felt that matters had now gone too far to be hushed up. Scores of officers in the War Office knew about it, and the members of the police department with which Gonse had had such futile dealings. A leak, Mercier reasoned, was now certain, and it would result in the press accusing them of condoning espionage. As War Minister he was already being heckled in the Chamber about certain bloomers he had made and he did not want any more trouble. In consequence he agreed that Gonse's arrangements should go forward.

Next morning at 9 o'clock Dreyfus reported to Major Picquart. He was taken in to du Paty who ordered him to take down a letter for the Chief of Staff's signature. The missive was so phrased as to contain many words which had been used in the *bordereau*. When he had done, du Paty, without even looking at it, charged him with high treason and arrested him.

The whole group of officers involved in the case had by now argued themselves into an unshakable conviction of Dreyfus's guilt so completely that they had actually placed under some papers on the table at which he was writing a loaded revolver. Revealing it, du Paty told him that he would save everybody a lot of trouble by doing the executioner's business himself. But the unfortunate man, taken entirely by surprise, violently protested against the charge and shouted: 'I won't do it! I am innocent! I am innocent!'

He was then searched, his keys were taken from him, and he was escorted by Major Henry to the Cherche-Midi prison. There, he became so overwrought that the Governor feared for his sanity and, convinced of his innocence, insisted that a doctor should be allowed to see him. Meanwhile a group of officers led by du Paty had searched his house. They found there not a scrap of evidence against him. His

76

wife was informed of his arrest, but they refused to disclose to her either with what he was charged or his whereabouts, and bound her to silence by telling her that if she mentioned his arrest, even to his family, that would assure his complete ruin.

During the fortnight that followed, by the interrogation of Dreyfus and an examination of his papers du Paty endeavoured to build up a a case, but by the end of the month he had unearthed nothing new and could only report that he considered Dreyfus's guilt to be established. Next day the *Libre Parole* broke the story to the public and in a matter of hours the rest of the Press was running leading articles upon it.

As the Press knew only the bare outline of the story it was not to be wondered at that there was an immediate outcry against the unfortunate Dreyfus.

The facts were that he was an Alsatian Jew but came of a family so completely integrated with their adopted country of France that after 1870 they had abandoned their home in order to retain their French citizenship; that he was an able and efficient officer about to be appointed to the General Staff and so had a career before him that was full of promise; that, although it was ferreted out that he had for three brief spells had mistresses, he was respectably and happily married and had two young children; that at the time of his arrest he had a bank balance of 400,000 francs—and the franc was then 25 to the £1. Therefore anyone less likely to have sold military secrets to a foreign power could hardly be imagined. But these facts were not reported at the time and did not emerge until long afterwards.

It was not until later, either, that his being a Jew played any considerable part in the matter. Both Colonel Sandherr and Major Picquart admittedly had a prejudice against Jews; but there were at that date over five hundred Jewish officers in the French Army. Neither in it nor among the public had there as yet developed anything approaching an anti-Semitic movement, and when it did come it was due not to the soldiers but to the Press.

The thing which weighed most heavily against Dreyfus was his unattractive personality. Several officers vouched for his intelligence, industry and, to the best of their belief, honesty, but not a soul could be found to say that he was a jolly good fellow.

He was of medium height with high shoulders; his hair and moustache were light and he had a broad forehead, but his eyes were small and close-set. He wore pince-nez and his voice was high-pitched, toneless and weak. His manners left much to be desired. He was extremely inquisitive, dictatorial and so boastful that he would lie about imaginary exploits with women. Finally, he had no interest whatever in music, literature, art or sport; so his sole contact with his fellow officers was the work they were engaged on, and in no other way was he one of them.

The crux of the matter was that the War Office staff was convinced, the Press reported and the public believed that an officer had been caught selling information to the Germans. Had the accused been an ex-jail-bird—as were many of the meaner kind of spies—yet a Frenchman, that would have been bad enough; but the fact that he was a Captain of Artillery made the crime heinous. The French nation felt shamed before the world, and officers of all ranks displayed bitter anger that one of them should have cast such a slur on the honour of the Army.

Early in November Major d'Ormeschville, of the Paris garrison's Court-martial Section, took over the investigation from du Paty and, finding that Dreyfus persisted in his denials, represented to the War Office the weakness of their case. This appears to have been the point at which the originators of the charge, fully believing Dreyfus guilty, decided that he must not be allowed to get off from lack of evidence, even if much of it could not be completely substantiated. Colonel Sandherr, presumably, and probably with the help of his loyal assistant Major Henry, then combed the Statistical Section's files for every leak of information which might conceivably be attributed to Dreyfus, and added to this dossier every scrap of material they could gather which might help to blacken him in the eyes of his judges.

Meanwhile Madame Dreyfus had been allowed to communicate with her husband's two brothers, who at once came to Paris and sought the assistance of Edgar Demange, one of the most brilliant barristers of the day. Demange interviewed Dreyfus in prison and, convinced of his innocence, agreed to undertake his defence; but, in the interests of national security, the authorities allowed him to see only a few of the papers which were to be put in as evidence for the prosecution.

Hanotaux's prediction, that the Germans would take umbrage if it was publicly asserted that their Embassy was being used for espionage purposes, proved correct. Their ambassador published an official statement that Schwartzkoppen had at no time either met or communicated with Dreyfus, and on direct orders from Berlin protested to both Hanotaux and the President of the Republic. Then Italy and Austria followed up with assurances that their Military Attachés also had had no dealings with Dreyfus. Nevertheless the preparation for the court martial went on.

It opened on December 19th, and the Military prosecutor at once asked that the case should be heard *in camera*. General Mercier had insisted on this, as he knew the weakness of the evidence but was now persuaded that should Dreyfus be acquitted the inference would be that someone else, still at large, was the traitor and that would make suspect the honour of every officer employed at the War Office, thus creating an intolerable situation. Demange protested, but the President of the Court, knowing the War Minister's wishes, overruled him; so the court was cleared of all but the military, and defending counsel.

Among the seven judges not one was an Artillery officer; so none of them possessed the technical knowledge to point out to the others that had the *bordereau* been written by a gunner he would have expressed himself differetnly, and that the only printed document mentioned in it, far from being secret, was not even classified as confidential.

Twenty officers were called for the prosecution, among them Gonse, du Paty and Henry, all of whom distorted the evidence with a view to blackening the accused. The Chief Rabbi, a few friends and half a dozen officers next testified to Dreyfus's good character. Henry then asked to be recalled. Knowing how important to the honour of the Army his superiors considered it that a verdict of guilty should be secured, he proceeded deliberately to perjure himself.

In spite of this, at the end of the second day, Picquart who was acting as observer for Mercier and de Boisdeffre reported to them that the judges appeared to be doubtful about the prisoner's guilt, and that he would be doubtful about it himself if he had not heard about the secret dossier that Colonel Sandherr had compiled.

It was this secret dossier which clinched the matter. On the third day the judges went through it in private. They were all honourable soldiers, but none of them had had any legal training, otherwise they would have realized that they should not have done so unless they were prepared to allow the defence to see and dispute its contents; but this they could not do because many of the papers would have disclosed the secret operations of the Statistical Section. Now convinced by the sheer mass of this supporting material that the evidence of Gonse, du Paty and Henry had revealed the truth, the Court brought in a unanimous verdict of "Guilty".

The death penalty for political crimes having been abolished in 1848; the prisoner was sentenced to be cashiered, degraded, deported, and confined for life in a fortified place.

On January 5th the first part of the sentence was carried out in one of the courts of the École Militaire. Detachments from all the regiments forming the garrison of Paris were paraded as a hollow square facing inward. In its centre Dreyfus standing to attention had his badges of rank and buttons cut from his uniform, and his sword was then broken in front of him. He gave a loud cry of: 'Soldiers, an innocent man is being degraded!' but his thin voice was half drowned by the shouts of hatred from the mob which had assembled outside the gates. His wrists were then tied and he was taken in a police van to the Sureté.

On January 18th he was removed to La Rochelle, where another mob learning of his presence tried to lynch him. Then on February 21st he was deported to the penal colony in French Guiana, and, shortly after his arrival there, permanently incarcerated on Devil's Island.

Once the sensation of his trial had died down, he was forgotten by all but a few people for nearly three years. But a time was to come when his name would cause suicides, duels, the wrecking of many careers, riots, widespread looting and the fall of a government.

CHAPTER IX

A RAKE'S PROGRESS

D E QUESNOY, like most of his companions at St. Cyr who knew only what the papers reported, felt it a great pity that the law did not permit of Dreyfus being shot or, as a more suitable end for such a loathsome traitor, hanged; but at the time of the trial he had much more pleasant thoughts to occupy him.

Just as he was in need of it, he had found in the vivacious and alluring Madeleine de Frontignac the perfect foil for his amorous propensities. During the fortnight that followed their first encounter they met either in secret or at the Marquise's home as frequently as de Quesnoy could get away from St. Cyr. Then the college broke up for the winter vacation, but the lovers had already made their plans for that. Madeleine had taken an early opportunity to present her new beau to her husband, and the cynical old Marquis did not disguise the fact that in this instance he approved her choice. In consequence she had no difficulty in getting him to invite the Count to join them at their villa at Cap Ferrat, to which they went each winter so that the Marquis could indulge his love of gambling during the height of the Monte Carlo season.

Immediately after Christmas they left for the South of France and nothing could have enhanced their romance more than the exchange of furtive meetings under the leaden skies of Paris for an unchallengeable and continuous companionship under the blue ones of the Mediterranean.

The house-party at the villa consisted of the Marquis's two elderly sisters, the husband of one of them, a young married couple who were friends of Madeleine's and a middle-aged bachelor of the type who spends his life battening on his richer friends but pays for it by making himself either useful or inconspicuous as required. They were all perfectly well aware that young de Quesnoy was their hostess's latest lover, but none of them even hinted at it; and, exercising an equal discretion, Armand and Madeleine never displayed before the others any greater degree of intimacy than could be attributed to tastes in common having led them to become close friends.

The age of travel for people of modest means had not yet dawned, but no major war had disturbed Europe for nearly a quarter of a century; so unhindered commerce had greatly increased the number of well-to-do families in every country, and many thousands of them now came each year to the Riviera. Among the wealthier nobility of Britain, Russia, Austria-Hungary, Scandinavia and the Balkans there were scores who either had their own villas or hired one for the season, and accommodation in the luxury hotels, although new ones were added to their number every year, was always at a premium.

Every sunny morning beneath the palms outside the *Cercle Nautique* at Cannes, on the terrace at Monte Carlo, on the *Promenade des Anglais* at Nice, and along the sea-walk at Mentone, fashion parades took place which were rivalled hardly anywhere else in the world. In the afternoons there were tea parties in innumerable beautiful private gardens, heady with the scent of mimosa, roses and carnations. In the evenings the lights were lit along the lovely coast while scores of wealthy hostesses entertained as many as thirty guests to ten-course dinners. Then in laces and satins, perfumed and bejewelled, their bare shoulders protected from the cool night air by ermine and sables, the ladies accompanied their men folk to the casinos, where hundreds of thousands of pounds changed hands nightly.

There were, too, visits to friends who entertained on the luxury yachts that crowded the anchorages of the harbours; drives in open landaux up to the beauty spots in the hills or to the scent factories at Grasse; rallies at which the curious could see ten or twelve of the new smelly, ugly, horseless carriages known as automobiles; and high spots in this riot of pleasure, the Battles of Flowers, in which the crowds bombarded the long processions of flower-decked carriages with every variety of bud and blossom.

This life of luxury, elegance and gaiety, ministered to by thousands of servants and brought about by the wealthy of half the world coming together for a few weeks in a tiny area, had only two more decades to run; but while it lasted it provided the perfect setting for two rich young people who were in love, and de Quesnoy and his beautiful Marquise enjoyed every moment of it.

Early in January the Count learned that his father was staying near Cannes at the villa of the Grand Duke Michael; so he wrote asking if he might call, and in reply received an invitation to lunch. After the meal they had a long talk, during which de Richleau endeavoured to persuade him to resign his commission in the French Army and accept a Captaincy that the Grand Duke had generously offered him in one of the regiments of which he was Colonel-in-Chief. Politely but firmly de Quesnoy refused; but the meeting had broken the ice after his year of estrangement from his father. He volunteered to send back the Cross of St. Louis that lay in a safe-deposit in Paris, and the Duke responded by raising his income to a thousand a year—which for a young bachelor was great affluence in those days—and thus the breach between them was healed.

While de Quesnoy was at Cap Ferrat there occurred another political crisis. Casimir-Périer, exasperated beyond further endurance by being ignored by the Dupuy Cabinet and libelled in the Socialist Press, resigned the Presidency. In his place another mediocre politician, Félix Faure, was elected. He was a handsome man, a great dandy, a fine figure on a horse and, although in his middle fifties, still an inveterate pursuer of women. Ten days later a new government was formed with M. Ribot as Prime Minister, and General Zurlinden succeeded Mercier at the War Office.

By then the Count had torn himself from Madeleine's arms, and the other joys of the Riviera, to return to St. Cyr for the opening of another term. But as a second year student he enjoyed still more latitude about going into Paris, so when she got back there at the end of February they had ample opportunity to continue their liaison.

The main interest of the students at St. Cyr now lay in Madagascar. The Hovás, who were the dominant race in this great island had accepted French protection during the Second Empire, and had again submitted to it in 1885, but recently they had been giving a lot of trouble; and Britain, owing to the activities of her missionaries, was well on the way to ousting French influence from the island. In consequence, General Duchesne had been despatched with a considerable expeditionary force, to overawe the Hová warriors and firmly establish France's rights as the protecting power.

The Hovás did not prove formidable antagonists, so Duchesne found little difficulty in penetrating to their capital, but Paris was much amused by the contretemps he had with their Queen when he got there. Having decided that the trouble was largely due to the pro-British Prime Minister, Duchesne exiled him and appointed a pro-French one. Unfortunately the new man was old, fat and ugly, which resulted in the Queen's descending on the General in a fury. She had no objection to the change of policy, but she had to this change in advisers, as it was the custom of the country that the Queen should marry whoever she took as her Prime Minister, and her subjects would dethrone her if she refused to comply. The embarrassed Duchesne, called on to adjudicate, ruled that she must marry him but need not sleep with him.

Only twenty French soldiers lost their lives in battle during Duchesne's operations; but, owing to Mercier's most reprehensible negligence in organizing the expedition, over five thousand of them died from privation and disease. So ultimately it proved a costly failure, and eighteen months later the subjugation of the island had to be undertaken all over again.

De Quesnoy continued to see Angela from time to time as, having in the past accepted Syveton's pressing invitations to lunch and dine, he could not now, with decency, always refuse them. They sometimes met, too, at the houses of friends and, in view of this social relationship, it would have been churlish not to appear occasionally at her Thursdays. But they never embarked on an explanation of her having given him a rendez-vous then sending a substitute to it.

For some months, fearful that he might broach the subject, she took considerable care to avoid being left alone with him, even for a few moments; while he, conscious that he had come well out of the matter and that she must know it, generously refrained from taking any special steps to corner her. Gradually she became less nervous that one day he would suddenly take his revenge by twitting her about her futile trick; so they slipped back into their old relationship, except that he no longer made even mild love to her.

Nevertheless, each was in secret still strongly attracted to the other. Although Angela continued to deplore Armand's morals, she was slowly growing out of her inhibitions and, while she would not have admitted it to herself, she was now desperately jealous of Madeleine. Armand, in spite of the physical delight he took in his passionate French mistress, was still fascinated by Angela's more perfect beauty, and he was convinced she was worth a dozen of the vivacious Marquise. But there the matter rested, and was fated to do so for some time.

In the summer the Frontignacs went to Deauville and there had been a suggestion that de Quesnoy should join them there for his vacation; but Madeleine had not pressed it and Armand spoke vaguely of some family visits he ought to make. The fact was that the passion of both was cooling somewhat and he was spoiling for another spell in his spiritual home, Vienna.

Once more he spent a hectic month with his Austrian friends and it was not until some two months after Madeleine had left Paris that he saw her again. During their separation each of them had been flagrantly unfaithful to the other, but their nine weeks apart and a number of amorous episodes which had meant little to either had the effect only of stimulating anew their desire for one another; so they happily resumed their affaire and continued it through the autumn, although with a more subdued pleasure in their meetings than had been the case in the early part of the year.

That suited de Quesnoy admirably for, at his age and with his temperament, had he remained long without a mistress his mind would have become too much occupied with thoughts of securing a new one; and the last thing he wanted at this juncture was to have to employ it laying siege to some new charmer with all the attendant intrigue that would have involved. Now that he was in his final term at St. Cyr he was anxious to concentrate on his studies, and his pleasant relations with Madeleine enabled him to do so to the best advantage, as she was always pleased to see him yet, realizing the importance he attached to doing well in his examinations, did not now press him to come into Paris so frequently as he had formerly.

All the same, when the results of the examinations were made known he received an unpleasant shock. His instructors had backed him to pass out amongst the first three students of his year, but he came in fifteenth. However, this blow to his pride was greatly offset by the wise old Commandant's telling him in private before he left that he had many qualities of value to a soldier which could not be assessed in any series of examination papers and was, in the opinion of his instructors, the most promising officer-cadet they had had at St. Cyr for some years.

Towards the end of October yet another government had fallen. M. Ribot's ministry was brought down by a vote of censure for having interfered with the course of justice through ordering certain judges to be changed in the middle of a trial.

Owing to continual dissensions among the parties of the Right, ever since the seventies the Conservative elements in the Chamber had been gradually losing ground; and, now for the first time, a Cabinet entirely composed of Radicals took office. Its Premier was Léon Bourgeois and for his Minister of War he chose a civilian named Cavaignac.

In December, lured by memories of the happy weeks that he had spent on the Riviera the previous winter, de Quesnoy again accepted an invitation from the de Frontignacs to accompany them to Cap Ferrat. Immediately after Christmas they all left with well-stocked picnic baskets, and other convenient utensils, on the long journey South; for the trains, although comfortable and luxuriously upholstered in the first-class compartments, as yet had no restaurant cars, corridors or lavatories. But de Quesnoy was still digesting a gala dinner to usher in the New Year of 1896, held at the Hôtel de Paris, Monte Carlo, under the auspices of Monsieur Fleury—then the most famous *maître d'hôtel* in the world—when he received a telegram cancelling his leave and ordering him to report to the War Office.

The officer-cadets passing out of St. Cyr had all had to fill in forms stating any special qualifications they possessed, among them foreign languages. The Count had put himself down as speaking German fluently, a little colloquial Polish and Hungarian, some English but only as learned from text books, and Russian as his second native tongue. It was the last ability which was the cause of his being sent for.

In 1891 a treaty of friendship had been signed by Russia and France; and this had been greatly strengthened two years later by a secret military convention. These diplomatic *coups* had led the French General Staff to reconsider the strategy which should be employed in the event of another war with Germany. With Russia even as a neutral friendly to France, Germany would not dare to denude her Russian frontier of troops, and with Russia as France's active ally sufficient weight should be taken off France to enable her to open the war with an offensive. In consequence, as the Franco-Russian alliance became steadily more concrete the plans of the French were constantly being redrafted into bolder patterns, and the more the need was felt of keeping close contact with the Russian General Staff.

De Boisdeffre was a great Russophil. It was he who in November

'94, during the most critical fortnight of the Dreyfus investigation, had gone to St. Petersburg to represent France at the funeral of the Czar Alexander III and to be present at the marriage of his successor, Nicholas II. And it was up to the ante-room of his office that de Quesnoy was taken after a brief interview with a Russian interpreter.

Raoul François Charles Le Mouton de Boisdeffre, to give the Chief of Staff his full name, was a member of one of the old families and he and de Quesnoy had already met socially. In consequence, when he had the young Count brought in to him he did not keep him standing at attention in front of his desk, as he would normally have done when addressing a junior officer, but shook him cordially by the hand and asked him to sit down.

The General then spoke at some length about the Franco-Russian military alliance and disclosed the fact that it was to be still further strengthened during the course of the year by a State visit to Paris by the Czar Nicholas and his young bride. He added that in the French Army there were lamentably few officers who spoke Russian; that he was much handicapped by having no one of good social standing on his personal staff who could entertain for him Russian visiting officers whose French was poor; and that in view of the Czar's forthcoming visit it was now more important than ever that he should have someone of the kind to attach to their Household. He ended by saying that he wished de Quesnoy to join his staff as an additional A.D.C.

The Count was much surprised and far from pleased. To appoint an officer to such a post straight from St. Cyr, without his having had even a few months' regimental experience, was an unheard-of thing although no doubt justified by the special circumstances—and anyway that was the General's affair. But de Quesnoy was quick to see that his principal duties would consist of playing host on tours of Montmartre to little parties of Russians, who were notoriously heavy drinkers and apt to become quarrelsome when drunk, and also probably having to procure women for the older ones who did not care to go out on such sprees. It was not to be employed in such a manner that he had become a soldier, and he said so as tactfully as he could to the Chief-of-Staff. In the hope of giving greater point to his objections he added:

'Since you have sent for me, Sir, I would like to take this opportunity of asking your good offices in connection with my posting to a regiment. I am aware that it is usual for officers on leaving St. Cyr to serve with one stationed in France for at least a year before being sent overseas; but I put in a special application to be sent at once on foreign service, and if you would arrange the matter for me I should take it as a great kindness.'

It was the General's turn to be surprised. The great majority of officers of good social standing not only preferred to serve in Metropolitan France, and if possible somewhere within easy reach of Paris; they actually looked down on those serving in the Colonies, much as the officers of the British regiments in those days considered their colleagues in the Indian Army to be of a slightly lower caste.

'What an extraordinary request,' he said, after a moment. 'It is only poor devils who have nothing but their pay to live on who need to exile themselves for years in the deserts of North Africa or the jungles of Indo-China.'

De Quesnoy smiled. 'I have no wish to spend a great part of my life in either, *mon Général*; but at present that is the only way to see active service. And should another European war break out officers who have never done so will prove of far less use to their country.'

'Yes, yes; you are right about that,' de Boisdeffre replied a little impatiently, 'and such sentiments are very laudable. But you have all your life before you and since you wish it can be given an opportunity later to serve abroad. Now, however, I require you here; and, if necessary, I must give you an order to comply with my wishes.'

Discipline having been invoked, the Count stood up, clicked his heels and said: 'In that case, Sir, I await your further instructions. I need hardly add that I shall serve you to the best of my ability.'

'That's better,' nodded the General. 'And now perhaps I can console you a little for your reluctance to accept this post that most young officers would have jumped at. The position you will occupy requires that you should have a certain military standing; so I intend to exercise the powers vested in me to make special promotions. I am sending your name in to be gazetted at the end of the week as a Captain.'

De Quesnoy could hardly believe his ears. France having become a Republic, the days had long since gone when, owing to wealth or influence, youngsters were allowed to hold rank in her Army above their years. To be gazetted a Captain straight out of St. Cyr and while still only twenty was something of which he could not even have dreamed. For that he was prepared to drink any number of Russians under the table and, if need be, organize a special harem for their exclusive use. Having thanked his new master profusely, he retired extraordinarily elated by this piece of good fortune that had befallen him.

After looking at several apartments he leased a very pleasant, well-furnished one in the Rue de Lille. Then he paid a formal call on the Russian military attaché, a bearded Colonel with bright blue eyes who exuded a mixed aroma of Havana cigars and eau-de-Cologne. As soon as the Colonel learnt that his visitor's mother had been a Princess Plackoff he treated him with the warmest regard and presented him to the Ambassador. Both of them then asked him to dinner and assured him that he would always be *persona grata* at the Embassy.

But at the War Office, for the first month or so, he took his new duties cautiously, as he was anxious not to arouse the ill-will of the older officers in the department that ordinarily dealt with the foreign Military Missions. This, and the fact that de Boisdeffre was often away for two or three days at a stretch, meant that he had very little to do; but, temporarily, he did not mind that, as his leave had been cut short and after the hard work he had put in before taking his examinations at St. Cyr he felt that he had earned an easy time.

Part of it he spent getting to know the Paris galleries and museums; then when he had a letter from Madeleine in which she mentioned that she had met a charming Spanish grandee whose financial interests necessitated his living for a good part of the year in Paris, he knew what that meant; so he began to look round for a new *chère amie*.

He thought that he had found her in the flaxen-haired wife of a Danish diplomat, but she had no sense of humour and, on closer acquaintance, proved so disappointing that he soon tired of her, and turned his attentions to a lady considerably older than himself named Josephine Pollit who, as she was married to a banker, was of the *haut bourgeoisie*.

Josephine was in her early thirties, but she had kept her looks and was gifted with an unusually high degree of intelligence. Not the least of her attractions for him, as he had recently become interested in painting, was her wide knowledge of art, and during the spring, with her fine critical appreciation, she opened a new world to him.

On Madeleine's return, by tacit consent, they made no attempt to renew their liaison. They had had a wonderful year together, but at its end had both been ready to seek pastures new; so they ceased to be lovers without heartache on either side and in the happy knowledge that their memories would always keep them cherished friends.

That spring a more than usually violent battle raged in the Chamber. M. Doumer, the Finance Minister in Bourgeois's Radical Government, endeavoured to bring in Income Tax. The Senate threw the bill out. Four times in five days Bourgeois had to ask for votes of confidence and got them only by the narrowest margins. In the meantime the nation had been aroused. Innumerable small shopkeepers might vote Left at the elections because they were anti-clerical or had theories about giving the under-dog a fair deal, but they were not standing for any nonsense about disclosing their incomes, much less paying a tax on them. On April 22nd Bourgeois's government was forced to resign, and he was succeeded by Jules Méline, an old type Republican. Méline put into the War Office General Billot, a man of nearly seventy, who for the past twenty years had been a Senator, and War Minister once before for a short period in the early eighties.

By this time de Quesnoy was becoming bored by having little to do except act as his Chief's personal intermediary with the Russians, entertain them, and sometimes translate secret Russian documents; so one day he asked to be allowed to improve his future prospects by working as a part-time Staff learner in one of the departments. De Boisdeffre, having considered the matter for a moment, agreed and said that as his work was so nearly related to diplomacy the Statistical Section would prove the most profitable for him in which to spend his spare time, then wrote a chit for him to take to its chief.

Since the Dreyfus trial there had been several changes in the personnel of the Section, the most important being that in the preceding June Colonel Sandherr had been retired on account of a paralytic stroke. Although Major Henry was still there, he had been passed over by the transfer of Picquart from the Third Bureau to the Section, as its new chief with the rank of Lieutenant-Colonel.

Picquart had so far had a quite outstanding military career and was regarded as one of the most promising officers on the General Staff. He was a good-looking, cultured bachelor, and he and de Quesnoy soon took a liking to one another.

For some time no mention was made between them of the Dreyfus case—which had now been forgotten by most people other than the unfortunate man's family and those immediately concerned in it—but

90

one day it cropped up, and Picquart revealed that although the case was officially closed certain members of the War Office staff were still not altogether happy about it.

Having given de Quesnoy a resumé of the inside story, as then known to himself, he went on to say that when he had taken over the Section de Boisdeffre had told him to follow up the case, as no plausible motive had ever been produced to account for Dreyfus's treachery, and it was unsatisfactory that there should be no document containing convincing proof of his guilt.

Picquart had never believed in Dreyfus's innocence, but he obeyed the orders he had received and kept inquiries going. Nothing of importance had emerged, but he had been made uneasy by reports that staff papers were still being stolen. Then, only a few weeks before, among the material still being collected by Henry from Schwartz-koppen's waste-paper basket, there had been found a *petit bleu*—as the flimsies used in Paris for delivery by special messenger were called. It had never been dispatched but instead torn up, and when pieced together it indicated that a Major Esterhazy had been in secret communication with the German military attaché.

Later it emerged that it was in fact Esterhazy, and not Dreyfus, who had offered to sell information to Schwartzkoppen in July '94. As an officer and a gentleman the German had been extremely shocked at finding himself confronted with a French officer who was proposing to betray his country. He had even endeavoured to dissuade him from doing so; but Esterhazy had persisted, and on submitting the matter to Berlin Schwartzkoppen had been ordered to deal with him. Actually he had produced nothing of any real value, and the material he supplied was now deteriorating to such a degree that Schwartzkoppen was on the point of telling him that he would buy nothing further.

But at this time it never occurred to anyone in the Statistical Section that Dreyfus might have been arrested in mistake for Esterhazy. They jumped to the conclusion that they were on the track of a second traitor.

Esterhazy's past was then investigated and orders given for him to be shadowed. It emerged that he was a thoroughly bad hat. He had, between '78 and '81, actually been employed in the Statistical Section, thereby acquiring a considerable general knowledge of espionage and War Office procedure. But he claimed falsely to have been decorated for gallantry in North Africa, had married a young woman with a dowry of two hundred thousand francs, which he had since dissipated on vice, had for some years always been hard up, and was living with a registered prostitute known as Four-Fingered Marguerite.

The shadowing of Esterhazy continued during May, June and July without producing any incriminating evidence, and as the *petit bleu* had never been dispatched there was really no case against him; so Picquart felt that it was, as yet, pointless to raise the matter with his superiors.

In the meantime young de Quesnoy was leading a far from creditable life and one by no means satisfactory to himself. He fulfilled de Boisdeffre's purpose admirably by serving as an intelligent and reliable link with the Russians; but, as he had foreseen, that entailed acting as cicerone to every new Muscovite officer who was sent either temporarily or permanently to take part in the secret discussions connected with the military alliance. A few among them were serious or elderly men, but the majority displayed an unflagging zest for "wine, women and song"; and to win their confidence meant once or twice a week accompanying them on wild bouts of dissipation which did not end till dawn.

It was not that the Count objected to seeing pretty girls served up in huge pies and then dancing naked on the table. The trouble was that the night life began to get hold of him and, although having no regular office hours he could sleep off the effects of these orgies, he found himself losing interest in more sober pleasures. Towards the end of May Josephine broke off her liaison with him, and instead of seeking another respectable mistress he gave himself over to the allurements of any *demi-mondaine* who momentarily took his fancy.

He now did little work in the Statistical Section but when he was in there one afternoon towards the end of August, Picquart showed him two letters and, covering up their signatures, asked him if he recognized the writing. He did, and said at once:

'It is the same as that of the *bordereau*. They must have been written by Dreyfus.'

'You are wrong,' replied Picquart, and uncovering the signatures disclosed that they were written by Esterhazy.

'*Mon dieu!*' exclaimed the Count. 'In that case it must have been Esterhazy who wrote the *bordereau*; so Dreyfus is innocent.'

Picquart shook his head. 'Not necessarily. Du Paty is of the opinion that they are forgeries made by Dreyfus's brothers in the hope of fathering his guilt on his fellow spy. And Bertillon of the Sûreté maintains that a professional forger has been employed with the same object.'

'How did you come by them?' asked de Quesnoy.

'Through another Jewish officer named Weil. He is on General Saussier's staff and is a friend of Esterhazy's. Recently he has also become suspect, and we have had his correspondence tapped.'

'Have you managed to get anything at all against Esterhazy?'

'No, nothing. That is just the trouble. Whatever may have been the case in the past we are quite certain that he has not been in communication with the German Embassy for the past few months.'

'What view does General de Boisdeffre take about him?'

Picquart replied a shade uneasily, 'Not wishing to raise a mare's-nest I did not even inform him of the finding of the *petit bleu* until the beginning of this month; but now I shall put in a full report and recommend a new investigation. After all, this does make it possible that Dreyfus was wrongly condemned, and we cannot allow an innocent man to suffer.'

'I fully agree,' de Quesnoy nodded. 'But, by Jove, what a rumpus there will be in the Chamber if it does turn out that way.'

For some weeks he heard no more of the matter as he now was really fully occupied in making arrangements for the visit of the Czar and Czarina. Paris was eager to welcome the Imperial couple, but when the visit took place it did not prove a great popular success. The timid young Nicholas cut a far from imposing figure and his German wife chilled people by her stand-offishness.

However, the horde of Generals, Admirals, Colonels and others that they brought in their entourage displayed no such nervousness about fraternizing with the French. As a number of them spoke only Russian de Quesnoy, although far from being the senior officer of the Committee appointed to entertain them, was the key member of it. For days on end he got no sleep at all and by the time they departed he was so sickened of everything to do with gilded vice that he hoped never to have to go up the hill to Montmartre again.

When he had recovered a little he asked his General to have him posted to a regiment, but de Boisdeffre said that the contacts he had made at the Russian Embassy were much too valuable to be thrown away. However, he suggested that as de Quesnoy had been a sitter-in with the Statistical Section for six months, he should in future spend his spare time in the Third Bureau, where getting an insight into operations would provide a new interest for him.

The Count had no option but to agree, yet he was still anxious to get away from Paris, if only for a while; so he asked for and obtained three weeks' leave. He had long wanted to visit the cities of the Rhine, and as this was the season of the vintage he decided that now was the time to do so.

Before leaving he inquired of Picquart how the Dreyfus-Esterhazy affair was progressing, and Picquart said:

'I am greatly worried about it. De Boisdeffre's view is that a second case of this kind would completely blacken the honour of the Army; so that even if we secure incontestable evidence against Esterhazy we should refrain from prosecution. He would, I am sure, like us to ignore the whole business.'

'But you must endeavour to find out the truth, on account of this wretched fellow Dreyfus.'

'That is what I told him; so he gave me reluctant permission to carry on, but added that I was to use the greatest possible discretion and handle the affair under the direction of General Gonse.'

De Quesnoy made a face. 'Gonse is both a fool and a spineless creature. What is more he and du Paty had a bigger hand than anyone else in getting Dreyfus condemned; so if a mistake has been made he is the last person to want it found out.'

'I know, and he has already indicated as much. But, justice apart, I think the attitude of the Generals is foolish. I expect you saw in the Press that the London *Daily Chronicle* had run a story that Dreyfus had escaped?'

'Yes; but I take it there was no truth in it?'

'No; none whatever. But it has brought the case to the attention of the public again, and there must have been some sort of leak about Esterhazy, without so far any mention of his name. This re-aroused interest has enabled the Dreyfus family to start an agitation for a retrial, and questions are to be asked in the Chamber.'

'You are right, then. Our masters would be much better advised to stop burying their heads like ostriches, get right to the heart of the matter, and if an honest mistake has been made admit it.'

Major Henry was not present at this conversation and, had he been, he would not have been in agreement with the conclusions reached. His only loyalty was to the Army. As he saw it Picquart was behaving like an interfering fool, and at all costs the reputations of the Generals must be protected.

He was one of the very few people who realized that the secret file contained no evidence against Dreyfus which could not have been torn to ribbons in an open court, and that if, therefore, the *bordereau* was proved to have been written by Esterhazy the whole case against Dreyfus must collapse. In consequence, at about this time, he began to manufacture new evidence with a view to protecting his superiors from being proved to have sent Dreyfus to trial without sufficient justification.

First he extracted from the files a letter written in March '94 by Panizzardi, the Italian military attaché, which had been intercepted on its way to Schwartzkoppen. In it a reference was made to some individual by the use of the initial P. Henry altered the initial to D.

After numerous other minor fiddlings he produced, on All Saints' Day—which being a public holiday enabled him to bring with him to the office without it's being known a professional forger named Leeman—his greatest effort at deception; a document that in due course became famous as the *faux Henry*. Taking two more flimsies intercepted from Panizzardi, the bottom halves of which had not been written on, he cut these off; then, having gummed them together, he had Leeman forge a note on them in Panizzardi's hand actually mentioning Dreyfus by name.

The fatal mistake he made, which later when discovered cost him his life, was his failure to notice that the two flimsies were of different paper. Although identical at a casual glance, on one the faint squared lines were blue-grey and on the other grey-claret.

Picquart, of course, had not the least idea that his subordinate was carrying on such nefarious activities, or that he was secretly warning the Generals that unless they got rid of the over-scrupulous head of the Statistical Section they might find themselves in serious trouble.

On de Quesnoy's return from the Rhine he saw his friend again and found him more worried than ever. He was now fully convinced that Dreyfus was innocent but he could not persuade anyone to do anything about it. De Boisdeffre had succeeded in persuading himself that Esterhazy must have been an accomplice of Dreyfus's and that, even if the legal case against the latter was weak, he had been condemned justly. General Billot who, as Minister of War, would have to answer for the Army to the Chamber if it was found that a miscarriage of justice had occurred, was still more strongly against the revision of the case, while Gonse had displayed panic at the very idea.

'The case cannot be reopened,' he had declared to Picquart. 'Owing to the senior officers involved that is out of the question.'

'But Dreyfus may be innocent,' Picquart persisted.

'By comparison that is a matter of no importance,' the General replied, then added: 'And if you keep your mouth shut no one will be any the wiser.'

At that Picquart had declared that he thought the General's attitude abominable, and that he refused to carry the secret of such injustice with him to the grave.

De Quesnoy congratulated him on the stand he had made, then went off to resume his own particular business. With the Russians he now dealt firmly, telling them that he planned to marry a great heiress and that her family would not agree to the match unless he gave up his life of dissipation. This was a situation they understood, so no umbrage was taken and his social relations with them were transformed into the giving and acceptance of a series of jolly but quite respectable luncheons and dinners.

Nevertheless, his life still being aimless, he continued to be ill at ease and discontented. After having paid only the most obligatory calls at the Salons in the Faubourg St. Germain for the past six months he returned to them; but he no longer radiated the unspoilt charm which had made him so popular while an officer cadet. He now had a blasé air which, in spite of his devilish handsomeness, attracted only the maturer women. Surfeited as he had been through the summer with *demi-mondaines*, experienced women of Josephine's age no longer had any appeal for him. Beauty with what might pass for innocence was what he craved, and he made a bad start on the young wife of a Senator named Trouverier, who responded to his proposals by threatening to slap his face and afterwards told all her friends that she had done so.

His next choice was more fortunate, as little Madame de Beaumont-

Arlon found him irresistible; but a cousin of hers who had adored her since she was a child, and had hoped that after marrying she might become his mistress, became furious with jealousy. It happened that he was a poet of mediocre ability, so he took his revenge by getting published some rather witty and decidedly derogatory verses obviously aimed at de Quesnoy.

The Count promptly threatened to cut off the writer's ears, but the lady's husband intervened. De Quesnoy was persuaded to forgo that pleasure in order to spare her the scandal which would have resulted, and, in view of the unfortunate publicity which had already been given to the affair, to transfer his attentions elsewhere.

His last venture that autumn was the Princess de Lodi. She was a lovely sylph-like creature of eighteen, but her husband was only twenty, and they had been married less than six months. As they happened to be in love with each other de Quesnoy's bid for the young Princess's favours was most untimely. But intrigued by the prospect of perhaps attaining the apparently unattainable he persisted in his endeavours; with the result that the Prince called him out.

The days when both principals took two friends with them to a duel, and all six men fought with a sword in one hand and a poignard in the other till a majority of the combatants had fallen bleeding to death upon the ground, were long since past. Duelling had become a farce in which pistols with very small bullets were used at quite a long range. In consequence it was the exception rather than the rule for either party even to wound the other.

In the chill hour of dawn the Prince and de Quesnoy met in a clearing in the Bois de Boulogne. Their seconds and a doctor took every precaution against either suffering any serious injury, they duly exchanged shots without hitting each other and honour was declared to be satisfied. But the story of the duel and the reason for it was all round Paris by mid-day, and it was not one which redounded to de Quesnoy's credit.

Now that he was attached to the Third Bureau he rarely saw Picquart and well over a month had elapsed since he had had an opportunity to ask him how the Dreyfus affair was progressing; but one morning early in December an enquiry took him to the Statistical Section. To his surprise he found Henry occupying Picquart's desk, and on his asking for Picquart the ex-ranker replied:

'He's gone, and won't be coming back.'

'Has he then met with an accident?' de Quesnoy inquired with quick concern.

Henry shrugged. 'You can call it that if you like; but it's one he brought on himself. People who start butting their heads against the policy decisions of their superiors are apt to break them.'

'Surely you don't mean that he has been kicked out of his job because he was pressing for the Dreyfus affair to be reopened?'

'That's just what I do mean. He got up against General Gonse, and Gonse went to old Billot. He told the Minister that either Picquart must go or he would.'

'But this is disgraceful! Picquart is a first-class man and he was acting in accordance with his conscience. From the moment it was discovered that the writing on the *bordereau* was Esterhazy's it became at least possible that Dreyfus had been wrongly condemned, and . . .'

'Oh, let the damned Jew rot,' cut in the bullet-headed Major. 'He has caused us more than enough trouble already.'

'But if he is innocent that was no fault of his; and it is disgraceful that he should be made to suffer for something he did not do.'

'You have a lot to learn about the Army yet, Count,' Henry replied with a tolerant smile. 'When I was a sergeant in the Zouaves, the son of a Colonel got involved in theft. His officer wanted him charged, but his seniors thought differently. The officer was broken and the culprit set free. That's the way things go, and it's no good trying to alter them. The sooner you get it into your head that the chaps on top are always right, the better.'

Seeing that it was pointless to argue de Quesnoy asked where Picquart had been sent, to which Henry replied:

'They bunged him off to Corps Headquarters at Châlons-sur-Marne; but that's only a temporary measure. I happen to know that they mean to send him to Tunisia, and I expect they're hoping that an Arab bullet will put an end to there being any chance of his talking out of turn.'

De Quesnoy was horrified, but he forbore to comment and marched out of the room. For the next hour he sat in his own office thinking the matter over. The suggestion that Picquart was deliberately to be put in the front line of battle was an iniquitous business. After much deliberation the Count decided that he could not stand by and see a friend so unjustly treated without attempting to do something about it. Drawing a sheet of paper towards him and heading it: "Personal; for the Minister of War only", he wrote to General Billot as follows:

This morning I learnt from Major Henry that Lieut.-Colonel Picquart has been deprived of his post as head of the Statistical Section owing to his having pressed for a possible miscarriage of justice to be fully investigated and, if necessary, rectified.

I desire to represent that, if the above is true, such treatment of an officer is not only indefensible upon moral grounds but, should questions be asked about it in the Chamber, is liable to bring the Army, and particularly yourself, into grave disrepute.

Knowing himself to be bound to secrecy, he had been shrewd enough not to imply that it was his own intention to get a Deputy to raise the question; but owing to the number of people concerned in the Dreyfus-Esterhazy affair several leaks had already occurred, and there might well be further ones. Counting on the fear in which all Generals went of political criticism, he hoped that the threat would induce the War Minister to reconsider the matter and, even if he did not reinstate Picquart, compensate him for removal from his post by promotion to a better one.

Having despatched his letter he left the War Office and, after lunch, did not feel like going back there that afternoon. It then occurred to him that it was one of Angela's Thursdays and, as he had not called on her for a long time, he decided to do so.

He was not surprised that she greeted him rather coldly and therefore all the more so when, after he had been there for about twenty minutes, she beckoned him over to her and said in a low voice: 'Armand, I want to talk to your privately. Can you come back about six o'clock?'

'With pleasure,' he replied at once and left shortly afterwards. At six he was back again and, much puzzled about what she could want with him, was shown up to her boudoir, to which he had never previously been admitted.

When they had settled down he said with a smile: 'Now, tell me. In what way can I be of service to you?'

She shook her head. 'None. It is yourself that I wish to talk about.'

'Really!' He raised his devil's eyebrows. 'What have I done? Nothing, I hope, to offend you.'

'Nothing to offend but to distress,' she replied sadly. 'We have known one another for nearly three years now; so I look on you as an old friend, and I am worried about you. I know you to have so many fine qualities and it pains me to hear of the life you have been leading.'

'Oh, come! It is true that in this past year I have racketed round quite a bit with my Russian friends; but to show them the sights was part of my job.'

'It's not that. It is the attitude to life that you have adopted which I find so distressing. From all accounts you have become completely cynical and think of nothing but chasing women.'

He shrugged. 'What the devil else is there to do as long as I am stationed in Paris? If only they would send me out to fight the Arabs, no one would be more pleased than myself. If only France were like Russia I could now and then hunt wolf and bear. During the two years I was at St. Cyr I read enough military history to last me a lifetime, and I am interested in neither cards nor horses. You must know that prose poem of Oscar Wilde's in which the "Doer of Good" restored the sight of the blind young man, then came upon him looking with desire upon a beautiful woman, and asked him why he was eyeing her like that. The young man replied: "But I was blind once, and you gave me sight. At what else should I look?" Well, like him, as long as I am in this city of amorous delights at what else should I look? I am the victim of my circumstances.'

Again Angela shook her head. 'That is not true, Armand; or only partly so. I make no criticism of your affair with Madeleine, or of your having become the lover of a woman like Madame Pollit; but of recent months your behaviour has been abominable. There was that episode which led to Claude Trouverier slapping your face.'

De Quesnoy grinned. 'She said she did, but she was lying.'

'No matter; it is clear that she found your attentions unwelcome. Then there were those poems published by Julie de Beaumont-Arlon's cousin; and more recently the duel in which you might have killed or wounded that poor young Prince de Lodi.'

'He is not a real Prince, only a Napoleonic one.'

'Armand, please be serious. No matter where he gets his name he is in love with his wife and she with him. For you to attempt to come between them was inexcusable.'

He sighed. 'Yes, my dear, I suppose you are right, and I have been behaving like a blackguard. In the circumstances it is sweet of you to be concerned for me; and to tell the truth I have derived little pleasure from these adventures. But I am all at sixes and sevens with myself; so what would you have me do?'

'Why, pull yourself together. Become again the man you really are, then find some nice girl to marry. Or, if you are averse to that, an attractive woman, with a complaisant husband, who needs a lover; and be faithful to her.'

'I have no mind to marry yet awhile,' he declared, then added with a smile: 'From your last recommendation it seems that you have overcome your old prejudices against adultery?'

'In three years, Armand, one's sense of values are apt to change,' she smiled back. 'I still regard it as a sin; but not such a terrible one as I used to. I have since met many women I respect whose characters have not deteriorated because they have taken lovers. There is, too, much point in the old saying: "When in Rome . . ." And the special circumstances in which most French marriages are made makes it difficult not to condone it.'

After a moment he said: 'If only I could adopt your suggestion it would, I know, mean recapturing the happiness I have lost; but the problem is to find such a woman, and one to whom I should be likely to remain faithful for any length of time. I . . . well, why should I not say so; I thought that I had found one once.'

Angela quickly looked away. 'I know, and I tricked you very badly. I have often regretted it.'

In an instant de Quesnoy was on his feet. 'D'you mean that? Angela, tell me! Do you really mean . . .'

'No! No!' Quickly she thrust him away from her. 'I meant only that I regretted the childish, vindictive trick that I played upon you.'

With a sigh, he sank back in his chair. 'I was a fool to hope anything else. But, tell me, do you intend never to take a lover?'

She hesitated, then replied in a low voice. 'I don't know. I would no longer have any scruples of conscience about doing so. Gabriel freed me of these some months ago.'

'Indeed! How did that come about?'

'Our personal relations have never been happy ones, and for a long time past he has bothered me very little—for which thank God. I think I would have died if I had had to continue to submit to the sort of demands which I have reason to suppose he makes of his young mistresses.'

The angry blood came rushing to de Quesnoy's face; but before he could speak she hurried on: 'Still, that is beside the point. What I was about to tell you is that during the summer a youngish banker with whom he does a great deal of business began to pay me marked attention. Then one night Gabriel gave me the strongest possible hint that if I liked to take this man as my lover he would be grateful to me, because it would help his financial interests.'

'My God! The swine!' De Quesnoy exclaimed. 'I'd like to wring his neck.'

Angela smiled. 'You need not be so fierce. Apart from his sadistic tendencies he is not a bad man. Normally he is kind, understanding and very generous. He is, too, a great patriot. He is always neglecting his own affairs to appear at rallies of the *Ligue* and attend Royalist conferences. As most women have lovers, too, there was nothing so terrible in his suggestion, and he did not press it in the least. I simply said that I did not feel that I could help him in that way, and that was the end of the matter. But I decided that his attitude freed me from any obligation to be faithful to him in the future.'

'Then Angela,' De Quesnoy leant forward earnestly, 'will you not take me for your lover? Oh, I beg you to! You, and you alone, have the power to rescue me from this stupid vicious life with which you so rightly reproach me. I have loved you for years, more than any woman I have ever known. And at the bottom of your heart you must still care for me, otherwise you would never have sent for me to talk to as you have this afternoon. Oh, please, my dear. Just think how happy we could be.'

'I . . . I don't know,' she stammered, the blood mounting to her face. 'Oh, Armand, if I could be really sure that you would keep on loving me I might. The idea of saving you from yourself that way had not occurred to me; but it is one that would appeal to any woman who has been as fond of a man as I have been of you. Don't press me for an answer now, though. No, please, I'll have to think about it first.'

'For how long, darling! For how long? How long?'

Suddenly she laughed. 'Armand, at heart you are still only a boy, and have all a boy's impatience. Give me a week. And if I do decide to give you a rendez-vous, this time I promise to keep it.'

Seizing her hands he kissed them, but she stood up and said firmly: 'I don't want to discuss this any more for the moment. I want to be alone; so please, my dear, go now.'

Regretfully he took his leave. But as he walked downstairs he felt a different man from the one who had come up them only twenty minutes earlier. Totally unexpectedly his whole outlook had been changed and he was in the seventh heaven of delight, for Angela's parting smile had left him with little doubt that he had only to wait a week and, after all these years, she would become his at last.

When he strode down the Rue Saint-Dominique to the War Office the following morning he was still walking on air. As he entered his room, one of his fellow A.D.C.s told him that their General wished to see him; but with his head still full of Angela he had forgotten all about the letter he had written to General Billot until he walked into de Boisdeffre's spacious sanctum.

As he approached the desk the General pushed a flimsy paper towards him and said: 'Read that.'

It was the *faux Henry*. Having read the few lines of writing on it, without even a suspicion that they might be a forgery, he murmured: 'I see. Then Dreyfus was guilty after all.'

De Boisdeffre nodded. 'Perhaps that will teach you not to form judgments contrary to those of your superiors.'

'Has Colonel Picquart seen this, Sir?' de Quesnoy inquired.

'No; it has come to hand only since his departure. But what concern is that of yours?'

'Only that from your showing it to me, Sir, I assume you have been told about the letter I wrote yesterday to General Billot. If Picquart has not seen this document it is still true that his dismissal is indefensible.'

'Again, your superiors are the best judge of that, and General Billot takes the strongest possible exception to your insolence in daring to criticize his decisions. He is also determined that no rumours of any kind shall reach Deputies, at all events from you. I recall that you wished to see foreign service. Well, you shall. But I fear you will not find much chance of winning any glory.'

De Boisdeffre paused for a moment, then delivered the *coup de grâce.* 'The Minister for War has charged me to convey to you the following order: You are to leave Paris tonight for Marseilles. At Army Headquarters there they will have been instructed to allot you a passage on the first ship leaving for Madagascar. It is to be hoped that you will have a better understanding of the word discipline after you have done a few years' garrison duty in the fever-ridden swamps of that most unattractive island.'

CHAPTER X

RIP VAN QUESNOY

T was not until January 1903 that de Quesnoy returned from exile. When one is still in the early twenties six years seems a lifetime, and as he strode down the crowded Cannebière a few hours after landing at Marseilles he felt like Rip van Winkle.

At twenty-seven he made a more than ever gallant figure, for he wore the sky-blue uniform and flowing scarlet cloak of the crack African cavalry corps; on his chest there were ribbons for gallantry, and his kepi carried the four gold rings of a Lieutenant-Colonel. His face was bronzed, his eyes bright and the muscles of his slender, medium-tall body as strong as whipcord.

As he ate his *bouillabaisse* at the Mont Ventoux, looking out towards the fishing boats in the Vieux Port, he well remembered the anger and despair with which he had eaten his last meal there. To have disobeyed the orders he had received would have meant court martial, and de Boisdeffre would not grant him even a twenty-four-hour postponement. That afternoon he had called on Angela but, to his fury, he had found Syveton's old mother with her; so they had had to part without a chance to say what was in their hearts.

He had seriously considered resigning his commission, as the only way of saving himself from the War Minister's fear-inspired vindictiveness, but to have done so would have meant losing face with his father. Much as he hated the idea of going to Madagascar, he would not give the Duke the satisfaction of believing that, after three easy years in Paris, he had thrown his hand in when called on to face the discomforts of real soldiering.

His first few months in Madagascar had been grim; for he had not even the comparative solace of the sort of books he liked, and other small luxuries which his private income enabled him later to have sent out from Europe. The huge island, larger in area than France, was thinly garrisoned and its population hostile. It was only in the preceding year that the famous Colonial soldier, General Galliéni, had succeeded in stamping out widespread rebellion. There was no proper accommodation for the troops, supplies of all kinds, particularly medical stores, were hopelessly inadequate and fever was rampant.

The French, having made a treaty with the Hová Queen, had expected to be able to administer the island through her officials, in the same way as they were now successfully running Tunisia through those of its Bey. But it transpired that the Hovás controlled only the big plateau of Imèrina; so Galliéni had had to start again from scratch, and set up an organization which would reconcile the divergent interests of several different races before order could be brought out of chaos. Moreover the Malagasy population was rapidly falling. It was of such poor spirit that it would not work to improve its condition, and the island had been declared unfit for white settlers. So a more depressing station for a young officer could hardly be imagined.

The Count had again contemplated sending in his papers, but had put off doing so owing to a friendship he had struck up with an English missionary: a fine, intelligent and broad-minded man with whom he spent many of his evenings converting his text-book English into a fluent command of that language.

This parson, like many of his kind at that time, was compiling a bulky treatise on the folklore and customs of the natives among whom he worked, and that entailed an examination of their priests' claim to occult powers. As the island's people were an admixture of Pacific and African races, its witch doctors had become the repositories of the magic of both, so were among the most advanced occultists in the world. The many strange feats they performed so intrigued de Quesnoy that by the early summer he had embarked on a serious study of the subject.

White magic was practised as extensively as Black, the only difference between the two being that whereas the latter is for personal ends the former is for purposes of healing or the benefit of others, and after a while de Quesnoy decided to become a neophyte under the direction of the most celebrated White Magician in the island. Henceforth the long empty hours between his dull routine duties were filled with mental exercises, tests of physical endurance and a gradual building up of the will-power which is necessary to all occult operations.

Originally he had made up his mind that in no circumstances

would he spend more than a year in Madagascar, but so fascinated did he become by his penetration into the vast domain of the supernatural that month after month slid by and, even after two and a half years, he hardly knew if he was pleased or sorry when an order at last arrived for his transfer.

The order was accompanied by a personal letter from General de Galliffet, who had just become Minister of War in a government formed by M. Waldeck-Rousseau. The General wrote that he had long wished to rescue his protégé from exile, but that had not been possible while de Boisdeffre had remained Chief of Staff, and even after his retirement in the preceding November opposition had been met with from other officers in the War Office. Now, however, as War Minister, his desires had to be complied with without argument. He added that on de Quesnoy's arrival in Europe he might take two months' leave, but that he was not having him posted to a Metropolitan regiment as he considered that his career would now be better forwarded by his seeing some active service; so when his leave was over he was to place himself at the disposal of the G.O.C. Algeria.

For his leave the Count had not gone to Paris. Instead, as his father was now resigned to the career he had chosen, he had taken ship from Suez via Constantinople to Odessa and thence travelled up to Jvanets. After a stay of some weeks there he had spent the rest of his leave in Budapest and Vienna, then by way of Trieste recrossed the Mediterannean to the scene of his new activities.

It was just at this time that the Dreyfus affair boiled up to the greatest of all its crises. In the summer of '97 the Dreyfus family's efforts to secure a retrial had begun to bear fruit, the agitation being led by an Alsatian Senator named Scheurer-Kestner. Esterhazy was publicly denounced that autumn and the War Office reluctantly compelled to bring him to trial early in '98. The court martial was held *in camera*, he was found "not guilty", and the mobs, which had now been whipped up by the Press into an anti-Semitic fervour, screamed with delight at his acquittal.

Emile Zola had then published his famous letter under the banner headline "*J'Accuse*" in the newspaper *Aurore*. In it he charged the judges at the court martial with having acquitted Esterhazy at the order of the War Office. This public "insult to the Army" resulted in anti-Semitic riots in nearly every town in France, while in Algiers the mobs got completely out of hand and for four days sacked the Jewish quarter.

Generals Billot and de Boisdeffre retaliated by prosecuting Zola for libel, but they feared that Picquart might prove awkward if he were called as a witness, so they decided that they had better tackle him before the trial came on.

In the preceding year Picquart had been ordered to a post of great danger on the frontier of Tripoli. The local C.-in-C., General Leclerc, on learning what lay behind the order, indignantly repudiated it, and told him that he was not to go farther south than Gabes. Now he was recalled to Paris, placed under arrest, forbidden to see his friends and brought before a Court of Inquiry. Then, having rejected the overtures of the Generals to save his career at the price of perjuring himself at the Zola trial, he was dismissed the service.

The trial of Zola lasted a week. He was not a very likeable personality. Having insulted the jury he spent most of the time that he was in the box singing his own praises; but the only way the Generals could get the better of his counsel was to refuse to answer questions on the excuse that to have done so would have given away official secrets. Zola was sentenced to twelve months' imprisonment and a heavy fine. The acid comment of the *Berliner Tageblatt* when reporting the case was "The French Army has won its first victory since its defeat in 1870–71".

Zola escaped prison by flight to England, but Dreyfusists and anti-Dreyfusists continued to hurl abuse at one another. There were numerous duels, especially between the journalists. Clemenceau and Drumont fired three times at each other, but all six shots missed. Picquart challenged Henry and Esterhazy Picquart. The only result was a slight wound in Henry's arm. The day before he received it his tame forger, Leeman, was found hanged in his lodgings. Perhaps he had committed suicide, but a lot of people later thought that he had been put out of the way.

That summer and autumn there had followed the fall of two Governments, Picquart's arrest on a charge of having disclosed official secrets, and the discovery that the *faux Henry* was a forgery. Henry was arrested, confessed and blew his brains out. Esterhazy was then dismissed from the service and fled to Belgium. Finally there came a government decision that the Court of Criminal Appeal should examine the arguments for reopening the original case.

108

In February '99 M. Félix Faure died while in amorous dalliance with a pretty woman in his private office. Soon after half-past six the lady's screams for help brought his Chef-de-Bureau running, but the President had been stricken by a cerebral haemorrhage and it was too late to do anything for him.

He was succeeded by Emile Loubet, who was known to be in favour of revision, which led to further riots. But after their long struggle the Dreyfusists were at last gaining ground. In June the united Appeal Courts gave their verdict in favour of a retrial. Another government fell, du Paty was arrested and Dreyfus brought back in a cruiser from Devil's Island.

The new court martial was held at Rennes and opened early in August. It lasted for over a month, while the seven officer judges sought to unravel the incredibly tangled skein which had evolved from five years of misunderstandings, lies, forgeries, suppressions and false accusations. An ex-President, an ex-Premier, General Mercier and all the War Ministers subsequent to him, a dozen Generals, scores of other officers, police, warders, experts, women and pushful publicity seekers were called to give evidence. Madame Dreyfus was hounded from her hotel and a fanatic attempted to assassinate Dreyfus's counsel; but, to the fury of the greater part of the French people, the World Press was solidly of the opinion that Dreyfus's first conviction had been a flagrant miscarriage of justice.

Nevertheless he was found "Guilty" again by a majority of five to two but, on "extenuating circumstances", his sentence was reduced to ten years' detention. He had already served four and three-quarter years and had returned from Devil's Island broken both mentally and physically. De Galliffet, as Minister of War, requested that the balance of the sentence should be remitted, and on September 19th the President issued a pardon. By this step de Galliffet hoped to end this shocking affair for good and all, and he issued a manifesto to the Army and the Press to the effect that it must now be regarded as closed.

But it was far from closed. For years Dreyfus's supporters endeavoured to clear his name by agitating for another retrial; or, alternatively, the trial of Mercier, de Boisdeffre, Gonse, du Paty and others for the parts they had played. There were more duels, more riots and many thousands more hours spent by leading jurists re-examining the evidence. It was not until July 1906 that Dreyfus's innocence was finally admitted in a special Bill passed by the Chamber, and he was decorated with the Legion of Honour (4th class). Picquart fared better. In a Bill of the same date he was reinstated with the rank of Brigadier and a few months later, when Clemenceau became Prime Minister to spite the Army, he made him his War Minister.

De Quesnoy reached Algiers while the Rennes trial was in progress, and read the reports of its later stages there; but he was soon posted up country and attached to the Headquarters of a regiment of Spahis. His early promotion to Captain now stood him in good stead, as his Colonel, finding him a born cavalry officer, soon gave him a squadron.

Then fate favoured him further by a decision of the Government to send forces across the Atlas mountains for the occupation of many thousands of square miles of territory to the south of them. Not only did this give him a chance to show his mettle in active warfare, but during their mountain and desert campaigns squadrons often operated a day or more's march apart, so he was virtually in command of an independent unit. It was not many months before his brilliant exploits became the talk of the frontier region and were reported to General Lyautey. Within eighteen months of landing in North Africa he was promoted to brevet Major, and three months before his recall to France he had been given another step to brevet Lieutenant-Colonel.

As the waiter helped him to the flaming *Omelette au Rhum* that he had ordered to follow the *bouillabaisse* he was thinking not of the past but of the future, and particularly of a letter that had been handed to him by a military messenger immediately his ship had docked at Marseilles that morning. It was from a General Laveriac who was now Assistant Chief of Staff at the War Office; but it was on private paper headed "Château d'Albaron, Camargue, Bouches du Rhone", and simply said:

Before you proceed to Paris I wish you to report to me here. Please telegraph the time of arrival of your train at Arles and a carriage will be sent in to meet you. Make no arrangements for the next few days as our host would like you to stay over the week-end.

Having never met the General, de Quesnoy was considerably puzzled by this semi-official, semi-private missive, and the fact that he was evidently supposed to know who "our host" was; for until that morning he had been unaware that such a place as the Château d'Albaron existed. However, as soon as he had parked his baggage at the Hôtel du Louvre et de la Paix, he made inquiries about trains, and as Arles was only some fifty miles distant he sent a telegram saying that he was proceeding there that afternoon.

One of his interests being ancient civilizations, he had during his three and a half years in North Africa spent two of his leaves in Rome and others in Athens, Sicily and Crete; so Arles being a Roman city he would have liked to visit its Colosseum and other remains; but a servant in plain livery was on the station platform to meet him, which gave him no option but to set off for Albaron as soon as his belongings had been loaded into a wagonette.

Not liking to confess his ignorance, he refrained from asking the coachman or groom the name of their master, but he learnt from them that Albaron was a good ten miles distant so he settled down to make the best of the hour's drive.

The pale winter sunshine was quite pleasant but the country was flat and uninteresting; so he was glad when the coachman pointed ahead with his whip to a distant building on a slight eminence and told him it was the Château.

As they approached, the Count saw that it was one in the original sense—a sixteenth-century castle with pointed turrets and battlements—although not a very big one; but perched up on its hillock it dominated the country for many miles around. At length the horses drew the wagonette slowly up the steepish drive that almost circled the big mound, and with every metre they advanced de Quesnoy was able to survey a greater area of the castle's surroundings.

About a mile to the east of it lay a small compact town, but there was hardly a building to be seen in any other part of the landscape. There were no woods or cultivated land; coarse tussocky grass divided into fields by water-filled ditches made up the immediate prospect, while away in the distance to the south lay the vast waterlogged Camargue, with its innumerable lakes and marshes straggling down to the sea. This desolate region, as de Quesnoy was aware, supported only herds of semi-wild cattle and a very sparse population; so it struck him that it was particularly well suited for meetings which it was desired to keep secret, and he had no need of his psychic faculties to tell him

111

that there must be some very special reason for his summons to this lonely castle.

But, as he entered the spacious hall, he got a pleasant surprise. The wagonette had been observed crawling up the drive and his host was there to greet him. One glance at the tall, stooping, bewhiskered figure, who looked much more than his age owing to his premature baldness, and de Quesnoy exclaimed:

'Why, Vicomte, how stupid of me! I should have realized that since you take your title from the Camargue, you might have a château in it; but I must confess that I had never heard your name associated with Albaron. I had not the faintest idea whose guest I was to be until this moment.'

'Fanthy that!' the Vicomte lisped. 'Well, well, no matter. After all ith quite understandable. When you were stathioned in Paris we had the pleasure of seeing you only occasionally; so even if we ever mentioned Albawon to you, after so long you might well have forgotten it. Gilles should have mentioned it in hith letter. By Gilles I mean, of course, my bwother-in-law General Lavewiac.'

At that moment Madame de Camargue and her brother appeared. Having kissed his hostess's hand and murmured how delighted he was to see her again, de Quesnoy was presented to the General. Like his sister, he was short and dark, a typical Gascon, with a hooked nose, black eyes and an animated manner. To meet he proved much more congenial than his letter would have suggested. He explained that, being due for a fortnight's leave, he had decided to spend it with his relatives in the southern sunshine, and that knowing de Quesnoy to be a friend of theirs it had occurred to him that the Château d'Albaron would be a good place to discuss the Count's next posting.

After de Quesnoy had been refreshed with that forerunner of the dry Martini, a glass of the dry Vermouth made near Marseilles, he was taken to his room, where a footman unpacked for him and laid out his things for dinner. Having changed, he was first down-stairs, and he had been in the Vicomtesse's drawing-room for only a few minutes when he received another surprise—Gabriel Syveton walked in.

De Quesnoy's heart gave such a bump that he had difficulty in controlling himself sufficiently to greet the politician with composure. He jumped to the conclusion that since Syveton was staying at the

Château, Angela would also be there, and that it might be she who had secretly stage-managed his being invited to Albaron.

During his six years in exile they had written to each other once in every three or four months, although only to exchange news and ideas. This regular correspondence had strengthened their long established friendship but the epistles of neither of them could have been classed as love letters. Had they actually become lovers de Quesnoy might have returned to Paris during his long leave in '99 in the hope of renewing their affaire; but he had felt certain that Angela would not consent to become his mistress for what could have amounted only to an amour lasting a few weeks.

And now, after the first moment, in view of their long separation, he could not give serious credit to his wild idea that, having learned of his imminent return, she was still sufficiently interested to have entered on an intricate intrigue in order to come south and welcome him. Nevertheless when, in answer to his enquiry, Syveton told him that Angela was not even at the Château, but staying with English friends in a villa at Mentone, he felt a sharp pang of disappointment.

For some years now Syveton had been the Treasurer of the *Ligue de la Patrie Française* and, as de Quesnoy knew from Angela's letters, had in the previous May been elected Deputy for the Paris Bourse district; so he congratulated him upon it.

It transpired that there were no other guests and the Vicomtesse, being the only woman of the party, declared at the end of dinner that she would release them from attendance on her in the drawing-room afterwards, as she had letters to write and would go straight upstairs.

The habit of smoking after dinner was now spreading rapidly; so as soon as she had left them cigars were handed round with the cognac, Chartreuse and Kummel, and the men lit up. When the servants had withdrawn there was a little desultory conversation, then Laveriac looked across at de Quesnoy and said:

'I expect you have been wondering, Count, why I should have asked you to report to me here rather than at the War Office; but it really is to discuss your future employment. General de Galliffet, I know, was anxious that you should enter the *École Supérieure de Guerre* as soon as you were qualified by age to do so, and you are now old enough. However, before I proceed further I should like to have your assurance that everything which may be said here tonight will be regarded by you as confided to a man of honour.'

De Quesnoy having given his assent, the General went on: 'De Galliffet's time at the War Office was all too short and his retirement for political reasons in May 1900 was a sad blow to the Army. Unfortunately his successor, General André, is not only a most unlikeable personality but a menace to the safety of the State. No one would seek to challenge his right to hold private views of a Leftist and anti-clerical nature; but the wicked thing is that he is allowing his political prejudices to operate against the Army's senior officers. Generals and Colonels of proved worth are being deliberately passed over, because they are either monarchists at heart or practising Catholics, and mediocre men are being put over their heads solely because they are people of no breeding and atheists.'

'That is bad,' de Quesnoy murmured, 'very bad. Because among the officers of the Army there must be at least ten Catholics for every free thinker; so if all the most responsible jobs are being given to the latter it will reduce the operational potential of the service by a really alarming degree.'

'Exactly,' the General nodded. 'Of course, as Assistant Chief of Staff, I am in a quite strong enough position to provide you with a nomination should you decide that you would like to enter the *École Supérieure de Guerre*. There is, however, an alternative; and about that I think it more fitting that my brother-in-law should speak to you.'

De Camargue gave a slight cough, then asked de Quesnoy: 'Duwing your campaigns in the desert, Count, have you followed our kaleidoscope politics, or have you found yourself too occupied with militerwe matters?'

'When stationed in the outposts of the Sahara,' the Count replied, 'the news from Paris sometimes does not reach one until it is several weeks old. Stale news loses much of its interest; so out there we don't bother to follow events very closely. But what General Laveriac has just been saying about General André's policy is entirely in keeping with all I have heard these past six months. Since the fall of the Waldeck-Rousseau government it has become obvious that the Church is to be afflicted with another wave of persecution.'

'The greatest mistake ever made,' Syveton chipped in, 'was His Holiness's initiation of the "*Ralliement*". By telling French catholics

114

to accept democracy and rally to the Republic, Rome put our chances of a restoration back ten years; yet in the long run has failed to get the protection for her interests that she expected from the unwritten bargain. Even under the Ribot ministry during '95 it became apparent that the Centre had no intention of compromising itself through standing by the Church; and now that Combes is in the saddle she will be made to pay the full price for siding with the "Slut" instead of helping to give France a monarch.'

'What sort of man is the Prime Minister?' inquired de Quesnoy. 'I know little about him except that he is over seventy and said to be strongly anti-clerical.'

'You understate the case. Emile Combes is probably the most fanatical atheist in France. In his youth he was a seminarist, but he was unfrocked and took to medicine. He has little interest in foreign policy, finance or even social problems. His one ambition is the destruc- tion of the Church and that he may have the maximum opportunity to enforce the measures he means to put through he has taken over the Ministry of Public Worship personally.'

'The tragedy ith that we might have been spared him,' de Camargue commented. 'Waldeck-Rousseau had done so well. Many of us gwumbled when on forming his government in '99 he took the socialist Millewand in as his Minister of Commerce. But the move pwoved a wise one. Millewand ith an able fellow, and although he had twouble with his own people for accepting office hith inclusion kept Guesde and Jaurès and their extremist followers weasonably quiet. And for thwee years too; the longest term that any Ministwy has lasted since 1870. Having won the general election last summer Waldeck-Rousseau had an ample majowity to carry on. His wetirement while still Pwemier was unpwecedented. I suppose he had hith pwivate weasons, but without him hith cabinet fell to pieces; and it ith that which has landed us with the unspeakable Combes.'

Laveriac rapped the table sharply with his knuckles. '*Mon ami*, I must call you to order. We have got away from the matter we are here to discuss. Besides, regrettable as Combes becoming Prime Minister may be for the immediate interests of the Church, it cannot fail to excite reactions which, in the long run, will prove most favourable to our designs.'

'You mean that it will put an end to the *Ralliement*,' de

Camargue replied, 'and bwing back to us the support of Catholics of all classes. That ith bound to happen and, in fact, it ith upon such a falling away of loyalty to the "Slut" that we are largely counting. I had not lost sight of that, but was perhaps a little cawied away by the thought of the disgwace it is for Fwance to have such a Pwime Minister. To proceed then ...' Turning, the Vicomte looked across at de Quesnoy, and asked:

'Does the title Duc de Vendôme mean anything to you?'

'I know it as one of the greatest in the *ancien régime*. Apart from having been created by Henry of Navarre for his son by Gabriel d'Estress, Bourbon blood has several times since been introduced by females into the Vendôme family. The present Duke must now be a young man. His father died when he was quite young and his mother was a Spanish Princess. If I remember she remarried and her second husband is a Spanish nobleman.'

'All that ith correct. Hith mother is an aunt of the pwesent King of Spain; so he has Bourbon blood on her side too and as first cousin to the King he ith styled His Highness. *En secondes noces* she married the Conde de Cordoba y Coralles, a gentleman who combines with an ancient title the Pwesidency of the Banco Coralles, and ith said to be one of the wichest men in Spain. The young Duke was brought up there, but he was born in Fwance and by weturning to enter the Fwench Army he has duly established hith Fwench citizenship. However, what I asked you was:—"Does the name Fwançois de Vendôme weawaken in your mind any special memory?"'

The Count thought for a moment, then exclaimed: '*Mon Dieu*, yes! It was just before I left Jvanets to start at St. Cyr; and both you, Vicomte, and Monsieur Syveton were there. On the last night of your visit the men of the party all agreed that the only hope of restoring honest government in France was for her to have a King again. They agreed, too, that it was useless to attempt anything on behalf of the Comte de Paris, and it was stated that the secret Monarchist Committee wished to adopt my father as candidate for the throne. When he refused, a suggestion was made that they should wait a few years and then approach the Duc de Vendôme.'

De Camargue nodded his bald head. 'That ith exactly what happened. Well, the few years have gone. This young Prince ith now nineteen and an officer-cadet at St. Cyr.'

116

'Indeed! A start has been made, then, in bringing him up in a manner which will help to make him popular with the nation.'

'Yes.' It was Laveriac who spoke. 'His mother was secretly influenced into sending him there. But she knows nothing of this, and he has not yet been approached. If you are of the same mind as ourselves, we feel that you might be the right man to approach him.'

'Why should your choice fall on me, General?' asked de Quesnoy, greatly surprised and with sudden caution.

'For several reasons. Our young Prince has been brought up most strictly; so even for his age he is very inexperienced in worldly matters. If the approach was bungled it would be disastrous. He might think it a trap intended to test his loyalty to the Republic, and flatly refuse to have anything to do with us—or even report the approach to his Commandant. It must therefore be made by someone he will instinctively trust—someone who is a member of a family as distinguished as his own, not too far removed from him in age, and if possible a brother officer whom he would have reason to look up to and admire. You, Count, fulfil all those conditions.'

De Quesnoy bowed his acknowledgement and the General went on: 'But there is much more to it than that. He has just completed his first year at St. Cyr. During it, not wishing to give him big ideas unnecessarily early, we deliberately held our hands; but from now on he will be coming more into Paris, and we wish to provide him with a suitable bear leader. I do not mean in the social sense, as every door will be open to him; but someone who will be constantly at hand to advise him, and to whom he can talk freely at times when the secret he will be carrying becomes a burden to him. Earlier, I mentioned to you that there is an alternative to your going to the *École Supérieure de Guerre*. It would be easy for me to secure your appointment as the Chief Instructor on the Cavalry side at St. Cyr. You are now well qualified for such a post; and, without appearing to take too much notice of the Prince, you would have him under your immediate supervision.'

For a moment the Count did not reply, then he said: 'It was, I recall, General de Galliffet who put forward de Vendôme's name that night at Jvanets. What does he think of these proposals?'

'He has not been consulted.' Laveriac spread out his hands. 'He detests the Republic and all the corruption that it stands for; but he has made it a rule of his life never to act against the government which is employing him. I have no doubt at all that in the event of a successful *coup d'état* he would immediately give our new provisional government his support, and later, for the sake of the Army that means so much to him, accept again the portfolio of War Minister. But, knowing his principles, we felt that it would have been wrong at this stage for us to make him privy to our plans.'

'I appreciate that.' De Quesnoy nodded. 'As for myself, I must have time to think the matter over.'

Syveton had been pulling nervously at his drooping moustache. He now leaned forward and said earnestly. 'Monsieur le Comte, I would like to stress how invaluable your help would be to us. In fact there is no one else who could play this role even half so effectively. As General Laveriac has pointed out, it is certain that owing to your distinguished lineage, coupled with the reputation you have already made while young as a gallant and experienced soldier, the Prince will place his confidence in you. But that is not all that is required. If we attempted to place an instructor over him who might be suspected by the government of being a nominee of what they call "the old gang at the War Office" General André would soon get to hear of it and veto the appointment. You will be immune from such suspicions; but I can think of no one else of your rank and achievements who would.'

'Then the reason for my being sent to Madagascar got out,' smiled the Count. 'And in consequence they now account me a Dreyfusist and a radical.'

Laveriac laughed. 'That was bound to happen. I am told that your sudden departure set every tongue in the War Office wagging. Your friendship for Picquart was of course known, and that old fool Billot stupidly refrained from destroying your letter; so in the course of a few days everyone knew the inside story. Naturally it will be assumed that you have come home with a grudge against de Boisdeffre, du Paty, and the rest of the Army's aristocratic pro-clerical element. That is why, having sounded General André, I am already certain that he would approve your appointment as one of the Chief Instructors at St. Cyr, and not have the faintest suspicion that you might be grooming our young man to play a royal rôle, with the object of throwing him and all his crooked colleagues out into the gutter.'

Again Syveton spoke, his pale eyes beneath the broad forehead boring earnestly into de Quesnoy's bright grey ones. 'It is only fair to

118

warn you, Count, that should you decide to work with us, until we can come out into the open, you will be called on to make certain sacrifices. I mean as far as your social life is concerned. It would be unnatural if, having returned to Paris, you refrained from calling on your cousins and more intimate friends of the past. But in view of what we have just been saying, while you are acting as mentor to the young Prince it is an essential precaution that you should have as little as possible to do with the Faubourg St. Germain circle. Only so can you maintain the impression that you continue to bear resentment for the scurvy trick that the Generals played upon you, and are therefore a reliable watch-dog who will prevent your pupil from being made political use of by what our enemies term "the reactionaries".'

'That ith so,' de Camargue nodded. 'As known woyalists my wife and myself will have to deny ourselves the pleasure of your visits. Thith also applies to all the other members of the Monarchist Committee whose names I will give you. And above all to Syveton; as he ith now Treasurer of the *Ligue de la Patrie* and the most active of all of us. But he ith wight that you have a perfect excuse for appawently having taken umbwage against the people with whom you would normally be in political agweement, so you are doubly waluable to us on that account.'

De Quesnoy drew heavily on his cigar, let the smoke trickle gently out from the corners of his mouth, then said: 'I appreciate now that few people are so circumstanced that they could fill your particular requirement with as good a chance of being successful in it as myself. But, as I have already said, I must have time to think the matter over. How long can you give me?'

Laveriac's quick black eyes flashed approval. 'If you do decide to do as we wish I shall be all the better pleased that there will afterwards be no question of our having rushed you into it. We have the week-end before us; but I leave for Paris on Monday. Do you think you could give us your decision by Sunday night?'

The Count agreed to do so; after which they talked of more general matters for an hour or so, then went to bed.

On the Saturday morning they were driven some distance then, taking to broad-bottomed punts, were poled by muscular peasants almost silently through narrow alleys between tall screens of bulrushes, which enabled them to get a fine bag of wild duck, in which the lakes

119

abounded. In the afternoon they rode out to witness a rounding up of cattle by the Camargue horsemen, who were as accomplished riders as Spanish *garrochitas*, and to admire the young wild bulls that were a feature of the district.

On Sunday de Quesnoy excused himself from accompanying the others to Mass. He was more than ever a believer in an after life and the power of Good over Evil; but since his two-year long concentration on contemplating the mysteries, in Madagascar, he had given up participating in the rituals of the Catholic Church. He asked if instead he might have a carriage to take him into Arles, and his host at once arranged the matter for him.

On arriving in Arles he spent a quarter of an hour looking round the Arena; then he went to the outskirts of the town where, below the remains of the Roman rampart, lay the ancient burial grounds. Most of the tombs dated back to the Roman occupation, and many of them were great carved stone sarcophagi which had lain there for upwards of fifteen hundred years.

It was a sunny morning and trees threw a dappled shade on the walks between the rows of tombs. At that hour the spot was deserted, peaceful and friendly. For over an hour he strolled slowly up and down, turning over in his mind the proposal that had been made to him.

The rôle he had been asked to assume would, he knew, be a difficult and far from pleasant one to play. It would entail cold-shouldering many of his old friends, and Angela among them. Moreover, the Duc de Vendôme might prove an awkward young man to handle or, perhaps, an unlikeable one. There was also the risk of discovery. If the conspiracy misfired its ringleaders would be tried for treason and perhaps be condemned to imprisonment for life, or, in certain circumstances, to death.

On the other hand if the Prince turned out to be a tractable and pleasant youth, and the *coup d'état* resulted in his being placed upon the throne, his principal supporters would be able to claim from him practically any rewards they liked to name. To de Quesnoy that meant the command of a Cavalry Division before he was very much older; and later the War Office, with the power to throw out incompetents like Gonse and, with the assistance of Galliéni and Lyautey, the possibility of remaking the whole French Army on a more efficient system. And there was much more to it than that. Under a young King with honest advisers, the whole administration could be purged of crooks and the name of France again made respected throughout the world.

By mid-afternoon he was back at Albaron, just in time to join the others, who were setting out for the nearby town in which a Saint's day was being celebrated. For a couple of hours they drank wine with the Mayor and a number of hearty fellows representative of the local notables, while watching the fiesta. Then they returned to the Château.

As soon as the Vicomtesse had withdrawn after dinner that night, General Laveriac said: 'Now, Count, may we hear your decision?'

De Quesnoy smiled. '*Mon Général*, having given deep thought to the matter, I am fully convinced that my duty lies in doing as you wish.'

At that de Camargue got quickly to his feet, raised his glass, and said: '*Mes amis*, I give you a toast. Let us dwink to Monsieur le Duc de Vendôme crowned in Rheims Cathedral as Francis the Third of France.'

CHAPTER XI

RED ROSES—BUT FOR WHOM ?

N arriving in Paris de Quesnoy put up at the Meurice. He then began a cautious build-up of what was to be his new social circle. As it was January most of the big houses in the Faubourg St. Germain were shut and their owners basking in the sunshine of the South of France, but one of his cousins had remained in the capital to conclude the merger of a company he controlled with one of its rivals. Through him, the Count had it put about that, while he would be happy to accept invitations from members of his family and close friends to small intimate dinners or lunches, he was anxious not to meet any of the General Staff who belonged to the nobility, so he did not mean to attend any larger functions.

He also made it clear to several old acquaintances whom he chanced to meet that, while he had no intention of mixing himself up in the Dreyfusard agitation, which was still going on, he considered the Generals who had handled the affair most culpable, and was more than half inclined to suspect that there was some truth in the rumours to the effect that their actions had been inspired by their Father Confessors as part of a Jesuit plot to stimulate anti-Semitism. That, he knew, would in due course get passed on to the anti-clerical War Minister, General André, and establish him as a "safe" man to have as one of the Chief Instructors at St. Cyr.

However, he was quick to appreciate that, if he gave the impression that he was living almost the life of a hermit, it would be regarded as unnatural; so he paid an early call on Josephine Pollit and had the good luck to find her in Paris. During the few months that Josephine had been his mistress he had met many interesting people in her salon. Painters were her speciality but she also gathered round her some of the more respectable literary lions of the day and a number of the younger members of the *Académie Française*. Having greatly widened his reading during the past six years de Quesnoy was much better equipped to hold his own with writers and savants than he had been in '96, and it was now his intention to cultivate these gifted people.

Josephine received him most kindly and, while there was no suggestion on either side that they should reopen their affaire, she told him that he would always be very welcome at her receptions. He attended an evening *soirée* at her house two days later, meeting there a few old acquaintances and making several new ones. By the time he left he had both given and accepted several invitations, and was pleased to think that, through his ex-mistress, he had provided for himself a social cover which should prove most rewarding.

By the end of January he had settled in at St. Cyr and was hard at work picking up his new duties. As he was a strong believer in discipline the students to whom he played the part of headmaster soon found that they could take no liberties with him. He was sharply intolerant of both slipshod work and the least slackness in appearance; but he never gave punishments without reason. Once this became generally realized his young men put their backs into their tasks and gave him little trouble.

To many of them, too, he was already a hero, as his reputation as a fighting soldier had gone before him. Moreover, lean and handsome, still wearing his Spahi uniform with its scarlet cloak floating from his shoulders, and with the ribbons of the Légion d'Honneur and the Croix de Guerre on his chest, he looked the part. About his own exploits he was reticent, but to encourage valour in his youngsters he would sometimes go to their mess in the evening and tell them stories of endurance in the desert, and of courageous deeds performed by the men he had led.

With regard to the Duc de Vendôme he exercised great caution, treating him exactly as he did the others, and for a while hardly ever addressing an informal word to him. Like de Quesnoy the young Prince was slim, well built and a little above medium height, but his hair was fair and he was endeavouring to grow a moustache. His eyes were blue, and the Bourbon blood in him had come through more strongly than it had in the case of the Count; for he had not only the beaky nose but also the heavy jowl of the royal race, and it detracted somewhat from his otherwise pleasant looks.

Unfortunately he had been educated entirely by priests, and not

ones of the broad-minded variety like the old Abbé Nodier. In consequence, while he was deeply religious and could easily have passed the
examinations to graduate from a seminary, he was abysmally ignorant
upon many subjects which were of importance in a worldly career.
This, however, when de Quesnoy discovered it, provided just the sort
of excuse for which he was seeking to get into closer touch with the
young man without arousing the jealousy of the other students. All
the more conscientious Instructors gave a certain amount of their own
time to coaching the more backward of their charges and the Count,
having set de Vendôme a special course of reading, made him come to
his private room for an hour every Monday evening to talk over what
he had read.

It did not take many of these talks to convince the Count that if
de Vendôme did become Francis the Third he would not set Europe on
fire. He was a kindly natured and polite young man with a great fondness for animals, and particularly horses. In fact the only natural
affinity between master and pupil was their love of hunting; but even
this was limited to hunting in its conventional sense, for the Prince
was too shy to hunt women and too timid to hunt men.

Yet, even if he was no throw-back to the amorous and brave
Vert Gallant, he had quite a will of his own and his fair share of ambition. He was devoted to his mother and stepfather and most anxious
to please them by doing well at St. Cyr; moreover, as a really expert
horseman, he had set his heart on later making a name for himself by
carrying off prizes for jumping at the international horse shows.

After a while de Quesnoy became quite fond of him, and decided
that he would fill the bill of King very well. He would never dominate
his ministers, but when he got over his shyness he would fulfil his
duties with considerable charm; on horseback in a brilliant uniform
he would make just the sort of showy figure to appeal to the populace,
and he was reasonably intelligent, honest and good tempered. Such
qualities made it much more likely that he would make a successful
constitutional monarch than had he been a lusty, boisterous determined schemer like his great ancestor. Nevertheless, it was not until
April that the Count disclosed to him the high destiny which might
be his.

He chose a fine Saturday on which to do it, and as the setting the
garden that Marie Antoinette had laid out about the Petit Trianon.

It was less than twenty minutes' ride from St. Cyr, and horses could be left in the stable at the rear of the little palace; so on several occasions he had ridden over to stroll there, and this time he invited de Vendôme to accompany him.

The crocuses were over and the lilac buds only just bursting; but the cherries and double peaches were in full blossom and drifts of daffodils and hyacinths made gay the lawns. The tourist season had not yet begun, so there were few people about and there was no chance of their being overheard as they walked slowly between the trees which thrust up branches covered with tender spring green towards the pale blue sky.

They had been talking of Premier Combe's recent visit to Brittany. He had gone there to unveil a statue of Renan, and his ferocious measures against the Church were already well under way. Brittany, being a Catholic stronghold, had given him a hot reception—so hot that a pitched battle had resulted between the devout peasants and the police. De Vendôme was saying what a terrible thing it was that France should be ruled by men who were so obviously the tools of Satan, when de Quesnoy remarked:

'If you have the courage, and are prepared to accept the direction of certain older men who will work loyally in your interests, I believe that in a year or so from now you could be in a position to drive every one of these atheists from office.'

De Vendôme first looked puzzled, then laughed, thinking that his senior had made a joke the point of which he did not get, but should have understood. The Count, having expected some such reaction, went on quietly to explain how the leaders of the monarchist party, realizing that there was no longer anything to be hoped from the legitimate heir to the crown, now wished to place their hopes in him.

The young man would hardly have been human had he not been momentarily dazzled by the prospect held out to him; but it did not take him long to realize that should a *coup d'état* to seat him on the throne succeed, he would have to pay for the glory by carrying great responsibilities and leading a life hedged about with every kind of restriction. For some while they discussed the pros and cons, then he said:

'I am greatly honoured, Count, but really I would rather not. It would be wonderful, of course, to be able to revive the Royal hunts at Fontainebleu and Compiègne, and to own the finest racing stables in the world. But my Ministers would always be at me about one thing or another, and I'd have practically no life of my own.'

De Quesnoy did not seek to persuade him by dwelling on the allurements of power and immense wealth; but he did say:

'I can understand your rejecting this offer on personal grounds. Have you considered, though, what your acceptance might mean to France?'

'No,' the Prince admitted reluctantly. 'I fear I have been thinking only of myself. You mean that it is my duty to accept in order to restore honest government. Perhaps you are right; although it is quite possible that I might find the task beyond me. I think the best plan would be for me to consult Father Thomas and find out if he considers me fitted to attempt such a great undertaking, or if I may refuse with a clear conscience.'

Father Thomas was one of the chaplains at St. Cyr and the Prince's spiritual director, to whom he confessed regularly every week. As a restoration of the monarchy was so obviously in the interests of the church, de Quesnoy thought that all the odds were on Father Thomas telling his penitent that he should accept. But one could not be certain, as some priests were still in favour of the *Ralliement* and so supporters of the Republic. His own duty, as he saw it, not for the sake of the Church but for the sake of France, was to persuade de Vendôme to play the rôle planned for him. Knowing how deeply religious the Prince was, although inwardly wincing at his own hypocrisy, he played his trump card, by saying:

'This is so dangerous a secret that I must ask you to refrain from mentioning it even to your confessor. And, indeed, you are under no obligation to do so; because by accepting you would not be committing yourself to a course of action which would necessarily lead you into sin. On the contrary it seems to me that you are God's chosen instrument. If we succeed in placing you on the throne you will be anointed with the Holy Oil at Rheims, and become His champion with the power to protect His Church from the persecution it is now suffering. In my view, to allow any other person, even His Holiness the Pope, to dissuade you from taking up the sceptre would be wrong. It is a matter entirely for your own conscience.'

For some moments the Prince was silent, then he said solemnly: 'You are right. I would not accept for any other reason, but I see that as a good son of the Church I must.'

That evening de Quesnoy went into Paris and called at Laveriac's private apartment to report his success. He had already been there on two occasions to give the General his opinion of the young Prince and inform him how he was shaping. Now, on the conclusion of his account of the conversation, the bright-eyed little Gascon exclaimed:

'God be thanked that we are over that hurdle! You were right, of course, not to rush matters; but the Committee are anxious to go ahead with their secret campaign to make him a popular figure with the public. I take it you are fully satisfied that he won't back out.'

'No, I feel sure you can count on him to go through with it,' de Quesnoy replied a shade unhappily. 'Although I had to turn the screw to get his consent, and I'm none too easy in my own conscience about that.'

Laveriac shrugged his broad shoulders. 'Forget it, *mon ami*. Most of us have to do things at times of which we do not approve, for the good of the cause. What matters is that we can now start to work in earnest for a man who you are convinced will make a good, if not spectacular, King.'

'Yes; he'll make a good King,' de Quesnoy agreed. 'Perhaps almost too good in one sense. He would never have agreed but for the bait of becoming the protector of the Church; so he will have to be watched. Otherwise he will fall completely under the domination of some Father confessor and the Jesuits; and that would be almost as bad for France as leaving the country to the mercy of Combes and the Socialists. I would be happier if instead of being quite such a saint he had a bit more of the devil in him.'

'It may be that he is only a slow starter,' remarked the General. 'That is often the case with youngsters brought up as strictly as he has been; and sometimes such types turn out the worst rips of all. Now that he is in his second year he will be coming into Paris much more frequently and he'll be a very abnormal nineteen-year-old if he doesn't become interested in some young woman.'

'Yes; I suppose that's true. Unless things have greatly changed since I was a student at St. Cyr, nearly all his class mates will have their grisettes or ladies with complaisant husbands. The discussion of such matters among themselves may lead him fairly soon now to risk his confessor's anger by succumbing to some pretty charmer's wiles.'

The General drew thoughtfully upon his cigarette. 'That's about what will happen. Seeing that he is a Duke, too, and by no means a bad looking one, I expect there are quite a number of the fair but frail already setting their bonnets at him.'

'You need not limit it to the frail,' de Quesnoy smiled. 'There are plenty of mothers in the Faubourg St. Germain who would like to get him for their daughters. And being the sort of chap he is he might decide to marry instead of taking a mistress.'

'God forbid!' Laveriac almost jumped out of his chair, 'If he made an unsuitable marriage before we can get him on the throne that would ruin everything.'

'I think that unlikely, and only mentioned it as a possibility. In families such as his marriages are always a matter of arrangement and lengthy negotiations. He is devoted to his mother and I cannot see him rushing into anything without her consent.'

'I hope you are right. If so we could disclose to her the high destiny that is intended for him, and no doubt she would restrain him from spoiling his chances of the throne. But one never knows. And now it has cropped up the whole question perturbs me. Say he does take a mistress; being such an innocent he will probably regard her as a twin soul. Even the most stupid of women are capable of making boys like him believe them to be persecuted angels with hearts as pure as gold. He would naturally be tempted to confide in her and if she proved indiscreet that, equally, might ruin all our plans. I tell you, Count, at this stage, if the wrong woman got hold of this young man she could prove more dangerous to us than a dozen priests.'

De Quesnoy shrugged. 'I fear that is a risk we must accept. Apart from continuing to impress upon him the imperative need for secrecy, I see no way in which we can counter it.'

'Neither do I, at the moment,' agreed the General. 'But I shall speak to the Committee about it; and at least we can arrange to have him watched whenever he comes into Paris.'

As a result of this talk the Count took even greater pains to gain the confidence of his charge and by skilful questioning find out how he spent his time when in the capital. As he had supposed, apart from a few hours passed at one or other of two aristocratic clubs, of which he had been made a member, de Vendôme devoted his week-ends to a few noble families to whom he was related. Unlike most of his companions, he never spent a Saturday night in Paris, was usually in by twelve o'clock and invariably attended early morning Mass at the college chapel on Sundays.

Meanwhile Combes launched himself against the Church with iconoclastic fury. The old "Law of Associations" which made it obligatory for the religious houses to have permits was re-applied with fresh vigour. For years the courts had been arguing hundreds of cases, aimed at confiscation of Church property, in which final judgment had been postponed owing to legal technicalities skilfully put forward by the lawyers. Now, the Prime Minister declared publicly in so many words that he did not give a fig for justice; he wanted action.

Only ten teaching Orders, which could not possibly be spared, were temporarily reprieved. Monks and nuns by the thousand were driven by the gendarmerie from the monasteries and convents which for many were the only homes they had known during the greater part of their lives. Great numbers sought refuge abroad, others went unhappily to live a new life, contrary to their vows, as lay members of their families, while others again, who lacked relations to care for them, were rendered entirely destitute and compelled to beg for food and shelter.

In some cases, as an alternative to confiscation, indemnities were accepted; but the valuations for them were carried out with calculated intent to harrow the feelings of the religious. Sacred relics that had been venerated for centuries were handled with contemptuous carelessness, or deliberately broken, and many precious vestments were spoiled.

Such measures aroused a strong feeling of sympathy for the Church among a large proportion of the French people who were not normally devout. These, mainly middle-class families, while far from priest-ridden, set a high value on the rites of christening, marriage, and burial, and considered that the religious orders did more good than harm; so they would have helped to stay the persecutions if they could. But Combes had succeeded in forming a combination in the Chamber which gave him a big majority; so he could not be stopped.

For the summer vacation de Vendôme returned to his home in Spain, while de Quesnoy spent his partly at Jvanets and partly in looking up old friends in Vienna. Both came back to St. Cyr the better for their holiday—the student determined to do his best during his last term so that when the results were published his future subjects should see that he had passed out well, and his instructor anxious to help him by private coaching to the utmost of his ability.

So keen was the Prince now that soon after the opening of the term he began to spend most of his Saturday afternoons working, But he always went into Paris on Saturday evenings; and by chance one week-end towards the end of September de Quesnoy discovered where the young man spent them.

He had some work of his own that he wanted to catch up with, so he too worked through the Saturday afternoon. Then, soon after six o'clock, he caught the same train as de Vendôme into Paris. On arriving at the Gare des Invalides, they discovered that they were both dining in the same part of the city, so they shared a fiacre to take them across the Seine. De Quesnoy was going to a house in the Avenue de Wagram, and de Vendôme to one in the Rue de Lisbonne; so the latter being nearer, the obvious thing was for the Count to drop the Prince.

On the far side of the Pont Alexandre an old flower seller was still sitting on a corner under her big sun umbrella hoping for late trade. Stopping the carriage de Vendôme got down and bought from her a big bunch of red roses. De Quesnoy observed the transaction with considerable interest, as it suggested that the young man might be going to a rendez-vous. It was, of course, equally possible that he was taking flowers to a sick friend or a hostess who frequently entertained him; but somehow the Count had a feeling that the red roses were intended for an *amant de cœur*, and it was strengthened by his recalling that during the past few weeks he had several times caught de Vendôme day-dreaming.

When they reached the Rue de Lisbonne, the Prince asked to be set down on its north side opposite the broad alley that led into the Parc Monceau. At that de Quesnoy immediately revised his guess about the roses. He had many a time in the past been set down himself in the same spot, as Angela lived in one of the two corner mansions the garden walls of which formed the alley. All the Committee behind the *Ligue de la Patrie Francaise* would by this time have made the acquaintance of the young man they hoped to make their King, Syveton among them. Evidently the Prince was dining with the Syvetons and taking the roses to Angela as a compliment.

With an inward sigh de Quesnoy wished that he was in the Prince's place. Interesting as he had found it during the past eight months to cultivate Josephine Pollit's literary and learned friends, he had still felt it a hardship that his rôle in the conspiracy necessitated his appearing to be out of sympathy with the people who would normally have formed his social circle.

On his arrival in Paris he had written to Angela telling her that greatly as he had looked forward to seeing her again after all these years he was, for the time being, debarred from calling on her owing to certain circumstances connected with the League of which her husband was now Treasurer. She had written back to say that she too was disappointed not to see him, but she fully understood, as she had asked Syveton about it and he had confided to her the hopes that were now being placed on a certain student at St. Cyr.

There they had had to leave matters; and although they had since exchanged two or three letters, giving each other their general news, now that de Quesnoy was back in France neither had felt called on to write the many-page dissertations on life, books, politics, and so on that they had when he was several thousand miles distant. As he no longer attended large social functions he had not even seen her in a crowd since his return, and when the carriage pulled up for de Vendôme to get out he would have given a lot to have accompanied him into the house; but he knew that to be out of the question.

However, as the carriage bowled on he chanced to look back and, to his surprise, he saw that instead of going to the front door of the mansion de Vendôme had turned into the alley leading to the park. Evidently then he was not, after all, dining with the Syvetons; so the odds were once more on the roses being for some young woman with whom he had started an affair.

Recalling Laveriac's remarks on the importance of being informed about any amatory relationship upon which the young Prince might enter, so that steps could be taken promptly to counter any danger to the conspiracy likely to arise from it, de Quesnoy instantly decided that it was his duty to follow his charge and, if possible, find out with whom he meant to spend his evening. Calling to the *cocher* to pull up and wait for him, he jumped out and walked quickly back to the entrance to the alley.

When he reached the alley it was empty. Dusk had already fallen, obscuring at its far end the park, but there was still sufficient light to see for a hundred yards or so, and the slim figure of the Prince should have been visible somewhere in the shadows ahead; but it was not. Fearing that he might lose him altogether de Quesnoy broke into a run, yet when he reached the park gates he could still see no sign of his quarry.

The Parc Monceau was the Kensington Gardens of Paris, as in it the children of the rich were taken for their airings; but it was made much gayer than its London equivalent by the picturesque clothes of the nurses. They all wore the costumes of the provinces from which they came; beautifully goffered bonnets of stiff lawn, huge bows of black watered silk and long streamers pinned to their back hair, or richly laced caps of a dozen varieties; so in the daytime the little park was one of the sights of the capital. But now it was almost deserted. The only people in sight when the Count pulled up in the gateway were a pair of lovers seated on one of the benches, and the man was certainly not de Vendôme.

Puzzled by the Prince's disappearance, de Quesnoy peered ahead of him, and was just about to run on when away to his right he caught the sound of a door slamming. On his right, as he stood there, was the corner of the wall of the Syveton's garden, the bottom of which was adjacent to the park. Turning, he strode along it and after covering thirty yards came upon a low door in the wall. Walking quickly on he came to another door, and then another. They were set in the wall regularly at intervals of about a hundred and twenty feet, and it was clear that all the houses in that section of the Rue de Lisbonne had private entrances from their gardens into the park.

All the doors were locked, and the question now was, through which of them had de Vendôme gone? The Count felt that it must have been through one of the two nearest to the alley as having run through it himself would have brought him almost on to the Prince's heels; so he could hardly have had time to get farther. Retracing his steps, he stood well back from the wall and stared up at it.

He saw that every eighty feet or so the wall merged into a higher structure, the outlines of which were only vaguely visible against a background of dark trees. These, obviously, were large summer-houses at the bottom of each garden, the upper storeys of which formed gazeboes with windows giving them a view over the park. At once he recalled the pavilion in the Syvetons' garden, and realized that he was now looking at its back and the backs of a row of others similar to it.

132

As his glance ran from one to another he saw that they were all in darkness, with one exception—the Syvetons'. Curtains were drawn across its windows but at their edges could be seen faint chinks of light. In amazement he stared at those tell-tale chinks. People did not receive their friends for ordinary social reasons in summer-houses at this hour on autumn evenings. Could it . . . could it possibly be that young de Vendôme was having an affaire with Angela?

CHAPTER XII

THE PRINCE'S MISTRESS

IKE the elephant's child, one of de Quesnoy's characteristics was a "satiable curiosity", and as this matter now concerned, perhaps, not only the young man of whom he was in charge but also the woman he had thought of for many years with an emotion very near to love, he knew that he would never be satisfied until he had found out the truth.

The wall was a tall one and although he could have scaled it he was averse to acting the spy on any love scene. Again, he could have excused himself soon after dinner at the house where he was to spend the evening and returned to watch from which door de Vendôme would come out. As the Prince made a habit of getting back to St. Cyr by midnight on Saturdays it was unlikely that the wait would have been a long one, and such a move would have enabled de Quesnoy to make certain whether the young man had gone into the Syvetons' garden or one of the others: but that would still not disclose the identity of the woman he had gone in to see.

Angela's parents had long since left Paris and, when de Quesnoy had last heard of them, were *en poste* in Stockholm; but from time to time she had her two younger sisters, now pretty girls of twenty-two and twenty-four, to stay. It might be one of them with whom de Vendôme was having a romance, or perhaps Angela had lent the pavilion to one of her friends as a place of assignation. Again, while visiting the Syvetons the Prince's fancy might have been caught by some pretty maid, with whom he had started an intrigue, and who was now using the pavilion in which to meet him without her mistress's knowledge. There was, too, still the possibility that the lights in it had nothing to do with him, and that he was by now being taken up the back stairs to his mistress in one of the houses farther along the Rue de Lisbonne.

Greatly intrigued by this problem the Count made his way back to the waiting *fiacre* and was driven on to dine in the Avenue de Wagram with a famous explorer whom he had met through Josephine. But it bubbled intermittently in his mind over the week-end and, with the unscrupulousness which gave him no qualms of conscience once he had determined on a course of action, on the Monday he took the first step towards solving the mystery.

Having waited till the afternoon, when de Vendôme and the rest of his class had changed into fencing kit, and were hard at it in the *Salle d'Armes*, he went to the Prince's sleeping quarters and, taking care to disturb things as little as possible, ran through his belongings. To his considerable satisfaction he came across a large key typical of the kind made for use in garden doors. This being one of the things he had hoped he might find he had come prepared with a lump of soft wax, upon which he took an impression of the key. Replacing everything as he had found it, he took the impression along to his Sergeant-Farrier and told him to make a key from it.

His next move did not take place until the following Saturday. In accordance with routine, after the last class in the morning, he spoke to his students about the weekly reports upon them put in by the junior instructors, and returned to them with praise or blame their Friday's essays, which he had glanced through himself on the previous night. When he came to the Prince's he said:

'Monsieur de Vendôme, your style is improving, and the substance of this essay is by no means bad. But your writing is appalling; positively appalling. And that an officer should write clearly is of the greatest importance. Imagine yourself commanding troops in action. You are hard pressed by the enemy and send back a message to your Colonel asking if you may retire or if it is imperative that you should hold your ground. The runner returns an hour later to say that the Colonel has been unable to read your message. What do you do? Retire and perhaps get yourself cashiered for having given away a valuable position; or stay where you are and perhaps sacrifice your life and the lives of your men quite needlessly. This is by no means the first time that I have spoken to you about the carelessness of your writing; so I must now take steps to make you improve it. Instead of going into Paris this afternoon or this evening you will remain at your desk from three o'clock until dinner time, and again afterwards until half-past ten, copying out this essay several times in a legible hand.'

There was nothing in the least abnormal about the giving of this punishment, and by having failed to improve his slipshod penmanship the Prince knew that he had laid himself open to it. He knew, too, that from time to time his fellow students were caught out in some slackness and, at the last moment, deprived of the permission to go into Paris on Saturday, or for the whole week-end. Usually that meant having to cut appointments, but their friends knew that they were under military discipline, so made allowances on occasions when they were forced to do so.

By half-past six de Quesnoy was again in the gateway of the Parc Monceau, now with a free field in front of him. He had come early as he wanted to have ample time to reconnoitre the ground before either being discovered or disclosing himself. On reaching the door into the Syvetons' garden he tried the key that his Sergeant-Farrier had made for him. It fitted, as he had felt the odds were that it would, and turned the well-oiled lock easily.

Slipping inside he closed the door gently behind him, then glanced quickly about him in the twilight. The houses at the far end of the gardens were partially obscured by trees and little more than dark blocks in which a few lighted windows showed through gaps between the leafy branches. No one was about, and immediately to his right stood the pavilion. In its side wall there were no windows, so as yet he had no means of telling if it was occupied.

Moving cautiously round to the front he tiptoed in under the arches of a low open arcade that ran along the garden side of its ground floor. An open door invited inspection of the interior; but it was dark in there, so before gliding in he took from his pocket a useful, fairly recent invention—a flat flask-like case with a small bulb in its top, which on pressing a button connected with a battery and gave out a beam of electric light.

Shining the torch round, he saw that to one side there was an ornamental staircase leading up to a closed door and that the rest of the ground floor was used partly as a garden store-room, for chairs, tables, etc., and partly as a machine shop. Later he learnt that the array of tools on a long bench, lathe and petrol engine belonged to young Henri Syveton, who had pursued his hobby of engineering there before being called up to do his military service. He was just about to advance to the stairs when he heard sounds above. Switching out his torch he dived down behind a stack of garden chairs and crouched there holding his breath.

It was the sound of the door above being opened that had given him just time to get under cover. As he stared upwards through the chair legs, in a band of pale light before the door was shut again he caught a glimpse of a woman's skirts and ankles. As she was wearing stockings of some thick black material, he knew that she must be a servant. She came quickly down the stairs humming a cheerful tune, and without the least suspicion of his presence walked past him out into the garden.

Having given her time to reach the house, he tiptoed up the stairs, eased the door open a crack and listened intently. Hearing no sound he went in and closed it behind him. The room he had entered was a tiny kitchen. It was lit by an oil lamp and against one wall stood an oil cooker. On it a crock of coffee was simmering gently, and a glance into its interior showed that a casserole and plates were being kept warm there.

He found the next room in darkness except for the faint glow from an oil heater. The room had windows on both its longer sides, which faced towards the house and park; but curtains were drawn across all of them, so he could risk a few flashes of his torch. They showed it to be a well-furnished sitting-room with cabinets, a sofa and arm-chairs against its walls. At one end a small table was laid for two, and on it there were silver candlesticks. A first course of caviare and crisp rolls was placed ready on a side table, also a big bowl of fruit. A bottle of champagne stood nearby in a long-legged ice bucket. Picking it up he glanced at the label. It was Moêt et Chandon Dry Imperial 1889. As he slipped it back he gave a rather grim little smile and thought: "Fourteen years; just turning the corner to perfection. With luck I shall enjoy that."

Another door at the far end of the dining-room led to a small but comfortable bedroom, warmed by another oil heater. De Quesnoy stood there for some moments, his glance fixed on the neatly turned-down pink silk sheets of the bed, and protruding from them the mahogany handle of a copper warming pan. Then, muttering to himself 'I wonder? I wonder?', he closed the door and retraced his steps to the ground floor of the pavilion.

Taking up his position beside the bottom of the staircase he settled himself to wait with as much patience as he could muster. Ten minutes, a quarter of an hour, drifted by; then he heard light footfalls on the gravel path. As he strained his eyes towards the grey oblong made in the darkness by the open doorway, he could feel his heart pounding in his chest. Next moment the silhouette of a woman appeared in the opening. Stare as he would, it was impossible to tell in that dim light whether she was Angela or someone else. She was still some twelve feet away from him and, whoever she was, he was anxious not to give her a nasty shock; so before she took another step he gave a faint cough.

Pausing in the doorway, she said quickly: '*François chéri*, you are early.'

It was Angela's voice. In reply he gave a low laugh, and said: 'I trust you will not be too disappointed but this, *chérie*, is Armand.'

'Armand!' she exclaimed. 'Why! What . . . what does this mean?'

'Simply that your little Prince will not be coming to sup with you tonight, and that as I have long wished to see you I took the opportunity to keep his appointment for him.'

'D'you mean that he told you he was coming here?' Angela's voice held an angry note 'I would never have believed him capable of being so careless of my reputation.'

'No, no! Please do not think ill of him,' the Count said quickly. 'He has no idea that I know of his affaire with you. In fact until you spoke just now I was not certain myself that it was you he comes here to meet.'

'Then how . . . ?'

'I found out by accident that he spends his Saturday evenings either here or somewhere very close by. As you are aware, I am his instructor and . . .'

'That does not justify your prying into his private life.'

De Quesnoy smiled in the darkness. 'I will confess that the possibility of your being concerned enormously stimulated my curiosity. But the special circumstances surrounding this young man do make it important that those interested in him should inform themselves about any close friends he may make.'

'Yes,' Angela admitted, a shade less annoyance in her tone. 'I appreciate how anxious you must be to guard against his becoming intimate with the wrong sort of people. But if he has not told you of his visits here, how do you know that he does not intend to come tonight?'

'Because, when it was too late for him to let you know that he would be unable to keep this rendez-vous, I suddenly dished him out a punishment lesson which will keep him busy all this evening.'

'Armand, really! What a beastly and unfair advantage to take of your position.'

'Not in the least. He is lucky that I did not keep him in for the whole week-end. I have more than once threatened to do so unless he took the trouble to improve his writing. If he sends you *billets-doux* you must know how atrocious it is.'

'He does, and his writing is quite frightful.' Suddenly Angela laughed. 'Poor boy, I fear that if you saw them you would criticize the matter in them too. They are pathetic compositions compared to the ones you used to send me when you were his age.'

'Thank you, my dear, for your memory of them. And how good it is to hear you laugh again. It makes me hope that you are not too grievously disappointed at my having deprived you of the Prince's company this evening.'

'No, I'll not fall into a decline from thwarted longing because I'll not see him for another week.'

'Then let us forget him for a while; and instead of remaining here talking in the darkness, make ourselves comfortable upstairs.'

'What leads you to believe that it is more comfortable up there?'

'Angela! Angela!' he exclaimed, burbling with laughter. 'Please do not seek to persuade me that after only a little private conversation with de Vendôme in the shadows here, you take him to dine in the house with half a dozen people. Twenty minutes ago I saw your maid come down these stairs. As a soldier it was my natural instinct to reconnoitre. All that I saw inclined me to suppose that the Prince is an extraordinarily lucky young fellow.'

'You had no right to pry,' she admonished him; but her tone was one of amused resignation. 'I might have guessed, though, that I would not be able to keep from you the fact that I am his mistress.'

'My dear, why should you? If I ventured any criticism at all it would only be that I could have wished you a more amusing lover. But we have just agreed to forget him. And I was hoping that you were about to ask me to supper.'

139

'Armand! You are incorrigible. Does not your conscience smite you for making such a suggestion, when you have condemned the poor young man for whom the meal was intended to spend his evening drawing pot-hooks and hangers?'

'Oh come! You must eat yourself and so must I. It would be absurd for us to bid one another a polite farewell and each spend the evening in sober solitude.'

'You deserve no better. And as the Prince has no means of getting his own back, I can at least do so for him by turning you out.'

'But Angela,' he pleaded. 'Does our old friendship mean nothing to you? Not having met for so long we have a thousand things to talk about. I'll be truthful now, and admit that simply by following de Vendôme I could have found out what I wished to know without him or his *chère amie* being the wiser. It was the possibility that she might be you, and if so the chance that I might steal you from him for a few hours, that has made me think of nothing but this moment during the whole of the past week. The fates have been unkind enough in depriving me of even seeing you since my return. Surely you will not be so harsh as to send me away now without so much as a glimpse of you?'

'All right, then.' There was a smile in her voice which told him that she had meant to relent all the time; but as she led the way upstairs she added firmly: 'Please do not get any false ideas, though. We will sup and talk; but nothing more. Is that quite understood?'

'Of course, my dear, of course,' he murmured. 'You may be sure that I would not seek to take advantage of your kindness.'

In the tiny kitchen she gave him a taper and told him to light the candles in the dining-room. When he looked up from doing so she was standing on the far side of the table. Catching his breath, he stared at her. She had thrown off a light wrap and her bare shoulders rose out of a foam of pink tulle. The candle flames caught the gold lights in her high-piled hair, and were reflected in the limpid depths of her brown eyes. Among her massed curls sparkled a diamond star, diamond and sapphire drop ear-rings drew the eye to the firm pale column of her neck, more diamonds glittered in the bracelets on her wrists, and a cluster nestled in the tulle above the cleft between her breasts.

'*Grâce de Dieu!*' he breathed after a moment. 'How beautiful you are!'

She laughed, showing her white even teeth. 'Did you then expect to find me an old woman?'

'No, no! But like a great wine which was admirable when young maturity has made you superb. I know you to be twenty-eight, but as in the case of many English women you have kept your figure, and you look at least three years younger than your age. I had known that you must still be beautiful but not that I should find you positively devastating.'

Angela lowered her lashes demurely, dropped him a curtsy, and murmured mockingly: 'I am flattered at having earned the approbation of such a connoisseur in wine and women as Monsieur le Comte.'

'But seriously,' he protested. 'In Paris, in all France, there cannot be a lovelier . . .'

'Enough, Armand! Enough, my dear.' She cut him short with a wave of her hand. 'I am anyway quite old enough not to allow my head to be turned by your compliments. And this is a meeting between old friends; no more. Now let me have a look at you.'

Coming round the table she stood within a foot of him. The heady scent she was wearing made him check his breathing. He was terribly tempted to take her in his arms; but he kept a tight hold on himself as her eyes ran over his face, and she said slowly:

'Yes; I can return the compliment. You must be as attractive to women as ever; if not more so. You have lost that slightly puffy, dissipated look that you were getting before they sent you into exile. But you look more than your age. I would put you down as thirty.'

'That does not surprise me. The life I led during the six years I was abroad was a hard one.'

'So I gathered from your letters. I expect, too, that those strange disciplines you practised on yourself while you were in Madagascar took a lot out of you. I was terribly intrigued by the accounts you sent me of some of your occult experiences.' She smiled suddenly and added: 'Recalling them sends quite a shiver up my spine; I should have remembered that you may have it in your power to bewitch me.'

For a moment his grey, yellow-flecked eyes held hers, as he replied, seriously: 'If I could do so by normal means, I would. But nothing would induce me to break the law which forbids the use of such powers for one's own ends.' Turning abruptly away he took the bottle of

141

champagne from the ice bucket and began to open it. Then in a lighter tone he said:

'I can never thank you sufficiently for the letters you wrote to me so regularly through all those years. You have no idea how much they meant to me. But all the same they never told me much about the real you, and how your life was shaping.'

She gave him an enigmatic smile. 'Perhaps I may when we have had supper. We'll see. I hope you like caviare?'

He nodded and she helped him liberally, then herself, and they sat down to their first course. *Perdreau en casserole* and cheese straws followed, after which he peeled for both of them Doyenne pears. It was a light meal as meals went in those days, but appropriate to its setting.

During it they talked, at first a shade awkwardly; but very soon the strangeness of being together again wore off, and they were laughing as happily as they had during that fortnight long ago at Jvanets, when they had first come to know one another. After the meal they stacked all the plates in the little kitchen; then Angela, skilfully forestalling her guest from occupying the sofa with her, settled herself in one corner of it and put her feet up. Waving him to a nearby arm-chair she said:

'Now, sit there and tell me of all your wickedness.'

He smiled. 'There is really not much to tell. In Madagascar I learned, thank God, how to sublimate my passions into will power. Had I not, Heaven knows what I should have done; for the Malagasy women are ugly beyond belief, and the handful of Europeans quite impossible. In North Africa, of course, my whole life was different, as it was no longer lived almost entirely on a mental plane. But by far the greater part of the time I was in small frontier towns or the desert. Now and then I got back for a week or two to civilization. In winter, particularly, the big hotels are always full of visitors, and I generally found some pretty woman who was willing to let me show her the sights; but, by and large, for a young officer, my life was quite a model of rectitude.'

'Armand, I can hardly believe that. Do you mean to tell me that in your six years abroad you did not have one serious affaire?'

'Well, not really serious. There was a singer in Oran. A real little gamin. As wicked as sin, but amusingly so, and possessing extraordinary powers of fascination. For a bet I took her away from one of the richest men in the city, then got caught myself. For a few weeks I was quite mad about her and became insanely jealous every time I suspected her of deceiving me, which I am sure she did quite frequently. Fortunately I was recalled to the frontier and the desert air soon cleared my brain again.'

Angela smiled. 'It must have been very good for you to meet your match for once. But were there no others?'

'During one of my leaves to Rome I met a charming Contessa. She was a young widow. One night we slipped away from a dance and drove up to the Palatine Hill in the moonlight. It was one of those sudden things and terrific while it lasted. We were both broken-hearted when my leave came to an end; but she wrote me a few months afterwards that she had fallen in love with an American, and meant to marry again; and by that time I too had got over it.'

'And what else?'

'Nothing. Nothing that could count as an affaire, I assure you.'

'You amaze me.' Angela shook her head. 'I would never have believed that the leopard could change his spots; yet, by comparison with the life you led during that year you lived in Paris, it seems that you have. And now, since your return, I gather that you have again become the respectable lover of that clever Madame Pollit?'

'Dear me, no! You are quite wrong about that. As your husband must have told you, I have had to pose these past eight months as a staunch supporter of the government. To do so I had to cultivate a quite different circle of friends; so I made use of Josephine's good offices to that end, that is all.'

'Really! Are you trying to persuade me that you are now endeavouring to qualify for canonization?'

'God forbid!' he laughed. 'Let me still your fears that I am becoming abnormal by telling you that I took a fortnight of my summer's leave in Vienna; and I found the girls there as beautiful as ever.'

'I am being silly,' Angela declared. 'Having sowed your wild oats why should you not have settled down to take your pleasures in moderation? In any case I have no right to catechize you.'

'Oh, but you have! You gained that right from having once tried to save me from going completely to the Devil. Besides, I mean to catechize you. When was it that you first came to your senses and decided to enjoy life like other people?'

'Not very long after you were sent abroad. The night that we had our talk I made up my mind to give myself to you. I was conceited enough to believe that although other women couldn't hold you, I could, and that I would be able to bring out all the best in you.'

'And you could have! Oh, Angela, my dear, just to think what I missed through the scurvy trick those Generals played on me. It makes me feel like seeking out old Billot and strangling him.'

She laughed. '*Mon ami*, be sensible. All this is ancient history. Fate decided that we should not become lovers, and had not General Billot been to hand the blind goddess would have used some other instrument to separate us. But, as I was about to say, looking back on it now I don't think my decision was based solely on the urge to save you from yourself, or even the fact that I had never ceased to have a great tenderness for you. I was twenty-two and, subconsciously at least, becoming increasingly aware that my natural instincts were being thwarted.'

As she paused, he supplemented: 'So someone blessed of the gods came into the paradise which should have been mine. Tell me, did he deserve it?'

'Yes. After you had gone I was very miserable for a while. You see, once I had taken my decision about you I had spring-time in my heart, if only for a few hours, and when the blow fell the following evening that it was not to be, I felt that for the second time in my life I had been wickedly cheated.

'Then some three months later I met a young attaché who had just been posted to the British Embassy. He was a sailor, and like so many Englishmen rather shy. At first we were just friends, drawn together by the same sort of childhood background which is so very different from that in which French people are brought up. After we had known one another for about ten weeks, one night in June he suddenly asked me to run away with him.

'Of course, I had known for some time that he was in love with me; but I had not realized the depths of his passion. His other love was the Navy, but he was quite prepared to send in his papers; so that we could start a new life, perhaps in the United States, and he was rich enough for us to have lived in comfort there. I must confess that I was tempted, because I had really come to care for him and knew him to be the

144

faithful kind. But it would have meant the wrecking of his career, so instead I—don't laugh Armand—I persuaded him to become my lover.'

De Quesnoy closed his eyes. 'You had to persuade him! Really the English are extraordinary! And how long did it last?'

'Nearly two years. Until he left Paris to go to sea again.'

'And then?'

'I missed him sadly; but after a few months I also missed being made love to. I had an affaire with a German Prince; but that was a mistake. I won't go into details but one night he behaved like an absolute brute. It brought back to me all the horror of my honeymoon; and for a long time after that I was too scared to venture myself again with anyone else.'

'My poor sweet. You seem to have had the most appalling luck.'

'No, not really. That was over four years ago, and I have known several charming men since. Three were quite brief affaires, but two lasted for some time; and one of those was a most talented musician of whom I became extremely fond.'

The Count nodded. 'So you have had seven lovers in seven years, and as four of them were only flashes in the pan you can hardly be said to have become a Messalina. Tell me now about de Vendôme? He is a pleasant enough youngster but hardly one calculated to give an experienced woman much pleasure. That is unless her tastes had become so jaded that she required innocence to stimulate her passions. From what you have told me that cannot possibly be the case with you; so read me this riddle.'

Angela smiled at him. 'Seeing that you are up to your neck in this conspiracy to make him King, I should have thought that you would have already guessed it.'

'No; I am completely puzzled. Unless it is that you have suddenly become ambitious and are counting on his making you a Duchess. He has all the right instincts about such matters and has already volunteered, once he is on the throne, to make me a Marshal of France. I've no doubt that he would be delighted to follow the good old Bourbon tradition with regard to mistresses and, for your sake, decorate the horns you have given Syveton with a ducal coronet.'

She shook her head. 'That's a poor guess. I've not the least desire to be a La Vallière or a Diane de Poitiers. In fact, though I hope that he will always remain my friend, once he is King I shall tell him as kindly as I can that he must find another mistress.'

'That makes the matter all the more mysterious. Come Angela, please unravel for me this mystery.'

'Very well then. Do you remember that just before you went abroad I told you how Gabriel had suggested to me that I could help him with his financial transactions if I would take a banker friend of his as my lover?'

'Yes; and the very idea that he should ask you to prostitute yourself for him made me see red.'

'Perhaps. But I think you put it too strongly. In France many women whose morals are lax, and who are themselves ambitious, help their husband's careers in that way. Anyhow, I had not then taken a lover, I felt that I owed nothing to Gabriel and I did not find the man attractive; so I would not even consider it. But now things are very different. I made no attempt to hide from Gabriel my affaire with the sailor, and he knows that I have had other lovers since. So when he approached me again on the same subject this summer I listened to what he had to say.'

'Ah! Now I understand!' exclaimed de Quesnoy, recalling his conversation with General Laveriac. 'Syveton asked you to take our young man in hand, so that he should not fall into the clutches of some woman who might endanger the conspiracy.'

'Exactly. And it was just as well that I did, as he was ripe for mischief. I expect you know a fellow student of his named Raoul Dampierre?'

'Yes; a most amusing young rogue. De Vendôme has become much attached to him.'

'Well, Dampierre is keeping a young woman in an apartment out at Versailles. She has a sister who lives with her and is no better than herself. On several occasions at the beginning of this term Dampierre took François with him to see these girls and, of course, the idea was that the sister should become our young friend's mistress. It so happens that they are the daughters of a Socialist Deputy; so you see how dangerous such an association might have proved.'

'I do, indeed.'

'Fortunately, General Laveriac had been having François watched. It was after he had reported this to the Committee that Gabriel explained matters to me and asked me if I would save the situation. Of course, I already knew François as we had entertained him a number of times during the past year. I had found him very sympathetic and . . . well, I was not involved in any romantic attachment.'

'So you sacrificed yourself on the altar of a great cause, and took over his education.'

Angela laughed. 'I suppose you could put it that way but it wasn't a very great sacrifice. Only rather embarrassing to begin with. You see although, as he told me himself afterwards, he was just on the point of taking the plunge with the lady at Versailles, he hadn't screwed up quite enough courage to do so. I have never before played the rôle of temptress, and I didn't much enjoy doing so to an innocent. But I'm glad I did now, because he is a very sweet person, and he appeals to all my protective instincts.'

They were silent for a moment, then the Count said: 'Angela, does our situation this evening remind you of anything?'

She nodded. 'I think I can guess what you mean. You are thinking of that night years ago when you were expecting me to dine with you at the Ambassadeurs, and I played a trick on you by sending Madeleine de Frontignac in my place.'

'That's it. And tonight our positions are reversed. You were expecting de Vendôme to dine with you here and I have played a trick on you by turning up in his place. Don't you think . . .'

Raising a slender hand that sparkled with diamonds, she checked him. 'No Armand, no. You have no need to remind me of what happened between you and Madeleine afterwards. I have no intention of allowing the parallel to go any further.'

Standing up, he went round behind the end of the sofa and bent above her. Intrigued as he had been by their conversation, for more than two hours he had had to use the greatest restraint to prevent himself from suddenly advancing on her and taking her in his arms. Once more the scent she wore and the sight of her bare shoulders, upon which he was now looking down, drove him nearly to distraction.

'Angela!' he pleaded. 'Angela, my dear. From the moment these candles were lit I have known again the magic of your eyes. They stir me to the depths of my being. They draw me to you like lodestones. More than ever before I long to feel my lips on yours. You can no longer plead fear or ignorance of love. I . . .'

147

'Stop!' she cried. 'I beg you to say no more. It's no use going on. I mustn't let you. I can't ...'

'You can; and you will.' His normally well-modulated voice took on a husky note. 'After all these years we are together again. I have never craved for anything so much as for this moment. I want you desperately, and I'll not let you deny me.'

Stooping, he threw his arms round her shoulders, grasped her wrists, and buried his face in the tender flesh at the base of her neck.

CHAPTER XIII

"LONG LIVE THE KING!"

WITH a violent movement Angela broke his hold, sprang to her feet, then turned and faced him. The sofa was now between them. She was trembling slightly; but her brown eyes held no anger, only determination, as she said:

'I am not made of stone either; but I'll not do as you wish. I warned you before we came up here that it would be for supper only.'

'I know it. But when you said that we were standing in the dark and had not exchanged a word for close on seven years.'

'What difference does that make?'

'Why, that in such circumstances you cannot regard my implied promise not to make love to you as binding, Now we have talked again and I've seen how more than ever beautiful you have become, my old passion for you has returned with redoubled ardour. We are alone here. I'd not be human if I didn't seize upon this God-given chance to . . .'

'Armand!' she cut him short. 'It is true that by allowing you to come up here I have placed myself virtually at your mercy; but I know you too well to believe that you would attempt to take by force what I am unwilling to give.'

His grey eyes flashed. '*Mort de Diable!* I'm mighty tempted to. Some women prefer to be taken by assault, and I believe you must be one of them.'

'I am not!' Her breath was coming quickly, but she strove to control it, and hurried on: 'The very thought of such a thing conjures up again the horror of my honeymoon with Gabriel. If you tried I'd fight you tooth and nail; and all you would succeed in doing would be to end the friendship of a lifetime.'

'But why? Why? Why?' he cried desperately. 'I was your first love! You can't deny it! Before I went abroad you had decided to give yourself to me. I love you now no whit less than I loved you then.

149

What is there to stop our becoming lovers? Surely it cannot be that you have fallen in love with this stupid boy?'

'No. I don't love him. But I am his mistress. As I have just told you, Armand, while you have been away I have had several lovers. But that does not mean that I am a wanton. I regard promiscuity as degrading. For men, I know that it is different. But no woman can slip out of one man's bed into another's overnight, then back again into that of the first without losing her self-respect. I have never yet been on with a new love before I have decided to finish with the old; and I never will. If I let you make love to me tonight I must write to François in the morning and tell him that I have finished with him. Now that I have made him into a man he will be easy game for the first pretty woman who sets her cap at him; and you know what that might lead to. Please, please, Armand, try to understand.'

De Quesnoy's hands dropped helplessly to his sides. After a moment he nodded. 'Against what you say there is no argument. If it were possible I would love you all the more for your high principles. It seems then, that since we are both caught up in this conspiracy we must see it through to the end. But what then? What of the future?'

Her breathing eased and she smiled again. 'For a while the rôles we must play will keep us apart. But you mean more to me than any man I have ever known. Nothing now will make me change in that, so I'll give you a solemn promise. I will become your mistress the night that François is proclaimed King of France.'

Five minutes later de Quesnoy re-locked the door in the garden wall behind him. His brain was still whirling. Up till this evening he had thought of Angela as a girl—lovely and well educated but with an immature mind prejudiced by fear; now she was a woman of the world—gracious, generous-hearted and in the full splendour of her magnificent beauty; but still unattainable. And that despite the fact that she loved him. His sense of frustration was almost unbearable. Yet he knew she had been right to say him nay. Even had she been willing to forgo her principles for his sake, they could not have become lovers for only a single night. Once broken, the dam so long between them must open the flood gates of an overwhelming passion, and de Vendôme would have been swept away by it like a wisp of straw. Angela could never again have accepted his caresses and he, de Quesnoy, would not have allowed her even to think of it. Had all the crowns in Europe been at stake he would not have shared her with any man.

Now, he could only pray that before many months were past the conspiracy would reach maturity, and endeavour to possess his soul in patience until he could claim the glorious promise she had made him.

From the summer on, unrealized by all but its organizers, the conspiracy had gradually been taking shape. De Vendôme had first been brought to the attention of the general public as a competitor in the annual *Concours Hippique*, held in the *Grand Palais*. He had won second prize for display riding and come third in the jumping.

As so frequently occurred at that period Italian cavalry officers secured the first two places; so the young Prince's achievement was a considerable one, and could be written up almost as though he had come first. For any Frenchman to have done so well would have delighted Paris and his being a direct descendant of *Henri le Grand* surrounded him with additional glamour.

The monarchists controlled big secret funds, which meant that they could ensure a wide Press for their protégé, and once they had launched him as a public figure they saw to it that he was kept in the limelight. In view of the great wealth of his family and his upbringing in Spain where, as a cousin of King Alfonso, he could have lived the idle life of a grandee, much praise was bestowed on him for returning to claim his French citizenship, choosing the Army for a career and submitting himself to the rigorous regime of a student at St. Cyr. Accounts were given of his shaving in cold water in the morning and other imaginary hardships which he was said cheerfully to endure; while the clerical Press needed no urging to publicize his genuine piety.

The cause, of which he was still the hidden pivot, was also gaining ground owing to Emile Combes's ferocious attacks on Christianity. These had driven the Press of the Right into a frenzy of protest and abuse; but, more important, they had brought to the fore several new champions of conservatism, who possessed considerable ability.

Charles Maurras was the greatest of these. He was by conviction a Pagan, so he did not seek particularly to defend the interests of the Church; but he believed intensely in autocracy as practised in the ancient civilizations. He openly advocated a return to monarchy as the only means of cleaning out the sink of iniquity which the government of

France had become, and his writings were so lucid, consistent and sincere that he won many thousands of converts.

Another was Léon Daudet, the son of a famous father and the husband of a grand-daughter of Victor Hugo. He possessed a brilliant wit and a remarkable nose for the innumerable scandals in the venal administration; so his articles were very widely read, and he also enjoyed great influence in literary circles.

As the autumn advanced the Faubourg St. Germain began openly to lionize de Vendôme. Ambitious mothers among the noblest families battled and intrigued to secure him as godfather to their children. Hardly a Sunday passed without his being the central figure at one of the elaborate pageants proper to such christenings in those times; and, as the custom was, afterwards throwing handfuls of sugared almonds from the church steps to the cheering crowds.

His status at St. Cyr had also gradually altered. During his first eighteen months there, in accordance with the Republican tradition, his fellow students—apart from a very few who sought his friendship out of snobbery—had treated him as an equal. But since the Press had taken him up more and more of them began to show him deference, relieve him of his turn at unpleasant tasks, and look to him as a leader in many of their activities. Some of the junior instructors, too, took to showing him an unwarrantable degree of favour.

This worried de Quesnoy and he did his best to counter it, both by reprimanding the instructors who were at fault and, now and then, giving the Prince some particularly hard row to hoe. In private he explained that he greatly regretted having to appear harsh to him, but it was the only way he could counter the growing tendency to regard him as royalty; which, if it came to the ears of the War Minister, might seriously jeopardize their plans for the future.

De Vendôme said that he fully understood but there was little he could do to check the movement as so many of his fellow students were royalists and, whether it was due to a leak from the Committee, or simply an idea that had arisen spontaneously, quite a number of them were now speaking of him among themselves as their future King.

All the Count could do was again to urge him to use the utmost discretion, and pray that conditions would make it possible to stage the *coup d'état* before the government began to regard the Prince as a serious menace. Otherwise there was the possibility that they might fake up some excuse for depriving him of his commission and sending him back to Spain.

Combes, meanwhile, blinded by his fanaticism to any risk of a revolt against his government, was lavishly sowing the seeds calculated to ferment one. Heedless of honour, patriotism, or even loyalty to the men who had placed him in power, finding that his anti-clerical laws were alienating many of his Left Centre supporters he entered into a pact with the Socialists, and adopted measures which could have been conceived only by a cunning crook.

To guard himself against being swept from power by a Chamber now having a majority hostile to him, he formed a body which was called the *Délégation des Gauches*. On this Committee were Deputies representing all groups from Radicals to Communists, and before each fresh move Combes drove a bargain with them. In this there was nothing particularly reprehensible, as it was no more than a method of securing support in anticipation instead of letting one government after another fall, then entering on the usual cut-throat auction to buy the backing of enough groups to form a new one.

The iniquitous thing about it was that as soon as all the representatives of the groups had accepted their bribes to give Combes a free hand for another month or so, they turned themselves into an Inquisition. Each had to make certain of the votes of his group, and for this the most unscrupulous methods were employed. The rank and file in the groups were kept under observation by the police then, on information so obtained, were blackmailed by their representatives. As comparatively few of these professional politicians lacked skeletons in their cupboards the bringing to light of which would have caused their ruin, they had to toe the line and vote as desired by "papa" Combes.

In addition to this stranglehold on the centre of power the Prime Minister's nefarious tentacles writhed out over the whole country. It had, in the past been the practice of governments to fill vacancies among the Préfects with men of their own political colour but, once appointed, the Préfects had a free hand to put into the posts under them such men as they considered would serve their Departments with the greatest credit and efficiency.

Combes was not content to follow this precedent. To the scandal of the nation he issued a circular to all Préfects warning them that in future State paid posts must be given only to friends of the government. He then issued an order that in communes where the Mayor was a member of one of the Right or Centre parties, a prominent local Socialist should be empowered to go over the Mayor's head in advising the Préfect about local appointments.

These police-state measures coupled with the tyrannous old atheist's war upon Christianity in all its forms naturally provoked violent reactions. The *Ligue de la Patrie Française* numbered several hundred thousand members, but in '99 it had suffered a set-back owing to an abortive conspiracy and the exiling of its old leader Paul Déroulède. Moreover, like all great political movements, the looseness of its organization made it of no great practical value except if called on for a general rising. In consequence a number of the leading monarchists decided that a more militant association was needed, and for this purpose organized the *Action Française*.

Henri Vaugeois, its leading spirit, found many able lieutenants in his fellow professors at the University and such men as Jacques Bainville, the distinguished writer on foreign policy. But publishing pamphlets and articles, holding meetings and canvassing for new supporters were by no means their only activities. Thousands of young men of the upper and middle classes were ready to fight the tyranny of Combes and were enrolled to do so.

These monarchist shock-troops were known as *Camelots du Roi*, and were the spiritual heirs of such Societies as the Companions of Jesus and the Companions of the Sun which, when the reaction came after the great Revolution, had hunted out and lynched the petty tyrants of the Terror. They roved the streets at night in bands, singing royalist songs, shouting abuse under the windows of Combes's colleagues, and fighting with stones, clubs and bottles the Communist youth groups which Jules Guesde had years before organized to frighten the bourgeois from going to the polls at election times.

With the approach of winter riots and street fighting became of daily occurrence and it was obvious to the Committee that final plans for the *coup d'état* could now be entered upon.

On several occasions General Laveriac sent for de Quesnoy to come to his private apartment, in order to inform him of decisions that had been taken. The Committee had excellent grounds for believing that the present agitation against the government, far from declining,

154

would gather greater momentum during the next few months. Moreover, at the turn of the year a number of changes in postings in the War Department would take place, and it was important to get certain royalist officers firmly established in key positions before launching the *coup d'état*; so it was provisionally timed for May.

At the end of December de Vendôme would pass out of St. Cyr and it had been decided to gazette him to the Guard Republican. Then, when the time came, with the connivance of its colonel who was in the plot, he could take command of that famous regiment and be seen deploying its red-plumed horsemen in the Place de la Concorde and other great open spaces of the capital.

But until the day, again with the connivance of the Colonel, his duties were to be nominal. A great mansion had been taken for him in the Avenue du Bois and he was to move in there at the end of January. The government could take no exception to such a step as, in the circumstances, there was nothing exceptional about it. The Prince's mother, the Condessa de Cordoba y Coralles, was coming to Paris to play hostess for him; and the immense funds of the Banco del Coralles amply justified the family's enjoying palatial accommodation, and entertaining lavishly. This move was the final one to sustain the publicity campaign as, by it for a few months, de Vendôme would occupy in Parisian society the all but royal position that the Comte de Paris had forfeited in '86 by the intrigue with Boulanger which had led to him being exiled.

However, as the General pointed out, the part the Prince played in the affair, provided he did not make a fool of himself, was of little moment. The success or failure of the *coup* would depend on the smooth working of arrangements in the War Departments. In ninety-nine cases out of a hundred troops could be counted on to obey their officers, and officers to obey the orders they received from above; therefore, no government could hope to resist for more than a few hours once the army was under the control of those making a new bid for power.

The Chief of Staff was not privy to the conspiracy, but his known sympathies made it probable that at the last moment he could be brought over to it without much difficulty. If not Laveriac, who had a score of officers pledged to do his bidding without question, intended to deprive him of his functions, take over, and issue orders in his name.

A similar situation existed in the other key point—the offices of the Military Governor of Paris. But there the little junta of trustworthy officers was not quite so strong; so although de Quesnoy's appointment as a senior instructor at St. Cyr was for two years, it was decided that an excuse should be made to transfer him early in January to strengthen the group. Then, once the *coup* there had been achieved, he could rejoin his royal pupil and be on hand to advise him in the event of any emergency.

For the rest, Combes, the War Minister, André and the other members of the Cabinet were to be arrested in their beds. Two senior police officials would hold the gendarmerie in check until the military had full control. Posts and telegraphs were to be seized and a general censorship of news temporarily enforced. The *Camelots du Roi* were to be given the task of smashing up the printing presses from which issued the newspapers of the Left, and it was hoped that within twelve hours, with very little bloodshed, the *coup d'état* would be accomplished.

De Quesnoy felt that he could not have improved on these arrangements. The little Gascon was shrewd, efficient and bold; and as Assistant Chief of Staff he was already number two at the War Office. The *Action Française* was daily stimulating resistance to the government, the *Camelots du Roi* were constantly increasing in numbers, and when the time came Syveton could swing his great civilian army of the *Ligue de la Patrie* into action behind the spearheads. Unless some quite unforeseeable development took place in the next two or three months it did not seem that things could go wrong.

It was thus that matters stood in mid-December. The students of de Vendôme's year were now taking their final examinations and, it being important, for publicity reasons, that the Prince should pass out well above average, de Quesnoy had arranged to mark the papers of his group himself; so that if necessary he could do a little cooking of his charge's marks.

He was so employed one evening when de Vendôme came to the door of his study and asked if he might have a word with him. After accepting a seat, the Prince said:

'I hope you won't be annoyed about it; but as we are breaking up next week a number of my friends have arranged to give a farewell dinner in my honour. It is to be held at the Hôtel du Roi Soleil in Versailles on Monday next, the 19th.'

The Count's eyes showed a sudden uneasiness. 'Do you mean they are planning some form of demonstration?'

'I'm afraid so,' the Prince admitted. 'Raoul Dampierre, and one or two others, got hold of the truth from somewhere. After the new year they will all be posted to regiments scattered over France. He and his friends, unknown to me until this morning, have been organizing a sort of secret society. The idea is that each member should sing my praises among his new brother officers wherever he is sent; then in a score or more of garrison towns there will be a little clique ready to declare for me when the news of the *coup d'état* reaches them.'

'The idea is praiseworthy enough,' the Count admitted, 'but all the same I wish that Dampierre had never thought of it. The success or failure of the *coup* depends entirely on what happens here in Paris. The readiness of a few junior officers to shout your name in provincial cities will not influence the issue in the least; whereas this party might result in the authorities taking a most unwelcome interest in you.'

'I realize that. It is why I came to tell you about it.'

'That was very sensible of you.' De Quesnoy fell silent for a minute, then he resumed: 'The trouble is that I have no authority, or even an excuse, for forbidding a private party of this kind; and I don't see, either, how you can very well refuse to accept such an invitation from your friends. In view of the monarchist slogans that the *Camelots du Roi* are shouting all over Paris in these days, I suppose it is unlikely that any serious notice will be taken of a gathering of officer-cadets that does the same thing. It wouldn't matter in the least if it were not that you are to be present, and the possibility of allusions to a *coup d'état* in your favour being made in your hearing. It is that you must try to check, particularly while the waiters are in the room.'

'I was wondering,' said the Prince after a moment, 'if it would be a good idea if I got them to ask you to come to this dinner.'

The Count raised his eyebrows. 'I hardly think they would welcome the suggestion, seeing that the part I have played for the past year must have led them all to believe me a staunch Republican.'

'But that's just it! Your being there would restrain them from getting out of hand and doing anything really silly. And politics apart, I know they would love to have you. Even if you have been a bit on the strict side it is recognized that you are the best instructor in the place; and you're looked upon as a model of the sort of soldier they would all like to be.'

'Thank you for the compliment,' smiled de Quesnoy, 'and I am happy to be able to return one. Your idea, *mon Prince*, has the ring of true statecraft. If, then, Dampierre and his friends care to ask me I shall accept with pleasure.'

As a result of this conversation, on the evening of December 19th the Count joined the party at the Hôtel du Roi Soleil. It was held in a private suite on the first floor, which consisted of a cloakroom, an ante-room having big double doors, and beyond them a spacious dining-room with tall windows that looked out on an inner courtyard. There were some thirty young officers present but no other instructors. All of them had been working exceptionally hard until a few days before, but now their examinations were over and in forty-eight hours they would be leaving St. Cyr for good; so it was a merry, laughing crowd that, after drinking aperitifs in the ante-room, went in to dinner.

All these young men belonged to the cavalry side; so they came from good families and had private means. In consequence no money had been spared in choosing the dinner and the wines to go with it. The Prince was placed at the head of the table and Raoul Dampierre took its foot with de Quesnoy on his right. The meal ran its course most pleasantly, differing in no way from an ordinary social occasion. Somewhat to the Count's surprise, and much to his relief, there were no speeches. While the dessert plates were being cleared away an upright piano was carried in, then the waiters retired. An amiable young giant named Léon de Jassy, who had a gift for remembering catchy tunes, sat down at the piano and began to strum. Soon they had all gathered round him and were singing the old bawdy favourites at the tops of their voices.

The time passed quickly and de Quesnoy was beginning to hope that the meeting would end without any open reference being made to the reason that lay behind it; but, at about ten past eleven, having stopped playing for a minute de Jassy, unheeding of shouted suggestions from those round him, began to hammer out the tune of *O Richard ô mon Roi.*

It was the famous royalist song that the *Garde du Corps* had sung in the banqueting hall of the Palace, only half a mile away, on the last occasion that Louis XVI and Queen Marie Antoinette had accepted the homage of their loyal officers before, a few days later, being taken as prisoners to Paris by the mob.

Instantly the tempo of the meeting changed. The laughter ceased; with serious faces but full-throated voices the song was sung as though it was an anthem. Evidently, too, de Jassy's playing of it had been planned beforehand; for as the song finished several of the officers went to a side table, opened some more bottles of champagne and began to refill all the glasses, while Dampierre stood up on a chair and addressed the company in ringing tones.

'Gentlemen! It was agreed that we should exchange no speeches this evening; but there is one toast that we all wish to drink before we leave this room. In a few minutes now we must do so, as it is still incumbent upon us to be back in barracks by midnight. But I have left just enough time for you to raise your glasses to the distinguished companion who has honoured us by being our guest.

'Before doing so I should like to say what a pleasure it has been to have with us another guest, Colonel the Count de Quesnoy. I must, too, now remark that while his political opinions are no concern of ours, whatever they may be, we need no assurance from him, as a member of one of the greatest families of the *ancien régime* and our guest, that he will not disclose to anyone that we have met here tonight for the purpose of drinking this toast.

'Lieutenant His Highness the Duke François de Vendôme has been one of our brotherhood. I will not dwell upon his qualities. It is enough to say that as our companion for two years, he has, by his simplicity, kindness and honest good fellowship, won the love of us all. I will not dwell either upon the sad state of France. A change must come. When, none of us can say. It may be in a few months; we may have to wait with what patience we can for several years. But when it does it will be upon him that we shall pin our hopes for the salvation of our beloved country. In his service we will if need be lay down our lives, and be proud to do so. May the day when we can acclaim him openly come soon.

'Gentlemen, I give you the toast: *François le Troisième, Roi de France.*'

As he ceased there was a second's silence, then the room rang with thunderous applause, and voices shouting: 'The King! The King! François the Third. Long live the King!'

It was at that moment that the double doors burst open and the police charged in.

CHAPTER XIV

NIGHT OF DISASTER

WHO had betrayed them de Quesnoy never discovered. Since Dampierre had enrolled as many as thirty enthusiastic adherents pledged to support the Prince, it seemed certain that he must have approached at least a few others without success; and, perhaps, quite a number. Once having broached the matter to them he could have done no more than do as he had with the Count—put them under a moral obligation to refrain from talking of it.

At least ninety per cent of the cavalry students were practising Catholics which, as a result of Combes's pogrom on priests and nuns, meant that nearly all of them now had monarchist sympathies; so it could be taken for granted that most of those who had rejected Dampierre's overtures had done so not from antagonism to them, but from caution. It might possibly be that one of them was a sincere Republican, and had felt it to be his duty to report the matter to the authorities; but de Quesnoy thought it much more likely that one of them, or perhaps one of the young men who had just drunk de Vendôme's health with such enthusiasm, had been indiscreet. It might even be that Dampierre had boastfully confided to the young woman he was keeping his hopes for himself from his friendship with the future King of France, and that she had passed on what he had told her to her father, the Socialist Deputy.

One thing was certain. The police had not broken in on the spur of the moment to suppress a riotous assembly. There was nothing riotous about it; and nightly in Paris now at meetings organized by the *Action Française* a restoration of the monarchy was openly being advocated. Not only had the police learned of Dampierre's activities but also they must since have followed the matter up and formed a very shrewd idea of what was likely to happen at the dinner. Obviously they had bided their time and posted someone outside the doors of the dining-room to wait until the toast was proposed, before rushing in to seize red-handed these enemies of the Republic.

Had de Vendôme not been present no Magistrate could have taken a very serious view of the proceedings. All through the last century, except during the years when the throne had been occupied, the healths of claimants and pretenders to it had been drunk with acclaim in innumerable private houses, and quite frequently at semi-private gatherings such as this. The authorities had never attempted to prevent it, any more than those in England during the latter half of the eighteenth century had tried to stop people still loyal to the Stuarts passing their wine across a finger-bowl both in public and private and so, symbolically, drinking to "the King over the Water".

But in this case a body of young officers had toasted a claimant to the throne in person. And he was still standing there in their midst, smilingly accepting their homage as the police broke in. Some police-man, or police spy, must have bent at the keyhole listening to Dampierre's speech, and would be prepared to give a résumé of it in evidence. That meant that everyone in the room would be found guilty of both con-spiracy and treason. De Quesnoy's mouth suddenly went dry as, having summed the situation up in a matter of seconds, he visualized the consequences.

Few of the young officers present could have been said to be drunk, but nearly all of them had consumed during the evening a bottle and a half, or more, of wine. On top of that their minds had been stimulated by the excitement of hailing the man they hoped would be their future King; so they were in no mood to submit tamely to arrest.

Still standing on his chair, Dampierre shouted over the heads of his companions at the leading police officer: 'Get out of here! This is a private party.'

The officer, who was a Captain of Gendarmes, halted a few paces inside the door, with his men bunched up behind him. Pulling his revolver from its black holster, he cried:

'Messieurs. In the name of the Law I arrest you for subversive activities against the Republic. Put your hands up, all of you. Put your hands above your heads.'

A young officer named de Rougemont, who had the physique of a small bull but only an apology for a chin and a sharply-receding forehead, was standing within a few feet of the Captain. Springing forward, he seized the policeman's wrist and, in a trice, had wrested the revolver from him. Next moment there ensued pandemonium.

As the police surged in the officers surged forward to throw them out. Like two tidal waves clashing head on, they met in the open space at the foot of the table.

De Quesnoy was some way back. His brain was working overtime. Swiftly, he realized that the outcome of the affray was of comparatively little importance. If the police succeeded in lugging the officers off to prison, that would be that. But if the officers succeeded in overcoming the police their escape could be only temporary; for it was certain that the police would have a list of the names of those who had been present at the dinner and would arrest them next day.

The thing that mattered was, if possible, to save de Vendôme. The others, defended by their counsel as young, irresponsible, led astray, and having toasted a pretender to the throne only when they were drunk should, as they would be tried by court martial, get away with a caution or, at worst, a few months' confinement to barracks with specially onerous duties. But the Prince, if arrested, would be accused of plotting the overthrow of the government, and having involved the others in a conspiracy to assist him in so doing. For that he might easily be sentenced to ten years' imprisonment in a fortress.

Even as these thoughts flashed through the Count's mind, matters took a more serious turn for all concerned. As de Rougemont snatched the Captain's revolver several of the other gendarmes drew theirs. Two levelled them at de Rougemont, who had swiftly reversed the weapon he had captured and now held it by the butt. Thinking, no doubt, that they meant to shoot him, he fired first.

The policeman nearest to him received the bullet in the throat. With a strangled cry he staggered back, then fell. The second policeman fired at de Rougemont but hit him only in the left shoulder.Three or four others who had drawn their guns now aimed them at his head. Realizing that in the next few moments he must be shot dead, he emptied the remaining five bullets from the revolver at random among those who menaced him.

Every one of his bullets found a mark. The right-hand side of the human wedge formed by the attacking police was thrown into complete confusion. One, shot through the head, died instantly; two others, each of whom had received two bullets in the body, lurched and crumpled. Their nearest comrades caught them as they fell but could not get them out of the crush to staunch the bleeding from their wounds because the doorway was choked with more police trying to force their way into the room.

In spite of the terrible diversion de Rougemont had created he did not escape. One bullet smashed through his cheek-bone and another through his forehead; a third sang past his ear and killed an officer who was just behind him. Within the space of a few seconds three men had been shot dead and three others seriously wounded. Grimly de Quesnoy re-assessed the situation. Now, it might be the guillotine for any of them that the unscrupulous government liked to pick upon and, at best, a long prison sentence for them all.

But he had not merely been looking on during the few moments since the police had burst into the room. While the swift thoughts were chasing one another through his mind, he had run to the nearest window. It was stuck and he could not get it open. Having wrestled with it ineffectively he tried the next. The twist and wrench he gave the iron handle was so violent that, this centre window being in frequent use, the half that opened flew inward causing him nearly to fall backwards. Recovering his balance he slipped through it on to a narrow balcony that had a wrought-iron balustrade.

It was dark outside, but not too dark for him to see as he peered over that there was a crowd of people in the courtyard. They were mostly hotel servants brought out there by the din, but a shaft of light from a downstairs window showed that there were police among them; so there was no escape that way, even if one could have accomplished the fifteen-feet drop without serious injury.

Swinging about, his glance roved over the dense, writhing mass of men at the other end of the room, searching for the Prince. After a moment he saw him. The room was not broad enough for all the combatants to take part at once in the hand-to-hand struggle that was now being waged. The officers were three deep and de Vendôme was among them in the third row. Running down one side of the long table de Quesnoy seized him by the arm and dragged him back.

Turning, the Prince exclaimed: 'Oh, it's you! How terrible this is! Had I had the least idea . . .'

'You hadn't,' de Quesnoy cut him short. 'Don't blame yourself.

163

But somehow you must get away. How, God knows, as yet! Meanwhile come back here and get down behind the piano.'

De Vendôme's eyes flashed: 'How dare you! Is it likely that I would crouch in a corner and let my comrades do all the fighting for me?'

The Count was much the stronger of the two. Giving the younger man a violent push he threw him off his balance, then swung him round and tripped him, so that he sprawled into the angle that the piano made with the wall. Standing over him, he cried angrily:

'*Ventre du Pape*, boy; do as I tell you! Your case was bad enough before that fool de Rougemont started shooting. Now, if Combes likes to pin one of these killings on to you, he can send you to spit in the basket. There is no sense in getting your head chopped off while there is the least chance to save it.'

The Prince struggled to his knees, but he had now gone very pale, and gasped out: 'I . . . I suppose you're right. But I'd rather die than have the others think me a coward.'

'So would any fool with more courage than sense,' snapped the Count. 'But he who fights and runs away . . . The question is, where the hell can we run to?'

As he spoke he was watching from across the top of the piano the development of the fight. Screams, shouts, curses blended in a hideous uproar. None of the officers was armed, so after the killing of de Rougemont the police had put up their guns. But they were now using their truncheons, and the conflict raged with undiminished violence. Several of the officers' heads had already been broken, that of Dampierre's among them; but the breaking of heads was not all on one side. The young giant, de Jassy, had seized a heavy chair by its back and, whirling it above his head as though it weighed no more than a camp stool, was bashing with its legs at the line of angry faces before him. Several of the officers, too, had now grabbed up bottles and were using them as clubs.

With growing anxiety de Quesnoy saw that the police were getting the best of it. There were too many of them for the students to make, as he had hoped, a break-out through the bottle-neck of the doorway, and there was no other entrance to the room. The police, too, were using their experience of suppressing riots to overcome the officers. Two of them would suddenly rush at one of the young men and each grab him by an arm; then, while their companions protected them, they would drag their captive forward through the door to the ante-room and slip a pair of handcuffs on to him.

After five minutes of this fierce encounter, of the thirty officers who had sat down to dinner less than half were still free and fighting. The rest were dead, lying on the floor bleeding and groaning with smashed heads, or captives. With a sinking heart, the Count decided that it was now or never. While all the police were still occupied, he must make his bid to get the Prince away.

Looking down, he asked: 'Do you know the position of Madame Syveton's bedroom window, or that of her husband?'

De Vendôme stared up at him round-eyed with astonishment.

'Answer me!' snapped the Count, 'I know of your affaire with her, and this is no time for chivalrous denials. Her good name is safe enough with me.'

'I . . . I don't know where Syveton's room is,' the Prince faltered, 'but hers is on the second floor at the back. It is the end room, reached through her boudoir.'

'Good! I thought that was probably the case. Now listen carefully. If I succeed in getting you away from here you are to make for their house. Go in by the garden and remain hidden there until all the lights in the house are out. Do nothing for at least an hour after that, to give the servants time to get soundly to sleep. Then collect some small gravel and throw it a piece at a time at Madame Syveton's window. When that rouses her and she comes to the window to see who it is, ask her to come down to you. Tell her then all that has occurred and that she should pass it all on to her husband. You can spend the rest of the night in the pavilion. I've no doubt they will be able to keep you hidden there for some days, until arrangements can be made to have you smuggled out of France and back to Spain.'

'What about you? I don't see how either of us is going to get out of here; but if I can you can too.'

'If I do get away I'll join you in the Syvetons' pavilion. Anyhow for the night. But the odds are I won't. My part in this is to protect your rear; so that you can get a good start. I mean to . . .'

De Vendôme broke in with an unhappy protest. 'I can't let you sacrifice yourself. I refuse to run off while . . .'

'You must,' the Count replied in a kinder tone, giving his shoulder a friendly squeeze. 'My life is not in danger whereas yours is. Besides, it is your duty to save yourself. This betrayal tonight has blown all our present plans sky high; but in a few years' time another chance may arise for you to save France by becoming her King.'

'Very well then,' the Prince agreed reluctantly. 'Tell me what you intend to do?'

'I mean to jump over their heads; and as soon as you have seen me land you are to jump after me.'

Again de Vendôme's blue eyes popped with astonishment; but de Quesnoy pulled him up and hurried him to the window end of the table. As they reached it, he said quickly:

'I ought to be able to land well outside the doors. How many police there are in the ante-room it is impossible to say. That's where our gamble comes in. I imagine, though, that they are taking our poor friends downstairs one by one as they overpower them; so there may be only one or two. Anyway, it will be my part to tackle them and keep them busy while you run straight through. When you reach the landing don't go downstairs. There are sure to be more of them with a prison van outside. Dash upstairs then along the upper floor until you find a service staircase. Come down it cautiously and out to the yard. There are police there, too, but they will be watching the windows, and provided you keep in the shadows, you ought to be able to slip away.'

Swift as their talk had been, it had occupied a good two minutes. During this time another policeman had gone down, his face battered and bleeding, to join the horrid tangle of dead and still writhing bodies on the floor; but the police had dragged three more officers through into the ante-room.

Realizing that not a moment must now be lost, lest the remaining officers, seeing that the battle was going so hopelessly against them, should suddenly decide to surrender, de Quesnoy said no more. Giving de Vendôme an encouraging smile, he scrambled up on to the table.

It was no affair of trestles, but a great mahogany piece of many legs and leaves, six feet wide and thirty long, at which successive generations had celebrated red-letter days of all kinds for well over a hundred years. Grabbing an empty champagne bottle by the neck, the Count ran swiftly down the table, then sprang from its end high into the air.

Until the very last moment no one except de Vendôme had an

inkling of his intention. Officers and police, cursing, wrestling, striking at one another, were still embroiled in a dozen individual combats as he sailed over their heads. He landed with a thud a good two yards beyond the open doors, staggered and pitched forward on all fours.

Luckily for him there were only two policemen in the ante-room and both were struggling to get handcuffs on to an officer named Moreau-Sala. Picking himself up, the Count rushed in, swung the empty bottle on high and brought it crashing down on the kepi of the nearest policeman. The bottle shattered, and the man went down like a pole-axed ox.

At the sound of a thump behind him, de Quesnoy swivelled round. It was de Vendôme, who had landed almost in his tracks, and was now lurching to his feet.

'Quick!' the Count shouted. 'The doors! The doors!'

Together they covered the few paces towards them. Six feet beyond the doors the fight still raged. The majority of the battling police had glimpsed the two figures that had sprung over their heads, but were so heavily engaged that they dared not turn to see what had become of them. The Captain of gendarmes had early been smitten down, but his Lieutenant and two Sergeants who were directing operations from the rear swung about and were now within a yard of the Prince.

"Poor devil" was the thought that flashed through de Quesnoy's mind, as his eyes met those of the Lieutenant from a distance of about eight feet. "He is only doing his duty; but I must do mine." Then he flung the jagged neck of the bottle, which he was holding, straight into the Lieutenant's face.

With a screech of agony the wretched man reeled away. The two Sergeants halted in their tracks. The Count's act had saved the situation for the Prince. Each of them seized one half of the double door and swung it shut.

'Go!' cried de Quesnoy. 'Now's your chance! Run for it! Good luck!' And he shot the bolts of the heavy doors, imprisoning the still-fighting officers and police in the dining-room.

But as he turned about he saw that two more policemen, just returned from taking a captive downstairs, had entered the ante-room. They now blocked de Vendôme's path. One of them drew his revolver and pointed it at him. The Prince leapt at the policeman and they went down together. The revolver went off as they crashed to the floor.

167

The bullet passed harmlessly over the Prince's shoulder; but Moreau-Sala gave a piercing cry and fell shot through the back.

De Quesnoy's instinct for battle told him instantly that the next few moments would prove critical. If his protégé could not get away very swiftly, more police would arrive on the scene and they would both be caught. As it was the collapse of Moreau-Sala had freed another gendarme; so they were already two against three.

Snatching up a small potted palm from a marble console table, the Count hurled it at the man in the doorway. It caught him in the midriff, doubling him up winded and helpless for a few precious moments. De Vendôme meanwhile had smashed his fist repeatedly into the face of the man with whom he was struggling on the floor. Gasping and howling the man writhed under him, then lay still. Springing to his feet the Prince dashed out on to the landing.

With a shout of triumph de Quesnoy made to follow him, but the policeman who had been endeavouring to handcuff Moreau-Sala struck out a foot. The Count took a header over it and crashed full length on the floor. The breath was driven from his body. Before he could recover it the two remaining policemen flung themselves at him.

A terrible tussle ensued. Both the representatives of the law were strong men well versed in tackling tough customers; but de Quesnoy's early training stood him in good stead. Wrestling was the Russian national sport and while in his 'teens he had had many a bout with the stable-hands and servitors at Jvanets.

For a moment he lay flat on his face and let himself go limp. One of his antagonists descended like half a ton of coals on his back, the other seized one of his wrists to handcuff it. Snatching his wrist away he suddenly tensed his muscles and drew up his knees. The man above him shot over his head, but before he could get to his feet the other fellow had grappled with him, and they went down together.

While a referee could have counted ten they rolled back and forth, first one on top then the other. Meanwhile the policeman he had shaken off was up again, and striving to kick him first on the head then in the ribs. Only two kicks got home, and they were not hard ones as the man had not dared to put any great force behind them lest they should strike his comrade.

In such a conflict there were no holds barred. Thrusting out his hand de Quesnoy suddenly seized the ear of the man with whom he was wrestling and gave it a violent wrench. His antagonist let out a howl of pain and instantly loosed his grip.

To put him out of the game for good the Count, levering himself up by his hands, half rose above him, then kneed him hard in the groin. Giving an ear-piercing cry he passed out. But the other man, seeing the extremity of his comrade, had pulled his gun and was pointing it at de Quesnoy.

Faced with death in a flash he threw up his hands, and came to his feet. But the policeman did not back away, keeping him covered, quickly enough. As the Count got up he pretended to lurch sideways, and brought the hard edge of his right palm down on the man's wrist. The stroke might have cost him his life, but in spite of what he had told de Vendôme he knew that this night's work might cost him his life anyway, so he took the chance.

It came off. With a blasphemous oath the man dropped his gun and with his good hand gripped the injured wrist. Swift to seize any opening that offered de Quesnoy resorted to the rudiments of British boxing, which he had also picked up in his 'teens. Clenching his right fist, he drove it with all his force at the policeman's jaw. The man's eyeballs flickered upwards, he sagged at the knees and gently collapsed upon the floor.

Victor of the field, the Count took a swift glance round. Two policemen lay still, the other two and Moreau-Sala were groaning feebly. But there was a violent hammering on the doors to the dining-room, and police whistles summoning assistance now shrilled above the din that continued to come from behind them. Gasping in a deep breath, the Count dashed out on to the landing.

His appearance there was met by a shout. In response to the shrilling of the whistles three more policemen were running up from the ground floor. Before they could draw their revolvers de Quesnoy pulled a fine old Venetian mirror from the landing wall and flung it down among them.

It shattered on the head of their leader. Stunned, he stopped dead in his tracks, fragments of glass flying in all directions about him; then, like the tall trunk of an axed tree, he fell gracefully backwards on to the two men in his rear, bringing them down with him. The Count did not wait to see the full effect of his missile. Taking the stairs three at a time he was already bounding up the flight that led to the floor above.

169

On the landing there he glanced swiftly to right and left. He had secured for de Vendôme a good two minutes' start; but, all the same, he did not want to lead the police on his track, as he might have found difficulty in getting out of the hotel unseen, and so still be lurking somewhere below in the kitchen quarters.

Turning left the Count ran towards the front of the hotel. As he came level with each door he quickly tried its handle. The first two were locked; the third swung open revealing an elderly couple sitting up in bed. Their faces told that they were listening in apprehension to the sounds of the riot below. Leaving the door wide open de Quesnoy sped on. His only object in opening it had been to let his pursuers know the direction he had taken, so as to keep them away from the back of the premises. The couple would do that, as the sight of the Count's bruised and bleeding face had already set the man off shouting: 'Help! Murder!'

Before turning in that direction de Quesnoy's quick glance had shown him that the corridor led into another at right angles to it. All the same, he had taken a big risk; for the other might prove a dead end. As he swung round the corner into it he saw that it extended for about sixty feet and was then closed off by a red velvet curtain. Fearful now that the curtain might conceal only a cul-de-sac, he raced on, wrenched it aside and peered into the darkness beyond it.

His heart sank. The faint light that percolated from a gas bracket twenty feet behind him was just enough to show that the last twelve feet of the corridor had been made into a small room. In it he saw that there were a gas stove, a sink, plate-racks, and a table on which were several trays already laid for *petit déjeuner*. Evidently it was the domain of the floor waiter, in which he prepared the breakfasts and cooked up light meals for anyone in his corridor who was taken ill.

With an oath de Quesnoy stared about him. There was nowhere there where he could hide, and if he turned back he could not now hope to recross the landing before the men at whom he had thrown the mirror reached it. They should have got there already. Striving to control his breathing he listened for a moment. The elderly couple were still shouting, but he could not hear the pounding footsteps he expected. That made it possible that instead of giving chase to him the police had thought it more urgent to answer the call for help being shrilled out by the whistles, so turned into the ante-room. If so, the couple's shouts were now an added danger, as they would soon bring other police up to the second floor.

All this went through de Quesnoy's brain in a few seconds, and he was still grasping the red curtain while weighing two alternatives. He could turn back in the hope of recrossing the landing unseen, or slip into a bathroom that he had passed, get through its window, and risk his neck attempting to shin down its drainpipe. The latter would not only be dangerous but futile if there were police on the watch nearby the spot where the drainpipe reached the ground; but he should be able to find that out from the window. Deciding to reconnoitre, he was just about to let the curtain drop when he chanced to glance up. His eyes, now better accustomed to the dim light, discerned a square recess in the ceiling. It was a trap-door.

There was a kitchen chair beside the gas stove. By standing it on the table he could reach the trap-door. If it led only to an attic containing a cistern he could not hope to escape capture by hiding up there because the chair would give away the way he had gone. But it might lead to the roof. To find out would take a few precious moments, but he decided that it would be worth the gamble.

Grasping the edge of the table he tipped it up. With a clatter and crash all the trays slid from it to the floor. Swinging the chair up he clambered on to it and thrust hard at the trap-door. One side of it opened a few inches, and a blast of chill air came through. Another minute and he had it wide open, had hoisted himself through and was out on the roof. His gamble had come off.

But his tribulations were far from over, and that he survived the next ten minutes was due only to his iron nerve. It was almost pitch dark, the roof was steep and dangerous, and the icy cold numbed his fingers as he slowly made his way forward, testing every foothold cautiously and clinging at times to the most precarious holds.

At last, having crossed a deep gulley, he found another trap-door in the roof of an adjacent building and lowered himself through it. He had had to leave his cloak behind so he was shivering as though he had the ague. Flailing his arms he tried to warm himself up a little, then when his teeth stopped chattering he struck a wax vesta and looked about him.

Before the flame died he had time to see that he was in a loft, in which awnings, garden chairs and sun umbrellas were stored. Striking

171

several more vestas, he found it to be a large place, and he had to use half a dozen before he came upon a steep wooden staircase leading below. At its bottom another vesta revealed a short passage at the end of which there was a faint glimmer. Proceeding to it de Quesnoy reached a wide landing. Two sides of it consisted of panes of clear glass and a proper staircase leading down from it. It was through the panes that the faint light, originating in the street lamps, penetrated. Beyond them was a great room with at least a hundred tables in it on which chairs were piled, and a row of tall windows.

De Quesnoy then knew for certain where he was. It was the annex to the hotel, where in summer thousands of tourists ate a fixed-price lunch before being shepherded by their guides across the *Place* to visit the Palace. It would remain closed and deserted until the tourist season started, as would the big café below it on the ground floor; so he had no hesitation in walking boldly downstairs.

After reconnoitring the back quarters of the annex with the aid of further vestas, he let himself out by a side door which gave on to a dark alley-way. Quickly he made his way down it in a direction away from the *Place*. It ended in a garden that had a low wall on one side of the path along which he was walking. Scrambling over it he found himself in another. He repeated the process three times, then dropped into a street.

Still moving away from the centre of the town he proceeded along it. The quarter before midnight chimed, but the noise of the shooting and rioting must have been audible for some distance as, although it had now ceased, there were quite a number of upstairs windows still lit, and here and there people were looking out of them.

A man perched on a bicycle was describing the scene in the square with graphic detail to a woman standing at an open doorway. As de Quesnoy passed the woman invited the man inside to warm himself up with a *café-cognac*. He got off his machine, propped it up against the side of the house and went in. The Count would cheerfully have paid five pounds for that *café-cognac*; but he would have given twenty times that sum for the bicycle. To have shown himself and tried to buy it would have proved disastrous. Having walked on a few paces, until the front door was shut, he turned back and took it.

The bicycle was an absolute godsend as, by pedalling hard, it enabled him to get back to St. Cyr just before midnight. Had he not done so he would have had to summon the sergeant of the guard in order to get in, and it was possible that the police had already telephoned to the Commandant asking that if he returned he should be arrested.

As it was he hid the bicycle some fifty yards from the main gate then went through it at a run. The lofty arch was lit only by a solitary lantern and, as there were several hundred cadets and instructors at the college, the odds were all against the sentry recognizing him. By running he aimed at giving the *poilu* the impression that he was a student who feared himself late and, although it was none of the man's business, one who had left his *kepi* and cloak behind rather than be shut out.

Slowing to a walk, he crossed two courtyards and ascended the stone stairs to his own rooms. Until he saw himself in the wardrobe mirror he had not realized quite what a state he was in. His uniform was smothered in filth, his jacket torn in two places, his collar ripped open and his face a sorry sight. Pulling off his jacket he poured some water into the basin. His three-mile dash on the bicycle had warmed him up, but the water was icy. Flinching a little he got the blood off his hands and face, then changed into a suit of civilian clothes.

Into a small valise he packed his shaving kit, a change of underclothes and a few things he valued. His revolver, and about fifty rounds of ammunition, he slipped into the pockets of his overcoat, then put it on and donned a curly-brimmed Homburg hat. Locking the door behind him he walked quickly downstairs and through a passage that led to another courtyard.

The upper floors on all four sides of it were students' quarters. Each student had one of the cells which had once been occupied by the religious inmates of the original establishment. Electric light had not yet been installed and after ten-thirty the pressure of the gas in this part of the college was reduced, giving only enough light by which to undress. But de Quesnoy met no one, as all the students, other than those who had been at the dinner, were already in bed. There were no locks to the cell doors, so he had no difficulty in entering that of de Vendôme's. Putting a match to the gas mantle, he turned it up as high as it would go, then by its pale blue light he began a hasty search of the tiny bedroom.

The drawers of the small bureau yielded nothing of interest, but on breaking open a carved box inlaid with ivory he found what he was seeking—a packet of letters in Angela's writing, tied up with a blue ribbon.

173

From what she had said of the Prince's writing *billets-doux* to her he felt certain that she would have sent some replies to them, and had it not been for that he would never have risked arrest by returning to the college. The police, he was confident, had no more reason to connect de Vendôme with the Syvetons than with any of a score of other wealthy families that he visited with some regularity; so sending him to hide with them was a move quite justified by the exceptional circumstances. But soon, and probably before the night was out, the authorities would seize and examine the Prince's belongings. If Angela's letters had been found among them, that would have led the hunt straight to him and, in de Quesnoy's view far worse, involved her in the conspiracy.

Precious as time was, he could not resist the temptation to pull one of the letters from the packet and glance through it. As he did so he smiled, for the phrases, charming and affectionate as they were, conveyed no hint of passion. Thrusting the bundle into his pocket, he picked up his valise and left the cell.

At the far end of each long corridor a wash-house had been installed. It contained a dozen cold water basins, a single bath and a big boiler, the function of which was to supply shaving water, the bath and a run of pipes that gave meagre heating to the cells. Turning into the wash-house, de Quesnoy opened the fire door of the boiler with his foot and, with a sigh of satisfaction, thrust Angela's letters into the glowing furnace. If de Vendôme was caught there would now be nothing to give away her association with him.

His mind passed swiftly to his next move. The gate now being shut he would have to get the sergeant of the guard to unlock it for him. As an instructor he was at liberty to leave the college at any hour of the day or night that he liked; but if the police had telephoned he might be held up and taken by the officer of the guard to the Commandant. For a moment he contemplated leaving the college by some unorthodox means—such as letting himself down from an outside window, or clambering over the stable-yard wall—but he decided against it.

As he was quite well known at the Roi Soleil, it was certain that, even if none of the police had recognized him, they would have learned from questioning the staff of the hotel that he had been at the dinner. But getting their prisoners away and attending to the wounded must have taken the police some time and in any case they would have thought it hardly likely that he had returned to the college; so there was still a good chance that they had not yet telephoned. If they had, he thought with a grim little smile as his right hand closed over the butt of the revolver in his pocket, he ought to be able to bluff or threaten his way out past a sergeant.

To his relief he was not called on to do either. The sergeant, stiff as a ramrod, reacting like an automaton, and speaking only when spoken to, produced his big bunch of keys and let him out of a side entrance. Two minutes later he found the stolen bicycle where he had left it hidden in the bushes, tied his small valise on to the back of its saddle and set off on it towards Paris.

It was close on three o'clock in the morning by the time he entered the Parc Monceau. Feeling that it would be impossible to hide the bicycle in the Syvetons' garden, and that its presence might give away to a gardener that someone had arrived there during the night, he had abandoned it in the Bois de Boulogne and walked the last two miles of the fourteen from St. Cyr.

Having let himself in through the door in the wall, he made straight for the pavilion. No chinks of light were showing at the edges of its curtains, so he thought it probable that de Vendôme had already arranged matters with the Syvetons, been installed there and gone to bed. Running up the stairs he turned the handle of the door that opened into the little kitchen, but found it locked. He knocked several times with increasing force, then called quite loudly, giving his name, but he received no reply; so it was evident that the Prince could not be there.

He remembered then that he had told him to wait in hiding for at least an hour after the lights in the house were out, before rousing Angela. In the hurry of the moment he had forgotten that by the time de Vendôme got there all the chances were that the lights would already be out; so it was just possible that the young man was strictly obeying the injunction to wait for an hour anyway.

Going out into the garden, de Quesnoy made a round of the shrubberies softly calling to him, but received no answer. And it could hardly be that, not having his key on him, he had boggled at climbing in over the wall, as that would have presented no great difficulty to any young man. His fears that de Vendôme had not yet arrived now being confirmed the Count became greatly worried. It was getting on for four hours since they had parted so, even if the Prince had had to walk the whole of the eleven miles from Versailles, he should still easily have arrived by this time. However, it was possible that he had been delayed in starting by having to hide in the hotel until the police had left it, and that might not have been until one o'clock or even later.

Comforting himself as well as he could with that thought, the Count tiptoed through the shadows towards the house. Collecting some small stones from a path he carefully checked up which of the windows on the second floor would be that of Angela's bedroom, then started to toss the stones up at it. To hit it in the dark at that height was not too easy, but at the third shot a sharp click told him that his pebble had struck glass, and in the next two minutes he scored two further hits. A light then went on, so he stopped throwing and waited. The curtains were pulled apart, the bottom of the window thrown up, and Angela's head appeared.

'Hist!' he called up softly. 'It is I; Armand! My pupil and I are in grave trouble. Can you come down?'

'Yes,' she called back. 'Give me a minute to put on a few things.'

He went up the conservatory steps and waited at the door that opened into it. After about five minutes a light showed through the greenery; then Angela appeared, unlocked the door and beckoned him inside.

She had tucked her hair under a mob cap edged with lace. Her dressing-gown was of crimson velvet; it swept the ground as she moved and at the neck was edged with a high collar of marabou which stood up under her ears like a light ruff. The modern age of make-up not yet having dawned she normally used only powder on her nose, so she looked no less lovely than when de Quesnoy had last seen her.

Putting a finger to her lips, she led him through a gap between two stages that held potted plants into a small room on the left. It was Syveton's study, and as she switched on the light there she got her first unshadowed sight of her visitor's face. It was badly scratched, there was an ugly bruise where a glancing blow had caught him on the side of the jaw, and his left eye was well on the way to closing.

'Armand!' she exclaimed. 'Your poor face is in a frightful mess. Whatever has been happening?'

'Tell me first,' he asked quickly, 'has de Vendôme been here?'

She shook her head. 'No. You know that he can never get off in the middle of the week; so why should you suppose he had?'

'I thought that he might have, and that perhaps Syveton ... But never mind. It is to be hoped that he will yet.' De Quesnoy shrugged wearily, then gave her a brief outline of what had happened, and added: 'Syveton must be informed of this immediately. Can you bring him down here without disturbing any other members of the household?'

'Yes. Stay here. I'll be as quick as I can,' she replied at once. Then as she turned away, she murmured, 'Oh poor François; I do hope he is all right! And you, Armand. What a frightful business.'

Ten minutes later she returned with Gabriel Syveton. He was buttoned into a tight-fitting smooth-faced black cloth coat with a red quilted collar and cross braids; but his hair was unbrushed and there were great pouches under his eyes, which made him look every day of his fifty-two years.

In greater detail, de Quesnoy repeated his story. Syveton heard him out, then angrily struck the desk near which he was standing, and exclaimed:

'The young fool! After all these months of planning! To ruin everything!'

De Quesnoy frowned. 'It was not his fault. If it is anyone's it is that of your precious Committee for having drawn attention to him prematurely by too much publicity. Naturally his friends jumped to conclusions and wanted to support him. Naturally, too, Combes's police have been led to take an interest in him. From that it was only a step to their learning about this party tonight, then waiting in ambush until these young hotheads had committed themselves.'

'But how could you have let them hold such a party?' Syveton groaned.

At that the Count flared up. 'I had no option. And he could hardly be expected to offend all his friends by refusing to go to it. We had no reason to suspect that the police had got wind of it, and by accompanying him to it I hoped that my presence would keep royalist enthusiasm within reasonable bounds. It is as well I did; for otherwise he would never have got away. He and I have far more reason for bitterness about this collapse of our hopes than yourself. It is we who are on the run, with our lives at stake, not you.'

'Forgive me,' Syveton murmured apologetically, 'but everything was going so well, and this catastrophe is so totally unexpected. You may count upon the Committee, though, to do everything possible to hide you and get you safely out of the country.'

177

De Quesnoy shrugged. 'I am more worried about that boy than myself. But tell me; what are the chances of your being compromised by this affair? I told de Vendome to come here because it was the only place I could think of where he could go to earth, at least for the night, in safety. What about tomorrow, though? It is likely that in their hunt for him the police will start a systematic search of the houses of all the members of the Committee?'

'No. I should be very surprised if they did; even if the names of all the members are known to them. None of us has had any communication with the Prince, except socially; and that applies to a hundred of the best families in Paris. The Senate would never permit them to turn the houses of so many influential people upside down.'

'But what of yourself, as Treasurer of the *Ligue*?'

'The *Ligue* is controlled by the Committee but separate from it; and there is nothing secret about the *Ligue's* activities. Even if the police suspect a conspiracy I doubt if they can have any evidence of it, and certainly none involving the *Ligue*. You see, you have acted as our sole agent throughout; so there are no trails leading back to anyone else.'

'Thank God for that!' murmured de Quesnoy. 'The last thing I would wish to do is to bring trouble on you and Madame Syveton. But it would be a great relief if he—that is if he turns up—and I could lie hidden in the apartment on the upper floor of your garden pavilion until you can make arrangements to have us smuggled across a frontier.'

Syveton raised his eyebrows. 'You are aware then, that the place is not just a loft.'

'I am; and this is no time to stand on ceremony. It has been my duty to keep myself informed about the Prince's activities.'

'In that case, Count, let us say no more. It is entirely at your disposal. You should be as safe there as anywhere; and I can assure you that you will not be involving us in any great risk.'

'What if François fails to turn up?' Angela asked anxiously.

'He will, unless he has been caught,' replied de Quesnoy. His mouth set in a grim line, then he added: 'If he has, whatever it costs we must rescue him. I would rather give my own life than leave him in Combes's hands to be sent to the guillotine.'

178

CHAPTER XV

ANXIOUS DAYS

H what an awful thought!' Angela's face went pale. 'That you ... That he ... That either of you ...'

'We've no need to contemplate anything so terrible, as yet,' her husband interposed quickly. 'After all, although Monsieur le Comte got the Prince out of the clutches of the police, he did not see him leave the hotel. He may have thought it best to hide for a while in some attic or cellar before setting out for Paris.'

'That is what I am hoping,' de Quesnoy agreed. 'You may take it, though, that he will not disobey my orders and strike out on a line of his own. That would be contrary to his nature. If he is free he will be here before daylight.'

'Daylight is still three hours away,' remarked Syveton. 'Where would you prefer to spend them—here or in the pavilion?'

'In the pavilion. From its back windows I can keep a lookout for de Vendôme; and the sooner you both return to your beds now the better. If any of your servants learnt that you had received a midnight visitor they might become curious; and the less they know about this the better.'

'Yes!' Angela gave a quick nod. 'And with the hue and cry that is likely to start after François and yourself we must take every possible precaution against any of them discovering that anyone is using the pavilion to lie low in. Apart from my maid, Lucille, and our butler, Octave, I would not care to trust any of them.

'Our gardener will be your worst danger,' Syveton added. 'He works here from seven till midday, then from two o'clock till five. Fortunately he is an old man and somewhat deaf; but you will have to be careful that he does not see you at any of the windows, or hear you moving about when he comes in to get his tools or to put them away.'

'I'll take every care; but if he does hear sounds I see no reason why

179

he should suspect that anyone other than a member of your household is up there.'

Angela shook her head. 'Oh, but he might! Only Lucille is aware that it is sometimes used in the winter months; and even then she goes to it only on Saturday afternoon, when he is not here, to prepare it for the evening; so you really will have to be very careful. We shall not be able to come to you whenever we wish, either; or stay with you for any length of time, even after he has gone home, for fear of arousing the suspicions of the other servants.'

'No matter,' replied de Quesnoy. 'As long as you can bring some food at night, and any news there is. While the gardener is away for his midday meal too, perhaps you could look in, anyhow tomorrow. If you will let me have the key I will go down there now and install myself.'

'Please let me give you a drink first;' Syveton offered, 'and some biscuits in case you get hungry during your vigil. I have both here in my cupboard.'

Without waiting for an answer, he produced a decanter of brandy, a quart bottle of Perrier and three glasses. The warming spirit was welcome to them all, but they drank in depressed silence. The Count pocketed a dozen of the biscuits, then Syveton said:

'I doubt if this affair will be reported in the morning papers, except as stop-press news; but first thing tomorrow I will send one of my agents out to Versailles to get particulars of exactly what is known to the hotel people. That will give us an indication of the sort of story that is likely to be published.' Turning, he gave Angela a somewhat embarrassed look, and added: 'The garden pavilion is yours, my love; so perhaps it would be best if I left it to you to put on a coat and show Monsieur le Comte the accommodation we can offer him.'

With a casual assent, Angela left them. For ten minutes Syveton bewailed the collapse of the conspiracy; although he took care not to criticize de Quesnoy further. Then she returned with a fur coat on, below which showed the hem of a thick tweed skirt and a pair of button boots. The Count bade Syveton good night and followed her out into the garden.

When they reached the pavilion she lit the oil stoves, showed him where everything he might need was kept, and insisted on bathing his face. She then suggested that she should sit up there to keep watch for de Vendôme, while he went to bed. Played out though he was, he would not let her, as it was by then after half-past four; so in another hour and a half the servants would be getting up and, perhaps, from one of the top windows of the house see her returning to it.

After she had left him he maintained a weary vigil till dawn; but it proved useless. Convinced that the Prince would not endanger his friends by seeking refuge there in daylight de Quesnoy now had every reason to fear that his protégé had failed to get away after all; but, as yet, nothing could be done about it. Sick and dispirited he undressed and stretched out his aching body between the cool pink silk sheets. In spite of his anxieties, he fell almost instantly asleep.

When he woke it was about half an hour after midday. Angela had roused him by laying a hand on his forehead. One of his eyes, now surrounded with a great purple bruise, refused to open; but with the other he looked up at her.

'Armand,' she said, 'I'm afraid I have bad news for you. I couldn't come to you until old Simon, our gardener, had gone to his dinner; but about an hour ago Gabriel's agent delivered his report of what he had picked up at Versailles.'

'Has the Prince been taken?' he asked quickly.

'I don't know for certain, but it sounds as if he has. Apparently he had never been to the hotel before; so only the waiters who served the dinner could have definitely identified him, and none of them admitted to having seen him. But a young officer who answers to his description was seen in a passage down by the kitchen quarters, where the waiters hang their overcoats, in the act of stealing one—presumably to put on over his uniform. A servant girl spotted him and started to cry: 'Stop thief!' He ran out of the building, but was caught before he could get across the yard.'

De Quesnoy groaned: 'That must have been de Vendôme. None of the others could have got as far as the ground floor. And what of them?'

'It must have been quite frightful. Worse even than most of these affrays that are taking place between the *Camelots du Roi* and the Communists. It is said that three policemen were killed and four of your students. Several more from both sides, suffering from serious injuries, were taken away in ambulances, and the rest of your party in prison vans. It seems that you were the only one who escaped.'

'Is it known where they took the prisoners?'

She shook her head. 'No; and even such facts as we have got were hard to get. The police threatened all the staff at the Roi Soleil that they would get into trouble if they talked; so Gabriel's agent had to spend quite a lot in bribes to get even a few general statements. I suppose the government want to put out their story of the affair, before our journalists have a chance to accuse the police of breaking up a harmless social gathering.'

'Have the morning papers got anything about it.'

'Only as stop-press items. Those of our side and theirs don't differ much. They just say: "A clash occurred between officers from St. Cyr and police in Versailles last night. It is reported that shots were exchanged resulting in several dead and injured. A number of arrests followed".'

'It is surprising that none of them mentions de Vendôme.'

'I don't think so. The party was held in a private room; so, as I have just said, only the waiters who served the dinner would have had a chance to recognize him. He was not received as royalty or called on by name while they were present, and they had all been bundled downstairs by the police sometime before Dampierre proposed his health; so it is even possible that none of them realized that he was one of the thirty young men at the dinner. Add to that the fact that the lower classes always go in fear of the police, and that the police have threatened to make it hot for these people unless they keep their mouths shut. Surely all this makes it unlikely that François's name would get into a first report?'

De Quesnoy ran a hand through his rumpled hair and sat up. 'Yes, I suppose you are right. But the journalists will ferret out the truth during the day. Anyhow, there can be little doubt that he was the young man who was caught stealing the overcoat; so we must lose no time in finding out to which prison they have taken him. It would be a bit too risky for me to walk the streets of Paris in broad daylight, but as soon as dusk falls I'll go out and start making enquiries.'

'You will do nothing of the kind,' declared Angela firmly. 'Either you will give me your word to remain here, or I shall take your clothes away. Gabriel will find out where François has been taken. The Committee have a special organization for doing that sort of thing; so it would be madness for you to expose yourself to getting caught quite unnecessarily.'

182

'Then you are right again.' He gave her a rueful smile. 'In that case I don't think I'll get up today at all. I'm still feeling pretty groggy from the rough handling I had last night; so twenty-four hours in bed will be welcome. I hope, though, you have brought me some *déjeuner* as I'm beginning to feel quite hungry.'

Angela returned his rueful smile. 'About that I'm afraid you are going to be disappointed. As I have never before been responsible for feeding anyone in hiding, I was quite staggered this morning when I realized how difficult it was going to be to get hold of a little food in my house without the servants knowing and wondering what I want it for. All I could do was to save you the *croissants* from my own breakfast, and sneak some biscuits and fruit from the dining-room.'

'Really!' He burst out laughing. 'Well, well! Never mind; that will do to go on with. I hope, though, you will think up some way to get me something a little more substantial for my dinner.'

'Yes; Gabriel is going to buy you some cold food this afternoon at a *charcuterie*. I couldn't even do that, as if I stopped my carriage and got out to make such purchases, my coachman would think I had gone crazy. When you think, too, that in the kitchen I have a head chef, a pastry cook, a vegetable man and half a dozen wenches to fetch and carry for them, it really is too farcical. But there it is. I'm afraid while you are here you will have to make do with picnics.'

'That will be no great hardship, and far better than arousing the suspicions of the servants. I thought, though, you said that you could trust your own maid.'

'Yes; but I've had no chance to speak to her yet. When I have she can do the shopping for you, and help us in various other ways. But you will have to look after yourself until Saturday, as that is the only day of the week she normally comes here. She can give the place a clean up then, because they must all know that I entertain a *chèr ami* here on Saturday evenings and that she gets the place ready for me. But for her to be seen coming here on other days would excite comment.'

While Angela had been speaking, she had taken from a large reticule she had brought with her the food she had mentioned together with an envelope containing what had been a pat of butter. As he gave it an amused glance, she said:

'This is not for you to eat, but for your poor eye.' Then, when she had fetched water and bathed his face, she made a small poultice of it over his closed and purple optic. Having finished her ministrations she stayed with him a while and, among other things, spoke of Syveton's bitterness at the collapse of the conspiracy. She said that for months he had been devoting his entire time to it and neglecting his business interests. In fact, although he said little about it, and refused to cut down his expensive establishment, she was rather worried by the idea that he might be getting into financial difficulties. Then a little before two o'clock she told him that later in the day Syveton would bring him food and the latest news, and left him.

Through the afternoon he slept again; then he got up and made an investigation of the resources of the apartment. To his disappointment they were extremely meagre. There were no books in it or anything else with which he could take his thoughts off his anxiety about de Vendôme. There were no edible stores in the kitchen and the only thing of that kind he came upon was half a box of candied fruits and some nougat and chocolates in a cupboard in the sitting-room. But there he did find as well four bottles of champagne and some small decanters containing liqueurs. Having opened one of the bottles he went back to bed and waited for his host.

Syveton arrived by way of the door in the garden wall about half an hour after darkness had fallen. With him he brought enough food to last a couple of days, three bottles of red wine and a fat sheaf of newspapers.

De Quesnoy restrained his impatience sufficiently to offer him a glass of his own champagne, and on his declining, asked quickly: 'What of the Prince? Have you found out where they took him?'

'Alas no,' Syveton replied with a shake of his square, powerful head. 'The others were taken back to St. Cyr and are all under close arrest; but I have a full list of their names, and his is not among them.'

'Perhaps, then, he escaped after all!' the Count exclaimed, his grey eyes lighting up.'

'It certainly seems possible. The more so as the government controlled Press makes no mention of his arrest; or even of his having been present at the party. At all events, for the moment we are acting on the assumption that he got away.'

'I don't quite understand. What action can you take?'

'This morning we held an emergency meeting of the Committee. It was unanimously agreed that pending an official statement mentioning him we must do our utmost to keep his name out of this. The public takes no great exception to bands of young royalists and communists breaking one another's heads and sometimes being killed in street affrays; but they regard shooting at the police in a very different light.'

'I see your point. As the police were only obeying orders the Prince's popularity would suffer a very severe setback should it come out that he participated in a fight in which three policemen lost their lives.'

'Exactly. So we have issued instructions to the monarchist Press that whatever stories their reporters may bring in about the party having been held in honour of de Vendôme they should not print them; and that should the government Press start rumours that he was present they are to deny them.'

'That is certainly very sound. In fact, providing he has not been caught and his hiding-place is kept secret, his cause is not irretrievably lost after all. When the others are court-martialled the police will give evidence about Dampierre's proposing his health as King of France, but if it cannot be proved that de Vendôme incited the act by his presence he cannot be held responsible for it. He will have some awkward explaining to do about not having returned to St. Cyr last night; but if only we could get in touch with him. I don't doubt we could provide him with a plausible story to get over that. What a pity that my goose is cooked for good as far as St. Cyr is concerned; otherwise I could have said that he had received a telegram saying that his mother was dangerously ill, and that as the term ends tomorrow I had taken the responsibility of giving him permission to go off to Spain at once.'

'My poor Count.' Syveton shook his head. 'Your goose is cooked indeed; and not only with the Army. For you France, too, is finished; and once we have got you out of the country you will never be able to return.'

As he spoke he opened out one of the evening papers, and added: 'I felt that since you would have to know the worst in the course of the next few days there was little to be gained by our making excuses to keep the newspapers from you. I can only say how distressed both the Committee and I are that this wretched business should fall so heavily upon you, and deprive us of the further help of so brave and valuable a colleague.'

185

On the front page of the paper there was a photograph of the Count, and a bold caption: "WANTED FOR MURDER! LT.-COLONEL THE COUNT DE QUESNOY".

Below, in the letter-press, the principal blame for the whole affair was fastened squarely upon him. It was stated that he had been suspected for some time of organizing an anti-Republican group among his students at St. Cyr, and had invited some thirty of them to an end-of-term dinner in Versailles the previous evening. The police, having reason to believe that a plot was to be hatched there for the assassination of Prime Minister Combes, had posted men in an adjacent room to listen to the proceedings. Having satisfied themselves that the gathering was of a treasonable nature the senior police officer had ordered the arrest of all present. A pitched battle had followed in which three policemen and four officer cadets had been killed. The Count had been seen to shoot two of the policemen at point-blank range, and had then escaped. Fighting had continued for some time until the police had got the upper hand and a number of arrests had been made.

De Quesnoy threw the papers down in disgust. 'There's hardly a word of truth in it. I shot no policemen; although I admit that I injured several. But why this business about plotting to assassinate Combes; and why am I singled out as the villain of the piece?'

'There are two possible explanations,' Syveton suggested. 'In this affair, as no mention has yet been made of the Prince, yours is the only name known to the public. The instinct of all journalists is to build their story round an individual, and you can imagine the avidity with which these Socialist scribblers would seize on the chance to vilify a nobleman like yourself. The other possibility is that it is government inspired. That they know the real origin of the party is certain; but if, as we now suppose, they are not even sure that the Prince was there, they would be wasting powder and shot in accusing him. But they know you were; and the War Minister must be furious with you for now turning out to be a monarchist after deceiving him all these months into believing you to be a staunch republican. As all the Press of the Left are running much the same story, I think the odds are that General André is behind it, and is preparing the ground to deprive you of your head if they can catch you.'

'Your last theory sounds the most plausible. And what have the Press of the Right to say?'

'They have panned the whole thing down as far as possible, and written of the dinner as a happy and law-abiding gathering brutally invaded and broken up by the police. But, of course, they could not ignore the fact that three policemen were killed and that you were the senior officer present. I will leave you the papers, and you can run through the different versions they give of the affair at your leisure.'

'Thanks,' replied the Count glumly. 'I think, though, that I have already gathered from you a clear enough view of my situation. Of course, last night I was quite well aware that a mine had exploded under me, but I have been worrying a lot about de Vendôme; so until now I've hardly faced up to what this will mean to myself. At best it means exile from France for ever, and soldiering in future with some foreign army—perhaps in the Balkans or in South America. I would not mind so much if I had been able to play a part in restoring an honourable and dignified government to France; but it is a bit hard that my career should have been ruined through the over-enthusiasm of a crowd of irresponsible youngsters.'

Syveton opened another bottle of wine and stayed on for an hour endeavouring to cheer him up. They had never talked so intimately before, and when he had gone de Quesnoy admitted to himself that there was something quite likeable about his host.

Before, he had always been prejudiced by his imaginings of what Angela had suffered during the first few months of her marriage; but that was years ago, and he realized now that it must largely have been due to her ignorance coupled with her husband's impatience and lack of understanding of how to treat a young girl. The fact that he had later attempted to exploit her was, too, as Angela had remarked herself, by no means exceptional in the sort of married lives lived by many wealthy Parisians. That at times he became a slave to his passions there could be little doubt, as his reputation for seducing young working girls was by no means an enviable one; but that apart, he had a kindly disposition, a considerable intelligence and was animated by a fervid patriotism.

Hoping that de Vendôme, after spending the day in hiding, might turn up there that night, the Count waited up on the look-out till past three in the morning; but he was again disappointed. On Wednesday he again slept late and he had not been awake for much over an hour when Angela arrived with some books and the morning papers for him.

The stories they carried differed little from those in the evening papers of the day before, except that three of the Liberal journals published a rumour that the Duc de Vendôme had been involved. But the Press of both Left and Right maintained their policy of making no mention of him; and to his anxious friends his whereabouts remained a mystery until that evening.

As on the previous night, shortly after dusk had fallen, Syveton came to the pavilion; and he said at once: 'Count, I'm afraid I have bad news for you.'

'It can now be only one of two things,' sighed de Quesnoy. 'Either the police are downstairs waiting to arrest me, or the Prince has been caught.'

'He was caught the night before last. In fact he never got away. We were right in our original assumption that it was he who was seen taking the waiter's overcoat, and was then seized as he tried to cross the courtyard.'

'I have feared that all along. I could not see how it could possibly have been anyone else; apart from the outside chance that the man was an ordinary thief, and a confused version of the episode was given to your agent. Has this come out in the evening papers?'

'No, no! There is nothing fresh in them, except that one of the Centre journals has unearthed the fact that the Prince disappeared from St. Cyr two days before the college was due to break up. No, this information comes from Laveriac, The Prince is in the *Cherche-Midi*. That came to the General's knowledge only through his chancing to overhear a few sentences exchanged between his Chief and General André; so it is being regarded as a matter of the highest possible secrecy.'

'I wonder why?' mused the Count. 'Since they've got him, and ample evidence that he allowed himself to be acclaimed King of France, and that he took a hand in the fighting, it seems extraordinary that they should refrain from doing anything about it. After all, it is bound to get out that he is a prisoner; so they will have to bring him to trial sooner or later.'

Syveton shook his head. 'I confess I am completely puzzled. The only thing I can suggest is that owing to his great popularity they fear really serious riots, perhaps even a revolution, if he is brought to trial. After the Dreyfus business the very word "trial" sends a shudder

188

through any French government. But I can hardly think they will give him his freedom and, as you say, they cannot detain him without trial indefinitely.'

'I think you are probably right. They are afraid of the larger issues bringing him to trial might raise and are arguing over how to set about it. If so, the longer they argue the better, as far as we are concerned. The *Cherche-Midi* is a very old-fashioned prison, so we should find it much easier to get him out of it than we would out of the Santé; and that is where they will probably move him to when they have faked up a filthy enough case against him to feel that they can risk a trial.'

'Yes; the *Cherche-Midi* is now used only by the military, and they rely more on bolts, bars and harsh discipline than on modern methods for prevention of escapes; but I expect special precautions are being taken to guard him. Of that I hope we will know more tomorrow. The Chaplain there is a fervent royalist, and we have asked him to find out all he can for us.'

Again de Quesnoy spent a lonely twenty-four hours, broken only by a belated visit from Angela. At mid-day it had been pouring with rain, so there was no possible excuse for her to take a walk in the garden. At three o'clock it had cleared, so she had come out then, set old Simon a job in the conservatory at the back of the house, to keep him away from the pavilion, then slipped into it and upstairs.

But she had no fresh news. A bloody riot the previous afternoon, in which a band of *Camelots du Roi* had endeavoured to rescue one of their leaders while he was being transferred from one prison to another, had taken precedence over the Versailles affair. It might even have died, had not de Quesnoy been associated with it and still at large. However, the paragraphs about it were smaller and the Press of the Right rebuked that of the Centre for associating de Vendôme's name with it. Syveton, when briefing his secret agents, had evidently made use of the Count's casual mention of what he might have done had he still been at St. Cyr; for two of them stated that the Condesa de Cordoba y Coralles had suddenly been taken ill, and that the Prince had been given special leave to depart before the end of the term to go to his mother's bedside.

The amazement of the Count was, therefore, all the greater when Syveton came to him at six o'clock and, without speaking, held up an evening paper. It carried the headline: "DEATH OF THE DUKE DE VENDÔME."

CHAPTER XVI

ALARMS AND EXCURSIONS

THE glaring headline was not based on rumour or any reporter's story. Below it was printed an official statement issued under the signature of the Minister of War. The accounts already given of the riot and its origin by the Socialist Press were substantially confirmed; but, instead of four, it was stated that five officer cadets had lost their lives as a result of the fighting. Their names were given, de Vendôme's among them.

The statement went on to the effect that examinations of the surviving officer cadets during the past forty-eight hours had convinced the authorities that they had assembled for a treasonable purpose not of their own free will, but under pressure from their Chief Instructor, Lieut.-Colonel the Count de Quesnoy. The President of the Republic had, therefore, accepted a recommendation by the Minister of Justice that they should not be held collectively responsible for acts committed during the riot, but should be disciplined individually under the powers held by the War Minister. It ended with an announcement that a reward of five hundred *louis d'or* would be paid to anyone providing information which would lead to the apprehension of de Quesnoy.

'What in God's name does this mean?' exclaimed the Count. 'Can it possibly be true? I suppose the police might have bludgeoned the poor boy while taking him prisoner, and that he has since died of wounds. Yet I can hardly believe that.'

'Nor I,' replied Syveton. 'My agent who went to Versailles secured an eye-witness account of the capture of the officer taken in the court-yard. He was grabbed from behind before he could put up a struggle; and it seems certain that he could have been no one but the Prince. Besides, if he had been seriously injured he would have been taken to hospital, not to the *Cherche-Midi*.'

'Have you yet been able to check up on Laveriac's information that de Vendôme is being held there.'

190

'In view of how he came by it, I see no reason to doubt it. I have, too, seen Father Pierre, the chaplain there, and I had from him the story of a curious happening at the prison on Monday night. The chief warder told him that at about one o'clock in the morning Captain Mollin, who is one of General André's A.D.C.s, arrived and had the Governor of the Prison got out of bed. They spent some time in private conversation, then Mollin had some police bring in from a prison van a man whose hands were tied behind him and with a sack over his head. The prisoner was put in a special cell that has an ante-room to it. Two warders were detailed to occupy the ante-room, with strict orders not to communicate with the prisoner and that only one of them should leave it at a time.'

'That settles it,' nodded de Quesnoy. 'Such precautions would only be taken to conceal the identity of a Prisoner of State. It must have been de Vendôme. God be thanked, then, that he is alive. But what devilish game are the Government up to in announcing his death?'

Syveton passed a hand over his broad forehead. 'It is impossible to say for certain; but it looks to me as if they have decided to adopt a policy dictated by the fears we felt they might have when we talked of the matter last night.'

'You mean they are afraid that if they brought the Prince to trial that might start a revolution?'

'Yes; and their statement about how they mean to deal with the other officers fits in. They could not bring them to trial without the Prince becoming the central figure of the case. They would have to produce him and that, equally, might lead to a monarchist uprising.'

'You are right. And, of course, as their trial might mean some of them being condemned to death, or at best long prison sentences for them all, none of them will be fools enough to demand a trial. They will consider themselves mighty lucky in being allowed to keep their commissions and get off with anything General André cares to give them. But what about de Vendôme? Evil as Combes and André may be we are past the days when such men could have Prisoners of State murdered, and they can't keep him a prisoner indefinitely without its getting out. His friends would start an agitation that would bring down the government. There is his mother too; and he is a cousin of the King of Spain. The King would intervene and there would be a first-class diplomatic incident.'

191

'Yes; whatever precautions they may take they could not possibly keep the fact that he is still alive secret for very long. Then they would find themselves in the very devil of a mess. Announcing his death seems sheer madness to me. I cannot conceive what they are up to. However, Father Pierre is coming to see me later this evening. He is the spiritual director of Colonel Roux, the Governor of the *Cherche-Midi*, and they are on excellent terms, so he may have got something out of him.'

When Syveton had gone de Quesnoy gave his whole mind to this extraordinary turn of events, but he could not form even a theory about the government's intentions. To fill a fifth coffin with bricks and have it buried with the other four before de Vendôme's mother could arrive from Spain to claim her son's body could only postpone the day when they must be called to account; for as long as he was alive he might escape, and sooner or later it was certain that his jailers would talk, or he would succeed in getting a message out to his friends.

It was after midnight when Syveton returned, and his pale blue eyes were alight with excitement. He was hardly through the door into the dining-room, in which de Quesnoy was sitting, before he cried:

'The Prince is still alive and the mystery solved! Father Pierre has only just left me. He dined with Colonel Roux and the Colonel was in a most distressed state of mind, so the Father managed to persuade him to confide in him. These people are devils! You would hardly believe what they plan to do to our poor young Prince. It sounds fantastic, but nevertheless it is quite logical.'

'Tell me!' said the Count sharply.

'You will have heard of the Man in the Iron Mask.'

'Of course. Dumas wrote a novel based on his sad history. He was the twin brother of Louis XIV and, fearing that when he was old enough disaffected nobles might start a civil war by persuading him to claim the crown, Cardinal Richelieu had him brought up in great secrecy.'

'Yes; and as he grew up the very image of the King, Louis, from fear of a plot to use the resemblance, had his head locked into an iron helmet and kept him a prisoner for the rest of his life in the castle on the Ile St. Marguerite.'

'You do not mean? You cannot mean . . ?'

'I do. But in this case it is to be a hinged leather contraption with a lock under the ear on one side. It arrived this morning and Colonel Roux showed it to Father Pierre. At the thought of what the young

192

Prince will suffer after the Colonel has put it on him tonight they wept together.'

'*Mort de Diable!* The iniquity of it!' exclaimed de Quesnoy, beginning to walk agitatedly up and down. 'But from what you say Colonel Roux is sympathetic towards his prisoner; and, anyway, as an officer and man of honour he will refuse to do this barbarous thing.'

Syveton spread out his large knobbly hands. 'What would be the use? If he did not Mollin, or some other jackal of André's, would. Roux, too, was given his orders yesterday by André personally, and told that failure to carry them out would mean the loss of his post. It was also intimated to him that if the prisoner escaped, or his identity got out, they would hold him, as Governor of the Prison, responsible, have him tried *en camera*, and get him seven years in a fortress.

'And, of course, once Roux has clamped this leather headpiece on the Prince he will keep the secret from shame of having to admit that it was he who did the ignoble deed. That must be why André has ordered him to do it instead of sending some crony of his own. What cunning swine these rulers of ours are!'

'You may well say that. The whole scheme is diabolically clever. If they had brought him to trial they would have had to risk a revolution in his favour. If they had dealt with him as they are dealing with the other officers, he might have resigned his commission and returned to Spain; but we could have retaliated by publicly acclaiming him as our choice for the throne and, given a fortunate turn of events, later brought him back to occupy it; so he would have continued to constitute a menace to them. As it is, by announcing his death, and condemning him untried to a living death, they will have disposed of him once and for all; and it will be years before we can build up another suitable claimant to the throne. This is a blow from which the hopes of a monarchist restoration may not recover for a generation; and they know it.'

'But wait!' cried the Count. 'All is not yet lost! We know the truth. Get your Committee together. Inform them of this and tell them to shout it from the house-tops. Get Charles Maurras or Henri Vaugeois to publish another article on the lines of Zola's *J'Accuse* at the time of the Dreyfus business. Call out the *Camelots du Roi*. Storm the prison and rescue the Prince. Launch your bid to put him on the throne as *François Troisième* now.'

Sadly Syveton shook his head. 'Alas, *mon chèr Comte*, that is not possible. The attempt was to be made in April or May. Only the basic plan has so far been agreed upon. There are a thousand and one things which yet have to be arranged if the *coup* is to be successful. To do as you suggest could only end in a débâcle. Our friends and I would promptly be arrested, the troops would obey General Andre's orders and the *Camelots du Roi* would be shot down. We should be playing into Combes's hands, and giving him just the excuse he would like to have to destroy utterly the monarchist party.'

'I do not believe that.' De Quesnoy stuck out his chin. 'Forty-eight hours should be ample for you to tie the strings together. What you may lose by measures taken so hurriedly will be more than made up for by the lesser likelihood of leakage of your plans than would be the case over a much longer period. And what a story to launch the attempt upon! No decent person in France could hear without feeling indignation of this plan to keep a young man's head in an inverted leather bucket for the rest of his life. Such a chance to rouse the masses in his favour will never come again.'

'There is much in what you say,' Syveton agreed. 'Yet I doubt if the Committee will see it in that light. They are mostly elderly men, and have had to act with caution for so long that caution has become second nature to them.' With a glance at his watch he added: 'After hearing Father Pierre's disclosure I sent messages to the key men of the Committee so that I might inform them of it. They are to meet at half-past one in a house not far from here. I must go now; but I will put your suggestion to them and let you know their reaction to it tomorrow.'

De Quesnoy's grey, yellow-flecked eyes bored into Syveton's pale blue ones, as he said harshly: 'Let us be clear about this matter. Either they adopt my proposal to launch a revolution within the next few days, with the forcible rescue of de Vendôme as the first move in it, or steps must be taken at once towards arranging his escape.'

'You are right,' Syveton agreed. 'We cannot abandon him to such a terrible fate. I may not get back until very late, but I will tell my wife what has been decided at the meeting and she will pass it on to you tomorrow at mid-day.'

Left alone with his thoughts, the Count brooded upon the living death that must be his young friend's portion unless he could be got

194

out of the clutches of his enemies. He knew enough of the Committee to fear that while its members would willingly provide money, and intrigue endlessly, in support of their political convictions, few of them would be game to risk their necks in the sort of bold stroke that he had suggested, so, after a while he turned his mind to ways in which it might be possible to rescue de Vendôme from the *Cherche-Midi*.

When Angela came up to him shortly after mid-day on the Friday he found her as distressed as himself. She reported that her husband, after a night of conferences which had kept him out of bed until early in the morning, had only just come downstairs. He sent a message to the effect that the Committee was convinced that to order a rising prematurely would jeopardize the whole monarchist movement for years to come, but that money, transport and courageous volunteers would all be made readily available for any scheme offering a fair chance to rescue the Prince.

Having heard what she had to say, de Quesnoy replied: 'During the night I have given the matter much thought, and of one thing I am certain; a military prison guarded by troops, such as the *Cherche-Midi*, cannot be broken into and a prisoner removed from it by half a dozen men, however determined. Either it must be stormed and the rescue effected by sheer weight of numbers, or some skilful deception practised which would need only two or three persons. Since the former has now been ruled out, we must resort to the latter.' He paused for a moment, then added:

'And now, my dear, I want an honest answer to a plain question. Just how much do you love de Vendôme?'

She turned her candid brown eyes upon him as she answered: 'I don't love him. Not in the true sense. I've told you how the affaire between us started. I liked him before that, and I have since become very fond of him; but that is not love.'

'Are you fond enough of him to risk considerable unpleasantness on his account? Perhaps even having to spend some time in prison?'

'If you mean will I help in an attempt to rescue him, of course I will. All of us who have had any hand in encouraging him to believe that he would become King owe him that. It is the least we can do.'

De Quesnoy nodded. 'That is what I feel; otherwise I would never have suggested that you should involve yourself in this. As it is, I hate having to do so; but no one else stands in the same relationship to him

195

as you do, so it would be impossible to carry through the plan I have thought out without your co-operation.'

'What do you wish me to do?'

'Get in to see him, on the plea that you are his mistress. Either through bribery or sentiment we ought to be able to persuade his jailers to allow you to say good-bye to him before he is removed from Paris. I shall come with you dressed as a woman and pretending to be your maid. Both of us will, of course, be heavily veiled. Are you willing to do that, and leave the rest to me?'

She nodded. 'Yes. If any single person can rescue him I am sure you will succeed.'

'Thank you, my dear,' he smiled. 'But we shall need one other: a coachman we can trust. Could Syveton drive his own brougham?'

'I greatly doubt it. I suppose he must have driven pony-carts and that sort of thing when he was young; but he has never been good with horses.'

'Then we certainly will not have him to drive us through the streets of Paris. Ask him to ask General Laveriac if he will do so. In any case I must see the General to discuss the guard arrangements at the prison with him, and the fewer of us who are in the plot the better. I would like to talk to Father Pierre, too. The best thing would be if Syveton could arrange a conference up here with the two of us, himself, Laveriac and the Father. If possible it should be for this evening, as they may move the Prince out of Paris at any time; so we must not waste an unnecessary moment.'

'Very well. I'll tell Gabriel that. Is there anything else?'

'You must buy a complete outfit of women's things for me. I should be able to get into the largest stock size of everything they keep. Black, of course; full-length skirts to hide my feet, bonnet, shawl and veil. I want to look as much like a respectable housekeeper, or elderly maid, as you can make me. You had better buy me a false bun with elastic to wear on the nape of my neck and some sausage curls to stick in the sides of the bonnet. I shall also want a pack of cards: the older the better. With regard to yourself, you should dress in a plain coat and skirt, and the coldness of the weather will justify a travelling cloak. Look out things of which you can provide, or get, more or less duplicates. I'll tell you why later. And one other thing; tell Syveton to ask Laveriac to bring with him if he can a plan of the *Cherche-Midi*.'

196

She was about to leave him, and he was accompanying her to the door, when he said softly: 'Just now I put the very worst complexion on things because no one can foresee every possibility. I mean, when I asked you if you would be willing to face a spell in prison. Actually I don't think there is any risk of that. You see, if Colonel Roux does let you in to see de Vendôme, he will have given hostages to fortune; so if things did go wrong, he would probably get rid of you as quickly as possible for his own sake. If it were not for that I would not have asked your help, but would have tried to think of some other plan.'

Her eyes shining, she took his hand and pressed it. 'I'm sure of that, *mon ami*; but I'm pleased and proud to be able to help in this. My only worry is about you, and that you mean to do something rash which may jeopardize your own safety.'

'Come now,' he chid her with a smile. 'Don't start to worry before there is any need. You promised to leave everything to me, and you may be sure that I shall not take any risks that I don't have to.'

Syveton succeeded in arranging the conference for six o'clock that evening, and brought the General and Father Pierre to the pavilion by way of the door in the garden wall. Angela was already with de Quesnoy, and when they were all seated round the dining-room table in the soft light of the candles he asked the priest:

'Do you think, Father, that if it were made worth Colonel Roux's while he would connive at the escape of his prisoner? If so, it would, of course, make everything much less difficult and dangerous for all concerned.'

Father Pierre was a vigorous-looking middle-aged man. As the *Cherche-Midi* was situated on the edge of the Faubourg St. Germain he combined his duties as Chaplain of the prison with that of spiritual director to a number of noble families; so he was very much a man of the world. Having taken a pinch of snuff, he replied with decision:

'No. Etienne Roux is a man of principle. He is a good Catholic and would certainly not be averse to a restoration of the monarchy. But forty years or more in the Army has imbued him with a strong sense of duty, and I am sure he would not be prepared to sacrifice it for personal gain.'

'I feared that might be the case,' said the Count. Then he intimated tactfully that the Prince had a deep romantic attachment to Angela, and asked if the Colonel might be persuaded to let her visit the prisoner,

197

in order that he should have the consolation of saying farewell to her.

To that the priest replied with equal assurance: 'Yes. Naturally I cannot guarantee that Colonel Roux will agree to allow Madame to see his prisoner, but I feel reasonably confident that I can persuade him to do so.' He made a little bow to Angela, and added: 'In fact I find it difficult to imagine a Frenchman who would be so ungallant as to refuse.'

With this hopeful opening to their talk they discussed the Count's plan. Its basis was that they should smuggle in women's clothes for the Prince similar to those that Angela would be wearing. He would then take the Prince out as Angela and she would remain behind until they were well clear of the prison. She would then declare herself, and Colonel Roux, realizing the futility of detaining her, would let her go.

His scheme was instantly assailed with a chorus of objections. Even if Angela was left alone with the Prince it might not be for long enough for him to put on the disguise. Anyway, when the cell door was opened the Colonel would see, apparently, two women and no Prince, And if Angela were left behind how could they be certain she would be released? Colonel Roux, finding himself a ruined man, would instinctively detain her, even if only to show how he had been tricked.

De Quesnoy dealt only with the last point. If the Colonel did detain Angela they would be able to get her out within forty-eight hours, because they would have rescued de Vendôme. With him free they could expose the official lie about his death and the whole of the atrocious government plot. Public indignation would be intense, and when the story of the way in which the Prince had been rescued was given to the Press Angela would be acclaimed a national heroine. The government would realize at once that if she were brought to trial no jury would ever convict her; so they would have to let her go.

His argument was unanswerable. The other points he refused to discuss, saying that he had thought of a way to trick the Colonel and had worked out the details of the escape with the greatest care; so he was convinced that, given reasonable luck, his plan was feasible. Laveriac and Syveton continued to have misgivings, but as he was insistent and declined to go into particulars they agreed to give him a free hand.

However, Father Pierre, who had taken no part in the argument, then said in a worried voice: 'I understood, of course, that we were meeting here to discuss the possibility of aiding the Prince to escape, but until Monsieur le Comte outlined his plan I had no idea of the form it might take. As both a Christian and a Royalist I am most anxious to help, but I cannot ignore my responsibility towards my good friend Etienne Roux. As this plan involves him personally it would cause his complete ruin. He would not only lose his post and pension but get the seven years in a fortress with which General André threatened him.'

'I was coming to that,' replied de Quesnoy. 'Should the Prince escape, however he may do so, the Colonel's loss of his post is inevitable. That is one of the reasons why I hoped that he might accept a handsome offer to give us a free hand. Since you feel sure that he will not, and my whole plan hangs upon our taking advantage of his compassion for the prisoner, I feel that he should be compensated afterwards.' Glancing towards Syveton and Laveriac, he added: 'Do you agree?'

Both nodded, and Syveton said: 'The Committee, I am sure, would be willing to pay him a pension equivalent to what he is receiving now. Would that meet your objection, Father?'

'It would if it were not for the fact that he is certain to be court-martialled, and will receive a heavy sentence.'

'No, no,' said de Quesnoy quickly. 'When Madame Syveton discloses herself she can tell him what has been settled about a pension for him and that instead of reporting the escape he must leave with, or immediately after her. No doubt, too, arrangements could be made to get him out of Paris that same night.'

'What about the Prince?' Laveriac asked. 'It is a long way to the Spanish border, or for that matter to any of the frontiers. If they get on his track and he is re-arrested before he can get across one of them that would be tragic. We shall have to organize his journey very carefully.'

'You have no need to worry about that,' smiled the Count. 'It was quite a problem but I think I have solved it. I suggest that you should drive him straight to the Spanish Embassy. He will then be out of danger within a quarter of an hour of leaving prison. Although he is a French citizen we can be quite certain, as he is a cousin of the King of Spain, that the Spanish Ambassador will never give him up.'

'Brilliant!' laughed the little General. 'Brilliant! Now, what about yourself?'

'I shall go still dressed as a woman to the Gare de l'Est. If I can get a night train for Metz, Strassburg or Basle so much the better. If not I shall wait in the buffet until one leaves early in the morning. I plan to go to Vienna, and should meet with no difficulty as this is not Russia.'

'What do you mean by that?'

'Why, to enter or leave Russia everyone has to have a passport; but, thank God, no other European country insists on that tiresome formality.'

'Unless Colonel Roux leaves the prison with my wife,' said Syveton, 'when he does let her go she will be quite alone. How do you propose that she should get home?'

'I see no reason why another carriage should not wait for her about two hundred yards away. In the Boulevard Raspail just by the *Mont de Pieté* would be a good place, then there can be no mistake. There is no need to tell the coachman anything; and if he does have to wait there all night it will do him no great harm.'

'Good,' Syveton agreed. 'I shall be anxious for her; so I shall go in the carriage and wait for her myself.'

The General then produced a plan of the *Cherche-Midi* and Father Pierre pointed out on it the cell occupied by the prisoner. It was at the back of the building, on the ground floor, and its ante-room gave on to a long L-shaped passage so; although it was some distance from the street, it might have been worse placed for an escape.

De Quesnoy asked the General what was being done about the other officer cadets who were under arrest. Laveriac shrugged and replied: 'The young fools got off far better than might have been expected; although their careers are ruined, at least for the time being. They have been split up and ordered into the wilderness, each to a different regiment, in New Caledonia, Martinique, Senegal, Madagascar, Saigon, and so on.'

For another hour they continued to discuss the proposed attempt at rescue, settling such details as where Laveriac should pick up Angela and de Quesnoy in a brougham that he meant to borrow from his brother-in-law, and the sending, when the time fixed for the escape was known, of an anonymous note to the Spanish Ambassador requesting him to prepare to receive a distinguished visitor who was travelling incognito. Then, as the loss of even a day might render the whole plan abortive, Father Pierre agreed to approach Colonel Roux after dinner that night; and the meeting broke up.

Next day Angela did not come to the pavilion until nearly half-past one. She said then that she had left her daily visit till late in the hope of hearing from Father Pierre and that he had turned up in person twenty minutes ago, giving the glib excuse to the servants for the unusual hour of his call that he was expected to lunch. He had persuaded Colonel Roux to receive her at the prison and allow her to take leave of her *chér ami*. The secret visit was to take place that night, and the Colonel had fixed the time for it as eleven o'clock, as that would give a full hour before the guard was changed; so only one watch of sentries would know that two women had entered or left the prison.

After telling de Quesnoy this, Angela said that she must hurry straight back to give the Father lunch; but, pausing at the door, she asked him what he would like for dinner.

He shrugged and smiled a little wryly. 'Oh, don't bother Lucille to get me anything fresh. I still have some bits of cold chicken, plenty of biscuits and a wedge of Brie.'

'You silly!' she laughed. 'Have you forgotten that this is Saturday—the night I dine here, and all the household know it. In an hour or so Lucille will be coming over to give the apartment its weekly cleaning, and I can send an order down for the Chef to prepare for us anything that will not spoil by being brought over and heated up.'

'What a delightful surprise!' he exclaimed joyfully. 'Let us have lobsters then. If cooked in plenty of cream they would heat up all right, and we can add the brandy at the last moment. For afterwards, pineapple with Kirsch. But would you like that?'

'Yes. What could be nicer.' She smiled again and ran downstairs.

At three o'clock Lucille arrived. De Quesnoy hardly knew her, but recognized her as the young woman who had shown him up to Angela's boudoir the evening before he had been sent into exile, and in this conspiratorial atmosphere they greeted one another as old friends. She had brought with her a valise containing the woman's outfit he had asked for, and while he tried the things on in the bedroom she set about cleaning up the rest of the apartment.

Later, he asked her to make a few adjustments to the clothes then, when she had gone, he lay down and had a couple of hours' sleep in preparation for the night's work. He was aroused by her return, bringing the food for dinner and to lay the table. While she was doing so he freshened himself up. Soon afterwards, having demurely wished him luck on "his outing dressed as a lady", she left again; and, ten minutes later, Angela joined him.

Tonight she was not *en décolleté* but wearing the clothes in which she meant to go to the prison. As she had on two skirts, two travelling cloaks, an extra veil and had numerous other things distributed about her she appeared much bulkier than usual; but her being so swathed up could well be justified by the cold outside. When de Quesnoy had helped her out of most of her surplus clothing they sat down to dinner.

It proved a strange meal: by no means a gay one yet not unduly solemn. Neither could altogether put out of their thoughts the anxieties and uncertainties with which they would be faced in a few hours' time; but by talking of the past they managed to keep quite light-hearted. Both realized that tonight they must not allow any emotional crisis to deflect their minds from the task before them; so by an unspoken agreement no mention was made by either of their feelings for one another, and at half-past nine, de Quesnoy went into the bedroom to change into his disguise.

Angela helped him with the final touches, then put on her extra garments. They pinned a small hat, like the one Angela was wearing, under his voluminous skirts and distributed a number of other items between them. Then they were ready.

They turned out the oil stoves, blew out the candles, and she produced a torch. As he took her arm to lead her to the door she said in a faltering voice:

'Armand. We have every reason to hope that I shall get away quite soon after you. Instead of going to the railway station why should you not return and . . . and spend the night here?'

His mouth suddenly went dry. Swallowing hard, he gulped. 'Oh, my beloved! If only I could. But I dare not. There is, I feel sure, a train that leaves for Basle at midnight. I must catch it if I possibly can. My life may depend on it.'

Throwing an arm round her he drew her to him; but she gave a little laugh that was near to tears and murmured: 'Dear Armand! Fate is against us. We have left it too late. Without unknotting these wretched veils we're wearing we can't even kiss.'

'If we are to rescue de Vendôme tonight,' he murmured, quickly releasing her, 'perhaps that is just as well.'

As they went downstairs she asked: 'When ... when can I hope to see you again?'

'Who can say?' He gave a heavy sigh. 'But somehow, sometime, somewhere, God will at last be kind to us, and allow us to make up for the years that we have lost.'

Hand in hand they went out into the darkness.

CHAPTER XVII

THE ONLY WAY

I T had been arranged that the brougham should wait for them a hundred yards down the Avenue Messine, which was only just across the Rue de Lisbonne from the cul-de-sac leading to the Park. Three minutes' walk brought them to it. On the box sat a figure they knew to be the General only by its shortness and broad shoulders, as a woollen muffler hid the lower part of his face and his cockaded top hat was pulled well down over his eyes. For that the chill of the night and a touch of fog was ample justification. He greeted them only by raising his whip. They got in, and the carriage moved off.

The streets through which they drove for the first few minutes were dark, but they soon entered the Madeleine district with its cafés and shops. As it was Christmas Eve many of the latter that sold food were still open; but France's present-giving festival being New Year's Day, the scene was not as animated as it would have been in the capitals of many other countries. To keep Angela's thoughts away from the hazardous business to which they were now committed de Quesnoy began to tell her about *Weinachsfest* in Vienna, with its Christmas trees, lighted candles in all the windows, and carol singers. That revived for her memories of her Christmas while still a young girl in England, and for ten minutes or so they talked of holly, mince-pies, stockings, snap-dragon and jolly, carefree parties.

It was not until they had crossed the river and were some way along the Boulevard St. Germain that he said to her: 'Now, I want you to listen very carefully. To begin with, as your maid, I can play only the part of an onlooker; so the whole initiative will lie with you. Should the Colonel suggest leaving me in some lobby while he takes you to see his prisoner alone, you must in no circumstances agree to that. Pretend to be very nervous and insist that I should remain within call. On the grounds of propriety that is a perfectly reasonable request, and it will ensure my being taken with you to the ante-room of the cell. Two warders are permanently stationed there. It is to be hoped that the Colonel will send them out into the passage. If he does not, tell him, again on the grounds of propriety, that you wish the door from the ante-room to the cell to be left ajar, but will he please spare you the embarrassment of anyone other than him and myself overhearing what passes between you and the prisoner. He can then hardly refuse to send the two men outside. Lastly, should the Prince have on this leather mask, you must persuade the Colonel to remove it. As he knows that you are aware who the prisoner is he can have no reasonable objection. Then, when you are alone with the Prince, you must on no account give him any idea that you have come there to rescue him. Until I join you act just as though you had got in only to bid him good-bye. Is that all clear?'

'Yes,' she replied in a low voice. 'And what then?'

'You can leave the rest to me. But whatever I may ask you to do you may be sure there will be a good reason for it; so please don't ask why, but do it quickly.'

The carriage was now within a hundred yards of the prison gates, and he went on: 'One thing more. I have decided on a slight change of plan. You are to come out first with the Prince, while I shall remain behind.'

'But why?' she exclaimed. 'The Colonel is much more likely to detain my maid than he is me.'

He gave a little laugh. 'Come now! Haven't I just asked you to do as I wish without argument.'

'But Armand!'

'Please! There is no time now to go into my reasons.'

As he finished speaking the carriage halted, and he threw open its door. Grasping his arm she said in a swift whisper: 'No, no! Are you mad! They would never let François and me out together dressed in almost the same clothes.'

Stepping down, he half pulled her out after him and whispered back: 'Don't worry. Leave everything to me.'

The gate-keeper had already come forward. Evidently he had been expecting them; for, without a word, he led them past the sentry and across a small courtyard to a pair of double doors through which he motioned them to enter. They passed through into a dimly-lit hall.

Near the door a sergeant was seated at a desk. Some way beyond him stood a tall grey-haired officer, with rather sad blue eyes and a walrus moustache. The number of gold rings on his kepi showed him to be the Colonel. He saluted casually and Angela, in the manner customary among her class, was just about to extend her hand for him to kiss when he clasped both of his behind his back and asked abruptly:

'You are the two nurses from the hospital?'

For a second she was taken aback, but quickly realizing that he was initiating in the presence of the sergeant some plan that he had thought out to cover himself, she replied: '*Oui, Monsieur.*'

'Be pleased to follow me, then.' Turning on his heel, he led them down the long L-shaped passage, that they had seen on the plan of the prison, to its far end and, opening a door there, showed them into a room about fourteen feet square. In it there were two warders: one a gaunt middle-aged man, sitting at a bare wooden table writing a letter, the other a somewhat younger red-headed fellow, dozing beside a glowing iron stove.

As Colonel Roux followed the visitors in the two warders came quickly to attention; then, to de Quesnoy's relief, the Colonel told them to go out into the passage but remain within call. Directly the heavy door was shut behind them he removed his kepi, bowed to Angela and said in a low voice:

'Madame, I am honoured to make your acquaintance. I only regret that it should be in such sad circumstances.'

She gave him her hand to kiss then, and said how deeply grateful she was to him for having agreed to allow her to say farewell to his prisoner.

He bowed again, and his pale blue eyes looked more melancholy than ever as he murmured: 'It was a request that no man of sensibility could refuse.' Then he produced two big keys from the pocket of his jacket and, while unlocking the two large old-fashioned locks on the iron-studded door of the cell, he said to her:

'I can allow you a quarter of an hour, Madame; no more. You will appreciate too that I must leave the cell door ajar, er . . . just in case of any unforeseen happening; but I will not listen to your conversation.' Pulling the door open, he stood aside for her to go in.

With a word of thanks, she stepped past him. Then she gave a low cry. It was answered by another, and the sound of chair legs scraping

206

back on the stone floor. Angela had paused in the doorway. Turning to Colonel Roux she cried:

'What is that awful box thing he has over his head.'

'It is a form of mask, Madame. The government has ordered that he shall wear it. Such treatment is inhuman; but what would you? They are determined to keep his identity secret at all costs. He is allowed to speak with no one but myself. Until yesterday, after I had put the mask on him, even the two warders were not allowed inside his cell; so I had to bring his food and perform other small services for him personally.'

Angela laid a hand on the Colonel's arm. 'But, Monsieur, his identity is no secret from me. I am his *chère amie*. Surely in this last interview you will permit me to gaze again on his face.'

With a heavy sigh, the Colonel replied: 'Madame, since you know who he is I would like to oblige you. But this morning when I removed his mask so that he could wash I had great difficulty in getting him to put it on again.'

'I am sure that he will make no such difficulties if you will relieve him of it now,' said Angela softly.

The Colonel accompanied her into the cell and spoke to the Prince. De Vendôme had come quickly to his feet and was staring through the slits in his mask at Angela as though she were a ghost. Stammering slightly, he gave the required assurance. Colonel Roux produced a key, unlocked the mask and came out almost closing the door behind him. The voices coming from within sank to a murmur.

De Quesnoy, meanwhile, had been standing quite still on the far side of the ante-room table. Up to the moment everything had gone in complete accordance with his wishes. He now took from a well-worn leather handbag that he was carrying the pack of cards. Holding it up for the Colonel to see as he came out of the cell he said:

'Will you permit me, Monsieur?'

The Colonel nodded. The Count sat down at the table, untied his veil and threw it back over his bonnet. It was a crucial moment. Although he had never before met Roux, the Colonel might recognize him from his photographs which had been appearing during the past few days in the papers. He could rely only on the extreme unlikelihood of a man wanted for murder deliberately walking into a prison, and his disguise. He had shaved with extra care, and Angela had said that although his arched nose, firm mouth and slanting eyebrows made his face a very male one, the side curls and high lace collar kept in place with whalebone supports did a lot to soften it. There was at least a more than even chance that he would be taken for a capable if unprepossessing middle-aged woman of the superior servant class; but, all the same, he kept his glance lowered as he began to lay out the cards on the table.

For about five minutes he tapped first one card then another of the layout, shuffled, cut, repeated the process, and all the time kept up an almost inaudible mutter; then, with a little cry of satisfaction, he swept the cards together.

Having nothing to do, Colonel Roux had been watching him, but only with casual interest. Without looking up the Count asked: 'Would *Monsieur le Colonel* like me to tell his fortune?'

It was the sort of invitation that few people will refuse; and, with a shrug, the Colonel replied: 'Why not, Madame; why not?' then sat down opposite him at the table.

De Quesnoy asked him to cut the pack and, when he had done so, said: 'It is important, Monsieur, that you should attune your personality to the cards. Please keep your eyes fixed on them and concentrate your thoughts upon the movement of my hands so that you will subconsciously direct the layout.'

He then began to deal the cards, first in one pattern then in another, while keeping up a low monologue of the rather vague type commonly used by fortune tellers—a remove; a slight illness; a dark woman who would make trouble; a journey; a new friend who would be a fat man having great influence; and so on—and all the time his slender hands with the long slim fingers flickered and flickered and flickered.

Having spent four or five minutes in this way he gathered up the cards, placed the pack face downwards in the centre of the table and said: 'Now your wish. Please cut the cards twice, so that they make three stacks; and at the same time, while you are making your wish, you must look into my eyes.'

All unsuspecting, the Colonel obeyed. He was already half mesmerized from his attempt to follow the constant flickering of those long pale fingers. Now, he lifted his eyes and met de Quesnoy's grey ones. After a moment he tried to look away; but it was too late. His gaze was held by that unwinking stare. The yellow-flecked cat's eyes of the Count seemed to him to grow larger and larger until he felt as though he was being engulfed in some gently shimmering grey sea. In his brain a soft voice said: 'Sleep. Sleep. Sleep.' His eyelids fluttered and closed; he thrust out his arms across the table and his head fell forward on to them; without a murmur he fell fast asleep.

Standing up de Quesnoy put the cards back in his bag, then rolled the Colonel's head over sideways, gently turned up one of his eyelids and gave a quick glance at the eyeball. Satisfied with what he saw, he let the head roll back, turned and walked into the cell.

Angela had undone and thrown back her veil, and was sitting beside de Vendôme on the narrow bed. Overcome with emotion at her having come to him in the midst of his ordeal, the poor youth had broken down and, his head bowed, was weeping. She had an arm round his shoulders and was making the little soothing noises that a mother makes to a terrified child.

At the sound of the Count's footsteps he cried: 'No, not again! Not again!' and thrusting out his hands shrank away from the table on which the great leather helmet now reposed upside down. Then as he lifted his terrified eyes they took in the black-clad female figure in the doorway. After a moment, knowing his ex-Chief Instructor so well, he penetrated his disguise. Springing to his feet, he ran towards him, crying:

'*Grâce à Dieu!* De Quesnoy! Oh, Monsieur le Comte, can it be that you are here to save me?'

'Yes, my Prince,' replied the Count. 'But please try to calm yourself, and give me your complete attention. I am about to give you certain instructions which it is all important that you should follow when you are free.' To Angela he added: 'I have put Colonel Roux into a deep hypnotic sleep; but we cannot be too careful. Please go into the ante-room and keep watch on him. If he stirs a finger let me know instantly.'

As she left them, he pushed the door to behind her. Turning back he saw that de Vendôme had picked up the helmet and was about to dash it to the ground. 'Stop!' he said sharply. 'Give me that. I want to look at it.'

The Prince handed it to him and he gave it a swift examination. It had evidently been modelled on the flat-topped saucepan-like type of *heaume* that many knights favoured in the late thirteenth century.

The leather of which it was made was so thick as to be almost rigid, so it could not possibly be torn; and its edges were strengthened with small brass studs. It had been fashioned in two halves: front and back. On the right hinges held the halves together. On the left, just below the level of the ear, was the lock. It had a grille on eye level to see through, and a slit like a pillar-box for conveying food and drink to the mouth. Inside it was padded where it rested on the top of the head and on the nape of the neck.

Throwing it on the bed, de Quesnoy said: 'Now we have to exchange clothes; and we have no time to lose.'

Suiting the action to the word he began to strip off his female garments as quickly as he could; but de Vendôme had off all but his underclothes long before him, for the cell was very well heated and he had been wearing only his uniform trousers and a white shirt.

As soon as the Count had the trousers and shirt on, he helped the Prince to arrange the bonnet, false curls and thick veil. It was not until he had done so that the still semi-hysterical young man suddenly gasped:

'But you ... ! But you, *mon ami*! If I am to go out in these things, what about yourself?'

De Quesnoy gave him a grim smile. 'I am not going out; at all events for the time being.'

'If you stay here God knows what they will do to you.'

'With luck, they will treat me no worse than they would have treated you.'

'You ... you mean to take my place?'

'Yes. We are much of a height and build. They will have no reason to suppose that an exchange of prisoners has been effected, and once I have put on the mask ...'

'No, no! I cannot let you!'

'You must. I insist upon it.'

De Vendôme violently shook his head. 'I cannot. It is too great a sacrifice to accept from anyone.'

'From most people, yes. But not from me. I owe you this. It is through me that you are here.'

'The dinner was no fault of yours. It was Dampierre who has brought us all to ruin. You did your utmost ...'

'No,' the Count cut him short. 'The dinner did no more than

provide an opportunity for the police to catch you allowing yourself to be acclaimed as King. It was I who set you on that path.'

'That is true. Even so . . .'

'Say no more! My mind is made up. And if we waste further time arguing we shall all be caught. That would mean not only the mask for you and death for me but a long prison sentence for Madame Syveton.'

'Oh God!' groaned the Prince, his resistance overcome by de Quesnoy's playing Angela as a trump card. 'Very well, then. Tell me what I am to do?'

'In a minute I shall rouse Colonel Roux from his hypnotic sleep. He will lock me in here, then see you and Madame Syveton to the entrance of the prison. A closed carriage is waiting there with General Laveriac acting as coachman. He will drive you to the Spanish Embassy. You know the Ambassador, of course?'

'Yes.'

'Who else do you know in the Spanish Embassy?'

'The Military Attaché, and the First Secretary, Don Ramon d'Avila.'

'They should prove as trustworthy as the Ambassador himself, I am worrying more about clerks, porters and other such people. Have you been to the Embassy much during your time at St. Cyr?'

'No; only once to dinner, soon after I arrived, and to a big reception on King Alphonso's birthday last May.'

De Quesnoy gave a quick sigh of relief. 'Then the servants there cannot know you well enough to recognize you when you enter it disguised as a woman. On their not doing so my life depends.'

'In what way? I don't understand.'

'The Government have fathered the dinner at Versailles on to me. In the fight afterwards three policemen lost their lives. It is alleged that I shot two of them, and a big reward has been offered for my capture. If it becomes known that you have escaped they will immediately send to find out who has taken your place in prison, and once the mask has been taken from my head it will mean the signing of my death warrant.'

'How can I let you run this awful risk for me!' exclaimed the Prince in fresh distress.

'There is no alternative.'

'Sooner or later it is bound to get out that I am free.'

'Yes. But if you and our other friends are careful it should be possible to keep the secret for several weeks, or even months. If you can gain me enough time I shall manage somehow to escape.'

'Oh, I pray that you may. I will do everything in my power . . .'

'I am sure of that. Now, this is what I suggest. You must tell the Spanish Ambassador everything and impress upon him that my life hangs on his concealing your identity. He has been warned to expect a distinguished guest travelling incognito. Leave it to him to provide you with a name, and to tell his staff that immediately on your arrival you were taken seriously ill. It means exchanging this prison for another but there will be little hardship in spending some days in a comfortable bedroom. As soon as he can he must arrange for you to travel, still disguised, with a diplomatic *laissez-passer* and accompanied by one of his staff, to Spain. But you must not go to Madrid. Choose some small place where you are unknown. Your mother must be in great grief about you. To alleviate her distress let her know that you are alive and well, but that she should tell only your step-father, and that if either of them breathes a word to anyone else it may bring about my death. To remain in hiding will mean a dreary time for you, but . . .'

'What does that matter! There is nothing I would not do to shield you from discovery.'

'Give me as long as you can, then. That is all I ask. My chance to escape will come when they transfer me to a fortress. Unless fortune has finished with me for good it won't be very long before I can send a message to your mother that I am free, and that you can come out into the open. Now, I must have a final word with Madame Syveton.'

Opening the cell door a few inches de Quesnoy called softly to Angela. As she came in she saw instantly that the two men had changed clothes. The blood drained from her face, and she gasped:

'This was not our plan! What in Heaven's name . . ?'

De Quesnoy cut her short. 'No, the one we arranged could never have worked. I'm afraid I deceived you from the beginning. I had to, otherwise you might have refused me your help; and that I had to have. I broke it to you partly just before we got here—that it was I who was to stay behind, not you. I could never have got the Prince out dressed in the extra things you brought, nor could I get out dressed in them myself after you have gone. For he and I to change clothes was the only way.'

Angela's mouth quivered. 'You . . . you mean that you're not going to attempt to get out at all?'

'Not tonight, anyhow. I hope to escape later; perhaps when they transfer me to a fortress.'

Suddenly her face brightened. 'With all these confusing changes you're forgetting how things stand. We can get you out tomorrow by the same means as we meant to use if I had stayed behind and the Colonel had detained me. With François free and safe in the Spanish Embassy, we can disclose the whole vile plot and force the government to release you.'

'No, my dear.' Sadly he shook his head. 'That is the one thing you cannot do. They would have had nothing against you except the part you had played in this, and that would have made you a national heroine. I am wanted for murder; and you may be sure that they will find some of those policemen willing to swear that they saw me shoot down two of their comrades.'

'Dear God!' With a little cry of despair Angela put one hand up to her head. 'Then . . . if Colonel Roux recognizes you . . .'

De Quesnoy pointed to the mask. 'He won't. That horrible thing can now be made to serve a useful purpose. My worst danger will be if it gets out that the Prince has escaped. He has agreed to remain in hiding both while at the Spanish Embassy and later for as long as he can. For the rest I must rely on you. Directly you have dropped the Prince at the Embassy, get Laveriac to bring you back to your own carriage. Collect your husband and tell both of them how things stand; and let Father Pierre know too. I'll still have a chance as long as they all keep the secret that the Prince is free.'

'But Armand! Every day, every hour, your life will be hanging by a thread.'

'I know it; but there was no other way. You must go now. I will wake the Colonel to take you out.'

'No!' Angela threw out an arm barring his passage to the door.

'You must! We have been here well over twenty minutes. Those two warders may already be wondering at the Colonel's having allowed you to stay so long. If one of them looks in . . .'

'No!' she repeated and swung round to de Vendôme. 'I wish to speak to Monsieur le Comte alone. Please leave us for a few moments.'

Obediently the Prince slipped out of the cell and closed its door behind him. Then she said:

'Armand. You are right that I would not have helped you in this had I known what you meant to do.'

'Please!' he begged. 'If you delay longer you may ruin everything.'

'I'll risk that rather than leave you here. I can't let you do this! I can't! I can't!'

'There is no alternative.'

'There is! The two of you must change clothes again.'

'What, and leave him here?'

'Yes. Since a choice has to be made I claim the right to make it. As a man, as a person, you are worth a hundred of him.'

'I love to hear you say so; but that has nothing to do with it.'

'Yes it has. And it was he who was arrested, not you. It will be terrible for him I know, but it is not fair that you should have to take his punishment on yourself.'

'Ah, Angela, my love, that is where you are wrong. He had no wish to be made King. It was I who . . .'

'I don't care. The choice was his, and he was beginning to glory in the prospect. He knew that he was playing for high stakes. Now that he has lost why should you pay up for him?'

'Because it is my debt. I have brought this on myself. For his own ends he would never have agreed to let us attempt to put him on the throne. By playing on his deep religious convictions I tricked him into it. The responsibility for his being here is mine, and no one else's. I would feel dishonoured if I left him here when I had it in my power to take his place.'

The tears were streaming down Angela's face. Throwing back her veil she dabbed at her eyes with a lace handkerchief, and sobbed: 'Oh the chivalry and the folly of it! You are another Bayard; but such men are derided, not honoured, in modern times.'

He shook his head. 'Right thinking has no period, and one does not have to be born of noble blood to follow the dictates of conscience. No, my darling, you must go. Otherwise . . .'

Suddenly she flung her arms round his neck, kissed him full upon the mouth and choked out: 'Armand! Armand! Your life is dearer to me than your honour or my own. If François remains here, his life will be in no danger; but if you do yours will be. That is my justification

for begging you to sacrifice your principles. I love you! I love you!
I always have! No other man has ever really touched my heart. Do as
I wish. What do I care if my name is dragged in the mud and I have to
live as your mistress. Let us leave Paris tonight and start a new life
together.'

For a moment he crushed her to him so hard that the breath was
driven out of her body. His mouth found hers again and hers opened
wide to receive his passionate kiss. Then releasing his grip he raised
his hands, seized her wrists, and in one swift movement broke her
hold. Still grasping her wrists, but now on a level with his chest, he
stared into her eyes and gasped:

'Never ... never in my life have I been so tempted. But if I succumbed this thing would always lie between us, and we'd hate each
other before another year is out. I love you too! Desperately! You know
that! Try to take comfort from having just given me a wonderful
memory to live upon. Pray for me, and I'll come back to you yet.'

Distraught with grief she no longer resisted as, with an arm about
her waist, he hurried her through into the ante-room. Colonel Roux
still slept with his head upon his arms. De Vendôme, in the black dress,
bonnet and shawl, his features obscured by the heavy veil, stood near
him.

De Quesnoy put his thumb on a nerve in the back of the Colonel's
neck, and said: 'In thirty seconds you will wake. You will have no
memory of your fortune being told or that you have been asleep; and
you will ask no questions of these ladies as you escort them to the street.'

Turning, without another look at Angela or the Prince, he walked
back into the cell and pulled the door to after him. Picking up the
mask he put it on. Then he lay down on the bed with his face turned
to the wall, as though overcome with emotion on account of his recent
interview; as indeed he was.

He had hardly done so when, outside in the ante-room, Roux raised
his head. For a moment he stared about him, then he stood up. Angela,
now sobbing as though her heart would break, was being supported
by de Vendôme, who had his arm about her shoulders. With a glance
at her the gallant old Colonel murmured: *'Pauvre petite Madame.'*
Producing his keys he went into the cell and relocked the helmet,
without the faintest suspicion that it had been transferred to de Quesnoy's
head, then he came out and locked the door behind him.

Two minutes later the warders were once more installed in the ante-room, and Angela, the Colonel and the Prince were half-way down the long corridor.

When they reached the angle in it Angela, still sobbing, paused, laid her hand on Colonel Roux's arm, and faltered: '*Monsieur le Colonel*, can you ... can you tell me when they mean to take him away from here?'

'Yes, Madame,' he replied without hesitation. 'Tomorrow. It was for that reason I arranged with Father Pierre for you to see him tonight. It was the last chance.'

Persevering in her bid to obtain information which would be useful in an attempt to rescue the man she loved, she went on: 'And where is he to be taken?'

The old Colonel shook his head. 'That I cannot tell you, Madame. But from the way the prisoner is being treated I think it unlikely that he will be released as long as France is a Republic, and wherever he is sent you may be sure that every possible precaution will be taken against his escaping; so I think you would be wise to endeavour to reconcile yourself to an indefinite separation.'

The advice was meant kindly, but had he struck Angela the physical blow would have been less brutal; for she could not ignore the soundness of his view of the prisoner's prospects. Leaning heavily upon the disguised de Vendôme, she stumbled out into the courtyard, half crazy with grief at the thought that she might never see Armand de Quesnoy again.

CHAPTER XVIII

NIGHTMARE JOURNEY

WHEN de Quesnoy had told Angela and de Vendôme that an opportunity to escape was certain to arise while he was being transferred to a fortress, he had done so only to hearten them. The extraordinary precautions being taken in the *Cherche-Midi* were indication enough that when he was moved he would probably be manacled and certainly never for a moment let out of the sight of armed guards.

Naturally he intended to watch like a hawk every move by his jailers and if a chance did come he was not the man to hesitate to take it; but, apart from some entirely unforeseen happening, his hopes lay in a relaxation of surveillance after he had been for some time in the place selected for his permanent captivity.

Its governor might be a humane man who would allow him some degree of liberty; one of his gaolers might be open to bribery; or, if he was not too closely watched, he might succeed in tunnelling his way out, as had Monte Cristo. Besides, Laveriac would be able to find out where he had been taken, and he felt confident that the Royalist Committee would do their utmost to effect his rescue, even had Angela not been certain to urge them to it.

With outside help and no lack of money for bribes, it seemed to him that, given time to plan and work in, a determined man must be able to escape from the deepest dungeon. But time was the all-important factor. And how much time would he be given?

Through treachery or ill chance it might get out within the next few days that de Vendôme was hiding in the Spanish Embassy. In any case rumours that he was free were bound to get about within a month or two, and if de Quesnoy was not also a free man by the time the French Government began to take these rumours seriously an investigation would soon afterwards result in his being sent to the scaffold.

217

So much for his future chances; but he had first to face a more immediate danger—namely the possibility of Colonel Roux's discovering that de Vendôme's place had been taken by someone else. As his voice might give him away he had decided to pretend to have been overcome by a profound melancholy and refrain from answering when spoken to, for some days at least. But there remained the risk that the Colonel might unlock the helmet in the morning for him to wash, and if he could not think of some way to avoid taking it off in Roux's presence the game would be up.

All this he had known when entering the cell and, as there was nothing he could do to avoid these hazards to his life, which was the price he had elected to pay rather than have de Vendôme's sufferings on his conscience, he was not even thinking about them. Instead, he let his mind savour in retrospect again and again those last passionate moments with Angela and the complete abandon with which she had avowed her love for him.

Still thinking of her, he mechanically undressed, pulled down the chain of the gas mantle and got into bed. The hard surface of the leather helmet, between the side of his face and the pillow, proved so uncomfortable that for some moments he gave way to a fit of rage, consigning to eternal damnation whoever it was that had thought of this cruel way of concealing de Vendôme's identity; then, realizing that the sooner he accustomed himself to the discomforts imposed by the mask the better it would be for his peace of mind, he turned over on his back. Even so, it was a long time before he fell into a fitful sleep, and then he twice woke from it sweating and gasping after nightmares, in the first of which he was being suffocated and in the second strangled.

The barred window high up in the cell wall had become only grey with the first pre-dawn light when he was aroused to full consciousness by the door being unlocked. Colonel Roux came in, lit the gas and said to him:

'I regret to arouse you so early, Monsieur, but you are to leave here today; and my orders are to have you out of the prison before the cleaning squads and day-staff are about. Please get up and dress. If you will give me your word not to make trouble about putting your mask on again I will unlock it for you.'

De Quesnoy sat up in bed, but followed his plan for continuing to deceive the Colonel by neither raising his eyes nor making any reply. Roux then repeated what he had said, upon which the Count only lowered his head mulishly and still made no answer.

'What has come over you?' the Colonel asked. 'You made no fuss about giving me your promise last night, when Madame Syveton came to see you. Why won't you do so now?'

With what the Colonel took for stubbornness, the Count remained dumb and unmoving. So, after a moment, Roux said with some asperity, 'Very well then! I've no more time to waste. You will have to go without a shave. If you make any trouble about dressing yourself I shall send my men in to dress you forcibly. Get up now.'

Still keeping his eyes lowered, in order to avoid the Colonel's direct glance, and with apparent reluctance, de Quesnoy got out of bed. His silence had unexpectedly relieved him of his worst anxiety, as to leave his face unwashed and unshaven was a small price to pay for not having to risk Roux's coming back into the cell while he still had the mask off. He was further cheered by the news that he was to be moved at once, for that meant that he would the sooner be subject to a settled routine, which was the necessary preliminary to planning a successful attempt to escape.

Concealing his satisfaction with a sullen shrug, he slouched over to the washstand and began to do his teeth with de Vendôme's brush. Then he washed as much of his neck as he could get at under the edge of the leather helmet, dried himself and proceeded to dress.

Roux had, meanwhile, left him but returned a few minutes later with the redheaded warder, who was carrying a breakfast tray. As the man set it down on the table the Colonel said:

'I can give you only ten minutes; so you had best make the most of them.'

A glance at the tray showed the Count that either the Government had issued an order that de Vendôme was to enjoy the full amenities of a Prisoner of State, or that Roux was treating him with special consideration, for the tray had evidently come from the Colonel's own kitchen. On it there were rolls, properly made pats of butter, honey, a dish of fruit and a pot of coffee the aroma from which guaranteed its excellence.

Neither danger nor anxiety had ever robbed de Quesnoy of his appetite, and he found no difficulty in eating with the mask on; but

219

when he raised his cup the lower edge of the mouth slit prevented his bringing it to his lips. Roux, who was standing nearby, picked up from the tray an implement that the Count had not noticed and, handing it to him, said: 'You seem very stupid this morning. Surely you have not forgotten that to drink you must use this.' It was a hollow glass tube about eight inches long, and through it de Quesnoy sucked up his coffee with considerable enjoyment.

This good breakfast was the last pleasant surprise that was to come his way for a considerable time, but there were plenty of disagreeable ones awaiting him. While he had been eating, the older warder had packed into a small valise a few underclothes and other personal belongings of de Vendôme's that had evidently been brought for him from St. Cyr. The other, meanwhile, had come into the cell carrying a pair of handcuffs and a sack.

De Quesnoy got up from the table and put on de Vendôme's greatcoat. As soon as he had done so he was handcuffed and the sack was put over his head. Grimly he realized the reason for the latter precaution. Had he been de Vendôme he might, once outside the prison, have shouted to passers-by that he was being martyred. The sack would prevent his knowing when there was anyone nearby to shout to and, if he shouted at random, muffle his cries; moreover, no stories of a prisoner whose head was encased in an inhuman leather helmet would get about, because the helmet was completely hidden under the sack.

Taking him by the arms the two warders led him from the cell, down the corridor and out through the front hall of the prison. For a few paces he could feel the cobbles of the courtyard beneath his feet, then he was half pulled, half pushed up a steep ramp. At its top he tripped over what seemed to be a wooden step but was saved from falling by his escorts, turned about and lowered into a sitting position on what he rightly guessed to be a narrow bed. Next there came a clanking of chain and a broad leather belt was fastened round his waist. His handcuffs were removed and the sack taken from over his head.

He saw at once that he was in another cell, but this one was smaller, had wooden walls and no window. It was about six feet high and seven feet square. Apart from the bed on which he was sitting, it was furnished only with a washstand, slop pail and a low wooden cupboard, the top of which could be used as a table.

As he sat on the bed he was facing the door. It was open but almost entirely blocked by the forms of the two warders as they went out and then that of the Colonel as he came in; yet before the latter closed the door behind him de Quesnoy caught a glimpse of the prison entrance. It gave him the impression that the cell was some feet from the ground and in the middle of the courtyard; but Roux proceeded to explain this strange phenomenon.

With a dour smile he said, 'This cell was specially made for you to travel in. Actually it is a large wooden box, and at the moment it is resting on a dray. The driver of the dray was sent away with his horses while we got you in here, but presently he will return and drive his load to the goods yard. There a crane will lift the cell on to a railway truck, and in this way you will be conveyed to your destination without our having constantly to guard against your communicating with people, or anyone's curiosity being aroused by the sight of a prisoner in a mask.'

As de Quesnoy cherished few hopes of being able to make his escape until he had been settled for a while in permanent quarters, this information was no great blow to him; but next moment he nearly gave himself away in his eagerness to find out where he was being sent. Fortunately, just as he was about to break silence and ask, the Colonel went on:

'The two warders and I are accompanying you, but naturally we shall travel in a railway coach, and it is not desirable that during the journey anyone should realize that this is a cell with a man in it. From outside it has the appearance of a large crate and in order to maintain that impression we shall not open its door again until we get to the other end. That will not be until some time tomorrow; so until then you will have to look after yourself.'

Opening the cupboard, the Colonel revealed that it contained bread, butter, cheese, some packets of cold meat, fruit, and two bottles each of red wine and mineral water, together with the things necessary for their consumption. Then he stepped back through the doorway, shut the door and locked it; upon which the cell, lit only by a dozen small airholes bored in its roof, became plunged in semi-darkness.

At the news that he was to be left on his own for twenty-four hours, and that meanwhile the cell would remain unguarded outside, de Quesnoy's spirits went up with a bound. They rose even higher when he saw that among the things in the cupboard there were two knives, a fork and a corkscrew. The possession of such implements and a day

221

and a night in which to work undisturbed seemed after all to offer a real chance of getting away during the journey.

Coming to his feet, he took a swift pace forward with the intention of examining the lock of the door. There was a clank of chain and he was brought up with a jerk while still three feet from it. He had not yet had a moment to examine the wide leather belt that had been fastened round his waist. Now, his fumbling fingers found that it was secured in the small of his back by a stout clasp from which ran a three-foot length of steel chain; then, turning, he saw that the end of the chain was padlocked to an iron staple bolted into the wall just above the level of the bed. Evidently the object of this contrivance was to prevent him from springing upon and overcoming anyone who entered the cell, then making a dash for freedom through the still open door. But, unless he could get free from it, the lock of the door remained just out of reach, which made it impossible for him to attempt to work back its tongue or pick it.

His first thought was to cut through the belt, but he soon saw that any attempt to hack through the leather with a table knife must prove hopeless because it was laced with strands of wire. He then tried to snap the chain by throwing his whole weight upon it, but he succeeded only in winding himself and the violent jerking did not even loosen the staple. As a forlorn hope he picked up the corkscrew and bored with it into the wall to get some idea of the thickness of the wood, on the chance that it might be thin enough for him to cut the staple and bolts out, but it proved to be inch thick planking, and he realized that with the meagre implements at his disposal the job would have taken him a week's hard work.

With bitter disappointment he had to accept the fact that the belt and chain not only prevented him from reaching the door but, even if he could have got it open, would still have held him prisoner.

For a while he sat on the bed, then he lay down upon it; but only to encounter a fresh discomfort. He had already discovered that if he lay on his side the hard leather of the mask hurt his cheek, and now it was impossible for him to lie on his back because one end of the chain and the big steel belt clasp came immediately beneath his spine. Vowing vengeance against Combes, André and their unscrupulous associates, he shifted about until he found a position which was just bearable, then, exerting his trained will power, he forced himself to sleep.

222

He was awakened by the cell receiving a sudden jolt. Then, as soon as memory flooded back to him, he realized that the dray on which it had been loaded was now slowly moving over the cobbles. How long he had slept he had no means of telling, but he had the feeling that it had been for quite a long time. However, daylight was still coming through the holes in the roof and since twilight fell so early at this nadir of the year he knew that it could not be much more than three o'clock in the afternoon.

For over an hour the dray rumbled its way through streets that he could not see or even guess at; then it halted. There came a jingle of harness as the big draught horses were taken from its shafts and after that, for a long time, silence.

Gradually the light faded, and as it did so he became increasingly conscious of a new distress. The cell had no form of heating, and when he had woken he had felt the cold. Now, it seemed to be seeping into his very bones. From time to time he stood up, stamped his feet and flailed his arms across his chest, but that brought him only temporary relief.

As a further measure for keeping some warmth in his body he opened one of the bottles of red wine and drank half its contents through a glass tube which had been provided. While he was supping it up he suddenly remembered that this was Christmas Day. Millions and millions of people in a hundred countries were now either sleeping off their Christmas lunch or preparing to enjoy their Christmas dinner; and here was he, locked up in a wooden box like a dangerous animal, shivering with cold and with his head encased in a grotesque mask as though he were one of the victims of the Inquisition in the Middle Ages. The cynical thought came to him that at least he could drink a toast, and he did: "To Combes and André side by side, roasting in Hell for ever."

It was shortly after that he heard faint sounds which might have been voices; then someone clambered on to the roof of the cell. From the occasional chugging and hissing of passing engines, he had already concluded that the dray must be parked in one of the Paris marshalling yards; so now he had half a mind to beat on the sides of the cell and call on the railway workers for help.

On second thoughts he realized the futility of such an act. Even if the men were willing they could not release him, and it was certain that

223

Colonel Roux would be somewhere in the vicinity. He would no doubt admit that there was a man in the box but account for this unusual way of transporting a prisoner by saying that he was a violent maniac. To have had to make an explanation at all about this most secret affair would be sure to annoy him, and it was even possible that to prevent a similar happening farther down the line he might resort to gagging his prisoner.

There came a faint shout. The cell was lifted by a crane and swung smoothly through a quarter of a circle. For a moment it hung swaying slightly, then it was suddenly lowered and came to rest with a heavy bump. The slop pail rattled and the water splashed out of the big enamel jug that stood in the tin wash basin, but nothing else in the cell responded to the jolt, and it was only then that de Quesnoy noticed that the rest of its modest furnishings were screwed to the floor.

Silence fell again. The cold seemed to grow more intense. No matches, candle or torch had been provided for the prisoner, so it was only by groping in the dark that he managed to make a scratch meal. Between mouthfuls he drank the rest of the bottle of wine, then crawled under the blankets of the bed fully dressed and tried to get to sleep.

An hour, two hours, perhaps four hours, later—for all he knew—the train jolted into motion and, after several false starts, chugged away into the night. At times it gathered quite a speed, then suddenly braked and slowed with a clanging of buffers; at other times it meandered on, then halted altogether for periods of up to twenty minutes. In Madagascar de Quesnoy had learned how to fall asleep almost at once simply by willing himself to do so, but to exercise such command over the mind at least a reasonable degree of quiet and physical relaxation were necessary; now to obtain either was impossible.

The result was that he slept only by fits and starts and between cold and acute discomfort spent the most miserable night of his life. A dozen times during it he vowed that, should he ever be a free man again, he would dedicate himself to the task of bringing about the fall of the Combes government and the public disgrace of General André.

At last a faint daylight began to percolate through the holes in the roof. Getting up, he washed as well as he could, spent some time in exercising to get his circulation going, then ate another scratch meal.

Soon after he had finished, a new trial beset him. It had begun to rain, and water now dripped from all the air-holes on to either the bed or the floor. Kneeling on the bed, he used the paper that the meat and cheese had been wrapped in to plug those over it, but there was not enough to do the others; so for the rest of the morning he sat in a chilly twilight while the drip, drip, drip on to the now sodden floor further added to his depression.

At what he guessed to be about mid-day the train rolled to a halt, remained stationary for a while, then went backwards several hundred yards. Suddenly the twilight in the cell became almost complete darkness, as had been the case for several minutes twice that morning when the train was passing through tunnels; but now it stopped again, and after half-an-hour had elapsed without its moving on, the Count decided that it had probably reached its destination.

An hour or so later his surmises were confirmed. The door was unlocked by Colonel Roux. Behind him were the two warders and over their shoulders de Quesnoy could see portions of a soot-grimed roof and girders, which told him that the truck carrying the cell had been shunted into a railway shed.

'Well!' said the Colonel. 'I hope you didn't find the journey too uncomfortable?'

De Quesnoy would have liked to reply that it had been hellish, and to pour vitriolic curses on both the people who had given Roux his orders and on him for accepting them; but he did not dare. It could not be much over forty hours since the Colonel had talked with the real de Vendôme, so his memory of the Prince's voice must still be too fresh for the false one to risk speaking to him. Instead of replying he again bent his head and stared at his feet.

'Still sulking, eh?' Roux commented with a shrug. 'It won't do you any good, my poor friend. You'd much better be sensible and give me your promise to make no trouble about putting your mask on again; then I will unlock it and you can have a proper wash.'

Receiving no response from his prisoner, he stepped back out of the cell and sent the two warders into it. One of them carried a basket, from which he renewed the supply of food and drink in the cupboard; the other emptied the basin and the slop pail, put disinfectant in the latter, and filled the big enamel jug with fresh water. When they had done, Roux came in again and said:

'I have just been told that we shall be here for two days or more;

225

so if there is anything you want now is the time to ask, and if my instructions permit I will get it for you.'

De Quesnoy made a pretence of shivering and, pulling the top blanket from the bed, held it up.

'I see,' said the Colonel. 'So you are feeling the cold. Well, that is not surprising. But why the devil can't you say so? All right, I'll do what I can to make things better for you.'

When Roux had gone the Count had another meal, and while he ate it he pondered the problem raised by the Colonel's statement that they would remain where they were for at least two days. Whatever fortress he was being taken to, there seemed no reason why two days should elapse in the middle of the journey before the truck carrying the cell could be hitched on to another train going in the right direction. His speculations failed to produce the solution to this mystery, but a few hours later he was given it, and it plunged him in near despair.

Late in the afternoon Roux and the warders returned. With them they brought an oil-stove and an oil lamp. When these had been installed the Colonel produced three paper-backed novels from his greatcoat pockets and said: 'These may help to occupy your mind until we can get you aboard the ship.'

At the last word the Count almost blurted out an exclamation of dismay. He managed to suppress it but could feel his pulses racing from shock, and fury at his impotence to parry this new blow, as Roux went on:

'I had expected the cruiser to be waiting to put to sea when we got here, but she was not; and her captain is most averse to having you put aboard until he is ready to sail. She will be coaling all day tomorrow, but from the latest information I have received we may be able to get you on to her the following evening.'

Left alone once more, de Quesnoy succumbed to a bout of acute dejection. He had expected to be taken to one of the old fortresses in which for many generations political prisoners had been confined Nearly all the jailers and staffs of such places were drawn from the local inhabitants, so it would have been easy for his friends to get in touch with and attempt to bribe some of them. And if, with or without outside help, he managed to escape he would still have been in France, with a very good chance of disappearing among the population.

Whereas now it was clear that he was to be sent to one or other of

France's penal colonies—French Guiana, on the northern coast of South America, or on Numea, an island in the Pacific. Both were so far from France that there could be no question of his friends helping him to escape; and if on his own he did succeed in getting away from the convict settlement, he would be in either a white man among natives, so specially liable to recognition and recapture. Still worse, before he could really count himself free he would have to face the desperate hazards of a month-long journey through primitive jungle or in a small boat across shark-infested seas.

His one rag of consolation was that in such places there were only small fortresses and these were not normally used as prisons, so that should make an initial escape easier; but against the dark background it was so small a ray that he spent the evening in abysmal gloom, and could not even bring himself to look at the novels that Roux had brought him.

The delay imposed by the cruiser's coaling aggravated him still further. As Roux knew the prisoner who had been brought to the *Cherche-Midi* with a sack over his head to be the Duc de Vendôme, and the two warders were also in the secret to the extent of knowing that a leather mask had been forced upon this special prisoner to conceal his identity, it had been sound policy on General André's part to avoid disclosing his inhuman treatment of the prisoner to others by ordering Roux, despite his rank, and his two men to act as escort to the port. Yet, once arrived, de Quesnoy could reasonably have hoped to be handed over at once to another officer, who was not in the secret. Even were he made privy to it, the odds were all against his ever having met de Vendôme; so, once Roux was out of the way, the Count could have spoken to his new jailers with no risk and allowed his mask to be removed with very little, but as long as Roux remained in charge of him he dared do neither.

The following day, and the next, dragged by with interminable slowness. On both, his escorts paid him visits morning and evening to clear his slops and replenish his larder. Then, on the evening of December 28th, they came again late at night. Roux told him that the cell was shortly to be loaded on to a tender, then the men removed the oil-stove, the oil lamp, the water jug and the slop-pail, as a precaution against any of them being tipped over during the move.

For the prisoner, the hour and a half that followed were extremely

227

unpleasant. The cell was first shunted about, then swayed wildly as it was transferred by a crane from the railway truck to the tender. For a while the deck heaved gently under it, then the tender cast off and no sooner was she clear of the harbour than she was bucking like a bronco. Actually it was not particularly rough but the little vessel was moving diagonally across the waves and de Quesnoy, imagining that a storm was raging, became considerably alarmed.

The transfer of bulky freight by derrick from one vessel to another in rough weather is a tricky business, and should a mishap occur in this case he saw himself being drowned like a rat in a trap. During the final stages, as the cell hung and spun in mid-air, his anxiety was acute, but it landed safely on the cruiser's deck and was soon after made fast.

During the past two days he had almost been counting the hours until, his journey over, he would be relieved of the discomfort of his belt and chain and transferred from his travelling cell to more spacious quarters. Cruisers, he knew, always kept a good cabin available to accommodate high government officials on special missions, so there seemed a reasonable hope that the one in this ship would be used as a cell for him during the voyage. There was always the unpleasant possibility that they would put him in the lazaret, but as he was a Prisoner of State he thought that very unlikely.

How he was treated during the next few weeks would, he assumed, depend upon the ship's Captain; and once the cell had settled on the cruiser's deck he began to wait impatiently for Colonel Roux to hand him over. It was not that he had any reason to complain of Roux, for the Colonel had behaved throughout with all the consideration that his orders permitted; but the Count was eager to see the last of him, so that he could speak again and—after making certain that the Captain had never met de Vendôme—have his mask removed so that he could wash properly at least once a day.

In all these hopes he was doomed to grievous disappointment. Ten minutes after the cell had been put on board its door was unlocked. There stood Colonel Roux and behind him the two warders; but they were not accompanied by a Naval officer. During the transfer from shore to ship a plate, a cup and a bottle of wine had been smashed. The men cleared up the mess, replaced the oil-stove and other things, then withdrew; after which the Colonel addressed his prisoner.

'I see no reason why I should not tell you now, Monsieur, that you are being taken to Guiana. The night you were brought to the *Cherche-Midi* was an unlucky one for me, as the knowledge of who you are was forced upon me and the government are determined to restrict that secret to as few people as possible. In consequence, I was ordered to convey you to your destination, and to use as escorts the two warders who have acted as your guards from the beginning; so that no story of a prisoner in a mask should get about Paris after you had left, or become known among the crew of the ship through having to employ marines to wait upon you during the voyage.

'On my return to France I am to be promoted to General of Brigade and appointed Inspector of Military Prisons; but I can assure you that I would rather have retired as a Colonel than perform this most unsoldierly duty. However, General André made it quite plain that, should I refuse the proffered bribe, the alternative was that he would find an excuse to break me and see to it that I was deprived of my pension. I can only hope that you will not think too badly of me for carrying out orders which disgrace those who gave them, rather than face poverty in my old age.

'At all events, by allowing Madame Syveton to take leave of you I have already shown my goodwill, and I am anxious to do what I can to make the voyage endurable for you. This travelling cell will have to remain your quarters, as only by keeping you in it can I be certain of preventing you from communicating with members of the crew. But I hope that you will be sensible and give up the sulky silence that you have maintained since we left Paris, as we could then discuss the possibility of allowing you to take some exercise, and at times giving you relief from the misery that wearing that leather helmet must cause you. Please consider this matter seriously, and for your own sake be prepared to talk to me when I come to you again tomorrow morning.'

In spite of the Colonel's friendly intentions, the things he had just said had the effect on de Quesnoy of a series of sickening body blows. His mind reeled under the impact as he grasped how completely they shattered his best expectations. In half-a-dozen sentences his optimistic day-dreams of a comfortable cabin, of being transferred to the charge of a Naval officer with whom he could talk without risk, and a good chance of being able to be rid of his mask for a while each morning, had been dissipated. For a fortnight or more he must remain chained like a wild beast in the narrow cell. For the last week of the voyage they would be running down through the tropics, so the heat up there on deck would become almost unbearable. Since the Colonel's orders were to keep him segregated, as though he were a leper, it was clear that he would not be allowed to go below to have a bath, and for his own safety he must deny himself even a proper wash or shave.

The fact that Roux—the one man who, on seeing his face, would know for certain that he was not de Vendôme, so feel compelled to take him back to France for trial and execution—should be accompanying him to his destination was the bitterest pill of all. That condemned him also to continued silence; yet only by talking could he hope to secure some amelioration of his unhappy lot.

The Colonel had hardly left him before the screws of the cruiser began to turn. To the accompaniment of their dull throbbing, and a slight rolling of the ship, he strove to think of some way in which he might minimize the acute miseries that lay ahead of him without giving away that he had tricked Roux by taking de Vendôme's place. For an hour or more he racked his brains in vain; they were dull and unresponsive. Then there recurred to him a means of obtaining guidance which can be explained only in terms of the supernatural, yet is widely practised by many down-to-earth people—namely that if one goes to sleep thinking of a problem one often wakes up with the answer to it.

Settling himself as comfortably as he could he concentrated his thoughts upon his predicament until he dropped off to sleep and, sure enough, on waking in a chilly dawn he had received good counsel. When Roux came to him some hours later, he still ignored his greeting; but used an index finger on the cupboard top to convey the idea of writing.

The Colonel sent one of his men for paper and pencil, and when they were brought de Quesnoy wrote:

I have committed no crime, so the punishment that I am receiving from men must be the will of God. Since it is His wish that I should suffer, I desire to acquire merit with Him by accepting even greater suffering than your superiors intend that you should impose upon me. I have therefore taken a vow that I will neither speak nor allow myself to be relieved of my mask until God is pleased to show His satisfaction with me by bringing about my release from captivity.

The Count had an uneasy feeling that he was taking the Creator's name in vain; but it was just the sort of line that de Vendôme, with his deep religious sense, might have taken, and Roux accepted it without question.

Looking up from the writing, he said, 'Monsieur, had you asked for paper and informed me sooner of this vow you have taken I would never have pressed you to speak; and you may rest assured that I shall do nothing which might tempt you to break it. Now I know the reason for your silence I will put to you the proposition that I had in mind.

'As you can see, through the doorway behind me, your cell has been lashed down on the stern deck of the ship. If an awning is rigged above this little semi-circle of deck, that would prevent its being over-looked from amidships, and by the erection of a few canvas screens it could be shut off from the rest of the deck. If I arrange for these measures to be taken, so that you can be let out twice a day to enjoy air and exercise, are you prepared to give me your word that you will neither seek to break away into the main part of the ship, so that the crew would see you, or, should we pass another ship, jump overboard in an attempt to escape to her?'

Taking the paper back, de Quesnoy wrote on it, *Yes. I give you my parole on both counts for the duration of the voyage; and I am deeply grateful to you for the consideration you are showing me.*

Roux nodded and gave his rather frosty smile. 'That is settled then. I only wish that for the nights, at least, I could relieve you of your helmet—as had been my intention. But the vow you have taken now precludes that.'

The Count nodded in reply. His fury of frustration at being unable to accept the Colonel's humane suggestion was almost unbearable, but he dared not do so.

That day he had to remain confined in his cell, for the cruiser had put out from La Rochelle, and as she ploughed south-westward across the Bay of Biscay the weather was too rough for the sailors to be able to rig up the screens on the stern deck; but on the second afternoon out they managed to do so, and that evening de Quesnoy, watched by Roux and one of the warders, but hidden from all other eyes, was able to stretch his legs for an hour.

Soon winter was left behind and from the New Year's Day of 1904 the ship ran smoothly through calm sparkling seas under nearly cloudless

231

skies. Given normal circumstances, congenial companionship, and freedom from worry, few things could have been more pleasant than to be a passenger aboard her; but the Count's circumstances were far from normal, his only companions three men to whom he was debarred from speaking and he was intensely worried.

During the few hours that he had been in the *Cherche-Midi* his prospects of making his escape within the next few weeks had seemed to him reasonably good, but, being a realist, he could not now help regarding them with much less optimism.

Since it was of such importance to the government to keep the identity of their prisoner secret, he felt certain that on arriving in Guiana he would not be sent to one of the penal settlements, but would be confined in the small fort at its capital, Cayenne. To break out of it should prove no more difficult than to escape from a fortress in France, although without aid that would have proved a formidable enough task. But other considerations made his chances in Guiana less good. Apart from the difficulties of escaping from the colony after having escaped from the fort, there loomed the horrible possibility that before he had had time even to plan an escape he might go down with fever.

He knew that the whole coast was infested with myriads of malaria-carrying mosquitoes and that few white men who went there got off without a severe bout of yellow fever, while a high proportion of them died from it. Confined in some dungeon or little-frequented tower, with almost certainly indifferent medical attention, his chances of survival would be poor.

The grim thought occurred to him that General André might well have chosen Guiana as the place of imprisonment for de Vendôme in the hope that the Prince would succumb to "Yellow Jack", and the government thus be rid of him once and for all. In any case, if he did catch the fever it would weaken him to the extent of putting any prospect of escape out of the question for some time to come. Meanwhile, at any time the news might reach Cayenne that de Vendôme was free; so a delay of even a few weeks caused by sickness might well cost him his life.

In addition to his dark forebodings about the future, he had to contend with his miseries of the present. For twenty hours out of every twenty-four he was cooped up in his box and the nearer the ship drew to the equator the more stuffy and breathless it became. In spite of his having given his parole, Colonel Roux would not allow him out except when he meant to remain on deck himself, and when the heat became tropical that was only in the mornings and evenings; so during the long torrid middle of the day his prisoner was condemned to sweat and stifle.

There was, too, the torture he endured from the mask. He had expected that with time he would become so accustomed to wearing it that it would cause him comparatively little inconvenience, but that proved far from the case. Considering it of the utmost importance to keep all his muscles in good shape against the time when he might attempt an escape, to begin with he spent long periods every day performing a variety of exercises, but as the temperature increased so did his sweating, with the maddening result that the tough leather edges of the helmet chafed sore places round his neck. Reluctantly he gave up doing most of the exercises, but in spite of that the sores refused to heal, and the dried sweat which he could not wash away from his scalp or the stubble of a growing beard drove him nearly mad with irritation.

It is possible that he would actually have lost his reason had it not been for the years he had spent in Madagascar. The supernormal powers he had acquired there, through endless hours spent patiently developing the techniques of the mind, now stood him in good stead. By concentrating his will he could make his spirit leave his body, which gave complete relief to both for several hours at a stretch. But the effort needed to perform this feat was considerable and sometimes he became exhausted before he could accomplish it. Nevertheless, these self-induced trances served to repair the mental and physical ravages he sustained far better than half-conscious, tortured sleep could have done; and as "hope springs eternal in the human breast" he managed to cling to the belief that patience, wit and courage would somehow enable him to escape from Cayenne.

At a little before seven o'clock in the evening of January 10th after a day of blistering heat, the cruiser suddenly dropped to half-speed, then slowed still further; an order was shouted from the bridge and her anchor was let go.

De Quesnoy was exercising in the presence of Colonel Roux and one attendant warder. Screened off as they were on the small semi-circular after-deck of the cruiser they could see only the open ocean that lay astern. But, after a few moments, the ship began to swing

233

with the tide. The Count stepped quickly to the rail expecting to catch his first glimpse of the South American coast and the little port of Cayenne.

Slowly a low coastline came into view, but it was a dozen miles away. Then, only a few hundred yards distant, there appeared a jagged spit of rocks upon which the waves were breaking in white foam. Another minute disclosed the spit to be the easternmost tip of a barren, sun-scorched island a bare four hundred yards wide by two miles long.

A good part of its flat surface was enclosed by a double palisade eight feet in height, the inner one having in its centre a single-storeyed stone building no larger than a cottage. The island had no harbour, but a short channel wide enough to take a good-sized boat had been cut through the reef to a flat slab of rock, upon which an officer and two men in warders' uniforms were standing.

As de Quesnoy stared through the eye-slits in his mask at the desolate scene, an icy hand seemed to grip his heart. Roux had come up beside him and, as in some awful dream, he heard the Colonel say:

'I had not the heart to tell you before, but it is here that you are to be permanently imprisoned. As you may have guessed, it is Devil's Island.'

The Count had guessed. The last hopes with which he had buoyed himself up during the past terrible days and nights were now gone. This was no fort with people going to and from it and outside its walls a town or jungle into which an escaped prisoner might hope to disappear. With awful certainty he knew that, once in that stone hut encircled by its palisades and surrounded by the ocean, short of a miracle, he must die there; for from such a place there could be no escape.

CHAPTER XIX

A TERRIBLE ORDEAL

THE night of de Quesnoy's transference from Paris to La Rochelle had been looked on by him as the most miserable he had ever spent, yet that following the arrival of the cruiser off Devil's Island brought him to even greater depths of misery. Before, he had spent the hours speculating unhappily on what the future might hold for him; now he knew the full horror of the fate to which he had been condemned.

In such circumstances the unruffled calm and concentration needed either to will himself to sleep or deliberately to project his spirit from his body were beyond his mental compass. Try as he would, he could neither keep still for any length of time nor succeed in completely emptying his mind. The itching of his scalp was so persistent that every now and then he was positively tortured into rubbing it against the inside of the helmet, and each time he endeavoured to check the working of his brain some thought of Devil's Island came to stir it into fresh activity.

He had had only a brief sight of the island, as Colonel Roux had declared his intention of going ashore at once to make arrangements for his prisoner's reception early the following morning. But before the Colonel had re-locked him into his cell he had seen two more islands in the distance on the other side of the ship.

The group was, he knew, called the Isles de Salut and they were about thirty miles from Cayenne. The largest was used as the penal settlement to which France's most dangerous convicts were sent, either to die of fever or to struggle with the barren soil for a miserable existence. The next in size had on it a primitive asylum, to which were sent criminal lunatics, and prisoners from the larger island who were driven mad by privation and despair. Devil's Island was much the smallest of the three and had been used until February 1895 for the internment of a handful of lepers, when it had been hurriedly evacuated to accommodate a single Prisoner of State—Alfred Dreyfus.

235

That most ill-fated of men had occupied a room in the little stone hut on it for four and a half years. For the first eighteen months of that time, while exercising each day, he had at least had the small consolation of being able to look at the other islands and watch the passing of an occasional ship, but in September '96 his captivity had been made still more rigorous.

His brother Mathieu, wishing to re-arouse interest in his case, had caused a rumour that he had escaped to appear in the British Press. André Lebon, the Minister for the Colonies at that date, although assured by cable that there was not the least possibility of Dreyfus's escaping, had sent an inhuman order to the Governor of the islands to build a double palisade round the hut, and that until it was completed the prisoner was to be shackled to his bed each night. So for six weeks the wretched man had lain in chains, and for his remaining three years on the island had been debarred from even gazing out to sea.

Later, accounts had been published of his sufferings. As the island was only five degrees north of the equator it had no seasons and the heat there was intense. Month in, month out, the sun blazed down from a brassy sky, making the little stone prison as hot as a furnace. Dreyfus's warders had been under orders not to speak to him. During the weeks he had been chained up, his manacles had rubbed raw places on his wrists and ankles. Each night the light in his cell had drawn myriads of insects to feast upon him and nearly drive him mad. A prison officer named Daniel, who was notorious as a sadist, had been sent specially from France to act as chief jailer. He had found the prisoner prostrate from heat and racked with fever, but had shown him no mercy.

As de Quesnoy recalled reading of these things he groaned aloud. His warders were not allowed to speak to him; he was chained in his cell; his flesh had been rubbed raw by one of the restraints put upon him, and he had no reason whatever to hope that the present French Government would treat him in other ways any better than its predecessor had Dreyfus. It even occurred to him that as it was only a little over four years since Dreyfus had been sent back to France, the officer whom he had seen on the landing place of the island might quite well be the infamous Daniel. In any case, the presence of an officer and two warders on the island at all showed that a cable must have been sent from Paris ahead of the cruiser to the Governor of the penal settlement, ordering him to prepare Devil's Island for a new Prisoner of State and, no doubt, giving special instructions about guarding him.

The thought of such a cable brought to the Count's mind the possibility that another might shortly be despatched reporting the discovery that someone had changed places with de Vendôme. It was now seventeen days since the exchange had been effected and every day that passed made it more probable that soon the secret must leak out. Now he felt that he would no longer care greatly if it did. A clean, quick death by a volley from a firing squad was to be preferred to a gradual destruction of body and mind by successive bouts of fever, dysentery, heat-stroke, hallucinations and derangement of the brain.

Yet his abnormally strict confinement had so far made no serious inroads on his quick wits or fine constitution, and when, at last, morning came it found him waiting almost with impatience to be taken to the island.

There he would, at all events, get a fresh deal. As soon as he had seen the last of Roux he would be free to speak again; and since none of the prison staff of the islands could know de Vendôme by sight, he could without risk accept the blessed relief of allowing his mask to be removed. Later he might even succeed in hypnotizing one of his warders and so compel the man to aid in his escape.

The insoluble problems of—How? In what? To where? What then? —pulled him up short, but, nevertheless, he refused to surrender absolutely to the depression which had almost overwhelmed him the previous evening, and when his breakfast was brought to him he ate it with his usual heartiness.

While he was eating, the two warders kept within a few feet of him but left the door of the cell open. Through it he saw that during the night another ship had arrived off the island. She was lying at anchor bow on to the stern of the cruiser and a good half mile away; so it was difficult to get a correct impression of her, but from the sharp angle of her bows, her white paint and squat yellow funnel de Quesnoy thought she might be a private yacht. It occurred to him that, in view of the importance the French Government obviously attached to him, she might perhaps have brought the Governor of Guiana out to satisfy himself that the prisoner was handed over in good shape.

When the Count had finished breakfast he was locked up again for an hour. Then Roux unlocked the cell and said to him, 'The cruiser has no boat large enough to take the cell without danger of it over-balancing; so we must leave it behind. That being so, I shall adopt the same measures for preventing you from attempting anything rash, or the curiosity of the crew's being aroused at the sight of your mask, as I did when we marched you out of the *Cherche-Midi*.'

As he spoke the red-headed warder was already undoing the padlock which secured the chain to the staple in the wall of the cell. A moment later its free end fell with a clank on to the floor. Stepping out of the cell, de Quesnoy tucked the end of it into his belt. The warder, picking up the valise that held de Vendôme's few belongings, followed. The older warder now appeared round the corner of the deck screen carrying a pair of handcuffs and a sack to put over the Count's head.

Roux gave a quick glance over his shoulder, then an exclamation of annoyance. Looking past him de Quesnoy saw that the ship that had arrived in the night had swung a little so that she now lay three-quarters on to the cruiser's stern, and at that angle his guess about her being a steam yacht was confirmed. At the same second his mind registered two other things—from her stern staff she was flying the Stars and Stripes, and a neat white gig, with four oarsmen and three men in her stern, had just put off from her.

'*Tonnerre!*' muttered the Colonel angrily. 'These accursed globe-trotters! Why must they choose this, of all days, to come and gape at Dreyfus's prison?' Turning back to de Quesnoy, he went on quickly, 'We cannot allow these people to get a close view of your being taken ashore; so we must postpone matters for a while, Be pleased Monsieur, to return to your cell.'

De Quesnoy's brain had been moving at the speed with which Marconi's invention of wireless telegraphy was soon to be transmitting messages all over the world. "Now that they had reached their destina-tion he was no longer bound by his parole. Could he break free of the Colonel and the warders? Surprise counted for much, so he might. The warders were both armed with pistols. Would the Colonel order his men to use them? Probably. Anyhow the chance that he would be shot down would have to be taken. But if he did get away could he possibly reach the yacht?

"No; there must be a boat alongside the cruiser already manned and waiting to take him to the island; it would overhaul him long before he could swim half-a-mile. The gig from the yacht was coming in this direction, though. Could he reach that? Perhaps. But what about sharks? That he might be attacked by them was another risk he would have to take. Say he did get through, what then?

"Would the men in the boat give him their protection? No, why should they? There could be no disguising from them the fact that he was an escaping prisoner. And, even if a generous pity inspired them with the wish to do so, how could they? As foreigners in French territorial waters they were subject to French law; and, unarmed as they were, how could they defy the cruiser and her crew?

"Yet the alternative was to be cast into hell upon earth—days and nights of unremitting torture from heat, insect bites and dysentery. And that could end only in one of two ways: either death from Yellow Jack or a cable about de Vendôme leading to a firing squad."

Desperation at these last swift thoughts swayed de Quesnoy into taking the wild gamble. To render Roux *hors de combat* would, he realized, contribute more than any other first move to his getting clear of the ship. Drawing back his clenched fist, he drove it with all his force into the Colonel's stomach.

They were standing facing one another only two feet apart, so the blow took full effect. Roux's melancholy pale blue eyes started from his head, his mouth gaped open; every breath of wind had been driven from his body. Without a sound he doubled up, then fell writhing on the deck.

Before his two men could recover from their surprise de Quesnoy had sprung over his body and was running for the stern rail. He covered no more than a couple of yards. As the Colonel had ordered him back into his cell the warder behind him had put down the valise and grasped the end of the chain preparatory to re-padlocking it to the staple. Now, seizing it with both hands, he threw all his weight on it and brought the Count up short.

The older warder had the sack in one hand and the handcuffs in the other. All he could do for the moment was to aim a blow with the latter at de Quesnoy's head. As the Count sprang past, the steel handcuffs caught him squarely on the back of the head and, had it been unprotected, might well have knocked him out. But the leather helmet saved him.

Brought up with a jerk, he swung left and returned the blow by a trick that he had learnt from an Apache back in '96, when he had been frequenting the low haunts of Montmartre. Instead of striking with his fist he stuck out his first and second fingers rigid and opened in the form of a V, then jabbed swiftly with them at the man's eyes. It was a risky stroke, as if the points of the fingers struck bone one or both of them might be broken; but if successful it was inevitably decisive. In this case it came off. As always happened, the man instinctively shut his eyes in time to save them, but they were severely bruised beneath the lids. Temporarily blinded, and in great pain, he dropped the things he was holding, gave a piercing cry, clapped his hands over his face and staggered away out of the fight for good.

Meanwhile the redheaded warder, still hanging on to the end of the chain with one hand, had drawn his revolver with the other. Raising it, he bellowed:

'Stand still! Put up your hands or I fire!'

As the Count swung about the chain wrapped itself half round his waist, bringing him within three feet of the man who held it. Although he was covered at point blank range, he was near enough to make a grab at the weapon. It was that or surrender. Simultaneously he shot out his left hand and kicked with his right foot. His thrust knocked the revolver aside just as it went off. The bullet hit the winch in the middle of the stern deck and ricocheted from it with a loud whine. His kick landed hard on the warder's left shin.

The man let out a yelp, lifted his injured leg, lurched, and dropped the end of the chain. Before he could recover and level his revolver to fire again de Quesnoy was upon him. Seizing his weapon arm by the wrist, he thrust it down, then brought his right fist in a smashing upper-cut to his jaw. The click made by the warder's teeth could have been heard twenty yards away. As his head came forward it rolled upon his shoulders. To make certain of him the Count repeated the dose. The revolver dropped from his nerveless hand, his knees gave and he slumped in an unconscious heap.

It was none too soon. The shot must have been heard forward of the screens as the Count caught the sound of shouting and running feet coming towards them. The Colonel too, although groaning and gasping, had recovered a little and was struggling to his feet. Springing at him, de Quesnoy gave him a violent push which sent him sprawling again, snatched up the revolver the warder had dropped and made his second dash for the rail.

As he reached it the Lieutenant of the Watch, followed by two *matelots*, came at the run round the end of the port side screen. For a moment they paused there, staring in astonishment at the scene of havoc on the deck and its evident cause—a figure made grotesquely inhuman from having a head the shape of an inverted bucket. But they had all heard that there was a mystery prisoner aboard, and guessed at once that this must be him.

Turning to face them, de Quesnoy levelled the revolver with a threatening gesture. They saw then that his strange headpiece was a mask, yet it seemed to make him more formidable. None of them was armed; so from fear of being shot down they pulled up a few yards from him.

He had injured the warders only because if he was to get away he had no option, and he did not mean to shoot at French sailors unless he was compelled to in order to keep his freedom. Having halted them, he threw a swift glance at the gig, then, to attract the attention of the men in her, he pointed the revolver upwards and, in rapid succession, fired three of its remaining bullets into the air.

As the shots crashed out the sailors made up their minds to rush him, but as they started forward he clambered up on to the rail. Balancing there for a second, he saw that the gig, which had been heading for the island, had suddenly altered course. She was now coming straight towards the cruiser, and could not be much more than a third of a mile away. The Lieutenant still had a pace to cover as de Quesnoy took a header into the sea.

He had never practised diving from any considerable height and was still clutching the revolver; so his awkward plunge might have resulted in his being temporarily knocked out. But the helmet protected his head from shock, and it served him well again in the next few moments for, although he went down as if he was never going to stop, the big bubble of air caught in it brought him to the surface more swiftly than he had expected.

When the water had poured from the slits in the mask, he gave a quick look round. Although the sea was fairly smooth, he could not see the gig; but he could see the yacht and the sight of her gave him roughly the gig's position. Exerting his muscles to the utmost, he struck out in a powerful sidestroke towards her.

The men in the stern of the gig had seen him dive overboard and were now urging their crew on in his direction. The cruiser's boat, a six-oared whaler, had been lying alongside her starboard beam; so her crew had so far seen neither de Quesnoy nor the gig. In consequence, although the sailors in the whaler had heard the shots, and were looking upward expectantly, they had no idea what had happened until the Lieutenant rushed to the rail above them shouting that the mystery prisoner had escaped and was swimming towards the yacht.

A Sub-Lieutenant who was in command of the whaler immediately ordered his boat away, but the delay in starting the pursuit gained for the Count several precious minutes. Before the whaler appeared round the stern of the cruiser he had swum a hundred and fifty yards and the gig had covered considerably more than that distance towards him.

There was still a gap of some two hundred yards between them and, owing to the pace de Quesnoy had been making, he was rapidly tiring; but he could now see the gig. In her stern a big, broad-shouldered, youngish looking man, wearing a panama hat with a blue spotted silk handkerchief round it, was standing up. With yells and excited gestures he was encouraging his crew to further efforts, and the sight of him put new heart into the Count.

With each stroke he should have been able to glance to his rear; but the mask prevented that. All the same, the shouts of the Sub-Lieutenant in the whaler told him that it was swiftly coming up behind him. Every wavelet that met him slapped against the helmet, then slopped through the eye and mouth slits, making his breathing difficult. His heart was pounding as though about to burst through his ribs, and every muscle in his body ached from the strain. For the last fifty yards the only thing that kept him going was the knowledge that the gig was racing to his rescue, and that if he could reach her before the whaler overtook him there was a chance that the people from the yacht might refuse to hand him over.

As he battled his way madly through the water, he was so blinded by spray that he did not catch another glimpse of the gig until it was nearly upon him. Just in time he saw her bows rise above his head, and flung himself on his back. His first grab at the gunwale missed, and as the boat's weigh carried her on he slithered along her side, dodging under the two oars until he came opposite her stern. There, willing hands seized him by the arms and shoulders and dragged him aboard.

'Snakes alive!' exclaimed the big man staring at the helmet. 'I was

wondering what he'd gotten on his head. Durn me if it isn't some kind of a mask!'

One of the yacht's officers was holding the rudder lines, and on his left sat a long-limbed young man with plump pink cheeks and a small fair moustache. As de Quesnoy collapsed on the bottom boards in the stern of the boat, the latter bent over him and cried:

'Why, look, Mr. Van Ryn, at that thick belt he's wearing and the chain fixed to it. He's been chained up some place. D'you think he's dangerous?'

'Could be, Harry,' replied the big man, who was still standing, and was now staring dubiously down at the Count. 'Looks as though that mask was clapped over his head to prevent him savaging people with his teeth.'

At that moment the whaler came level with the gig. Its crew backed water then rested on their oars. De Quesnoy, still choking up water and gasping for breath, then heard, but only as if at a great distance, a swift exchange of sentences between his pursuer and his rescuer.

'Many thanks, Monsieur, for saving our prisoner,' called out the Sub-Lieutenant in French. 'In another few minutes the sharks would have had him.'

'You're welcome,' called back the big Mr. Van Ryn, using the same language. 'But what's wrong with him? Is he a lunatic? Has he gotten rabies or something?'

'No, no; there is nothing wrong with his brain or health. At least, I do not think so. He is a criminal to whom special importance is attached.'

'What crime has he committed?'

'I cannot tell you.'

'D'you mean you can't, or you won't?'

'I cannot because I do not know, Monsieur.'

'What's the reason for the helmet thing he's wearing on his head?'

'I do not know that either. Until a few moments ago I had never set eyes on him or it.'

'Oh come, you can't expect me to believe that!'

'It is the truth, Monsieur. During the voyage none of the ship's officers were permitted to see this prisoner; not even our Captain.'

'What is the prisoner's name?'

'I have no idea. That he has been forced to wear a mask suggests

243

that he is someone quite well known, and that the Government wish to keep his identity secret.'

'If so, your Government is composed of inhuman monsters!' cried the American in a sudden burst of anger. 'To have forced him to wear a mask like that is torture, nothing less. And he's been chained; chained like a mad dog, to a wall.'

'Personally, Monsieur, I deplore these things,' replied the Sub-Lieutenant. 'But it is not for me to question the decision of my Government.'

'It is for every decent person to challenge such barbarous treatment of a helpless man, no matter what crime he has committed.'

'Monsieur, I have no wish to enter into an argument with you. I have a duty to perform, and the sooner I can get it over the better I shall be pleased. Be good enough to order your men to ship their oars, so that I can come alongside you. Then we will relieve you of the prisoner and take him back to the ship.'

'Not yet,' said the American firmly. 'What's the hurry? I'd like to know a bit more about this mystery man first.'

'There is nothing more I can tell you,' declared the Sub-Lieutenant.

'Then I'll get it first hand from him,' came the swift retort.

'You have no right to question our prisoner.'

'I've a right to find out how he comes to be wearing that hideous mask.'

'Monsieur, that is no concern of yours.'

'It certainly is. I oughtn't to have to tell you that such treatment of a prisoner is against every Christian principle. I mean to find out who is responsible.'

'Then I suggest that you should return with us to the ship, and put your questions to the Colonel who has been acting as the prisoner's escort.'

De Quesnoy had now got back his breath and grasped the substance of the argument that was going on about him. Struggling up into a sitting position, he gave a quick tug to the edge of Mr. Van Ryn's coat and surprised him by saying huskily in English:

'Sir! I beg you not to do so. It would be more merciful of you to throw me out of this boat and let me drown. If you take me back to the cruiser I must suffer the lingering death that they have planned for me.'

'Come, Monsieur,' called the Sub-Lieutenant. 'Be pleased to order your men to row you to the ship.'

Van Ryn looked down at the Count, and asked sharply, 'What crime have you committed that they should be treating you like this?'

'None! None! I swear it. I am the victim of a hideous plot. Take me to your yacht and I will tell you the whole awful story.'

'I see my Captain signalling to us,' cut in the Sub-Lieutenant. 'He is becoming impatient. Kindly delay no longer. Either put your boat about or hand the prisoner over.'

'What if I refuse?' asked Van Ryn truculently.

'Then I must order you to do so.

'Who the hell are you to order me about?'

'I am a French Naval officer,' cried the Sub-Lieutenant with sudden anger, 'and you are in French territorial waters.'

'And I'm a citizen of the United States of America,' shot back the big man. 'That means that wherever I am in the world it's a matter of principle with me to uphold the rights of man and the maintenance of human dignity. As I see it, in the case of this poor devil you people have outraged both; so I'm determined to hear his own story before I hand him back to you. What is more, while he tells it I'll not have him brow-beaten by this Colonel you speak of or anyone else; so I'm not accepting your invitation.'

'That is all very well, Monsieur; but I must warn you that you are making yourself liable to arrest.'

'The United States consul in Cayenne is going to make you look pretty foolish if you arrest me simply for pulling a man out of the sea and insisting on having ten minutes' talk with him afterwards.'

'It will be for my Captain to decide whether any action is to be taken against you. But you may be certain that strong measures will follow should you attempt to put to sea when you reach your yacht, or refuse to hand the prisoner over when his escort is sent to fetch him.'

With a shrug of his great shoulders Van Ryn sat down and, turning to the officer who was coxing the gig, said abruptly, 'Mr. Sarson, we'll not be going to have a look at Devil's Island after all. Have your boys pull for the yacht.'

As the gig swung about, de Quesnoy grasped his rescuer by the arm and exclaimed, 'I thank you, Sir, a thousand times for this. When you have heard my story I am certain you will not have the heart to give me up to my enemies.'

The American grunted. 'Get that idea out of your head, friend. I'll have to. You heard what that officer said. If I attempted to hide you they'd send an armed party to search the yacht; and if we weighed anchor they'd put a shot across our bows. No; the best I can do for you is to hear what you've got to say, and give the story of your inhuman treatment to the world in the hope of forcing your Government to give you a better deal.'

'I appreciate your goodwill, Sir; but what you propose would take months. Long before any relief could be secured for me by such means I should be dead.'

'Seeing the number of sharks there are in these tropical waters, I wonder you're not dead already.'

'Yes, I was lucky to escape them; but I won't be if you give me up. It would be better to have been dragged under and dead within a few minutes than to die by inches or be driven mad by heat and insects in that stone hut on Devil's Island.'

'That certainly is a terrible prospect. But I'm told that Dreyfus survived there for four and a half years. In that number of months I reckon I could stir up enough trouble to have your case reviewed.'

'Dreyfus was not condemned to wear a mask like this. I cannot describe the suffering it inflicts. Wearing it for only eighteen days and nights has nearly driven me insane. Besides, the fiends who devised it have already decreed my death. I have every reason to believe that within two months at the most orders will come from France which will result in my being executed by a firing squad.'

'Then you're in one helluva fix,' declared the big man glumly. 'One thing I can do is to have that durned helmet cut off your head as soon as we get aboard, and in a place like this it'll be a tidy while before they can fit you with another. But I'll have to give you up. About that I'll have no option. The yacht's not equipped to give battle to the French Navy.'

As they talked de Quesnoy had been studying his new acquaintance. He judged Van Ryn to be some five years older than himself. His face was large and chunky, with a broad forehead, a nose that was almost snub, a generous mouth and a bulldog chin. His eyes were brown, not very large, but full of vitality and intelligence. He gave the impression of a man who had plenty of courage but would be difficult to move once he had made up his mind.

Inwardly the Count groaned. It seemed incredibly hard that, having overcome Roux and the two warders, having escaped the sharks, having reached the gig before he could be caught and having found in it a man who had the desire to protect him, all this should go for nothing, and that within an hour or so he would again be a prisoner.

Yet that was the end to his desperate bid for freedom that he had himself foreseen during those hectic moments before he had decided to make it. That was no consolation, but there was no argument he could use to counter the American's reluctant logic; so, once more a prey to bitter frustration, he fell silent until they reached the yacht.

Directly they were aboard Van Ryn set some of his sailors to force the clasps of the Count's belt and to hack through the leather on either side of the lock to his mask. It proved so tough that their jack knives were blunted in the process, but after five minutes' hard work they managed to free him from both the belt and helmet.

As the latter came off, Van Ryn gave an exclamation of indignation. De Quesnoy's normally handsome face was now a horrid sight. A half-inch-long beard had sprouted untidily round his jowls; his eyes were red-rimmed; there were angry sores on his aquiline nose and the tips of his ears where the mask had rubbed them; his cheeks were yellow-stained from nightly contact with its leather, and his dark, wavy hair was so matted with sweat that it looked as if it had been glued down to his head. Taking him by the arm, his temporary host said:

'First thing you need is a good wash. Come along to my cabin. You can talk while you're cleaning yourself up.'

The Count followed him aft and soon, stripped to the waist, he was enjoying the almost forgotten luxury of plenty of warm water and scented soap. Between his splashings, knowing that there was all too little time, and hoping against hope that Van Ryn might yet be persuaded to give him a further chance by hiding him, he gabbled out the unhappy story of de Vendôme's abruptly terminated career as a pretender to the Throne of France.

When he had done, Van Ryn observed shrewdly, 'The French Government's having announced your death, Prince, provides a logical explanation for their trying to hide your face for good under a mask. I calculate your story is too circumstantial not to be true; and I'm glad to feel that, because up to a few minutes ago I had just a suspicion that I might be harbouring some particularly desperate criminal. My hat, though; what double-dyed swine old Prime Minister Combes and that General André must be!'

De Quesnoy was not listening. He was staring at his hardly recognizable face in the mirror. Suddenly he exclaimed, 'Holy Virgin be thanked! I believe I have it!' Then he swung round and asked: 'Would you be willing to tell a few lies, if by doing so there was a good chance that you could save me?'

Van Ryn shrugged. 'I'd lie like a trooper to save any man from more of what you've been through. But, oh boy, the lies have got to be good if they're to prevent your compatriots from the cruiser taking you off this yacht.'

'When they come for me I want you to tell them that on my failing to persuade you to hide me I threw myself overboard in despair, and that before the gig could be got round to this side of the ship I was taken by the sharks.'

'No, friend. What's the use? They wouldn't believe me unless they'd searched the ship and failed to find you. And the yacht's not all that big. They'd ferret you out wherever you were hid. You'd be no better off, and I'd have made myself liable to see the inside of a French prison. I'd risk that if we could get away with it; but we couldn't. Not a hope.'

'But I do not mean to hide. Owing to the mask none of them have seen my face. All I ask is that you get me a pair of ducks and a singlet. They will expect my hair to be long; so I must shave my head and trim my beard. I shall then be able to pass as one of your crew.'

The American stared at him round eyed. 'Snakes alive! I believe you've got something there. But we'll have to be mighty quick about it. My Jap valet will see to your hair, and I'll tell my Captain to pass the word to the boys to play along. They'll just love making suckers out of those Frenchies. Sorry, Prince, but your English is so good I'd forgotten you were one yourself.'

Dashing to the door of the cabin, he bellowed, 'Harry! Harry! Come here! Quick!'

As the tall pink-cheeked young man appeared at the run, Van Ryn said hurriedly, 'This is my secretary, Harry Plimsol. Harry, this is Prince Vendôme. We're going to save his bacon if we can. Find Mitso for me; then go along to the First Engineer. Get him to lend you a pair of soiled dungarees and a singlet. Later we'll smear the Prince's hands and face with coal dust, then he'll look like a stoker. But hurry, hurry! We've not a moment to lose.'

De Quesnoy had already snatched up the shaving brush from the fitted washstand and begun to lather his beard. With Van Ryn's razor he shaved the hair from the sides of his face, leaving only his moustache and a round patch on his chin. The Japanese valet arrived on the scene just as he was washing off the last soap suds.

'Come on, Mitso,' cried his master. 'I want you to shave this gentleman's head. Look alive, now!'

'No,' amended the Count. 'It will look more natural if it is close cropped all over with a short brush left in front, like many Baltic sailors wear theirs.'

As he spoke he sat down in front of the basin. The Japanese took a pair of scissors from a drawer beneath it, and Van Ryn ran from the cabin to tell his Captain what was on foot.

Within five minutes de Quesnoy's matted wavy hair had been shorn away, and his scalp showed unattractively through the short bristles that remained. Harry Plimsol then came running in with the borrowed garments. As he handed them to the Count he cried:

'Just throw your own clothes down any place. I'll lock them up with the helmet and the belt in the boss's safe, so there's no chance of anyone coming across them. But hurry, man, hurry! The cruiser's boat's no more than a dozen lengths away from our gangway.'

Two minutes later, as de Quesnoy emerged on deck, he was met by the First Engineer, who said to him in a low voice with a strong Scottish accent, 'Meester Van Ryn's compliments, an' wee're noo about tae raise a head o' steam preparatory tae sailin'. Your best chance if they come below lookin' fer ye is t'be seen doing a stint at a boiler. S'come wi' me, mon, an' take heed lest ye slip on the footin's.'

The Count followed his guide down into the bowels of the yacht; and there the real stokers, not having been told that he was supposed to be a Prince, indulged in some friendly horseplay, making him as grimy as themselves; then they gave him a shovel and set him to work.

Meanwhile the whaler had made fast to the gangway and up it came the cruiser's Captain, a bull-necked man with a black spade beard, followed by Colonel Roux, the redheaded warder and four marines.

Van Ryn met them on the quarter deck, and made a good tactical move by telling his story without delay. His chunky, normally cheerful face expressing suitable solemnity, he greeted them with the words:

'Gentlemen, I'm sure the treatment you've been ordered to mete out to your prisoner must be repugnant to you; so I think you may be relieved to hear that he has freed you of such unpleasant duties. You've come for him just too late. Five minutes ago he threw himself over the rail on the far side of the yacht; and before you could say "Jack Robinson" the sharks that were hovering round the waste chute from the main galley got him.'

He had spoken in heavily accented but fluent French, so the whole of the boarding party understood him. The Captain and the Colonel exchanged a swift glance. Roux gave a slight shake of the head and the sailor replied for both of them:

'We cannot accept your statement, Monsieur. My Sub-Lieutenant reports to me that you behaved most truculently towards him and showed an evident desire to shield the prisoner.'

'What! D'you call me a liar?' exclaimed Van Ryn, simulating swift indignation.

'No, Monsieur,' replied the French Captain tactfully. 'But perhaps you have allowed your imagination to run away with you.'

'Imagination be damned! I was beside him when he went over.' Van Ryn jerked a thumb at young Plimsol and the yacht's Captain, who were standing beside him. 'So did these two. Ask my secretary here, and Captain Oakie.'

The Captain spoke no French, but he nodded vigorously, and Harry Plimsol said that he too had witnessed the sudden tragedy.

The French officers stared at them, still obviously unconvinced, and Colonel Roux said, 'If he had intended to commit suicide, after plunging off the stern of the cruiser he would not have swum towards your boat. Since he did so, and you picked him up, his throwing himself into the sea again twenty minutes later does not make sense.'

'Oh yes it does,' countered the American swiftly. 'When he made his break from you he was hoping to find sanctuary on this yacht. He implored me to hide him in one of the coal bunkers. But I wouldn't.

He told me he was a Prince who was being persecuted, and I was mighty interested; but, all the same, I had to tell him that when you came for him I'd have to hand him over. It was then that despair clouded the poor feller's mind, and before we could stop him he took a header. Would that be true about his being a Prince? He said Vendôme, or something like it, was his name and that he was the rightful King of France.'

There was a sudden stir among the group of Frenchmen, and the Captain threw a swift glance of interrogation at the Colonel. After hesitating a moment, Roux said awkwardly:

'The Prince is dead, Monsieur. He was shot while resisting arrest some weeks ago, and it was all in the newspapers. But the prisoner has a strange resemblance to his late Highness, and was causing great trouble by impersonating him. That is why my superiors took measures to conceal his features.'

'Well, they're both dead now,' remarked Van Ryn with an air of finality. But the Colonel and the Captain were consulting together in undertones, and when they had done, the Captain announced:

'I regret, Monsieur, but I regard it as my duty to search your yacht. As a first move, be good enough to have the whole of your ship's company paraded up here.'

With a shrug of resignation, Van Ryn told Captain Oakie to have the boatswain pipe "all hands on deck". Most of the sailors were already standing about watching the proceedings, but soon after the whistle had ceased to shrill others, including the engine room staff with de Quesnoy amongst them, came tumbling up through the hatchways.

Altogether, including the Japanese valet and a Chinese cook, the ship's company numbered twenty. The men made no attempt to fall in, but, grouping themselves in a ragged line, stood eyeing the French intruders with either slightly hostile or faintly amused expressions.

De Quesnoy, now sweating and begrimed, was standing among the stokers. He needed no telling that for him, during the next five minutes, life or death would hang in the balance. It was only with a great effort of will that he managed to stand slackly, as though at ease, and to keep his eyes from riveting themselves on Roux.

The Captain of the cruiser gave the assembly a sweeping glance from end to end; then he said to the Colonel, 'I knew de Vendôme

251

slightly. My sister sold him a hunter and I was with her when he came to inspect the horse. There is no one remotely like him here.'

'I fear you are right,' Roux agreed. 'All the same, I am going to have a closer look.' Then, followed by the warder, he walked slowly along the ragged line, giving each man in turn a searching glance.

He peered with his melancholy blue eyes for longest at the stokers, striving to discern their features more clearly under the coatings of sweat and dirt. The Count dared not meet those probing eyes. His heart hammering in his breast, he feared that even now a memory of one of the many photographs of himself, which had appeared in the Press only three weeks before, might cause Roux to question him; and if that happened it might yet lead to his recapture and death.

Roux passed on. De Quesnoy's feeling of relief was beyond description. But it was premature. The warder was following close on the Colonel's heels. He now stared at the Count. His eyes widened. Suddenly he gave a shout.

'*Mon Colonel!* Here is our man!' He shot out an accusing finger. 'Look! Look! The sores upon his neck. Our prisoner had them. They were made by the rubbing of the helmet.'

Next moment, burning to get his own back for the blows that had knocked him out earlier that morning, he fell upon de Quesnoy, kicking and striking at him furiously.

Taken by surprise though he was, the Count's brain was quick enough to tell him that his only hope now lay in bluffing to the limit. In broken French and using the most atrocious accent, he cried:

'You make mistake! I no French convict! I Russian seaman.' Then, parrying the blows of the redheaded warder and lashing out in his turn, he gave vent to a non-stop flow of curses, protests and abuse in fluent Russian.

Before either of them sustained any serious injury they were pulled apart by the other stokers. Roux's eyes were once more riveted on de Quesnoy. Both Captains, Van Ryn and young Plimsol had all come hurrying up. To put his friends wise to the line he was taking, the Count shouted again, this time in broken English:

'I am Russian! Ivan Orloff is my name. I am Russian. I show you!' Upon which, breaking free of the men who held him, he folded his arms, bent both his knees and, kicking out his feet alternately, began to dance a Trepak.

252

His skilful antics, and mercurial change from anger to buffoonery, had the desired effect of easing the tension. Most of the men about him laughed and Van Ryn cried gamely:

'Sure thing he's a Russian. It's only folk who're born subjects of the Czar can dance those crazy dances as easy as we could a polka.' Then, having heard the Count's fluent swearing, he added: 'He can sing a good song, too, when he chooses. Come on, Ivan; give us a song.'

Ceasing his kicking, the Count stood up and obliged with the first few stanzas of a Russian folk song; but to his dismay he saw that the warder was still regarding him with malevolent suspicion, and Roux with a curious intentness. After a moment the Colonel waved de Quesnoy into silence and asked Van Ryn:

'For how long has this man been signed on by you?'

'He's a new hand,' replied the American. 'He came into Caracas in a grain-ship, got drunk, missed his sailing and was taken on by us because we were short-staffed in the engine room.'

De Quesnoy's heart was in his mouth again. Van Ryn's statement had been a wild gamble. There was no Ivan Orloff on the manifest, so if Roux asked to see it the game would be up. On the other hand the bluff must have collapsed right away had the Colonel received no reply.

The Captain of the cruiser had been thoughtfully stroking his square beard. Now, he gave a shrug and said to Roux, 'Why waste time on this fellow? He is a Russian all right; and anyhow he has not the faintest resemblance to the Duc de Vendôme.'

'No,' replied the Colonel slowly, 'but his face is strangely familiar. I cannot get it out of my mind that I have seen him somewhere before.'

'Cross-question him again later then. If we do not get on with searching the ship we shall still be at it into the hot hours of the day.'

It was a most welcome reprieve for de Quesnoy; but no more. With the warder, the marines and the sailors called up from the whaler to help, the two officers spent the next hour and three quarters poking into every corner, cubby-hole and locker in the yacht. Meanwhile, still a prey to almost unbearable suspense, the Count had to continue to act his rôle of a stoker, now lounging about off duty, with as much conviction as he could put into it.

Soon after ten o'clock the abortive search at last came to an end. Tired, hot and ill-tempered, the French boarding party straggled back on deck to be met with the now openly derisive grins of the yacht's company. Van Ryn was among the few who kept a straight face. Going up to the two officers, he said tersely:

'Well, gentlemen. I trust that you are now satisfied?'

It was the Captain who answered. 'We are satisfied, Monsieur, that the man we are seeking is not hidden in this yacht; therefore we must accept your explanation of his disappearance. But I am far from satisfied about your conduct in this matter. Had you not arbitrarily refused to hand the man over to my officer in the whaler, he would have had no opportunity to commit suicide, and we should not be saddled with the unenviable task of accounting to our Government for the loss of a most important Prisoner of State.'

'Now isn't that just too bad,' remarked Van Ryn sarcastically. 'It gives me a real pain to think that after all the kindness you two fellers showed your prisoner you're likely to find yourselves in the doghouse on his account.'

The Captain flushed above his black beard. 'It is true that on account of your act we may get into hot water, and that seems to me all the better reason why I should take steps to ensure your getting into hot water too. Your yacht is now under arrest and you will sail her to the port of Cayenne, to answer a charge in front of a French magistrate of having obstructed a Naval officer carrying out his duty.'

It was then that the hefty, thirty-four-year-old American showed to the full his true mettle. 'Like hell I will!' he positively roared. 'You'd best think again, and mighty quick unless you want the pants scorched off you. I pulled a man out of the sea. He was muzzled like a mad dog and had been chained up like a wild beast; yet he was as sane as I am. And you're going to charge me with wanting to know how come that the French nation, with all its vaunted civilization, was treating a human being as though it had not yet crawled out of the Middle Ages.'

For a second he paused for breath, then stormed on. 'All right! Try it! Try it and just see where it gets you. My name's Channock Van Ryn. Maybe you've never heard of it, but that name goes for something in the United States. My old man is President of the Chesapeake Banking and Trust Corporation. What's more, he is a Senator. You pull this on me and he'll have it taken up by our Ambassador in Paris. Can you guess what'll happen then? Don't bother; I'll tell you. I'm a banker, so it's my business to know about Governments and their reactions. Yours won't face the music. No Government would dare to admit to a thing like this. It's going to deny all knowledge of the mask and chain. It's going to father those bright ideas on you; and to appease world indignation it will have those gold rings off your hats and tunics just so quickly you'll think they've been ripped off by a hurricane.'

Again Van Ryn paused for a second. Then he launched his final broadside. 'As soon as my engineer has a head of steam, I'm sailing. But not to Cayenne. I am a citizen of the United States of America proceeding on my lawful occasions. On the stern staff of this yacht I'm flying, as is my right, the Stars and Stripes. Just you try firing at Old Glory as a means of stopping me. I guess Mr. Theodore Roosevelt would have something to say about that. As First Citizen the President would be liable to take that as sort of personal. So if you boys want to make dead certain of wrecking your careers that's what you'd better do.'

Under this terrible tirade the two Frenchmen had wilted visibly. Both were thinking how fortunate it was that all their men had already filed down the gangway, and so had not witnessed their being subjected to these appalling threats. They cast an anxious glance round, wondering how many of the yacht's crew understood French, then exchanged an unhappy glance. Each of them read his own thoughts in the other's eyes. This horrible American meant what he said; and he was right in believing that their Government would save its face by making scapegoats of them. They were faced with ruin or surrender.

In an endeavour to retrieve something of his dignity, the Captain said, 'Monsieur; this affair of the prisoner is our misfortune, not our fault. You are right in your contention that it is of much more importance that good relations between our two countries should be maintained. Be pleased to proceed whenever you wish.'

As he turned towards the gangway Roux said, 'You are right. But before leaving I would like to question further that man who says he is a Russian. In another five minutes' talk with him I should probably remember why it is that his face is so familiar to me.'

'To hell with the Russian!' exclaimed the black-bearded Captain, letting go against his military colleague the suppressed rage he was feeling. 'We know that he is not your prisoner, so what the devil does it matter who he is? For God's sake, let us get away from this accursed yacht.'

255

When the whaler was well on her way back to the cruiser, and de Quesnoy had for the past five minutes been pouring out his heartfelt thanks to the man who had saved him, Van Ryn suddenly gave him a quizzical glance, and said:

'Before that bunch came aboard you assured me that none of them would be able to tell that you weren't a member of the crew. Yet it was clear that the Colonel and the Captain were looking for the Prince Vendôme, and knew him well by sight. How come that you escaped identification?'

De Quesnoy smiled. 'Because I am not the man they were looking for. I changed places with the Duc de Vendôme after they had put the mask on him. All the same, I had a very narrow escape, because I am wanted for participation in this conspiracy and Colonel Roux very nearly recognized me.'

'And who may you be?' inquired Van Ryn with a lift of his eyebrows.

'I am Lieutenant-Colonel the Count de Quesnoy, and your most grateful servant.'

As the Count declared himself he made a graceful bow, but on drawing himself upright again he staggered slightly, put a hand to his head and murmured, 'Forgive me, but for the past three hours I have been under a great strain, and . . . and it is now nearly three weeks since I have been able to do more than doze in considerable discomfort. Would you therefore permit me . . . ?'

'Not another word, Count,' Van Ryn cut him short. 'I'm a poor host not to have thought of that. Come right along with me, and I'll put you in my best guest cabin. You shall sleep the clock round if you wish.'

Almost at once de Quesnoy fell into eight hours of oblivion. On waking he felt wonderfully refreshed, and found that a suit of white drill had been laid out for him. After luxuriating for a while in a hot bath, he dressed and joined his host, whom he found with Plimsol and Captain Oakie just about to go into dinner.

While once more savouring the joys of pleasant companionship, well-cooked food and excellent champagne, he told them the full story of the Vendôme conspiracy and its tragic outcome. When at length he had done and they were lighting up their cigars, Van Ryn asked:

'And what now, Count? It is clear that you are finished as far as the French Army is concerned. What do you mean to do with yourself?'

De Quesnoy's grey, yellow-flecked eyes suddenly became hard and his mouth determined. 'I intend to return to France with the least possible delay,' he replied without hesitation. 'I have taken a vow to ruin General André and bring about the fall of the Combes government. Either I shall succeed in that or die in the attempt.'

CHAPTER XX

THE LONG ROAD BACK

THE fates decreed that de Quesnoy should not, after all, return to France in the immediate future. In the first place, an hour or so after dinner on the night of his escape his new friends noticed that he was looking very flushed. At first they thought that it was the excitement of having regained his freedom coupled with the quantity of champagne he had drunk; but later he complained of pains in his head and it transpired that he was running a high temperature. Next day it was clear that he had used his last reserves of strength during his escape and, having already been seriously weakened by his eighteen days of extraordinarily harsh captivity, had now gone down with fever.

There was no doctor on board, but the tall, pink-cheeked Harry Plimsol was a young man of most diverse accomplishments. His father being a small town doctor, he had started life by studying medicine, but after a year thrown it up in favour of law, but then in turn abandoned that for accountancy; but his money having given out before he could qualify, he had had to take a job in the Chesapeake Corporation. It might therefore have been said that he was a "Jack of all trades and a master of none", but the fact remained that his unusually wide general knowledge, together with an excellent memory and a pleasant manner, made him a most efficient confidential secretary; and in the present case he was quite capable of taking charge of the invalid.

The yacht belonged to Senator Van Ryn, but his son, Channock, was using it to make a tour of the major cities of South America. In all of them the Chesapeake Corporation had branches and the Board had decided that, while carrying out an inspection of them, Channock could also make the acquaintance of many of the leading financiers of Latin America, which should lead to a valuable extension of business.

For a week after leaving Devil's Island the yacht ploughed her way steadily south-east until she reached Bahia. By then de Quesnoy's

258

fever had abated, but he was still too weak to accompany Van Ryn ashore during the eight days that the latter spent transacting business and meeting people socially in the Brazilian city. However, his mind was clear again; so he was able to draft cables, which Harry Plimsol sent off for him, to Angela, to his father and to de Vendôme care of the Condessa de Cordoba y Coralles, conveying to them all, without mentioning his name, that he had escaped and was enjoying the hospitality of an American friend in a yacht in South American waters.

On January 27th the yacht left Bahia, and three days later dropped anchor in the almost unbelievably beautiful harbour of Rio de Janeiro.

De Quesnoy's week of fever while crossing the equator had taken a lot out of him and, coming on top of the physical and mental strain he had already endured, had left him only a shadow of the man he had been before Christmas. In consequence, when they had been for about ten days in the Brazilian capital and he spoke of inquiring about sailings for France, Van Ryn would not hear of it. He pointed out that the Count's self-imposed mission must prove an exceedingly dangerous one, and that he would be mad to enter the lion's den before he was again one hundred per cent fit.

De Quesnoy admitted the sound sense of this and agreed to remain as Van Ryn's guest for at least another month. He still had to go carefully, but during the latter part of their time in Rio he was able to see the sights of the city and to accompany the banker to some very pleasant social gatherings.

With regret, on February 21st, they weighed anchor. Four days' sailing brought them to Montevideo, where they spent only six days, then they crossed the great estuary of the River Plate, arriving at Buenos Aires on March 4th.

It was now seven weeks since the Count's escape. He was well on the way to regaining his normal weight and mental alertness but his nights were still subject to terrible nightmares, in which he was again masked, chained and almost suffocated by heat; and these left him haggard and exhausted in the mornings. In Rio he had already collected a considerable sum of money that in his cable to his father he had asked should be wired to Van Ryn's branch there; so there was nothing to prevent him from booking a passage in a false name on a ship that was shortly due to leave Buenos Aires for a French port. But it was sympto-matic of his condition that he hesitated to do so; because he could not make up his mind whether he was not really sufficiently recovered again to take his life in his hands, or if the lazy and enjoyable existence he was leading had caused him to become subconsciously a malingerer.

Van Ryn made his mind up for him. They had taken a great liking to one another and eight weeks of constant companionship had resulted in a greater degree of intimacy between them than would have been the case after as many years of normal friendship had they lived for all that time in the same city. Unusual as it was in those days, they had even reached the point of calling one another by their Christian names. When the Count again tentatively raised the question of going back to France, the American said to him:

'Well, Armand, it's not for me to tell you how best to handle your affairs; but if it were me I'd be mighty cautious how I set about pitting myself against the all-powerful ministers of a great country when they already had my name chalked up to lose my head under the guillotine. To start with I'd grow a beard.'

De Quesnoy had long since shaven off the dark, wiry stubble that he had left round his mouth and on the ball of his chin for his impersonation of a Russian stoker, and he replied, 'To grow a proper beard would take months.'

'What does that matter? You're not all that old you need fear becoming tied to a wheel-chair before you can carry out your vow.'

'No, Channock. But I'd like to get it off my chest; so that I can set about reshaping my life on new lines.'

'Such as?'

'Oh, soldiering somewhere. It is the only trade I know; and although I don't have to work for my living I have a rooted objection to remaining idle.'

'Then you're sitting on the doorstep of the best market for your talents right now. The smaller Latin American Republics are always at one another's throats. There must be several of them who'd jump at the chance to get hold of a man who has been a chief-instructor at St. Cyr.'

The Count nodded. 'That is just what I had thought of as a possi-bility later. But I couldn't sign on with any of them with a quiet mind until I have been back to France. You are right, though, that when

I do go back I shall be risking my head and stand a very good chance of having it chopped off if I fail to keep from the police the secret of my real identity. The thing that worries me is the state of my nerves. I always used to sleep like a top, but now I quite frequently wake screaming. I am sure that I talk in my sleep, and there are times when alcohol has a much more rapid effect on me than it should have; so I am just a little scared that I might give myself away.'

'Then you'd be plumb crazy to go yet,' declared the American firmly.

'But, my dear Channock, I cannot sponge on you indefinitely.'

'Nonsense, Armand, I like having you around. If you are all that set on evening up the score you can entertain me sometime when I come to Europe in one of your old man's castles. But listen now. Much your best plan is to give plenty of time for the Vendôme business to die down. Come summer, people will have forgotten about it and about you. Then you'll be able to move around Paris without anyone giving you a second glance; especially if you've grown a beard. I'm keen on the beard. I'd like you to grow a real big one like the captain of that cruiser had.'

'Perhaps you are right; but, although the climate here is pleasant summer still seems a long way off.'

'You'll find the time go quick enough with all the new places and people we'll be seeing. I've told you my itinerary. Round the Horn to Valparaiso a fortnight there; on to the port of Arica and up country for a week in La Paz. Next a fortnight in Lima, then to Guayaquil and another trip inland for a week in Quito. Lastly, a third rail jaunt, from Buenaventura up to Bogota; then straight sailing for San Francisco and by the transcontinental home. I figure to be back in New York by early July; so you could be in Paris by the end of that month. By that time your nerves will be restored to normal and you'll have a beard as long as an early Christian Father's. Besides, think what a chance this is for you to fix up about your future soldiering. We'll be staying in the capitals of Chile, Bolivia, Peru, Ecuador and Columbia, and I've got chits to the big shots in all of these places. If I can't get you an offer from one of them to return in a year's time as an Inspector General or a Chief of Staff I'll eat my hat.'

De Quesnoy laughed. 'It seems to have been my lucky day in more ways than one when curiosity led you to put in for a look at Devil's Island. Anyhow, there is nothing I would like more than to accompany you on this fascinating trip; so I'll salve my conscience with the thought that it may lead to a new career, and that I'll be a more dangerous enemy to the men I've sworn to destroy when I take up the cudgels against them later.'

Thus the matter was settled. For three weeks the yacht lay in Buenos Aires, while they enjoyed the lavish hospitality of many rich Argentinians and Van Ryn entered into a number of arrangements advantageous to his firm. On March 25th they sailed, and a few days later for the first time met bad weather; but the yacht was well found and Captain Oakie a good seaman; so after the inside of a week of discomfort she was safely through the Straits of Magellan, and on April 5th reached Valparaiso.

There, however, a cable awaited Van Ryn which entirely altered their plans. His father sent him the news that his uncle had died in Paris, and asked him to return to New York as soon as possible. Their stay in Valparaiso was accordingly curtailed to two days, and the rest of the South American itinerary scrapped. They sailed again direct for Panama, arriving on April 16th, and there they left the yacht to circumnavigate again the Southern continent on her return journey to her home port.

Another ten years were to elapse before the Panama canal could be opened, but while crossing the isthmus by train they saw much of the vast work which had already been accomplished at the cost of thousands of lives and the savings of tens of thousands of French families. At Colon, on the Atlantic side, Van Ryn found that as a next step the quickest way for him to get back to New York would be for him to take a ship that was sailing the following day for Havana. From Havana, too, there would be frequent sailings for France and de Quesnoy, now fully recovered, spoke of booking a passage; but his friend again dissuaded him from doing so.

'I know you've been getting more and more boiled up for some time now to have the pants off those swine in Paris,' he said with his cheerful grin, 'but all the same I'd keep the lid on for another month or two if I were you. It's only six weeks since you started to grow that beard, and although it's good and thick it'll have more of a permanent look when it's long enough to trim. And there's another thing. I can't be sure yet, but I've a hunch that the reason my old man sent for me post haste like this is because he wants me to take over at our Paris office. If so, we'd be able to go over together, and I could provide initial cover for you by letting all and sundry believe you to be a member of my staff.'

As previous to the arrival of the cable the Count had agreed to postpone his return until July and it was as yet only the beginning of May, this new possibility of valuable aid in establishing a false identity at once decided him to remain with Van Ryn. So together they took a ship from Havana to New Orleans and completed their journey by rail, arriving in New York on April 26th.

Channock had a fine apartment of his own in the big old brownstone family mansion on upper Fifth Avenue; but whenever he could during the summer months he slept out at the Van Ryn home on Long Island, and it was there that de Quesnoy spent most of the fortnight that followed.

The Senator and his white-haired wife made him very welcome and he could not have been a guest in more delightful surroundings. The Van Ryns' forebears had settled with other Dutch families in New Amsterdam before the city's name had been changed to New York, and as they had prospered from the beginning the houses of the present generation contained old furniture, pictures, silver, china and other *objets d'art* which could have rivalled many private collections in Europe.

While Channock attended business conferences, the Count amused himself seeing the sights of the metropolis and mingling with the bustling crowds on Broadway, or riding in the woods of the eight-hundred-acre Long Island estate with its lovely views of Oyster Bay. In the evenings there were always jolly parties with one neighbour or another, and at week-ends Channock, who had a passion for sailing and kept a forty-foot yacht in the bay, initiated him into the mysteries of making the best of wind and tide.

The young banker's guess that his father wanted him to take over the post left vacant by his uncle's death proved correct. It was by the Paris office that all the major European transactions of the Corporation were handled, and the Board considered it important that a member of the family should live there. As the eldest of the younger generation Channock had been selected and, loath as he was to be parted from his wide circle of friends, he felt that he could not refuse. So passages were booked in the *Campania* and on May 20th Channock, de Quesnoy and Harry Plimsol arrived—via Liverpool, London, Dover and Calais —in Paris.

The Count travelled as Mr. Jules Dupont, an American of Belgian extraction, whose function it was to protect his rich master from undesirables, see to his comforts, arrange his pleasures and, more particularly, to acquire for him a small racing stable. The occupation of viewing bloodstock with an eye to its possible purchase was a cover which would serve indefinitely; and, owing to de Quesnoy's knowledge of horseflesh, the chances were high that when he did complete a deal he would get Van Ryn good value for his money.

For their first two nights in Paris they put up at the Scribe, then, as Channock's uncle had been a widower and his spacious apartment in the Avenue Victor Hugo seemed suitable, they took it over and moved in there.

As it was before the days when passports were required for entry into France, de Quesnoy had met with no difficulty about landing at Calais, and as soon as they were settled in permanent quarters he lost no time in making arrangements to contact his old associates. In the past five months he had written several letters to Angela, but had received no replies, and had expected none, because he had been unable in advance to give her any address at which a letter from her could have reached him before he had left it. He was therefore all the more anxious to see her.

The memory of the passionate avowals she had made to him in their last few moments together had been his only solace during his nightmare journey, and he had many times since recalled them with profound joy. To hear her repeat them had actually been a more potent factor underlying his impatience to return to France than his wish to be revenged on General André; although, having committed himself to achieve the latter's ruin, he knew that until he had done so he must not give way to the temptation to bring matters between Angela and himself to a head.

His three-months-old beard, now slightly curly and trimmed square, together with his eyebrows, from which he had shaved that outer upturned half-inch that normally gave him a likeness to the conventional idea of Prince Lucifer, had altered his appearance sufficiently for acquaintances not to know him if he passed them in the street; but he could hardly alter his height, walk or figure permanently, and his eyes and nose were such distinctive features that he felt that the risk of recognition was still considerable if he came face to face with anyone who had seen him frequently in the past. In consequence, he decided that instead of going to the Syveton mansion it would be safer first to get Syveton to come to see him.

To give the meeting the appearance of normal social intercourse, he got Van Ryn to invite Syveton and, on the same day, General Laveriac to lunch, giving as an excuse to both that, although a stranger to them, he wanted to convey messages to them from a friend in the United States. Both, piqued by curiosity, accepted; and when they arrived, on the only other guest being introduced to them as Monsieur Dupont, they thought him somehow familiar. A moment later they exclaimed almost simultaneously:

'De Quesnoy! Monsieur le Comte! What a delightful surprise! How good to see you again!'

The returned exile's pleasure in this reunion was largely marred a few minutes later by his learning that Angela was not in Paris, or expected back for some time, She had gone to England in May and intended to stay with her parents at their house in Great Cumberland Place until the end of the London season. Consoling himself as best he could for this disappointment with the thought that there would now be nothing to distract him from his self-imposed mission, he launched into an account of his escape, and throughout luncheon kept the Deputy and the General enthralled by it. After the meal Van Ryn, having played his part as genial host, excused himself and left the three Frenchmen together.

When they were settled in the library with liqueur brandies and cigars de Quesnoy said: 'Messieurs; it is just on six months since I took de Vendôme's place in the *Cherche-Midi*. Much must have happened since then. What are the present prospects of bringing about a restoration?'

It was Syveton who answered. 'Alas, none. De Vendôme, as you must have heard, got away safely to Spain. After you had escaped and he was able to come out of hiding a deputation from our Committee was then sent to ascertain his views about the future. He believes the disaster which put a premature end to our conspiracy to have been a direct warning from Heaven, and he refuses absolutely to continue to allow himself to be regarded as a claimant to the Throne. In fact, he declares that, even were it offered to him by the elected representatives of the French people, he would decline it.'

The little, square-shouldered Gascon General took up the tale. 'So that throws us back on the Duc d'Orleans, who has unquestionably been the legitimate heir since the death of the Comte de Paris in '94. But we went into all that years ago, and the son has proved no more willing than his father was to make a serious bid for his great inheritance. Since de Vendôme's defection, there has been some talk among us of inviting the Duc de Guise to accept our allegiance, but there are certain objections to that which cannot easily be got over; so I doubt if anything will come of it. In short, my dear Count, it is many years since we Royalists had so little to pin our hopes upon.'

De Quesnoy nodded. 'I am not surprised to hear what you tell me about de Vendôme; and even if it were possible to settle, in the fairly near future, on some other Prince of the Blood as being suitable it would take years to build him up as a popular claimant. Meanwhile, what of our poor country?'

'Things go from bad to worse,' Syveton gave an unhappy shrug. 'Except that Combes and his friends have not yet openly adopted torture and the stake, we now have a reversal of the Spanish Inquisition here. To be a Catholic is to invite certain persecution. Every city swarms with Government spies and informers. For anyone employed by the State to have his children baptized is quite enough for him to be hounded from his post and deprived of his pension.'

'Abominable!' murmured the Count, as Laveriac again contributed his piece.

'And the Army, *mon ami*! You would hardly credit the lengths to which that swine André has gone. He started, you will remember, by getting rid of de Castelnau, the best of all our younger Generals, from the War Office. Then he ousted Generals Delanne and Jamont from their seats on the *Conseil Supérieur de la Guerre*—the sole crime of all three being that they are practising Catholics. It was bad enough that he should meddle with the High Command, but he has since gone much further. He has suppressed all the Promotion Committees, and now holds the fate of every officer in the Army in his own hands.'

'But he cannot know personally more than one in a hundred of them,' protested de Quesnoy, 'and the fitness of officers for promotion cannot be judged entirely on written reports. How can one man, and a Minister at that, possibly find time to interview the scores of Lieutenants,

Captains and Majors whose cases become due for consideration every week?'

The General gave a bitter laugh. 'He does not attempt to. He goes entirely on information supplied to him by his spies. In all but a very few regiments there is at least one officer who is an atheist and a socialist. A high proportion of such men are not beyond putting in confidential reports about the private lives of their brother officers, if by so doing they can earn promotion for themselves. Every ex-ranker Lieutenant has been secretly approached with an offer on those lines. Should one of these stool-pigeons have a grouse against his Major he has only to report that the Major goes to confession once a month to ensure the latter's promotion being blocked for good—even if he is the most efficient officer in the battalion.'

'And the Freemasons,' added Syveton. 'Do not forget them. Their network of espionage penetrates every stratum of society, and we know that their organization is being used by André as a private information service. There are thousands of Freemasons in the ranks, others are Army Doctors, Army contractors, Civil Servants in garrison towns, and private servants in big houses frequented by senior officers. All of them are now under orders to report any conversations they may over-hear in which the Government is disparaged, or respect shown for the Church. Such is the basis upon which our Minister of War decides whether a recommendation for promotion should be approved or not.'

De Quesnoy raised his hands in horror. 'What you tell me is almost unbelievable. Political favouritism in making special appointments is deplorable enough; but to employ it as a standard practice is no less than a betrayal of France. What would become of us if the Germans picked another quarrel with us, and all our best soldiers were on half-pay or in subordinate positions?'

'We would hang André from a lamp-post,' remarked Laveriac cynically, 'but that would not save us from defeat'.

'These methods that you suggest he employs,' went on the Count. 'Are you certain of your facts? Is it really true that any General of the Army of France could have sunk to such depths?'

'Why should you doubt it, when the same General had no scruples about putting an innocent man in a head-mask and chains, solely to serve his political ends?'

'Yes; I suppose this picture of his wider activities is in keeping. But how is it that you have escaped his attentions?'

Laveriac shrugged. 'Because I married a Protestant, and for the past year and a half have denied myself the satisfaction of practising my own religion. I regard it as more important that, if war comes, at least some of the key posts should still be occupied by officers who are competent to carry out their duties. That, too, is why I will not risk being purged through producing evidence of the nefarious practices by which André is ruining the Army—although I am prepared to vouch for them to you.'

'If we could expose him, and show how his system of promotion based on secret denunciations and religious prejudice is endangering the safety of the country, surely popular indignation would drive him from office and result in the fall of the Government?'

Both the General and the Deputy nodded.

'To help in bringing those events to pass is my reason for returning to France,' said de Quesnoy impressively. 'My new identity is good cover, I am a free agent and have ample funds at my disposal. Tell me, Messieurs, how do you suggest that I should set about this patriotic undertaking?'

CHAPTER XXI

THE TREBLE LIFE OF
M. LE COMTE DE QUESNOY

FOR a few moments both the General and the Deputy remained in thoughtful silence, then the latter asked:

'I suppose you are not, by any chance, a Freemason?'

'*Mort de Dieu!* No!' replied de Quesnoy in shocked surprise.

'My apologies, Monsieur le Comte.' Syveton gave a slightly nervous smile. 'But many men get carried away in their youth by a desire to reform the world, and some, even of the aristocracy, are persuaded to become Masons. Later, of course, they realize that they have been snared into a secret society whose object is to bring about world-revolution, and cease to take any active part. I thought it just possible that . . .'

'And had I been,' the Count cut him short, 'what then?'

'You would still be one. Even those who come to disagree violently with the aims of Freemasonry and refuse all further participation in it are not allowed to resign. So had you ever been initiated you could return to the fold and, perhaps, secure for us concrete evidence of the devil's pact which has been entered into between the Masons and General André.'

After considering for a moment, de Quesnoy said, 'I imagine they take certain oaths and perform secret rites which would be anathema to my own beliefs. But for the purpose we have in mind I would be prepared to stomach that. I mean, of course, if it would be possible for you to arrange for my initiation.'

Laveriac sat forward quickly. 'I think I know a man who could. Syveton knows him too. I speak of the Deputy Guyot de Villeneuve. He was one of the earliest officers to be purged; so he bears a deadly hatred against André for ruining his military career. Not long ago I was dining with him and we were discussing Freemasonry. He told me then that, for the reasons Syveton has just given, as a young man he became

269

an initiate, and that out of curiosity he still occasionally attends their meetings.'

'Why, then, if this information is obtainable, should he not get it for us?' inquired the Count.

'Because, owing to his public utterances, now that he has become a Deputy of the Right, they no longer trust him. For that reason, too, it would defeat our object if it were he who proposed you. But he must be acquainted with other Masons. No doubt he could arrange for you to meet a few of the more important ones, as though casually, and simply introduce you as a Belgian acquaintance who has come to live in Paris. Then if you cultivate them independently of him you should be able to secure initiation under favourable auspices.'

'It will take time,' remarked Syveton, 'even for the Count to get himself initiated. And it is certain that they will not trust a new brother with their secrets right away. Much patience will be needed before there can be any hope of obtaining the evidence we want.'

De Quesnoy smiled. 'I may be able to think of ways to hasten matters, but the initial stages will certainly take some weeks; so the sooner we set the ball rolling the better.'

For a good while longer they discussed the general situation and two days later, as a result of their talk, Laveriac took the Count to see Guyot de Villeneuve, at the latter's apartment in the Rue Jean Goujon.

The Deputy was a distinguished looking man of middle age with a high forehead, an upturned moustache and a little imperial. When making the appointment, Laveriac had informed him of its purpose and after they had exchanged civilities he said to de Quesnoy:

'Monsieur Dupont, no one could have a better will to aid you in this matter than myself. But it is only right that I should warn you first that, should you succeed in penetrating the secrets of the Freemasons and then betray them, you will be exposing yourself to considerable danger. It might even cost you your life.'

De Quesnoy gave a tight-lipped smile. 'I thank you, Monsieur, but by coming to Paris at all I have exposed himself to arrest and execution; so this additional risk will not deter me.'

'I have made no mention of your circumstances,' the General put in quickly.

'Quite right, *mon ami*. The fewer people who are aware that I have returned to Paris the better; and I am sure Monsieur de Villeneuve will not press me for my real name. It is only that I wish him to know that I am in fact a Frenchman and, like himself, an ex-officer who has been forced out of the Army.'

De Villeneuve at once shook him warmly by the hand. 'I appreciate your trust, Monsieur; and what you tell me makes me all the more eager to serve you. But since you have adopted a *nom-de-guerre* that will add to our difficulties. Had you really been a Belgian they would have had only to make inquiries through their people in the town from which you came to check up on your antecedents. As things are, it seems that there is no background with which you can provide them; and I am certain that they would never accept you as an initiate without one.'

'I thought that would be the case,' replied the Count; 'so I have a suggestion which might enable this question of a check-up to be evaded. On my mother's side I am Russian, and I speak that language fluently. If you passed me on to one or two of them as a Russian who had recently arrived in Paris, I would later disclose that I was an atheist and a revolutionary who had been sent into exile by the Czar.'

'There are a number such, and the Masons would probably confront you with one or more of them.'

'No matter. None of them would be able to detect that I am not a Russian born; and Russia is such a vast country that if I say that I come from some quite small town the odds are a hundred to one against their even knowing if a revolutionary cell exists in it.'

'I think your plan a good one; and I happen to know a Past-Master who has a Russian wife. His name is Forain—Gustave Forain—and they used to dine two or three evenings a week at the Rotonde in Montparnasse. If they still do so we can pick him up there. But tell me, do you know anything about Masonry?'

'Practically nothing,' admitted de Quesnoy. 'Only that in France it is a secret society composed of freethinkers and fanatics who would like to see Church and State overthrown everywhere.'

'It is much more than that. Its membership runs into tens of thousands. All are sworn to promote such policies as are decided on by their superiors, and ninety-five per cent are slavishly obedient; with the result that it is a great hidden power. I am speaking now of Continental Masonry. The English variety is, I gather, non-political and mainly concerned with charity; but ours originated in Germany

271

and was brought here by Illuminatii in the middle of the eighteenth century. They were the founders of the Grand Lodge of the Orient, which now has over five hundred branches in France alone. It brought about the great revolution of 1789 and all those bloody upheavals that overturned half-a-dozen European governments in 1848 and '49. It is powerful enough to ferment such revolts at any time; but it will not do so here as long as the present government remains in office, because Combes's policies, being retrograde and destructive, are doing its work for it.'

De Quesnoy nodded. 'And what do you think my chances are of being able to secure evidence that the Freemasons are now largely controlling, through General André, promotions and enforced retirements calculated seriously to decrease the efficiency of the Army?'

'Far from certain,' replied the Deputy, pulling at his little imperial. 'In Masonry there are numerous grades. Many initiates, like myself, never advance farther than the lowest. By showing great keenness and making an intensive study of the rituals it is possible for one to get passed through the rest of the inferior degrees fairly quickly; by that I mean in a year or so. But even then I doubt if you would learn much of what goes on in the secret councils of the upper strata.'

'Then it hardly seems worth while for me to devote so much time and trouble to such an unpromising line of investigation.'

'That is for you to decide, Monsieur; but I think it might be. You see, once you have become an initiate you will meet any number of Masons. Even while still yourself of the lowest degree there will be nothing to stop your beginning to cultivate socially some of those who have passed the Chair. Being human, I don't doubt that certain of them are subject to flattery and the temptation to boast to their juniors in the Masonic hierarchy of the powers they wield. So, although it seems to me unlikely that you will learn anything officially, if you play your cards skilfully there would at least be a chance of your picking up enough information through private sources to damn General André.'

'To do that I shall find no trouble too much,' said the Count more cheerfully; 'so let us plan our campaign'.

The upshot of their deliberations was that the following morning de Quesnoy visited a number of second-hand clothes shops and bought himself a modest wardrobe of items suitable to the rôle of a middle-class Russian business man. After a patient search, he also secured

272

a large, round-lidded, cedarwood trunk that had some Russian labels on it. Returning to the Avenue Victor Hugo with his purchases, he changed into one of the suits and packed the rest of his new possessions into the trunk.

After lunch he called at the Russian Consul-General's and inquired about boarding-houses, preferably in the Montparnasse district, kept by Russians for people of moderate means. An obliging young clerk supplied him with a list of four and, having collected his trunk, he set off to inspect them.

His choice fell on the Pension Smirnoff, which was run by a widow of that name; and, suitably enough, was situated in the Rue d'Odessa. Introducing himself by the undistinguished name of Vasili Petrovitch, he told her that he had only recently arrived from Russia; and that he had already found a job as a commercial traveller; so he would frequently be away from Paris for varying periods, but wanted a *pied à terre* in which to leave his things, and in which to live whenever he returned to the capital.

As it was her custom to let rooms with full pension she at first demurred, but it happened that she had three rooms empty; so, on his offering to take one on the first floor and pay a month's rent in advance, a compromise was reached. In this way he secured a suitable accommodation address and background without having to face the miserable prospect of actually living, perhaps for many weeks, in a dreary boarding-house. However, it was important that he should know enough of the place to be able to talk about it and, it being Saturday, he spent the week-end there.

He had decided on taking a lodging in Montparnasse so that it would appear natural for him to frequent the Rotonde, and as this was a part of the Latin quarter he was by no means surprised to find that most of his fellow guests at the Pension were Russians who had come to Paris to study art. Madame Smirnoff turned out to be an easy-going, motherly body; so at mealtimes a cheerful Bohemianism reigned, and while de Quesnoy observed a deliberate reticence regarding his own affairs he was soon very well informed about those of his neighbours at table.

On the Monday he returned to the elegant comfort of the Avenue Victor Hugo, but in the evening he met de Villeneuve and they went to the Rotonde together. They were unlucky; Monsieur Forain and his wife did not appear. But on the Tuesday they were more fortunate. In the late sunlight of the summer evening the Forains came walking arm-in-arm up the street. De Villeneuve, as had previously been agreed, pointed them out to de Quesnoy, then slipped away down a side street, leaving the rest to him.

Having guarded against direct observation by going into one of the kiosk-like *pissoirs* which in those days were a feature of the streets of Paris, and from outside which the backs of gentlemen's heads and feet could be seen by passers-by, the Count, peeping over his shoulder and across the top of the green-painted iron body-screen, watched the Forains go into the restaurant. A few minutes later he followed them in and sat down on the *banquette* at a table next to the one they had taken.

While ordering his meal in fairly good French with a heavy accent, he ignored the faintly interested glances of the couple beside him; but when his first dish arrived, he deliberately, in taking up a fork, dropped it on the floor, then as he bent to pick it up gave vent to an apparently spontaneous exclamation of annoyance in Russian.

The little trick worked like a charm. Madame Forain smiled at him and remarked, 'I think you must be a compatriot of mine, Monsieur.' He bowed gallantly, addressed her in Russian and told her his name. She did likewise and introduced her husband. From that moment the game was in de Quesnoy's hands and, without showing undue eager-ness, he was soon in pleasant conversation with his new acquaintances.

Kemenets Podolskiy being the nearest town to Jvanets, he told them that he was a native of that place; so that, should he later be confronted with anyone who came from the district, he could not possibly be faulted on it. He had, he said, been a prosperous dealer in agricultural implements, and now followed that trade in Paris; but no longer as his own master. He gave them no reason for his having left Russia, but mentioned casually that he had regretted having to give up his work as an official of the local Co-operative Society; because he knew, and he knew Forain would know, that the Co-ops in Russia were regularly used by the revolutionaries as the means of distributing to the masses their bulletins and subversive propaganda.

Forain, who was a fair-haired, square-faced man of about forty-eight, disclosed for his part that he had been a master-printer and now owned his own printing works in the Rue de Rennes. He and his wife lived above the works. They had no children but seven nieces, ranging in age from seventeen to three, provided one of the major interests of their lives. Madame Forain was a great needlewoman and spent most of her spare time making these children pretty things: her husband worked long hours but, in the summer months, when he could get away from business, his great delight was to go rowing on the Seine.

Next night the Forains did not come to the Rotonde, but they came again on the Thursday and went straight to the table they had occupied two evenings before. De Quesnoy had already installed himself, but deliberately chosen a table near the door, and he exchanged a polite bow with them as they came in. Then, when they were getting towards the end of their meal, he sent a waiter over to ask them if they would honour him by joining him for coffee and a liqueur.

Madame Forain smiled an acceptance, and when they came over he displayed almost pathetic pleasure, making it clear that he had plucked up the courage to ask them only because he knew so few people in Paris and at times felt terribly lonely.

Over their Benedictine and *café filtre* they talked for a good hour and a half, mostly of Russia and Madame's girlhood there. She was a native of St. Petersburg and had become lady's maid to a Countess, who had brought her to Paris in the middle eighties. Forain had met her, on one of her evenings off, dancing at the Great Hall of Folly, and later persuaded her to marry him. Politics were not mentioned, but this second meeting paid de Quesnoy a good dividend, as before leaving the Forains asked him if he would like to join them for a picnic next Sunday in a boat that they kept out at St. Cloud. As it was contrary to custom for the French bourgeoisie to invite any but most intimate friends to their homes, this was better than anything for which he could normally have hoped, and he accepted with alacrity.

The Sunday proved fine, and the long hours on the river created just the atmosphere for disclosing confidences; so the fictitious M. Vasili Petrovich gave his reasons for leaving Russia. Having decided that the Forains were far from fanatical types, he made no pretence of being a nihilist, and even deplored the attempts by them to assassinate members of the Imperial family. But he spoke with great bitterness of the way in which the Czar's autocratic government denied the people a voice in the running of the country and deliberately blocked all progress. It was circulating pamphlets advocating a Socialist World-State that had brought him to grief, but fortunately a friendly police chief had warned him that he had been denounced so this enabled him to escape over the frontier with some part of his small fortune instead of being sent as a prisoner to exile in Siberia.

The Forains were most sympathetic. It transpired that Madame had a brother who, while demonstrating in the streets, had been ridden down by the Cossacks and crippled for life; and that Monsieur, although only a boy of fifteen at the time, had fought beside the Communists on the barricades in '71.

During the following week the Count returned their hospitality by taking them to a local café-concert, and they joined him on another night after dinner at the Rotonde. On the Sunday, he again went with them to St. Cloud but in the afternoon it came on to rain so they returned early. Madame then decided to visit her sister-in-law and nieces, and Forain took de Quesnoy with him to what he termed his "wet weather retreat".

Entering a small café, they walked through it and upstairs to a room in which there were two billiard tables and a score of men, a number of whom were sitting talking and drinking in its big bay window. Half a dozen of them called cheerful greetings to Forain, and he introduced "Monsieur Vasili Petrovich" all round as a good fellow who had recently been driven from his country by the tyranny of the Czar.

It was soon obvious to the Count that everyone in the place knew one another and that it was a form of club, although an unofficial one, as there was no formal electing of members; but on his leaving with Forain after spending several hours there, three of the other men with whom he had talked all invited him to come again any time that he liked.

Most of the men present had given the impression of being middle-class intellectuals and, while the conversation had touched on a wide variety of subjects, whenever politics cropped up the views expressed had been those of the extreme Left; so de Quesnoy judged that many of his new acquaintances were brother Masons of Forain's. In consequence, while keeping up with the Forains, he now gave more of his time to the billiards saloon and to cultivating its most regular occupants: three men named Héquet, Daguenet and Lazare.

It was the last who first spoke to him about Freemasonry, and said he thought he would find much in it to interest him. Playing for safety, he showed no great enthusiasm but asked to be told more about it.

Smiling, Lazare declared that the secrets of Masonry could not be divulged, but that all honest men who hated priests and oppression could be certain that by becoming Masons they would be helping to advance the cause in which they believed.

No more was said at the time; but three evenings later Héquet tackled him on the same subject, then drew Lazare and also Forain, who happened to be in the room, into the conversation. On the latter, as his original friend, promising to sponsor him, de Quesnoy agreed to have his name put forward.

A fortnight elapsed, then his friends took him by night to an underground Masonic Temple at the headquarters of the Grand Orient in the Rue Cadet, just off the southern end of the Rue de la Fayette, and there he was initiated into the first degree of the mysteries. Parts of the ritual he thought impressive and other parts childish. The oaths he had to take would have been binding, on account of the awful fate accepted as the penalty for breaking them, had he given them the weight they were expected to carry; but he did not. To him his word of honour meant a very great deal, as also did an oath in which God was invoked, but, as he had decided for himself before seeking initiation, the dictates of chivalry had no bearing on this matter and, since the congregation was composed of atheists, any oath dictated by their representative must logically be meaningless.

His initiation did not take place until the third week in July; so it had cost him two months' hard work even to penetrate the Masonic world as a neophyte, but the way was now open for him to become the repository of Masonic secrets if he could induce his seniors in the hierarchy to confide them to him.

In the meantime, he had been building up a very different personality which he felt might later have its uses should Masonry prove a dead end for him. He had soon learned that the Forains dined at the Rotonde only on Tuesdays and Thursdays and decided that to run into them there one night a week was quite sufficient. He had had to devote five Sundays to them, and had spent four weekends, as well as a number of odd nights, keeping warm his room at the Pension Smirnoff. Lastly, from mid-June, he had had to spend two or more evenings each week up in the billiards room. But it had been easy for him frequently to fit these activities in on the same night; so actually he had spent barely a third of each week in Montparnasse.

277

For the other two-thirds he had been living miles away on the north side of the Seine as Jules Dupont, in Van Ryn's comfortable apartment. A certain amount of his time he gave to seeing bloodstock put through its paces, and making arrangements concerning his nominal master's small stud. He also stocked Channock's cellar, engaged a good chef for him and made all the arrangements for his frequent luncheon and dinner parties, leaving Harry Plimsol free to concentrate entirely on the banker's business affairs.

Most of Van Ryn's guests were Americans, either resident in Paris or passing through it, but as his circle of acquaintances grew he also began to entertain the leading French financiers of solid reputation, and on two occasions when de Quesnoy was present he had M. Rouvier, the Minister of Finance in Combes's government, to dinner.

Listening to the talk of these men, who largely controlled the economic situation in France, gave the Count a behind-the-scenes insight into the affairs of the country which he felt might in due course prove of considerable value to him in his endeavours to bring down the government. Moreover, this cover of his in the Avenue Victor Hugo enabled him to see General Laveriac, Gabriel Syveton and Guyot de Villeneuve openly, to discuss progress, whenever he wished.

Early in June he received two letters. The first had been forwarded on to him from America through the Van Ryn office. It was from de Vendôme, in reply to one that he had written to the Prince from New York.

His ex-pupil first expressed unbounded delight at his escape, then undying gratitude for his sacrifice in having changed places with him in the *Cherche-Midi*. He went on to say that he was not content to leave matters as they were, with de Quesnoy exposed, should he return to France and be caught, to a charge of murder. He had, therefore, instructed a legal firm in Paris to engage private inquiry agents to make an exhaustive investigation into the fracas at Versailles. His idea was to pay out of his own pocket considerable sums as compensation to every policeman who had suffered injury in the affair. But before receiving the money they would be asked to write out a detailed eyewitness account of every act they had seen committed during the engagement, and swear to it.

By these means, de Vendôme reasoned, the malice of Combes and André might be defeated, as the combined statements must show how the three policemen who had died had met their deaths, and that de Quesnoy had had no hand in killing any of them.

The Count was greatly touched, for he felt that if the plan succeeded it would make a great difference to his future. As long as he was wanted for murder the French Government could, on locating him, demand his extradition from almost any country in the world; so there would be few places in which he could ever have settled down in safety under his own name. But if a dossier of sworn evidence could be compiled against which no murder charge could be sustained, then a prison sentence for assaulting the police was the worst penalty that could be inflicted on him, if he were caught while in France, and he could live in exile anywhere that he liked without fear of extradition.

The other letter was from Angela. He had not written to her from New York as he had planned to surprise her by turning up in Paris some two months earlier than had been his intention before reaching Valparaiso; so this was a reply to a letter he had sent her only a week after learning from her husband that she was in London.

In it she said how overjoyed she had been on receiving his cable from Bahia, and spoke of the frustration she had felt at not being able to reply to the letters he had sent her from South American ports on account of her uncertainty of his future movements. She went on to say that in February her father had begun a tour of duty at the Foreign Office; so her parents had taken a house in Great Cumberland Place, and she had gone over at the beginning of May for a long stay with them. At present she was greatly enjoying the gaieties of the London season, and did not mean to return to Paris until at least after Cowes week, as for this she was going to her grandmother, the Dowager Lady Chudleigh, whose home, Herne Court, was in the Isle of Wight.

De Quesnoy found her letter disappointing. Apart from a description of her relief when she had first learned that he had escaped to South America, and a plea that now he had returned to Paris he should take every possible precaution against being recognized, the tone of her letter was very similar to those which she had written to him while he was in Madagascar and North Africa. It was not that after this last five months of separation he had expected an outpouring of violent passion, but her declaration just before they had parted in the *Cherche-Midi*, and his own letters to her since, had led him to anticipate a much warmer expression of her feelings.

However, after some thought he decided that her restraint on paper was probably due to her English upbringing, and that being once again among her own people had re-aroused in her the virtue they made of concealing their emotions. He was, too, by this time launched on his campaign to cultivate the Forains, and felt that he must not allow his mind to dwell too much on Angela until he could make more concrete plans about his own future.

Nevertheless, now that he was again in Paris so many of its sights and scenes recalled her to him that he thought of her frequently, and towards the end of June he jumped at a chance that arose by which he might see her again earlier than he had expected. It came about through Van Ryn's announcing one evening that he intended to buy a yacht; so that he could enjoy his favourite pastime of sailing at Deauville, and perhaps for a while, during the coming winter, down in the Mediterranean.

Realizing at once the possibility of combining his friend's pleasure with his own desires, de Quesnoy said, 'What a splendid idea; and if in the next few weeks you could find something to suit you we could take her across to Cowes. The meeting there and the Kiel Regatta are the two greatest events of the sailing year; so if business does not interfere it would be a pity for you to miss either.'

Van Ryn agreed with enthusiasm. Enquiries were set on foot, and after inspecting three craft of about the tonnage he favoured he settled on a handsome cutter named the *Juliette* that was lying in Dieppe harbour, took over her crew, and left it to de Quesnoy to complete the arrangements for her sailing.

The Count's initiation as a Mason had by then been fixed for July 17th, after which discretion demanded that for a while he should not put himself forward too eagerly; so he told his sponsors and Madame Smirnoff that he was taking the last week in July and the first in August as his annual holiday, and meant to spend them at a little place in Normandy. Then he wrote to Angela giving the name of Van Ryn's yacht and telling her that they were coming to Cowes. She replied by return saying how greatly she looked forward to seeing him, and on July 21st the yacht set sail for England.

They had a good passage, and when she arrived the following evening Van Ryn found the Solent a sight to gladden his yachtsman's heart. Hundreds of small and medium-sized boats were practising for the races, and scores of larger ones with towering masts lay at their anchorages—among them King Edward VII's *Britannia*, her famous rivals, *Reliance* and *Valkyrie II*, and Sir Thomas Lipton's Atlantic challenger, *Shamrock III*.

Their application for an anchorage having been put in very late, the one allotted to them was a considerable distance from Cowes pier, but de Quesnoy got ashore as soon as he could and, having forced his way through the packed hall of the Gloster Hotel, found to his relief that Herne Court was on the telephone. After the initial difficulties connected with the use of this comparatively new instrument had been overcome, he managed to speak to Angela. Between buzzings and cracklings, she asked him to come over with his American friend to lunch next day, and told him that Herne Court lay in the south-east of the island, near the village of Brading.

On making further inquiries at the office of the hotel, he learned that Brading was a good twelve miles from Cowes by road, so he ordered a carriage for eleven o'clock the following morning; then, darkness having fallen, he spent two grim hours being rowed in and out between a forest of bobbing masts before the three French sailors who had brought him ashore succeeded in locating the *Juliette* at her moorings.

His excitement at the prospect of seeing Angela again, undiminished by his dinnerless and exasperating evening, he hustled Van Ryn ashore next day and, as the weather remained good, they had an enjoyable drive through leafy lanes, which brought them to Herne Court in good time for luncheon. They found it to be a not very large but charming Georgian mansion, and the house-party of some fifteen people, which had been assembled for Cowes week, was seated on the lawn under a great cedar.

Now that he was again outside France the Count had had no intention of asking Angela to keep his real identity secret; but, even so, he was distinctly embarrassed to find that she had told all her relatives and friends about the part he had played in the de Vendôme conspiracy, and how Van Ryn had rescued him. As a result both of them were given a welcome in which curiosity was only thinly veiled under good breeding, and Angela's grandmother, the formidable old Dowager Countess, voiced the desire of all her guests, although somewhat inexactly, when she declared that after lunch they must tell the story of how they had murdered all the warders on Devil's Island.

When they had enjoyed one of those meals the simplicity but excellence of which seems peculiar to English country houses, they adjourned to the garden and de Quesnoy gave a modest account of the events which had led to his diving overboard from the cruiser. Van Ryn then took up the tale and would obviously have been willing to spent the rest of the afternoon discoursing on his friend's sufferings and bravery; but the Count did his best to cut him short as he was anxious that the party should break up so that he could get Angela to himself.

In her light summer frock, a big picture hat and this, the natural setting for her English loveliness, he thought her more beautiful than he had ever seen her, and it made him all the more impatient to talk to her about the future; but in that, for the time being, he was infuriatingly frustrated. He was just about to ask her to take him round the gardens when a clock in a small belfry over the stables chimed three. The butler appeared behind Lady Chudleigh's chair and murmured with a bow:

'The carriages are ready, milady.'

A few of the party excused themselves on the plea of having letters to write, but the old lady lost no time in sweeping the others together and leading them through to the front of the house, where two carriages and pairs, and behind them the victoria which had brought the visitors, were waiting.

As she was assisted into the leading landau by a tall, grey-haired man, who was spoken to as "Jim-jam", "Newcombe" or "Sir Reginald" according to the age and sex of whoever addressed him, Angela whispered to de Quesnoy:

'To go for a drive every fine afternoon is one of Grandmama's rituals, and today she is taking us to Carisbrooke Castle. King Charles I was kept a prisoner there by the Roundheads, so she thought you and Mr. Van Ryn would like to go over it.'

'That was most kind,' murmured the Count, as he and Sir Reginald followed her into the carriage, while Van Ryn and the other members of the party got into those behind. Two minutes later the little cavalcade set off at a spanking trot, and after a drive of an hour through gently rolling well-wooded country reached the mount upon which stood the ivy-covered, half-ruined gate-house of the castle.

Old Lady Chudleigh said that she meant to remain in her carriage, but she refused to allow Sir Reginald to stay and keep her company, declaring that few people knew the castle better than he did, so he must take the party round it.

In other circumstances de Quesnoy would have been much interested in the misfortunes of Charles I, but now he silently cursed that monarch, and Sir Reginald for discoursing so loquaciously upon him. However, towards the end of the half-hour's tour he managed to get Angela a little behind the others, so that he was able to say to her, *sotto voce*:

'When can I see you alone?'

'I don't know.' She gave him an uneasy glance. 'To arrange that would be difficult.'

'But it was for that I came to England. Can we not make our excuses to your grandmother and go off together for a cup of tea in one of those little places we passed in Carisbrooke village?'

'No, no! That is impossible. A picnic tea will have been brought. Anyway, people like ourselves could not eat a meal at a table in a garden full of trippers.'

'My dear, what snobs you English are! But no matter. If I can engage a private room in one of the hotels in Cowes, will you come and dine with me?'

'No, Armand, no! What possible excuse could I give for going out at night on my own. That is quite out of the question.'

'Why should you have to give an excuse? Although you don't look it, you are twenty-nine years of age, and married.'

'Armand, things are different here from what they are in France. In England women of my class, single or married, never go out alone. I believe there are restaurants that have private rooms, and that men take chorus girls to them; but when a society woman has an *affaire* she has to conduct it in her own home or while staying with friends.'

'Can you not arrange, then, for Lady Chudleigh to invite me to stay for a few nights at Herne Court?'

'I could have at any other time of the year, but for the regatta week the house is always packed to the attics. Whether I would have dared to, though, I hardly know. You see, Grandmama has no idea that you are more to me than just an old friend, and she is frightfully strait-laced.'

'Very well, then. I noticed an inn when we drove through Brading. I will take a room there and meet you clandestinely in the woods, or at night in the garden.'

'Please, Armand! Please do no such thing,' she pleaded in a low, urgent voice. 'There would be tittle-tattle in the village. It would reach my grandmother's ears. Remember, you are a foreigner, so would be remarked by everyone in the vicinity. If she learned that you were living nearby and that we were meeting in secret she would be horrified. To her mind I should have put myself on a level with a servant girl with a follower who hangs about the area steps. She would never forgive me.'

'Then it seems the only thing is for you to come to lunch with me in the yacht; although that is anything but an ideal spot for private conversation.'

'Even there I could not go alone.'

'I appreciate that; but the table in the cabin will not accommodate more than six, so we cannot invite Lady Chudleigh and her whole party.'

'Provided I may bring another woman and you will meet us on the quay, that would be all right.'

The matter was satisfactorily settled a few minutes later, owing to Van Ryn's wish to see more of a charming Miss Fiona Mackintosh, with whom he had spent most of the afternoon. Fiona's mother gave her consent, providing Angela would go as chaperone; so Fiona accepted his invitation to lunch in the *Juliette* the following day.

De Quesnoy had been hoping that he and Van Ryn would be carried back to Herne Court to tea, and that after it another chance would arise for him to talk to Angela; but that hope was quashed by a picnic tea having been provided.

Lady Chudleigh directed that a pleasant spot on the Cowes road should be selected, so that the two visitors should have a minimum distance to travel afterwards; a pretty vale some half-mile from the Castle was chosen, the two footmen who had accompanied the party beside the coachmen on the boxes of the carriages spread the contents of the hampers on the grass; a carefree hour was passed in eating and light conversation, then the two guests made their adieux and drove back to Cowes in their hired victoria.

To de Quesnoy's fury he proved no luckier on the following day. Angela and the highly decorative Miss Mackintosh were duly met and taken off to the yacht, but, most unfortunately, a small sea was running and neither of them was a very good sailor. They only pecked at the excellent lunch provided and were both so obviously uncomfortable that there was no alternative but to take them ashore immediately afterwards.

Consoled a little by the thought that he would at least be able to take Angela for a walk through the town, the Count helped her up out of the dinghy, but a moment later they ran into some friends of hers who were just landing with Lord Dunraven from his yacht for the same reason as themselves.

After introductions had been made, Lord Dunraven declared that he could not possibly allow them to watch the races wedged in among the crowd, and that they must come with his party to the Squadron lawn; so, much against his wish, de Quesnoy had to submit to being signed in for the afternoon as a guest at the Royal Yacht Club.

In any other circumstances it would have been a delightful experience, for during Regatta Week this, perhaps the most exclusive club in the world, was the scene of the last great event of the Season. The broad greensward along the sea wall, opposite which the races finished, was crowded with the nobility and beauty of Britain. Fat, jolly King Edward was there, and gracious Queen Alexandra; Admirals Prince Louis of Battenberg and Lord Charles Beresford; famous hostesses such as Mrs. Ronnie Greville, Lady Cooper and Mrs. George Keppel; the Royal children and the young millionaire Duke of Westminster with his beautiful wife. The men were nearly all wearing white, with yachting caps, panamas or straw boaters; the women were in bright-hued, wide-flounced dresses with feather boas, and screening their complexions under gay parasols; so in the summer sunshine the brilliant colours of the constantly moving throng gave it the appearance of a human kaleidoscope.

After they had watched several races, Lord Dunraven offered to show de Quesnoy and Van Ryn the trophies, so they left the girls with the rest of Dunraven's party and went with him to the Club house. For a few minutes they admired the great silver cups and challenge shields, and were just turning away when King Edward came in, followed by half a dozen gentlemen. He gave a friendly nod and said:

'Not racing today, Dunraven?'

'No, Sir,' replied the famous yachtsman. 'We broke our spinnaker boom in yesterday's race, and couldn't get another fitted in time today; so we had to scratch.'

'Hard luck,' said the King. Then his glance took in Dunraven's companions and he asked. 'Are your friends sailing men?' which was tantamount to permission to present them.

Dunraven stepped aside so that they could come forward. 'Yes, Sir. This is Mr. Channock Van Ryn of New York, who has brought the *Juliette* over from Dieppe; and this, Colonel the Count de Quesnoy.'

In turn they bent over the royal hand. The King said to Van Ryn that he was always happy to welcome American yachtsmen, as it was they who provided the British with the best rivals in the great sport. Then, stroking his pointed beard with a thoughtful gesture, he said to de Quesnoy:

'Your name seems very familiar to me, Count; but I cannot recall in what connection. Wait! I have it. Surely it was you who played a leading rôle in the de Vendôme conspiracy last winter?'

De Quesnoy bowed. 'That is so, Your Majesty. I hope, though, that you will not believe the lies printed about me in the papers. I had no hand in shooting policemen, as was said, much as I would like to see a King upon the Throne of France again.'

'I would be a poor King if I did not incline to take the word of a royalist,' smiled the monarch. Then, his smile broadening, he glanced over his shoulder and added with a touch of wickedness, 'Although I can hardly expect some of these gentlemen to agree with me about that.'

With a pleasant nod, he dismissed Dunraven and his friends, turned to the others and said in French, 'And now, Messieurs, I will show you our trophies.'

As they left the Club house, Dunraven remarked to de Quesnoy: 'Those were some official visitors from France, invited here at the King's instigation. He has played a greater part than anyone in promoting this Entente Cordiale, and he is doing everything he can to cement it.'

The Count nodded. 'To have brought about the burying of the hatchet after six hundred years of enmity between our two countries was a remarkable achievement; and, personally, I am delighted by it.'

He was, however, far from delighted at having run into several French officials; and as soon as he could, in a low voice, he asked Van Ryn, 'Did you know any of those people? I thought I saw you nod to one of them.'

'You're right,' replied the American. 'The little dark man was Camille Pelletan, the Minister of Marine. I sat near him at dinner about three weeks back, at a party given by Finance Minister Rouvier.'

No more was said upon the matter until the early evening, after the girls had been seen off in the carriage that had brought them over. Van Ryn was in great form, for his afternoon on the Squadron lawn and having been presented to King Edward had more than made up to him for the ill-success of his lunch party. He was, too, making excellent going with Fiona, and it was only after he had been singing her praises for some minutes that he noticed his friend's unresponsive silence, so asked:

'What's wrong, Armand? Why are you looking so glum?'

'I'm greatly worried about our encounter with the King,' de Quesnoy replied. 'Having those French officials with him at the time could not have been more unfortunate. They must have heard my name when I was presented, and His Majesty's remarks about the de Vendôme conspiracy. As you told Colonel Roux that I jumped overboard, I have been hoping that my enemies believed me to be dead; but now they'll know that I am still very much alive. What is more, if Pelletan, or one of the others, sends a telegram reporting my presence here to the Minister of Justice, it is quite on the cards that he will apply for a warrant for my extradition.'

'They might try it; but I doubt if it would get them anywhere. The British make a great thing of refusing to surrender foreigners accused of political crimes who have taken refuge here. They even give sanctuary to Italian anarchists and Russian nihilists.'

'True, but not when those gentry have knifed someone or blown them to bits with a bomb; and unfortunately I fall into that category. The French Government will charge me, not with any political crime, but with murder. And under International Law, if the English police catch me they would have to give me up.'

'That's bad, Armand; that's bad. Fiona's not going back to her home in Scotland till the grouse shooting starts on the 12th; so I've been thinking of staying in these parts for a week longer than we planned. But it looks now as if we'll have to be moving on before the boys who are after you can get to work.'

'My dear Channock,' de Quesnoy smiled, 'after all your kindness to me, I would not dream of dragging you away. But they might send an Inspector from the Sûreté over specially to get me, and if they act at once he could be here with his warrant within forty-eight hours; so to be on the safe side I ought to be out of England by Thursday night.'

'Where'll you go?'

'Why, back to France. That is the last place they will look for me, and I have no intention of abandoning my vendetta against André.'

'Good for you. It's pretty hard, though, when you were hoping to see a lot more of that lovely Madame Syveton.'

Van Ryn had voiced the thing which was making de Quesnoy seethe with inward fury. So far, all his attempts to get Angela on his own long enough for a serious conversation had been frustrated and the next day, Wednesday, she was going with a party from Herne Court across to the mainland to lunch with the Stuart Wortleys at Highcliffe Castle. That left him only Thursday, and Lord Dunraven had asked them all again to the Royal Yacht Club on that day; so his chances of securing a tête-à-tête with her before he had to leave England now seemed extremely slender.

On Wednesday there was a race for yachts of *Juliette*'s class and she came in third out of nine. As Van Ryn had had, as yet, so little time to practise handling her, he was delighted, and encouraged to hope that he might do even better in another race for which she was entered on Friday.

The Count did his best to show interest in the race and enthusiasm about its result, but for most of the day his mind was on Angela. By exercising his imagination he thought of a dozen tricks by which he could have lured her away from her friends for an hour or two, but all of them involved either the use of high-handed methods or of her having to disclose afterwards that she had kept a secret rendez-vous with him. Had they been in France he would have had no scruples about adopting some bold design, but here he dared not do so. Her insistence that, should he disclose himself as anything more than an old friend, this would involve her in a most unpleasant scandal and be her ruin with her grandmother, tied his hands.

Thursday proved fine and again, both within and without the shadow thrown by Cowes Castle, the Squadron lawn was crowded. Once more for several hours de Quesnoy was compelled to play the tantalizing game of seeing but not touching. He could delight in the sight of Angela and smile at her, but he could not even press her hand, and could speak privately with her only between long intervals of airy general conversation and the distraction of fresh people constantly emerging from the social whirl to exchange pleasantries with herself and her friends

To his further annoyance, he learnt that she was not, as he had supposed, returning to France soon after Cowes Week She was staying with her grandmother until mid-September, and only going home then because her step-son, Henri Syveton, was to be married.

De Quesnoy had almost forgotten the boy's existence, as until the previous March he had been out of Paris for three years doing his military service. Angela said that his father had arranged a very satisfactory match for him with a Mademoiselle Clothilde de Vauclose who was quite a beauty, if one liked full-blooded southern types, and came of an old family that was still well endowed with this world's goods.

With a quick smile de Quesnoy said in a whisper, 'I wish them well; but it's about your own marriage that I have been so anxious to talk to you. It is a great disappointment to me that I must leave here without any idea what your feelings are about the future.'

Her big brown eyes intent and serious, she replied in a low voice, 'Please forgive me for having avoided an explanation, but had you insisted on seeing me alone it would have caused me great embarrassment. Besides, certain complications have arisen which prevent me from taking any decision at the moment. But by the time I get back to Paris I hope things will have straightened out. Anyhow, there will be nothing to stop us meeting in secret there and talking freely.'

With that the Count had to be content. The same evening he took affectionate leave of Van Ryn and crossed the Solent to Southampton in the pinnace of one of their recently made English acquaintances. Using the name of Jules Dupont, he crossed in the boat that left at midnight for Le Havre. No formalities were required for landing, and on July 27th he was again in Paris.

For a fortnight he resumed the activities that he had temporarily dropped to go to England. Most of his time he spent as Vasili Petrovitch with the Forains, Héquet, Daguenet, Lazare and a new acquaintance named Jean Bidegain, who always seemed to be at the headquarters of the Grand Orient whenever he went there. Both week-ends he slept at the Pension Smirnoff but during midweek he continued to enjoy the far greater comfort of the apartment in the Avenue Victor Hugo, with Harry Plimsol as his companion.

It was on August 9th that Plimsol received a telegram from his master, which read: 'Sailing today expect to arrive Paris on eleventh.'

At about nine o'clock on the morning of the 11th de Quesnoy was lying in his bath. A gentle tapping on the door surprised him into sitting up and calling out, 'What is it?'

Plimsol's voice came in a whisper. 'It's me—Harry. The police are here. They say they are expecting the Boss to turn up at any time, and mean to wait here so they can ask him some questions immediately on his arrival. But I've a hunch it's you they are after.'

CHAPTER XXII

THE LOYAL (?) WIFE

I N a second de Quesnoy was out of the bath. Flinging a towel round him he crossed to the door, unlocked it, beckoned Plimsol inside and asked in a whisper:

'How many of them are there? Where are they?'

'Two,' Plimsol whispered back, 'both plain-clothes 'tecs. Antoine let them in and came along to me. I took them into the salon. They said they meant to wait here till the Boss turned up and that they had a warrant to search the apartment in the meantime. I said they'd best have a café-cognac before they started in on the job. They fell for that, and I was able to slip away on the pretext that we keep the brandy locked up.'

'Well done! But what makes you think they are after me?'

'I figure they may be expecting you to turn up with the Boss. It's a dollar to a dime against his being wanted by the Sûreté; but you are, and . . .'

'You're right, Harry. Thank God they don't know that I'm back here already. I must get out at once.'

'I'll get your clothes, so you can dress here. Antoine will be taking them their coffee any moment now. I calculate you'll be safe for about ten minutes while they drink it.'

As the innocent-eyed, pink-cheeked young man gently closed the door, the Count hastily began to dry himself and think of possible ways of escape. The inner hall of the apartment was divided from the salon only by a pair of heavy red velvet curtains; so that the two rooms could be thrown into one for entertaining, The curtains were drawn in the evenings but at this hour were open, which made it impossible for him to pass through the hall without being seen. The fire escape for the whole block ran down its far end; so could be reached only by crossing the hall and the main landing and entering the apartment on its opposite side. The bathroom in which de Quesnoy, still naked, stood was three floors up and any attempt to climb down into the back yard was quite out of the question. It looked as if he was trapped and would have to fight his way out. Then, as he quickly brushed his hair, he remembered the tradesmen's lift that served the kitchen—but wondered whether it would bear him.

The door opened and Plimsol dumped a bundle of clothes on the towel-covered bathroom chair. De Quesnoy grabbed up his pants and said:

'I don't want to get you into trouble, and it may if you go on helping me to escape arrest.'

'Oh, shucks!' The young American grinned. 'Having pulled you out from under on the other side, the Boss wouldn't let you be collared here in Paris. Not if he could help it. And I go right along with him, every time.'

'Thanks, Harry. Then I'll get you to lower me in the tradesmen's lift; and we'll pray that the rope doesn't snap. If I get down safely, when Channock turns up tip him off somehow to say that he left me in England. None of the yacht's crew knew that I was returning to France; so if they are questioned the police will take what they say as confirmation of his story. If they swallow it there will be no hunt for me in Paris and I won't have much to worry about, providing I keep clear of this part of the city.'

'You'll drop being Jules Dupont altogether, eh?'

'That's it. I shall become Vasili Petrovitch permanently, and go to earth in the Pension Smirnoff.'

'Are you all right for dough?'

'I've enough to last me for about ten days. But I shall not be able to draw on my Dupont account any longer; so after that I'd be grateful if Channock would finance me till I can get fresh funds sent me by my father.'

'That'll be okay. I'll bring a wad of francs to the Pension.'

'No, no! If they question the servants while searching the flat they will find out that I've been here for the past fortnight. You can cover yourself by saying that no law compels you to volunteer information, and that I must have gone out before you were up this morning. But from then on both you and Channock will be under suspicion. They will shadow you, and probably intercept your mail, in the hope of tracing me through you. We had better not risk a meeting until next week, anyhow. And then it should be in some public place where neither of us is likely to be recognized. Let us make it a week today at mid-day at—let me see, yes—at the Brasserie Graff in the Boulevard de Clichy.'

As the Count tied his tie, he went on, 'Of course, if the servants give it away that I've been here it will be futile to get Channock to say that he left me in England. Build up for that, though, as far as you can. They will find nothing in my room to compromise me; but you must get the bed there made the moment I have gone. Tell them that the clothes I have left belonged to Channock's uncle. Now come and do your best to prevent my breaking my neck going down in the tradesmen's lift.'

Plimsol cautiously opened the door and peered out, while de Quesnoy pulled on his coat and made certain that his wallet was in his pocket; then, the coast being clear, they tiptoed quickly along to the kitchen.

The chef and Antoine, the butler, were both there. They gave Plimsol a surprised glance and he pulled up abruptly in the doorway. Wondering why, the Count took another pace forward and looked over his shoulder. To his consternation, round the corner of the door, he saw two men who had obviously been talking to the servants, and realized that they must be the detectives.

His glance met theirs. The sudden brightening of their eyes told him instantly that they must have been given a description of him, so knew him to be the man they were after.

He had heard no more of de Vendôme's plan to protect him from a murder charge; so for him arrest might still mean the guillotine. Immediately inside the kitchen door, on the left, lay a double door only the wire gauze section of which was kept closed in summer. Beyond it lay a small platform, then the tradesmen's lift. The two detectives were standing on the far side of the kitchen table, so would be twice as long as himself in reaching the lift—and more if they met with an obstruction.

His immediate instinct was to push Harry Plimsol forward so that he would block their path, then dive for the lift. But he judged that it was meant to carry, at the most, only a hundredweight of goods.

With Harry to hold the rope and check the lift's descent, but not so sharply as to endanger the rope's snapping under the strain, he might

293

have ridden swiftly yet safely to the ground. But if he jumped on to it while uncontrolled he would so greatly outweigh its counterweights that it would hurtle like a plummet to its base in the courtyard, burst its wooden sides with the impact and throw him violently from its shattered top on to the stone paving.

Next second the two detectives moved simultaneously towards him. At the same instant he gave Plimsol a swift shove in their direction. Then, instead of diving for the lift, he stepped a pace backwards, pulled the kitchen door to with a bang, and turned the key in its lock. Without waiting to draw breath he swung about and dashed back along the corridor.

He knew that there was a second exit from the kitchen, by way of the dining-room; so that he had no more than a flying start. But he reached the front door of the apartment before he heard the first sounds of pursuit. Out on the landing he saw that the lift was at some other floor. Taking the stairs three at a time, he fled helter-skelter down them. The concierge's wife gave him a startled glance as he dashed past her; but within two minutes of leaving the kitchen he was in the street.

A closed carriage was passing, its horses moving at a fast trot. With a run and a leap he landed on its back bar and supported himself there while being carried two hundred yards. Then he dropped off, stumbled, nearly fell under an approaching dray, but saved himself and reeled on to the pavement. Glancing back, he saw the detectives just emerging from the entrance to the block. Before they caught sight of him he dived down a side turning, then dropped his pace to a swift walk, breathless but elated at having eluded his pursuers.

Coming out in the Avenue Kléber, he walked down it to the Place du Trocadero, made quite certain that he was not, after all, being followed, then took the first omnibus going in the direction of Montparnasse. As it jogged across the river, past the Eiffel Tower and the Champ de Mars, he worked out in his mind the probable chain of events which had led up to his narrow escape from arrest.

The first link must have been a report by Camille Pelletan, or one of his party, that the Count de Quesnoy was in Cowes; but that would not have linked him with Jules Dupont. One of them must either have seen him in Paris while he was using the name of Dupont, or sent a description of his changed appearance which, coupled with being a guest in Van Ryn's yacht, had led to his identification as Dupont. It must have been some such evil chance which had enabled the Sûreté to put two and two together; for they must have already had on their files a report by Colonel Roux of how Van Ryn had pulled the Count out of the water, and declared that later in desperation he had jumped back into it.

Following their discovery that de Quesnoy was alive and had been living in Van Ryn's Paris apartment under the name of Dupont, they must have reasoned that the trouble and publicity entailed in applying to the English authorities for a warrant for the Count's extradition could be avoided by waiting until he returned in the *Juliette* to France and quietly arresting him on his arrival in Paris.

While the stuffy omnibus rumbled on over the *pavé* he began to worry about Van Ryn. The American had said that he might perhaps bring the *Juliette* up the Seine as far as Rouen, but he might equally well leave her at Le Havre, or her home port of Dieppe; so, not knowing his movements, there was no way in which de Quesnoy could prevent his walking in a few hours' time into the arms of the police. As he had brought the so-called Jules Dupont with him from the United States, and Dupont was now known to be de Quesnoy, that would make it next to impossible for him to maintain his assertion that the Count had jumped overboard. In consequence, he would probably now be arrested and charged with having deliberately aided a convict to escape. What the penalty was for such an act de Quesnoy had no idea, but it seemed quite on the cards that it would be a prison sentence; so he was made thoroughly wretched by the thought of the evil plight in which he had landed the friend who had given him such generous help.

His own situation was a further cause for considerable anxiety. By his early return to Paris, and Harry Plimsol's prompt warning that morning, he had had the luck to escape arrest. He was also fortunate in having the already established identity of Vasili Petrovitch into which to slip, and a bolt-hole at the Pension Smirnoff. But the police now knew him to be alive and in Paris, and it was impossible for him to make another radical change in his appearance unless he sacrificed the excellent contacts that he had built up with such patience among the Freemasons.

To remain as Petrovitch he must also remain—even if a shabby copy—as Dupont, and be liable to recognition by anyone who had known him as the Belgian. That danger would not only deprive him of the valuable insight into behind the scenes political moves that he had enjoyed through Van Ryn's banking contacts, but make it extremely risky for him to hold future consultations with Laveriac, Syveton or de Villeneuve, unless he could arrange to meet them secretly.

Greatly depressed, he went to the Pension and, to account for suddenly becoming a permanent inmate of it, told Madame Smirnoff that he had quarrelled with his employer; so he had been dismissed and, for the present, would be making no more short tours outside Paris as a commercial traveller.

During the week that followed time hung heavily on his hands. He had to leave the Pension each morning on the pretence of looking for a job; but he had nothing to do and dared not show his face in the more prosperous parts of the city. In the day-time all his brother Masons worked at one job or another; so he could not relieve his boredom, even in their company, until the evenings.

At last the week was up and, a prey to alternate fears and hopes, he set off across Paris to Montmartre to keep the rendez-vous at the Brasserie Graff that he had made with Plimsol. He had been sitting at a small table in a corner for only a few minutes when, somewhat to his surprise and greatly to his relief, not Harry but Van Ryn walked in and, spotting him almost at once, came over to join him.

After they had greeted one another casually, the Count said in a low voice, 'I don't think I've ever been so pleased to see anyone. I feared that even Harry might be in prison for abetting my escape, and that you definitely would be.'

'It was a near thing,' the American admitted. 'Those Sûreté boys certainly did their best to make things unpleasant.'

A waiter paused at the table so de Quesnoy had to contain his impatience while they ordered two *Vermouth-Cassis*, before he could say:

'What happened? I take it they accused you of having lied about my jumping overboard, and of having brought me to France under the name of Dupont, knowing all the time that I was the escaped convict, de Quesnoy?'

Van Ryn's big mouth widened into a grin. 'That is just what they did. But I wouldn't admit it. No, sir; I told them "you prove that if you can". And I knew they durn well couldn't; not unless they spent a fortune tracing up our tour round South America and shipping witnesses over from the United States.'

'*Mon Dieu*, how admirable!' murmured the Count. 'What splendid effrontery, and what an excellent nerve you displayed.'

'It didn't end there, though,' the American went on, tossing back half his drink and ordering a second round. 'Next day one of their big shots came to see me at the office. He said that maybe they couldn't prove anything against Harry and myself, but this was France, and they didn't have to have folks here that they didn't like; so he was giving us forty-eight hours to pack our bags and quit.'

'The Devil, he did!'

'Yes; but it didn't take me long to sort that one. I said that, maybe, I had dreamed about seeing you jump into the water, but I certainly hadn't dreamed about pulling you out; and that I had most distinct recollections of your head being locked into a leather helmet, as though you were not a man at all but a wild animal. I told him either to go tell his Government that I was staying put in Paris, or I would give an eyewitness account of its barbarity towards a political prisoner that would be featured by the Press of the whole world.'

They chuckled together over the success of this forceful blackmail; then Van Ryn inquired how his friend had been managing.

With a shrug the Count replied, 'I am leading a boring, uncomfortable and dangerous life; and I suppose it is a gross impertinence for a new brother, like myself, to hope to penetrate the secrets of the Grand Orient in the space of a few months. But there it is; I see no other way in which I might manage to achieve my object.'

'If the prospect is so poor, why not call it a day? After all, being in Paris wasn't all that risky while the Sûreté thought you dead. But now . . .'

'No. I made up my mind that I would bring this Government down, or pay the penalty of failure if I were caught while making the attempt.'

'Ah, but that was when your mind was biased from having your head locked in that hideous mask. Things are different now. Honestly, Armand, it's all wrong that you should risk a fine life like yours in a vendetta against General André and his pals. Remember what the Good Book tells us on that subject. "Vengeance is mine, saith the Lord." '

'I know.' De Quesnoy nodded. 'But there is something much more to this than vengeance. The root of the matter, Channock, is that these people are deliberately destroying the French Army's ability to wage war successfully. If they are not stopped, in another few years the Germans will be able to crush France like a rotten apple. That is why, although my chances of doing anything effective may be very slender, I can't possibly accept your advice to throw my hand in. Now, about money. I'm getting pretty low, so I hope that you have brought me some?'

Van Ryn took a thick envelope from his pocket and pushed it across the table. 'In that you'll find a wad of bills to carry on with, and a cheque book. I've had an account opened for you in the name of Petrovitch. Write your old man to send a draft in favour of that name to the bank. In the meantime I've told my people to honour your cheques up to any reasonable amount.' Producing a fountain pen and a slip of paper, he added, 'Just give me a couple of specimen signatures on this for my cashier.'

As de Quesnoy signed the paper he said, 'Channock, you are a friend in a million. I can never thank you enough. Tell me now, how did you enjoy the rest of your stay at Cowes?'

'Fine!' came the prompt response. 'Fine! In the Friday's race I brought *Juliette* in first by a length and a half, and collected a cup from Queen Alexandra's own hands. But that was just a nice dish on the side compared to the kick I got out of becoming acquainted with Fiona; and I've got you to thank for that. My, what a girl she is! I'm real sweet on her. I've got on the right side of her mother, too; so they've asked me up to stay in Scotland. I came back only to put through a few deals that required my personal attention; and by the end of the week I'll be off again to shoot a few grouse birds on Fiona's native heather.'

De Quesnoy smiled. 'You do seem to have got it badly.'

'I certainly have,' Van Ryn smiled back. Then he added with sudden seriousness, 'Tell me, Armand; d'you think if I asked Fiona that she would marry me?'

'I can see no earthly reason why she should not. You are a most likeable fellow, and from the worldly point of view what more could any girl want than the wealthy son of a United States Senator?'

Van Ryn shook his head a shade despondently. 'It's good to hear you say that, but Fiona is something very special. She was the loveliest

debutante of her season, and on top of that she is a niece of the
Mackintosh of Moy.'

The Count's knowledge of the *Almanach de Gotha* was extensive,
but this designation led only to his looking puzzled; so the American
proceeded to enlighten him.

'In Tudor times most of the nobles in Scotland had no titles. The
heads of clans were simply known as Lochiel, the Macduff, Cameron,
Macdonald of the Isles and so on. When the Stuarts came along and
joined Scotland to England under one crown they made most of them
Dukes and Earls, so they could sit in the House of Lords at Westminster. But some of them preferred keeping their name to any title,
and the Mackintosh of the day felt that way. As the chief of the biggest
of all the clans, I'm told that the present one still reckons himself
above any Duke; so that makes Fiona a sort of Scottish Princess.'

'I wouldn't let that worry you,' the Count advised. 'I have the blood
of most of the royal houses of Europe in my veins, but it is no more blue
than that of anyone else; and Fiona is just a pretty girl with the same
physical attributes and emotions as any other. Her mother would not
have asked you up to Scotland if she did not regard you as a suitable
match for her girl. And if Fiona hadn't a soft spot for you already, she
would never have let her mother invite you to stay. Nail your flag to the
mast, Channock, and sail right in. You have only to keep in mind the
old adage, "faint heart ne'er won fair lady," and next time we meet
you will be able to tell me that you are engaged to her.'

'Well, I hope you're right,' Van Ryn nodded. 'I've had a lot of fun
with the girls; but I'll be thirty-four next fall, and it's about time I took
life a bit more seriously. My old man would be pleased as Punch, too.
For years past he's been badgering me to get married. You see, I'm an
only child and he's mad keen to have a grandson. He's even picked on
a name for him. Wants him called Rex; though why, God alone knows.
I've recently been thinking myself that Mackintosh would make a good
name for a boy. Still, I suppose we could compromise and call him Rex
Mackintosh Van Ryn. That sounds pretty good, doesn't it?'

De Quesnoy gave a quick chuckle. 'Only a moment ago you were
wondering if you could persuade the girl to marry you, and now you
are christening her children.'

Van Ryn grinned back. 'You've put such heart into me, Armand,
that I guess I've let my imagination run off the rails.'

'That's all to the good. Keep it up, and the best of luck to you. Before you set off to capture Fiona, though, there is one thing that I'd be very grateful if you could do for me.'

'Give it a name.'

'If I do get on to anything through the Masons, and use it, there is always the unpleasant possibility that they will trace the leak back to me. As I can no longer resume the identity of Jules Dupont I should then be really up against it. Hundreds of Masons all over Paris would be ordered to keep a look-out for me, so that an Apache could be hired to stick a knife between my ribs. My only hope would be a quick get-out.'

'Sure; and with the police already watching the railway stations and the ports for you, I wouldn't give much for your chances of getting through.'

'Exactly. But I've thought of a way in which I could get safely to England within twenty-four hours. My idea is to take a leaf out of the enemy's book. You will remember my telling you how they shipped me out to Devil's Island in a big crate?'

'Do I not, the misbegotten swine!'

'I want you to have another made like it; but it needn't be quite so big. Six feet square would do. There should be a fixed bunk at one side for me to lie in, holes in the roof and sides for air, and a stock of drink and tinned food enough to last for several days in case of a hold-up in delivery—all well secured so that it doesn't rattle about. The door should be made flush with the planking, so that it does not look like a door, and made to bolt on the inside, so that I can let myself out when the crate arrives in England.'

'I get the idea, and it's a mighty fine one. But where will we keep the thing when I've had it made?'

'You could rent a coach-house to store it in and send me a key. Then all I'd have to do would be to let you know that I had gone to earth in it. You would have it collected right away and taken to the *Gare du Nord*. Your story would be that it contained some pictures that were too valuable to send by "goods", so you wanted it despatched to England by passenger train. Then you would take out a heavy insurance on it, so that they marked it, as they always do in such cases, for careful handling. If you could get it on the mid-day train it would be landed at Dover the same evening. It would be put into a Bonded warehouse to await clearance through the Customs and as soon as darkness fell I should let myself out with all the odds on being none the worse for the trip.'

Van Ryn gave his broad grin. 'With a mind like yours I believe you'll get the best of the boys you are gunning for yet. Anyhow, it seems you've thought of everything. I'm off to Scotland in a few days, as I've told you. But I'll get young Harry on to this. You'd better meet him some place, say in a week's time, to hear how he's gotten along fixing up a neat little private cabin for you.'

It was agreed that the Count should meet Plimsol at another café a few hundred yards down the street, at six o'clock in the evening a week from that day. Then the two friends took an affectionate leave of one another; and de Quesnoy made his way back to Montparnasse, greatly relieved to know that Van Ryn had so successfully bluffed his way out of trouble with the police.

Talking again with the cheerful, generous-hearted American had cheered him up enormously; but the stimulant was only a temporary one. That evening found him back in his cheap and depressing Pension, among the perpetually hard-up artists and others, some of whom he would much have liked to help, yet dared not from fear of its being rumoured that he was something other than the refugee of very modest means that he pretended to be.

It had, in fact, already occurred to him that Madame Smirnoff might become suspicious if he continued to pay his rent promptly while she believed him to be out of work; so he told her that he had got a job devilling for a professor who was translating a hand-book on agriculture from the Russian, and would in future be working for several hours each day in his room.

This ruse, and a small bribe to the slut who made a pretence of cleaning the upstairs rooms to do his room last, enabled him to lie late in bed in the mornings; and he spent several hours of every afternoon up there reading. But for the month that followed his meeting with Van Ryn his existence was wearily monotonous.

Twice he met Harry Plimsol; at their first meeting he approved the plans which had been got out for the interior of his travelling crate, and at their second received one of the keys of a coach-house in a mews not far from the *Gare du Nord*, in which the completed article had by then been installed. Soon afterwards, in the quiet of very early morning, he went there to inspect it, and found it in every way satisfactory.

But his social life, except for two Sundays spent with the Forains, was limited to the evenings, and bounded by the Masonic circle of which he had become a member. He went to every ceremony that he was entitled to attend at the Grand Orient headquarters in the Rue Cadet, and displayed there all the fervour of a neophyte; Bidegain, who was always there, he cultivated assiduously and in due course discovered that he was the principal assistant of M. Vadecard, the Secretary-General of the Order. Six evenings out of seven he spent in the upstairs billiards saloon with the mixed group of mostly decent and earnest, but limited and misguided, men whom he had now made his cronies.

Paris was hot, dusty and swarming with groups of goggle-eyed tourists. He would have given a great deal to get away from it to Vienna or the sea; or even to be able once more to enjoy freely the amenities of the Ritz, Maxim's, Paillard's and his other old haunts; but he dared not enter them, and on the rare occasions when, desperate for change of scene, he ventured across one of the bridges into central Paris, he went with his eyes constantly alert for anyone approaching who might have known him as Jules Dupont.

In mid-September he saw a mention in the social column of *Le Temps* of the forthcoming Syveton–de Vauclose wedding, and noted that it was to take place at the Church of St. Roche on the 20th. The frustration resulting from his abortive meetings with Angela during Cowes Week, and his long periods of inactivity since, had led to her occupying a large share of his thoughts throughout the past six weeks, and his longing to see her now grew even more insistent. She must, he knew, be back in Paris, but he decided that it was only fair to let her get through the wedding before approaching her again about the future; so he restrained his impatience until the night of the 21st, then he went again to the Parc Monceau, arriving there shortly after one in the morning.

As he no longer had a key to the garden door, he had to hunt about until he found a toe-hold in the wall, the use of which would enable him to grasp its coping and haul himself up and over it. Dropping down on the far side, he skirted the lawn till he reached the house, then picked up some small stones and began to throw them up at Angela's window.

After a few successful clinks a light showed round the edges of the curtains, the lower sash of the window was thrown up and Angela's head appeared. De Quesnoy called softly up to her:

'It is I—Armand. I've got to talk to you. Please come down; and put on clothes warm enough for us to go across to the pavilion.'

Without making any reply, Angela withdrew her head and shut the window. Five minutes later a light appeared in the conservatory, de Quesnoy went up the steps to it and she unlocked the door.

Taking her hand, he carried it to his lips; then, as his eager glance ran over her, he saw that she had only bedroom slippers on her feet and, apparently, a dressing-gown over her nightdress. With a laugh he said:

'I'll carry you to the pavilion if you like, but you had better fetch a a cloak, or I fear you will be cold there.'

She shook her head and held the door wider. 'We can't use the pavilion. It is being done up, and the workmen have the key. But come in, and we'll talk in Gabriel's study.'

Closing the door behind him, he followed her to the smallish room in which, nine months before, he had broken to her and to Syveton the news of the murderous fracas at Versailles and the collapse of the de Vendôme conspiracy. A large desk occupied a good part of it, shelves filled with reference books, official pamphlets and files gave it a cheerless, impersonal atmosphere and, by comparison with the main room of the pavilion, it was a miserable place for a lovers' meeting.

Nevertheless, with pent-up longing, the moment they had entered it de Quesnoy made a movement to take Angela in his arms. But she was too quick for him. Slipping into the swivel chair behind the heavy desk, she said:

'No, Armand; please! If we once let our emotions carry us away we shall become incapable of talking afterwards like rational beings. Since I returned to Paris ten days ago I have been most terribly anxious about you.'

'Syveton told you, then, that I had had to go to earth at the Pension Smirnoff in the Rue de Odessa?'

'No. As soon as I got home I rang you up as Monsieur Dupont at Mr. Van Ryn's apartment. The secretary there said you had gone abroad and that he had no idea when you would be back. Then I asked Gabriel if he knew why you had changed your plans. All he could tell me was that you had had a narrow escape from being arrested, but he had heard from de Villeneuve, who had heard from Van Ryn, that you were still in Paris. It was that which worried me so.'

De Quesnoy gave her a brief account of what had happened, and when he had done she said, 'If only I had known where you were I should have written urging you to give me a rendez-vous at some place to which you could come with safety.'

He smiled. 'I should have needed no urging.'

Impatiently she shook her head. 'I do not mean a *rendez-vous d'amour*, but one at which I might implore you to leave Paris immediately.'

'I am afraid that is out of the question.'

'Armand, you must! If you are caught they will sentence you to at least two years' imprisonment.'

'At least!' the Count repeated with a laugh. 'I wish I could be as optimistic. They'll have my head if they can get it.'

Angela looked at him in surprise, and asked: 'Have you not heard from François?'

'What, de Vendôme? Yes, early in June I had a letter from him which had been forwarded on from New York. In it he said that he had instructed lawyers here to draw up a *procès-verbal* of the fracas at Versailles, with the object of endeavouring to secure evidence from the police themselves that none of their comrades was killed by me.'

'And he succeeded. The day after I got back I received a letter from him telling me all about it. The deaths of all three policemen have been fully accounted for, and François has sent a sworn copy of all the statements to the Minister of Justice. He says that in the face of it there is no longer the least possibility of their bringing a charge of murder against you.'

'Holy Mary be praised!' exclaimed the Count. 'What splendid news!'

'Yes, yes; it is a great relief,' she said hurriedly, 'but remember, they can still charge, and convict, you of both assaulting the police and conspiracy.'

'They have to catch me first.'

'Oh, Armand, for pity's sake be sensible. You are one against hundreds of them; and there must be scores of people who knew you as Jules Dupont.'

'I know. Having to maintain the same appearance in my character

304

of Vasili Petrovitch is the only thing that worries me. I would feel much safer if I could make some radical changes in it; but to do so would arouse the suspicions of my Masonic friends and the people at the Pension Smirnoff.'

For the first time since they had met on the doorstep, Angela smiled. 'I wish you could resume your old appearance. Having lived so long in France, I don't mind your beard; but it is a pity that you had to shave off the points of those wickedly Satanic eyebrows, and to have cut your wavy hair except for that little brush in front makes you look like a German. I was quite distressed about it when I first saw you at Herne Court. And it doesn't really serve as a complete disguise. Anyone who has seen you often in the past, as for instance the servants here, would still recognize you as the Count de Quesnoy.'

He shrugged. 'It is the best that I can do, and no one saw through it when I was Dupont. As Petrovitch it is even less likely that I shall meet anyone who knew me as myself. But now that you have mentioned Herne Court, tell me why you treated me so badly while I was at Cowes?'

After a moment's hesitation, she replied, 'All that I told you about the difficulties of any woman of position in England carrying on an illicit love affair, except with a man who is staying in the same house as herself, was perfectly true; and if you had disclosed yourself as my lover by any Don Juan tricks I should have got into awful trouble with my grandmother. But, of course, I could have thought up some way for us to have had, anyhow, half-an-hour together on our own.'

'Then why, in Heaven's name, didn't you?' he asked, throwing out his hands in puzzled expostulation. 'You cannot have forgotten the wonderful things you said to me that night in the *Cherche-Midi*. How you offered to sacrifice your good name and publicly become my mistress if only I would come away with you. Yet when we meet again seven months later in the Isle of Wight, I find you as cold as marble, and unwilling even to risk the disapproval of your family in order to afford me a private conversation.'

'I know, and perhaps that was cowardly of me. If things had been as they were before the collapse of the conspiracy I should have been just as eager for us to be alone together as you were; but I simply could not bring myself to face up to the inferences that I felt you would have drawn from that terrible scene we had in the prison.'

'Why not, my dear? For mercy's sake don't tell me that while I was abroad you . . . you met someone else, and have ceased to love me.'

'No! No! That could never be. But on account of what I said, I felt sure you would ask me to leave Gabriel. That *was* your intention, wasn't it?'

De Quesnoy nodded. 'Yes. If you had kept that rendezvous years ago instead of sending Madeleine de Frontignac in your place and we had become lovers then; or if on my return to Paris young de Véndôme had not forestalled me with you, matters would have been different. Both of us might have been content, and either burnt out our passion in a year or two and remained good friends, or settled into the sort of steady relationship that is not uncommon in such affaires and often lasts well into middle age. But both of us know now that for you to become my mistress is not enough. From the moment when we parted in the *Cherche-Midi* I realized that my love for you was so lasting and profound that if I did escape no half measures could ever satisfy me; and from the things you had just said I believed that you felt that too.'

'Oh, Armand, I did! I do! But at the time I was desperate—driven crazy with the fear that if I left you there it would be to die. I couldn't bear the thought that I would never see you again, and to save you I would have promised anything.'

'Do you mean, then, that had you succeeded in persuading me to abandon de Vendôme, when we got out of the prison you would have gone back on your offer to run away with me?'

'Of course not,' Angela retorted with a flash of indignation. 'How can you think me capable of such baseness? But I was driven to make my offer by the belief that it was the only way in which I might save your life. God be thanked that after all you managed to save it for yourself; but the fact that it is no longer in danger entirely changes the situation. Then, I was too distraught to think of anything but your being shot or guillotined, perhaps within a few hours; since, I have had time to realize that if we eloped we might soon become millstones round one another's necks.'

For a moment he was silent, his mouth drawn into a thin, hard line; then he said. 'Since we appear to be agreed that to become lovers clandestinely would only increase our longing to be together always, am I to understand that when my business in Paris is done, rather than

306

leave your husband, you would prefer me to make a career abroad alone and endeavour to forget you?'

'If you did that I'd have nothing left to live for,' Angela sighed. 'Yet if we ran away together what sort of future could we hope for? Given the usual expectation of life Gabriel will not die for another twenty years or more, and until he does we could not get married.'

'I should regard you in every respect as my wife.'

'I am sure you would; but if we had children they would be illegitimate. Sooner or later we should have to tell them that they were, and to have placed such a handicap in life upon them might cause their love for us to turn to hatred.'

'Then we must make up our minds not to have children.'

'Very well. Let us ignore the fact that if we were living as husband and wife I should like to have children by you. There is still another aspect to the matter. As the heir to a great title you should already be considering marriage with the daughter of some other noble house, so that you can have children by her who *are* legitimate. And, dearly as I love you, I would find it hard indeed to share you permanently with another woman.'

'How can you suggest that when you had given up everything for me I should ever think of placing you in such an intolerable situation?'

'But Armand, it is your duty to beget an heir.'

'Maybe; but failing in that is part of the price I must pay to have you for my own, and in the circumstances I'd have few qualms about neglecting that particular duty.'

'Then you can have less feeling for your family than I have for mine. Perhaps the thought of your father's bitter disappointment that with you his line must end would not trouble you; but the thought of the shame my father would feel at the knowledge that I was living as a kept woman would trouble me acutely. And, of course, except for very occasional *sub-rosa* meetings with my sisters, I don't suppose I would ever see any of my relatives again. They would all decide to regard me as dead, or anyhow better so.'

'Do they mean so much to you?'

'Enough for me to be most loath to cause them pain, and to cut myself off from them for good. But that is far from being the end of it. I would never again dare to show my face in Paris or London. If I were known to be living with you openly I would be ostracized by society

307

in every capital in Europe; and between us you and I have far too wide an acquaintance to hope to establish ourselves as a married couple under another name. If we attempted to do so, just think of the never-ending anxiety we should suffer from fear that someone we had known in the past might suddenly turn up and give us away!'

'There would be little risk of that if we made our home in America—as I had planned that we should.'

'There would be if we lived in New York, or in any city that people of our own kind visit, or break their journey at while on their travels. That is unless we changed our habits entirely and resigned ourselves to live out our lives as *bourgeoisi* in a suburb of some provincial town.'

'No, no! We are not cut out for that. But it was South America I had in mind. I need disclose my real name only to the Minister of War of one of the Republics there to secure a staff appointment in its Army. My being a political exile would be excuse enough for me then to adopt a *nom-de-guerre*. There seemed to me no reason why, if I presented you under it as my wife, anyone should ever question your legal title to that position.'

Angela shook her head. 'Do you really think that a South American politician could be trusted to keep your real name secret from his friends. Besides, from time to time we should have to attend official receptions, and sooner or later some French diplomat or chance visitor to the place would recognize us"

'I suppose you're right,' de Quesnoy admitted reluctantly. 'I must confess that during these months we have been apart I have dwelt only on the broader picture. Heaven knows the countless hours I've spent building "castles in Spain" of you and I living together; but I fear I have tended to thrust from my mind the practical difficulty of two people as well known as ourselves managing to continue to live the sort of life that is congenial to us, and at the same time covering up indefinitely all evidence of our true identities.'

Stretching out a hand Angela took his and pressed it. 'My dear love, it distresses me most terribly to bring those "castles in Spain" you have been building tumbling down; but if we once embarked for this land of Cytherea there would be no turning back, we should deserve the reproaches of all who are dear to us and, I am convinced, soon have cause bitterly to regret our temerity.'

Hardly comprehending yet that the roseate prospect with which he had buoyed up his spirits for so many months had been shattered in even fewer minutes, he stared at her unhappily, then muttered in a miserable and puzzzled voice:

'What, then, do you suggest that we should do?'

For the first time that night she smiled right into his eyes, as she replied. 'I too have thought about our future a great deal and, if only you love me enough, there is a way in which by one stroke we could eliminate the possibility of any of these horrid situations of which we have been talking.'

'What is it?' he asked eagerly. 'Tell me?'

'That I should get an annulment of my marriage to Gabriel; then I'd be free to marry you.'

'An annulment,' he repeated, his face falling. 'Yes, I had thought of that. But even if you could get one it would take years; two at least, perhaps more.'

'I did say "if you loved me enough". In other words, if you are prepared to wait. After all it is now over nine years since we first fell in love. Surely it would be worth waiting a few more if by doing so we need not sacrifice our relatives and friends, can have children who would be legitimate, and instead of being outlawed by society remain respected members of it.'

'It would if we could be certain that your plea for an annulment would be granted. But, with long intervals between, such pleas are submitted to a succession of clerical courts, any one of which—even the last after years of waiting—has the power to throw it out. And, once refused, no appeal is allowed.'

'I know that; but I am sure it is largely a question of money and influence. Rome would not willingly go against a request made by the champions of Catholicism in France, and many of them are members of the Monarchist Committee; so my personal friends. A word in the right ear from some of them, and I have very little doubt that my plea for an annulment would be granted.'

'In that you are probably right,' he agreed thoughtfully. 'Much would depend, though, on Gabriel's attitude. His agreement and co-operation are essential to your building up a good case. Either that or being able to produce evidence of his having committed some gross infringement of the marital state, and the Church does not regard ordinary infidelity in that light.'

'An annulment would enable him to preserve his dignity; so I feel certain that he would agree to one rather than have me run away from him, and should he refuse I mean to threaten him with doing so.'

De Quesnoy gave a grim little smile. 'That certainly is sound psychology. When told that you mean to leave him anyhow, he will probably even be grateful for the chance to escape the humiliation the alternative would inflict on him. But on what grounds could you make your plea to the clerical court?'

'I lived with Gabriel only during the first year of our marriage, and it would be difficult for anyone to show proof that I did so even then. We have had no children, so we could declare that the marriage had never been consummated. Gabriel has stretched his conscience in other matters often enough not to make any bones about abetting me in that.'

With a cheerfulness that he had not shown since the beginning of their conversation, the Count admitted, 'I must confess that you've convinced me of the soundness of your plan; and handled the way you suggest I think now that all the odds are on its succeeding.' But a moment later his face clouded over as he added, 'All the same, to have to wait so long will be devilish hard to bear. We are already getting towards the end of our twenties, and the next two or three years should be the best in our lives. Now we are agreed that nothing short of living together as man and wife will satisfy us, to have to waste them while the annulment is going through is almost as hard as a prison sentence.'

Angela raised one eyebrow and her lips twitched in a smile. 'Aren't you being a little slow-witted, darling? Or at least being a bit too literal about your "nothing short of living as man and wife". I agree that to enter now on a back-stairs intrigue could lead only to frustration for us both. But on the day that I apply for an annulment I shall leave Gabriel, so there will no longer be any question of back-stairs. We would have to be very, very careful and we could live together only at intervals, but . . .'

Again de Quesnoy's face lit up. 'Of course! How stupid of me not to have realized that. The whole thing takes on a new aspect looked at in that light. The sooner you tackle Gabriel the better, then. I beg you to do so in the morning, and I'll return tomorrow night to hear how things have gone.'

Her smile faded and she shook her head. 'No, I'm afraid I can't do that. I told you when we met in the Isle of Wight that certain complications had arisen which prevented me from taking any definite step about my future. I was hoping that by now everything would have been straightened out, but it hasn't yet. There is no point in my approaching Gabriel until, given his agreement, we could go to our lawyers and set the ball rolling. Once we did that it would soon get out that we are separating, and I don't want to let him down.'

'Let him down!' echoed the Count, aghast. 'Angela darling! What the devil are you talking about? Why this sudden concern for him? There has never been even a shadow of love between you. As a bride you were treated by him abominably and for a year or more afterwards you went in terror of him. Then he went back to his practice of seducing young girls of the lower classes, and after a time you went your own way. Apart from having shared the same roof and name for ten years, you have nothing . . .'

'We have that. He is still my husband, and he is in trouble.'

'What sort of trouble?'

'About money. I have dreaded something like this for a long time. For years past he has neglected his own affairs to devote all his energies to the *Ligue de la Patrie*; and after his costly campaign to get himself elected as a Deputy he had to sell the foundry at Lens that was left to him by his father. Since then things have been going from bad to worse, and unless he can make some arrangement with his largest creditors he may have to go bankrupt.'

'He has only himself to blame,' commented the Count angrily. 'When he married you he had a fine fortune. The fact that he has given his time to politics instead of business has no bearing on its loss. By doing so he may have sacrificed his chance to increase it, but to keep it needed only common sense and that he should live within his income. As it is he has squandered it on keeping a succession of young women still in their 'teens, then, as he tired of them, paying them or their families off. On that, and on living beyond his means so that he might cut a figure in society and hobnob with people of birth and breeding. If he now goes bankrupt it will be through no fault of yours. You owe him nothing.'

'I do, Armand. It is true that, ever since I first suspected that he was overspending himself, I have urged him to sell this big house and let us live more modestly; and that he refused to do. But he has always been most generous towards me. Expensive clothes, equipages, masses of flowers, lavish entertaining; he has paid every bill that I have run up without a murmur.'

'*Mort de Dieu!* And so he should. He was only carrying out the unspoken bargain made when he married you. A hundred other men would have done the same, and made you far happier.'

'Nevertheless, my extravagance in the past must have done much to contribute to his ruin.'

'If, in you, he bought something that he could not afford, that is his funeral. Anyhow, what of it?'

'Simply that I feel under an obligation to help him, as far as I can, to get straight again. It was for that reason that I went to England in May and returned only for the wedding. My absence enabled us to cut out all entertaining for four and a half months, and to run the house with only a skeleton staff.'

'But what of the future? Should he fail to recover and be sold up, or even have to retrench to the extent of leaving here for some suburban villa, surely you do not intend to remain with him? The Saints themselves would not expect you to martyr yourself to that extent for a man who means nothing to you.'

Angela smiled rather wanly. 'No, I'm certainly not seeking a crown in Heaven, and there is a limit to what I am prepared to do. The crux of the matter is that if I left him now those who know of his difficulties would look upon me as a rat leaving the sinking ship, They are mostly money-lenders, for whom I have only contempt; so for myself I would not give a rap what they think. But it might lead them to suppose that his position is even worse than it is, and so wreck his last chance of recovery.'

Beneath his brown beard, de Quesnoy's lips curled cynically. 'So you prefer to put the interests of this husband of yours, to whom you owe little or nothing, before the feelings of the man whom you say you love?'

'Armand, you are unfair. Having been his wife for ten years, I am willing to give him a few more months; but that is all. Whereas if you were in difficulties I would stop at nothing to save you. Besides, say that I was willing to elope with you this very night, would you agree?'

He shrugged uncomfortably. 'You have me there. You know that

312

I cannot consider myself a free man until this chancy game that I have started has been played out to a finish.'

'You see! And you will not even leave Paris, although I beg you to. I am not now attempting to bribe you by saying that I would go with you; but won't you please reconsider that? For one man to attempt to overturn a government is surely tilting at windmills, and it could so easily lead to a long term of imprisonment. For both our sakes, please, please, give up this mad endeavour and go abroad again.'

'No,' he replied firmly. 'I'm sorry, but I can't do that.'

For a further half-hour they continued to argue without either gaining any concrete concession from the other. He grudgingly agreed that, if by Christmas he had failed to secure evidence of the connection between the Grand Orient and the Government, he would consider abandoning the attempt, and she that should Syveton's affairs take a turn for the better she would then put to him her wish for an annulment. Having reached this understanding, they parted.

As Angela let him out and watched his slim figure disappear across the lawn into the darkness, she wondered if she had been really justified in postponing the issue. Armand, she felt, had been so right in saying that these were the best years of their lives; so, now that both of them were convinced that they could never be really happy apart, it seemed out of all reason to allow even days, let alone months, to elapse before taking the action required to secure her freedom. Yet Gabriel, despite his many shortcomings, had in the main behaved very generously towards her, and she knew that she could not have abandoned him with a clear conscience as long as his difficulties remained unresolved.

De Quesnoy, on the other hand, was thinking only of how well Angela had made her case for annulment as opposed to an elopement. Now that he gave his mind to the down-to-earth aspects of the matter he realized how right she was in her contention that for them to attempt to live under false names as a married couple was not practical.

Either they would be a constant prey to fears of recognition—and perhaps even blackmail—or as the price of security they would have to submerge themselves indefinitely in the great mass of the middle classes. Living in suburbs or small provincial towns would mean that, to escape unwelcome comment, they must give up all the luxuries to which they had so long been accustomed. For her there could be no personal maid, or carriage, or clothes of the latest fashion; for him no hunting, no career, no fine wines and cigars. Above all, in such surroundings there could be little hope of making new friends who were able to share their interests, or even capable of understanding the thoughts and habits they had brought with them from having lived for so long in an utterly different world. They would be completely dependent on one another and without occupation or ambition to engage their minds. Being a realist, he acknowledged to himself that in such circumstances even the greatest love must wilt and die before many years had passed.

It irked him somewhat that out of consideration for Syveton Angela refused to set the ball rolling at once; but he consoled himself with the thought that even if she had taken immediate steps to break with her past, until he had completed his self-imposed mission he would be in no situation to reap the joys that her freedom promised.

During the month that followed he continued with dogged persistence to pursue the furtive and cheerless existence to which he had condemned himself. After nearly five months' association with the Masons he was now fully accepted by a wide circle of them as a keen and promising initiate, but he had made no progress at all towards their inner councils, and might not have done so for an almost indefinite period had it not been for a chance encounter one night in the third week of October.

He had attended a session at the Temple of the Grand Orient and afterwards, to relieve his boredom, he walked round the corner and spent an hour in the Folies Bergère. On coming out, he crossed the road and turned down the Rue de Trévise. Halfway along it he happened to glance through the window of a small café. Inside he saw Jean Bidegain seated alone at a table; so he went in and joined him.

Bidegain was a small, grey-haired man with mutton-chop whiskers and a sallow complexion. He was drinking absinthe, and it was soon clear to de Quesnoy that his mind was already befuddled with the insidious potion. Their talk naturally turned on Masonic matters and the Count's progress in studying to take his second degree. After ordering Bidegain another absinthe he asked him if he had a particular fondness for the drink.

With a shrug the little man replied, 'It is the cheapest way to buy forgetfulness, and I have many troubles. I often come here to put away enough to make me sleep at night.'

Tactfully, de Quesnoy asked if there were any way in which he could be of help, but Bidegain shook his head. 'Not unless you are richer than you look, and crazy enough to give money away. Money is my trouble. I've an invalid wife, and four children to educate. I'm up to my eyes in debt, and for two pins would throw myself into the Seine.'

'Surely the Grand Orient would help you,' the Count suggested. 'There is a big fund for assisting brothers who are in distress. Why don't you apply for a grant from it?'

'I did, and they made me one.' Bidegain picked up the carafe and let the water drip through the sugar on the pierced spoon into the clear green spirit, turning it to an opaque opal hue, then he added thickly, 'But they found out that I used it to buy lottery tickets; so they refuse to help me further. And the salary they pay me is a pittance.'

De Quesnoy raised his eyebrows. 'You surprise me. I should have thought that, as principal assistant to the Secretary-General, your services would have merited a very handsome remuneration.'

'You are right. But Vadecard is a mean swine. And when you think of the power I have. At times it makes me boil.'

'Yes, in your position you must have great influence,' agreed the Count quickly.

Bidegain sucked down a long draught of absinthe. His eyes were slightly bleary, and when he spoke again it was to blurt out boastfully, 'Not influence—power, I said! I can make or mar the careers of half the officers in the Army.'

'Oh, come!' The Count's eyes narrowed slightly, but he gave a quick laugh. 'You can hardly expect me to believe that.'

'I can,' Bidegain insisted. 'When Vadecard's been through the *fiches* he keeps a few, then passes the rest on to me for filing till . . . till they're ready at the War Office for another batch.'

'The *fiches*?' queried de Quesnoy innocently.

'Yes, man. The denunciations we receive about these accursed Catholics. And I select those that go in. By . . . by pushing one forward quickly I can . . . can get a General or a Colonel broken right away. If I hold up the *fiche* about him they . . . they forget about him, see. That's power, isn't it?'

'Yes; it would be if you had it. But you must take me for a simpleton if you think I'll swallow this tall story of yours that Vadecard leaves it to you to . . .'

'He does,' Bidegain broke in. 'At least, in most cases. I can put a *fiche* on ... on the top of the pile or ... or tear it up. There are hundreds of 'em. If I des ... destroyed a score, no-one'd miss them.'

'I'd like to see some of these *fiches*;' the Count murmured, 'just as a matter of interest. But I'm sure you're kidding. I bet you wouldn't really dare to remove a dozen from the files.'

Bidegain leaned forward eagerly. 'So I'm kidding, am I? All right, what'll you bet me?'

'Fifty francs,' replied de Quesnoy, after a moment's hesitation; judging that to be a tempting sum while not beyond his apparent means.

'Done!' The little man gave a hiccup then a laugh. 'It'll be the easiest fifty francs I've earned for a long time.'

Over another drink they sealed the wager that twelve *fiches* should be produced there by Bidegain the following night. Soon afterwards a neighbour of his who had been drinking at a nearby table came up, and the two absinthe addicts set out to see one another home. As de Quesnoy made his way back to his Pension, he was almost trembling with excitement. He felt that he had played his fish well, yet he hardly dared let himself hope that Bidegain was something better than a drunken boaster.

Next day he found it impossible to think of anything but the meeting for that night; and when evening came it was only with the greatest difficulty that he fought down the urge to set off early for the café. When he did arrive Bidegain was there and, having had only one absinthe, was still sober. But with a smile of triumph he produced from an inner pocket a packet of papers and slapped them down on the table.

De Quesnoy made a wry grimace, as though pained at the prospect of having to pay up; then he carefully read through the *fiches*. Most of them were on coarse paper and in only semi-literate writings. Five were from non-commissioned officers or privates, denouncing as regular Church-goers officers against whom they obviously had a grudge; the rest were from schoolmasters, men-servants and tradesmen in garrison towns, retailing tittle-tattle about senior officers' families. Visits from priests, the possession of rosaries, and crucifixes hung in nurseries were all mentioned as evidence of treacherous intentions towards the Republic, and such terms of abuse as "filthy Jesuit" and "priest's bottom-licker" more than once employed.

He was greatly tempted to stuff them in his pocket, or attempt to buy them from Bidegain there and then, but he knew that they would be of infinitely greater value if some proof could be obtained that such denouncements were actually acted upon by the War Office; so when he had finished looking through them he muttered, 'You win,' gave them back and, taking a shabby wallet from his pocket, counted out fifty francs in dirty ten and five-franc notes.

For the best part of an hour, while Bidegain consumed a second and third absinthe, de Quesnoy said no more on the subject then suddenly, he remarked, 'If you are really as pressed for money as you say, I marvel at your honesty. Were I in your shoes I would use some of those *fiches* as banknotes.'

While waiting for a reply, he held his breath. On that one sentence he had gambled the results of five months' uncongenial, painstaking work, for he had implied that for a price he would be willing to break his Masonic oath; and if Bidegain reported him the game was up. But the little man only shook his head and muttered:

'It would not be easy to turn these things into cash.'

De Quesnoy breathed again, but his heart was still hammering in his chest as he said in a low voice, 'It could be done. The officers whom they concern would pay handsomely to get hold of and destroy them.'

'They are scattered over France and the Colonial Empire. Without committing oneself to writing it would be impossible to get in touch with them.'

For a moment the Count remained silent, as though in thought; then he took a further plunge and said, 'You could sell them to the *Ligue de la Patrie Française*.'

Bidegain suddenly drew back and said in a scared voice, 'But the *Ligue* would use them for its political ends. It would make them public.'

'And what if it did? Why should you consider the interests of the Grand Orient when it has treated you so scurvily?' De Quesnoy sat forward, elbows on the table, his hypnotic eyes holding those of the little man opposite him. 'Listen to me. You are in urgent need of money and so am I. The funds that I brought out of Russia are almost gone, and the only work I can get brings me in little more than a starvation wage. Why should we not go into this together? You provide the *fiches* and I will market them. We will go fifty-fifty on the proceeds.'

After an attempt to draw his eyes away had failed, Bidegain gulped, 'Perhaps! Why not! It would have to be for a big sum, though. We could sell a few dozen privately for destruction and no one would be any the wiser; but if a batch were published things would blow up at headquarters. They would accuse me, or at least declare that I had been guilty of unforgivable negligence. No, no, I would not dare to face it.'

'You need not do so. I am sure I could get you enough money to go abroad and start life anew in the United States.'

'For me to emigrate with my whole family, and still have a nice little capital when we settled on the other side, would run to a lot of money. Do you think they would pay so great a sum?'

'Yes, but with the *fiches* we should have to provide proof that they were secured at the request of the War Office.'

Now under a light hypnosis, Bidegain disclosed, 'A Captain Mollin acts as our liaison with the Ministry. He is General André's most trusted A.D.C. There are letters from him in the files that I could steal: letters asking for more batches of *fiches*, and that we should dig up everything we could that would detract from the characters of certain generals.'

De Quesnoy had all his work cut out to conceal his delight; but when he withdrew his compelling gaze from Bidegain, the little man showed unwillingness to commit himself fully, and would do no more than promise to think things over.

For the next forty-eight hours the Count was a constant prey to mingled hopes, fears and impatience; but after a fourth night session at the café, the matter was settled. It was decided that they should ask one hundred thousand francs, but if pressed accept eighty thousand, and split the proceeds. But Bidegain flatly refused to steal the all-important letters until his accomplice had found out whether the *Ligue de la Patrie* was willing to deal.

That meant that, as a minimum, de Quesnoy would have to produce forty thousand francs. It was a very considerable sum and far beyond his immediate resources. But that did not concern him, as this was clearly just the sort of transaction which the *Ligue's* Fighting Fund had been established to finance, and he had no doubt that Syveton, as the Treasurer of the *Ligue*, would gladly produce it to secure the material for such a devastating attack on the Government.

The night following his final talk with Bidegain, the Count again crossed Paris to the Parc Monceau. On his way he endeavoured to put Angela out of his mind, as his only object on this nocturnal journey was to arrange with Syveton about the payment for the *fiches* and some of Mollin's letters. It was not until he was about to climb the garden wall that his thoughts were suddenly distracted from his mission. On glancing upwards he saw a streak of light at one side of the drawn curtains of the window which he knew to be that of the pavilion bedroom.

He drew in his breath sharply and stared up at the window, wondering what the light could mean. A month ago Angela had said that she no longer had the key to the upper part of the pavilion and that it was being redecorated. Why? And what was she doing up there now?'

Disquieting memories flooded back to him. Her deliberate avoidance of a tête-à-tête with him during his stay in Cowes. Her almost chilly self-possession when they had last met. The concern, which she had never before displayed, for the interests of her husband. Her refusal to ask yet for an annulment, or commit herself to a date when she would do so.

Could it possibly be that she was deceiving him? It was getting on for a year since de Vendôme had ceased to be her lover; and she had admitted to having had several in succession immediately before him. Could it be that, believing him, de Quesnoy, lost to her for good last Christmas, she had soon after, out of despair and for distraction, taken another lover and since come to prefer him?

Perhaps all she had said about Syveton's financial difficulties was untrue; a clever invention to excuse herself from taking any step which might upset a new liaison that now meant more to her than the never-fulfilled love of her youth. The pavilion was Angela's private province. Why should she have had it redecorated unless she meant to continue to use it? He knew that she often spent her afternoons there reading or sewing. But one did not read or sew at one o'clock on a chilly morning late in October. She must again be using it as a rendezvous. Who, in hell's name, was up there with her?

CHAPTER XXIII

AT THE ELEVENTH HOUR

WHEN François de Vendôme had been Angela's lover de Quesnoy had not suffered from jealousy; neither had he done so when, to his knowledge, certain of his past mistresses had occasionally had to sleep with their husbands in order to keep the peace. The morals of his class in the Paris of that day had made him cynical in such matters; and as far as Angela and de Vendôme were concerned, that had been a special case made supportable by the fact that she did not love the Prince.

But this was utterly different. If his suspicions were correct she now loved someone else, had told him a pack of lies and had deceived him with an unscrupulousness of which he would never have believed her capable.

As he stared up at the chink of light a pulse began to hammer in his throat. In his mind's eye he could see again every detail of the room. A Devil-inspired vision came to him of her lying naked between the silk sheets of the bed. Her hair, with its burnished copper lights, curled loose upon the pillow, making a frame for her fair, flushed face; her lips were partly open and her brown eyes wide with passionate desire, as the figure of a man bent above her.

His mouth went dry, he swallowed hard and thrust the tormenting scene from him with shame that, on so little evidence, he should think her capable of betraying him. But, at that moment, he caught the faint sound of voices from above. Two people were definitely there, then. His blood seemed to boil in his veins. The vision returned. He felt that he could not support the uncertainty a moment longer. Better by far to know the worst. Flinging himself at the wall, he scrambled up and over it.

Taking no precautions against the sounds of his approach being heard, he crashed through the shrubbery, strode round the corner to the entrance to the pavilion and ran up the stairs three at a time. On the landing that also formed the kitchenette he paused for a moment to get back his breath. Then he seized the knob of the door to the main room. The door was locked. He shook it violently. Stepping back a pace, he gave a savage kick that brought the flat of his foot over the keyhole. The lock snapped and the door flew open.

The room was gay with fresh paint and new chintzes, and had much more furniture in it than when he had last been there. But the table was a familiar sight. As of old, it had on it the remains of an excellent cold supper for two, a big bowl of fruit and an opened bottle of champagne in an ice bucket. That much he took in before pulling up with a jerk, to stare with astonished relief at a girl who stood just beyond it.

She was quite young; not more than twenty, he guessed, and striking looking in a rather Spanish way. Her complexion was rich, her lips very full, her eyes black and her dark, smooth hair was done in great coils round her head. She was short, plump and wearing a crimson negligée that set off her sultry beauty.

'I . . . I must apologize,' he stammered. 'I hardly know how to explain. May I . . . may I ask who you are?'

The scared look left her dark eyes, and she replied in a husky voice, 'I am Madame Syveton.'

For a second he was puzzled, then he realized that she must be Clothilde, the young woman whom Henri Syveton had married in mid-September.

He bowed. 'I see. Yes, of course. I can't attempt to say how sorry I am to have burst in on you like this. I didn't realize that the door was locked. I thought it had jammed; so I gave it an extra hard push. It is your father-in-law, Monsieur Gabriel Syveton, whom I want to see. The matter is one of the greatest urgency and . . . well, there are reasons why I cannot go and enquire for him at the house. I came in over the garden wall and, seeing a light in the pavilion, thought that he might be up here. I meant to rouse him by throwing stones up at his bedroom window. I had better go and do that.'

As he was about to turn awkwardly away, she said after a second's hesitation, 'It will be useless. He is not there.'

'Can you tell me, then, where he is?' de Quesnoy asked quickly. 'I have got to find him; even if I have to risk waking the servants and questioning them. It is of the utmost importance that I should see him before morning.'

At that moment the door to the bathroom opened and Syveton

walked into the room. He was dressed in a purple smoking jacket and held a newly lit cigarette in his hand. Without looking at the Count, he said to his daughter-in-law:

'Clothilde, my dear. I did not expect this gentleman tonight, but we sometimes have private matters to discuss together. You had better go to bed now. I don't suppose we shall be long, and if we are we will try not to disturb you when we leave. Sleep well, child.'

'Thank you, Papa,' she murmured. 'Good night, then,' and with a slight nod to de Quesnoy she turned towards the bedroom. As she did so her face, which before had been partly shadowed, caught the light, and he noticed that her eyelids were slightly swollen, as though she had been crying. But he thought no more of it as his mind was busy on what he should say to Syveton about having broken in. The Deputy knew well enough that for many years he had been much more than an ordinary friend to Angela, but he could not possibly admit to having forced the door in a fit of jealous anger, believing that he would find her in bed with another lover.

To his relief, he was spared having to offer an explanation, as Syveton immediately launched into one about his own presence there. He said that, his son having not been able to find an apartment exactly to his taste, Angela had agreed to give up the pavilion for a while to provide the young couple with temporary accommodation.

De Quesnoy at once guessed the truth to be that Syveton was in such low water that he could not afford to set his son up in a way which would have done him credit; so he had adopted this expedient to save his face. Meanwhile he was going on:

'As an engineer, Henri seems to have considerable promise. He has gone into a firm of automobile makers. Whether there will ever be any big money to be made out of that sort of thing it is as yet impossible to say; but he is very enthusiastic. It means his having to spend one night a week down at their factory at Le Mans, though, and poor little Clothilde has been far from well lately; so I came over to keep her company and see that she had everything she wanted.'

What he was saying had no interest for the Count and barely penetrated his mind. It was occupied with giving silent thanks to God that he had not found Angela as he had pictured her in his Devil-begotten vision. He was still upbraiding himself for ever having harboured such unworthy thoughts of her when Syveton brought him back

322

to the present by asking, for a second time, what the urgent matter was on which he wished to see him.

Swiftly recovering, de Quesnoy gave particulars of Bidegain and the *fiches*. As Syveton listened his delight increased until he could hardly contain himself for joy. Here at last was a club with which to beat the Government to death; the very thing for which, with his fanatical hatred of Combes, he had been longing to get hold of for years. But when he learned that Bidegain wanted forty thousand francs to betray the Masons, his face fell, and he said:

'That is a lot of money. I don't think . . .'

'Nonsense!' the Count cut him short. 'For years past you must have spent three or four times that amount each year, to live in the way that you have. And this little man, remember, has to get his family to the States, then start a shop, or buy a partnership in some small business. I am supposed to be getting a half-share, and were I doing so to start with I should have asked a hundred thousand francs. Even that would not have been too high a price to pay for these *fiches* and Mollin's letters acknowledging the use to which they are being put.'

'I know; I know.' Syveton held up his hand. 'I meant only that I could not lay my hand on such a large sum at the moment.'

'Why? You are Treasurer of the *Ligue de la Patrie* and its Fighting Fund must run into several million.'

'Yes, but I have only a running account at my disposal; enough to pay for the printing of handbills, agents' expenses and that sort of thing. For a draft of this amount I need the signatures of two out of my three co-Trustees who are responsible with me for the Fund.'

'How long will it take you to get them?'

'Only a day or two; but we may have to realize securities before such a draft could be met, so we could not count on concluding the transaction in much under a week.'

'But this matter cannot wait. The effects of absinthe drinking have made Bidegain unstable—otherwise it is unlikely that he would even have considered selling out his associates. He may change his mind again, unless I can clinch the deal within forty-eight hours.'

Syveton agitatedly ran a hand over the whispy, smarmed-down hair that only partly concealed his big expanse of bald forehead. 'We must on no account miss this,' he muttered, 'But what can I do?

323

Unfortunately I have big commitments to meet at the end of the month, otherwise I would try to raise the money myself; I take it that you could not raise such a sum at short notice either. But how about your friend Van Ryn, the banker? Do you think you could persuade him to help us?'

De Quesnoy nodded. 'That is certainly an idea. Yes, I think he might loan me the money on my note of hand. If he will, how soon could you enable me to repay him?'

'Today is the 24th. Shall we say the 30th? No, to be on the safe side we had better make it the end of the week, Friday 1st of November.'

'Very well, then. If you hear nothing further from me you will know that Van Ryn has acceded to my request. If all goes well, I will turn the material in to General Laveriac so that he can verify that the letters were actually written by Captain Mollin. Then, if the deal has gone through, you will pay the draft into my account at Van Ryn's bank as Vasili Petrovitch on November 1st. Can you find me a pen, or pencil, and paper so that I can write a note to Van Ryn now, and drop it on my way back to the Pension Smirnoff? I have been out of touch with him for some time; so we can only hope that he is in Paris, and not off on another trip somewhere.'

Opening the flap of a Dutch bureau, Syveton waved the Count towards it. Sitting down, he wrote a brief note asking the American to meet him if he possibly could at eleven o'clock in the Louvre, near the Winged Victory of Samothrace. Marking the envelope "Strictly Private", he put it in his pocket.

Five minutes later he was again out in the dark night. On his way across Paris he dropped his note into the letter-box of Van Ryn's bank. It was three o'clock before he let himself into the Pension Smirnoff; but even then it was a long time before he could get to sleep, his mind being filled with remorse for his unjustified suspicions of Angela.

Nevertheless, he was up betimes and strolling past the headless "Victory" shortly before eleven. As he halted to admire it, his friend approached from the other direction. They greeted one another in English with exclamations of surprise, as though they had met by the purest chance. Falling into step, they walked slowly down the long gallery, pausing now and then to look at the cases of Tanagra figures, and Grecian pottery with its archaic scenes sharply black on the red ceramic ground, while de Quesnoy gave a low-voiced account of the situation that had developed.

Having heard him out, the American said, 'Eight thousand dollars. That's quite a sum. You're still on the right side by about twelve hundred on that draft your father sent us early in September. Still, that's beside the point. You certainly must not miss the chance to get even now the risks you have been taking look like bearing fruit. Okay, then; I'll let you have the eight thousand against your note of hand.'

With a smile the Count produced his worn pocket-book and took out a folded paper. 'A thousand thanks. I felt sure you would; so I have it here already written out for you. My only real anxiety was that you might not be in Paris.'

Van Ryn's mouth widened into a broad grin. 'I wouldn't want to be any other place just now. I've a fiancée and her mother staying as my guests at the Scribe.'

'*Mon Dieu!*' de Quesnoy swung upon him. 'You pulled it off, then?'

'Sure; and I owe you a lot for urging me to go right out to get her. Queer folk one meets up in Scotland, though. No one there seemed ever to have heard of the Chesapeake Banking and Trust Corporation. But did I ever let on to you that I'm a crack shot with a twelve bore? Anyway, I am; and I slaughtered more grouse birds in a day than some of the fellers there did in a week. Not that that made any difference to Fiona, bless her heart. She wouldn't mind if I couldn't hit a tame cat with a water pistol. But my being able to beat the men of her family and their friends at their own game made things sorta easier all round. In no time at all they were treating me as though I were a long-lost brother.'

'I am delighted! Delighted!' The Count wrung his friend's hand with real enthusiasm. 'But you are no more lucky than she is. Had I a sister I could not wish for her a better husband. How I regret that I am not in a position to call on her and offer her my congratulations. Please convey them to her for me. And as soon as I am through with this business you and I will drink to your happiness the best bottle money can buy.'

De Quesnoy having been debarred from altering the appearance he had had while living as Dupont with Van Ryn, the greatest risk he could run was to be seen in his company; so they resisted the temptation to linger longer together. But they arranged to meet again after dark that evening in the south-west corner of the Palais Royal arcade, and in the shadows there the banker handed over a thick envelope containing the forty thousand francs.

Returning to the Pension Smirnoff, the Count went up to his bedroom, locked the door and took up a board under the bed that he had loosened to form a cache. As a precaution against having his pocket picked in one of the cheap haunts which his life as Petrovitch made it necessary for him to frequent, he kept there the bulk of his money for current expenses and also the precious key to the coach-house in which Harry Plimsol had installed his escape crate. Now, he took five thousand francs out of the envelope that Van Ryn had given him, then put it with the rest of the money into the cache, and replaced the board.

Three hours later he was again with Bidegain at a corner table in the little café where that unhappy man took his nightly potations. Having reported that he had found a buyer for the *fiches*, but could not induce him to go higher than eighty thousand francs, the Count, under cover of a newspaper, showed Bidegain the five *mille* notes he had taken from the envelope, saying that he had demanded that much as evidence that the buyer meant to go through with the deal.

At the sight of the big crisp banknotes that could have got him out of all his troubles, Bidegain lifted his rheumy eyes to de Quesnoy's and muttered, 'You have worked fast; but that is all to the good. The sooner we are through with this business now the better. I'll bring the papers here tomorrow night. I'll not part with them, though, without the money; so you must persuade your friends to trust you with the lot.'

'I think I can do that,' replied the Count quietly. Then, after they had had another drink, he went home feeling confident that his gesture of showing Bidegain as large a sum as he probably earned in a year had both removed his last hesitations and ensured his acting without delay.

Next morning he was up early and, having walked for the best part of a mile, went into a café where he was not known. From it he telephoned Laveriac's apartment but, to his annoyance, learnt that the General had been away for a couple of nights and was not expected back until mid-day. He then tried that of Guyot de Villeneuve and had better fortune. As it was a Saturday the Deputy had no plans for that morning that he could not put off, and he agreed to meet de Quesnoy at half-past ten at the west gate of the Luxembourg Gardens.

When de Villeneuve learned about the *fiches* he became almost as excited as Syveton had been. He said that, through Laveriac and other secret royalists at the War Office, it was known to the Committee that during the last few months the influence of the Grand Orient over General André had increased to such a degree that it now virtually dictated all promotions and appointments in the Army. If cast iron evidence of the connection could be produced it would, therefore, be more valuable than ever, and should provoke a storm of public indignation which would have disastrous repercussions on the Government.

Elated as de Quesnoy was to learn that his six months of uncongenial and dangerous labour were likely to be so well rewarded, he pointed out to de Villeneuve that the *fiches* would be of little value unless it could be proved that André acted upon them; so Mollin's letters to Vadecard were essential to the *coup*, and, although he had no reason to suppose them to be forgeries, it must be put beyond all doubt that they had been written by him. It was for that reason he had tried to get hold of Laveriac, as the General could no doubt have secured a paper in Mollin's writing from one of the files in the War Office.

De Villeneuve at once agreed the point and said that, the matter being of such importance, he would go to Laveriac's apartment and wait there until his return. It was further settled that the Deputy and the General should be at half-past eleven that night at the Café Nicole, which was only a few hundred yards from that frequented by Bidegain, and there await de Quesnoy's coming.

It was close on twelve o'clock when he joined them, and he had with him three letters from Mollin. For them he had given Bidegain twenty thousand francs, withholding the other half of the money for the time being, while the equally cautious Bidegain had retained the *fiches*. All three of the letters contained passages showing beyond dispute that Mollin had been acting on behalf of General André, and after a brief examination Laveriac declared himself fully satisfied that they were in Mollin's writing.

De Quesnoy then returned to Bidegain and, to his astonishment, on his handing over the second twenty thousand francs the little man produced from a canvas satchel a great bundle consisting of several hundred *fiches*. Seeing the Count's look of surprise, he gave a nervous laugh and said:

'From the time we started asking the branches for these things I've had over twenty-five thousand of them through my hands; but now I'm finished with the business I thought your friends might as well have their money's worth; so I cleared the files and brought you their whole contents. I only wish I could see that pig Vadecard's face on Monday morning.'

Having had a final drink with him and wished him luck, the Count hurried back with his treasure to the Café Nichol. There, he and his two fellow conspirators spent over an hour going through it to their great satisfaction. Many of the *fiches* were quite innocuous and a few even in praise of the officers reported on, as sound priest-haters and good democrats, but dozens were denunciations of men whose only crime was sending their children to one of the old-established Church schools instead of the new government *lycées*, and some, as Laveriac was in a position to know, were tissues of malicious lies invented with the object of sabotaging the careers of strict but highly competent officers.

They still had more than half of the *fiches* to go through when they noticed that the café was nearly empty and, not wishing to draw the patron's attention to themselves, decided that they had better soon make a move. As Vadecard could not fail to find on Monday that his files had been rifled, there was now a risk that he might take some counter action which would rob the *coup* of its surprise value; so it was agreed that de Villeneuve should enter the Chamber as soon as it opened on Monday, with Mollin's letters and a selection of the *fiches*, and intervene to produce them at the first opportunity.

Whatever the risk, de Quesnoy felt that he could not deny himself the pleasure of witnessing the outcome of his endeavours; so during Sunday he spent quite a lot of time considering various possible disguises. His choice fell on turning himself into an elderly asthmatic, and first thing on Monday morning he set about his transformation.

At a pharmacy he bought a pair of cheap steel-rimmed spectacles, a large black oval pad such as poor persons afflicted with asthma used to wear tied over their mouths with black tapes, and a tin of talcum powder. In a public lavatory, with the aid of a pocket mirror, he brushed some of the powder well into his beard and hair; then, satisfied that he looked a good fifteen years older, he bought a stick on which to lean, and, at a little before eleven o'clock, having the appearance of a confirmed invalid, made his way slowly up to the public gallery in the Chamber of Deputies.

The Chamber was two-thirds empty and engaged in winding up a dull debate that had been carried over from a previous session. But Deputies kept drifting in and it soon became clear that those of the Right had been specially mobilized. A scurrying to and fro on the Left showed that alarm had been taken there and a quarter of an hour later the benches on that side also began to fill up. Prime Minister Combes came hurrying in at midday and soon after him the Foreign Minister, Delcassé, the Minister for the Colonies, Doumergue, Pelletan and General André.

They had hardly taken their seats before de Villeneuve jumped to his feet and asked leave of the President of the Chamber to speak on a matter of urgent national importance. It was granted and, with the vitriolic eloquence of which he was a master, he denounced the War Minister as a traitor guilty of deliberately weakening the country's defence for political ends.

His attack was at first greeted with laughter; but having recalled how André had suppressed the properly qualified Promotion Committees to take the fates of twenty thousand officers into his own hands, he pointed out that no man could have personal knowledge of even one in fifty of them; so the Minister had found himself compelled to substitute other, less impartial, groups of advisers for the Promotion Committees. That he had consulted Prefects who owed their appointments to the Ministry was common knowledge, also that he had invited the *Bloc des Gauches* to make its recommendations; but it had been only rumoured that he had disgraced his high office by allowing himself to bécome a creature of the Freemasons.

There were cheers from the Right, boos and catcalls from the Left, but the Chamber was obviously intrigued to know what was coming next. As soon as the noise had died down he read out Captain Mollin's letters to Vadecard and followed them with a selection of the most slanderous of the *fiches*.

The Chamber heard him out with hardly a murmur. When he had

finished the Left sat in stunned silence, looking hopefully at the Ministry for a swift and categorical denial of these damning charges.

It did not come. General André got slowly to his feet and, white-faced and shaking, he cried in a tremulous voice, 'I have had no notice of this. I will look into the matter.'

Tough old Combes jumped up and shouted, 'Lies! Lies! Lies!' But he was howled down by the Right and the Centre, which now turned upon him with cries of 'Explain or resign! André is a traitor! Down with the Ministry! We are betrayed! The country is in danger! Refute the charges or resign! They have sold us to the Germans! Out with them; out!'

To de Quesnoy's grim delight it seemed that the Government was doomed; but, taking advantage of a temporary lull in the pandemonium, Jules Jaurès, the great Socialist intellectual, sprang up to the tribune and, with the skill of a born orator, succeeded in getting a hearing.

Eloquently he pleaded with the Radicals and Republicans not to be stampeded into withdrawing their support from the Ministry on a snap motion; not to lose their heads and help the "Caesarians"—the old military caste, the promoters of war, the rich manufacturers of arms and the oppressors of the common people—to overthrow the Government.

His impassioned plea saved Combes and his colleagues. A Radical put a motion that André should be allowed a week to produce an explanation. It was carried, although only by a majority of four.

De Quesnoy left the Public Gallery sadly disappointed. He endeavoured to cheer himself with the thought that André would find it no more easy to explain his associations with the Masons in a week's time; but he knew only too well that, now the mine had been sprung, scores of unscrupulous politicians would be holding small, agitated group meetings, with the object of keeping in power the Combes Ministry, because it suited their private ends.

Pocketing his spectacles and asthma pad, he went to a barber's and, giving as a reason for the white powder in his hair and beard that he had been to a fancy dress dance the previous night, he had them thoroughly shampooed. Then, early in the evening, he took his courage in both hands and went to the headquarters of the Grand Orient in the Rue Cadet.

It took considerable nerve to do so, as it was possible that Bidegain had been caught and, under pressure, given him away as the man who had tempted him to sell the secrets of the Brotherhood. Yet, if he suddenly terminated his associations with the Masons, knowing him to have been a crony of Bidegain's they might swiftly come to suspect him of acting as the agent for their betrayal. To appear boldly among them before they had had the time to carry out a full investigation, and find out how their minds were working, seemed therefore a high, but not unreasonable, stake to play against the certainty of being shadowed later and possibly having his identity discovered by fanatical amateur sleuths, who would either have him arrested by the police or knifed by an Apache.

He found the headquarters in a turmoil. Freemasons buzzed indignantly in it like a swarm of angry bees. They took the line that their Secretary-General had been performing a valuable service to the State in helping to Republicanize the Army—that last stronghold of aristocratic privilege, monarchism, and subservience to Rome—but, all the same, they were far from happy at having had his activities made public.

Bidegain, the Count learned much to his comfort, had made good use of the week-end. His family were still in Paris and refused to answer questions; but he had taken the Sunday morning train for Brussels with several pieces of luggage, and left behind him rude notes for his principal creditors intimating that he never meant to return.

Reassured that he, personally, was in no immediate danger, the Count returned to his lodging and put in a sound night's sleep. On Tuesday evening he went to the billiards saloon and spent a few hours with Forain and the rest of the little crowd there that he had come to know so well. They echoed the opinions he had heard at the Grand Orient the previous night, and it was evident that not one of them had the least suspicion that he was at the bottom of the scandal which had become front-page news under inch-high headlines, and was now agitating all France.

Two mornings later, as he left his room to go out, Madame Smirnoff, meeting him on the landing, told him there was a letter for him in the rack. Had she not mentioned it, he might not have known of its arrival for some days, as during the whole time he had had a room at the Pension he had not received a single letter there, and he expected none. Wondering what could have caused one of his fellow conspirators, or

331

Van Ryn, to write to him, he hurried downstairs, to find to his surprise that the envelope was in Angela's writing.

Tearing it open, he saw that it contained only a single sheet of paper with a few lines on it, which read:

Something has happened about which I must talk to you. Please come to the pavilion at ten o'clock tomorrow, Thursday, night. I will see that the door in the wall is left unlocked. If you cannot come on Thursday I shall wait there at the same time each night until you can.

For the rest of the day his thoughts were never far from her, but he speculated in vain upon what it might be that she wished to see him about. He was still feeling great contrition over the unjust suspicions of her that had driven him to break into the pavilion the preceding Thursday night, and weighed in his mind if he ought to tell her about that. Finally he decided that no good could come from doing so; but it was possible that Syveton had already told her of his unexpected and violent entry. If that proved the case, rather than attempt to explain it away by lies, he was quite prepared to confess the truth and grovel. As things turned out the matter did not arise, and from the moment of his arrival upstairs in the pavilion his mind was fully occupied with a startling new development.

On reaching the door of the sitting-room he saw that its lock had been repaired, but it was only latched; so he walked in. He had jumped to the conclusion that Angela had asked Clothilde to go out and lend her the pavilion for the evening; but he took in at a glance that, although none of the additional furniture had been removed, none of Clothilde's small personal possessions was lying about, as they had been when he had last been there, and that tonight no enticing supper was spread upon the table.

As he closed the door behind him, that of the bedroom opened and Angela came in. Her face looked strained and tired, and she smiled a little wanly as she said, 'I've an awful headache; so I have been lying down in the dark until you came.'

Then walking quickly towards him she took both his outstretched hands in hers and burst out, 'Armand, I sent for you to tell you that I have told Gabriel that he must assist me to get an annulment.'

'My darling!' he exclaimed, taking her gently in his arms. 'This is wonderful news. Last time I saw you I feared it might be months before you could bring yourself to abandon him. Now, at last, we'll have a definite future to look forward to. I cannot begin to tell you how much that means to me.'

'I know,' she murmured. 'And to me. You have been sweetly patient for so long. But soon, now, I'll be able to start making that up to you.'

For a few moments she lay against him, while he softly kissed her cheek and forehead; then she drew away, and said, 'Come; let's sit down. I must tell you the reason for my decision; although it's so horrible that I can hardly bear to think of it.'

Greatly puzzled, he led her to the sofa, and when they had settled there with her head against his shoulder, she went on: 'It is Clothilde. Of course, she is just the sensual-looking type of young girl that would appeal to him. I could tell that from the way I caught him eyeing her now and again when he thought no one was watching. But I never dreamed. . . .'

De Quesnoy stiffened slightly. 'Surely you can't mean . . .?'

'Yes. Last Thursday, when Henri was spending the night at Le Mans, Gabriel came here and . . . well, I think he as good as forced her. At least, that is what she says.'

'*Mon Dieu!* His son's wife! It is unbelievable!'

The Count's exclamations of horror were spontaneous. Yet even as he made them, the brief scene that had taken place after he had broken in that night flashed back to him, and little things he had noticed almost subconsciously now took on a new meaning.

It had been one o'clock in the morning, so long past the hour at which a man would normally have remained with his daughter-in-law if, as Syveton had said, he had only come over to keep her company because she was not feeling very well. She had been wearing a negligée, which was hardly a conventional garment in which to entertain one's father-in-law to supper. Her swollen eyelids had suggested that she had been crying. And Syveton, instead of demanding an explanation from his visitor for breaking in, had rushed into one to explain his own presence there.

'Whether he really forced her, as she says, or she let him seduce her and is now suffering from remorse, is really immaterial,' Angela was going on. 'It is their relationship which makes what took place so unforgivable.'

'How did you learn of this?' de Quesnoy asked.

'From her mother. Apparently Clothilde went to confession on Sunday and her director told her that she must confess her sin to her husband. She didn't ... at least, not at first. Instead, on Monday afternoon she poured out the whole awful business to her mother. On Tuesday morning Madame de Vauclose came to see me. She asked me to send for Clothilde, then made the girl repeat her story. It was most terribly embarrassing. Clothilde wept and her mother raved. She said that if her husband had been in Paris he would have come round to horsewhip Gabriel, and that they would bring an action against him. Then she declared that Clothilde should never spend another night under a Syveton roof and carried her off.'

Angela's voice quivered slightly at the memory of this totally unexpected and most harrowing interview, but she controlled it and continued, 'In the afternoon she sent her maid and a footman to pack and remove all Clothilde's things. When Henri came home and found that both his wife and her belongings had vanished, he could hardly believe his eyes. He came rushing over to the house and I had the horrible job of breaking it to the poor boy that I feared his marriage had broken up; but when he pressed me to tell him why, I said I felt that I must leave Clothilde to do that; so he went dashing off to the de Vauclose apartment.'

'Where was Syveton all this time?'

'He had gone out before Madame de Vauclose paid her call on me and was still out when Henri came home in the evening. In fact, he didn't get back till after Henri returned from seeing Clothilde.'

'Poor fellow, this is a terrible thing for him. Perhaps, in a way, worse even than for her. Did he take it very badly?'

'Yes. I had hoped till then that it might not be true; that she was one of those unfortunate people whose minds are both unbalanced and lascivious, and that the way Gabriel used to look at her had caused her to make these accusations in a fit of hysteria. But it wasn't like that. She mentioned to Henri that Gabriel has a big mole on his chest, and there is no way she could know that unless she had seen it. Henri was absolutely distraught, and swore that he would kill his father. I had a terrible time with him, and when Gabriel did get home I insisted on remaining with them while they had it out, from fear that if I left them on their own one of them might do the other a serious injury.'

De Quesnoy drew her closer and said with a frown, 'What a rôle for a woman to have to play! I'd like to horsewhip Syveton myself, for being the cause of your suffering such an ordeal.'

Angela sighed. 'It was shattering while it lasted. They went for one another like pickpockets. After what seemed an interminable time, Henri declared that he meant to leave the house and would never enter it again. I came up here with him and helped him pack a bag, and he asked me to have the rest of his things sent to Le Mans. I did that today. I only wish I could have done something more, I feel so terribly sorry for him.'

'What did you do when he had gone?'

'I went back to the house and confronted Gabriel. I told him that I meant to apply for an annulment. He begged me not to, urging that if I did and it got out, his creditors would take it as a sign that it was all up with him. I told him that Henri had confirmed that the de Vaucloses meant to bring an action against him, and that a wife could have no better reason for leaving her husband than this shameful act of his, which will be the talk of Paris within the next few days; so there would not then be the least cause for his creditors to suppose that I was abandoning him because he could no longer afford to keep me in luxury.

'There was another terrible scene, but I stuck to what I had said— that the moment this scandal about Clothilde breaks I mean to act. And, of course, to have his aid in getting an annulment is no longer essential. Even if he opposed my plea his crime provides sufficient grounds for me to secure a favourable verdict. It is a hateful thought that anything so horrible as this should have to happen in order for me to have a clear conscience about freeing myself from him; but now it has, nothing will induce me to remain his wife one moment longer than I have to. First thing next morning I wrote to you, asking you to come here tonight, or as soon as you could.'

Almost exhausted with emotion, Angela lapsed into silence. For a while de Quesnoy petted her, then he began to speak quietly of his own affairs. Whether the Government would fall as a result of the scandal of the *fiches* still remained on the knees of the gods, but he declared himself content with having been responsible for the great blow which must at least weaken it and shorten its life considerably.

She praised him now without stint for the persistence he had shown, and spoke of the general feeling of people with whom she had talked during the past few days that the coming Monday would witness the downfall of Combes and André.

He told her that once the crisis was over, one way or the other, he had intended to see her, then leave Paris; and about the fitted crate, by travelling in which he would escape the watch that might still be maintained for him at railway stations and ports. But that now she had made up her mind to leave Syveton, he would either join her, if she meant to go abroad, or remain in France, just as she wished.

'I shall go to my family in England,' Angela said, 'but not for a little while yet. I have no intention of scurrying out by night as though I were doing something to be ashamed of. I mean to pack at my leisure and, without referring to the reason for my departure, make farewell calls on all my friends before I go. That will enable me to keep at least some shreds of dignity.'

De Quesnoy nodded. 'You are right, my love. That is just the way in which I would have wished my future wife to act.'

'But you, dearest,' she said quickly, 'you must not delay on my account. I beg you not to linger for a single day after the fate of the Government is decided. I shall be following you very soon, and think what a joy it will be for me to know that you are waiting in England to welcome me.'

'The prospect makes me disinclined to take the least risk that might prevent that,' he smiled, 'so I will do as you wish. All the same, I would be happier if we were going to some country other than England.'

'How could I go anywhere else? Directly I tell my parents that I am leaving Gabriel they will naturally expect me to come to them in London. What possible excuse could I give for not doing so? Besides, England is my true country, and I love it. We've had no chance yet to discuss where we'll live when we can get married, but I do hope, darling, that you are willing that we should make our home there.'

'With you,' he declared, 'I should be happy to make my home anywhere; and as your family and friends live in England that is the obvious choice. In any case I can never return openly to France. But, apart from the fact that I shall regret not being able to visit Paris, I am not really sorry. Ten years ago my father told me that France was finished. He said that the Revolution, the Napoleonic wars and other troubles since had either sent into permanent exile or destroyed all the best elements in the French people. That they were now a different race from what they were under our great Kings, in the days of our glory. That the leaven of courage and honesty and chivalry had gone out of them, and that the avarice, the meanness and the trickery of the unenlightened peasant now dominated all their dealings, both with other nations and among themselves. I did not believe him. And, of course, there are still many fine, brave, upright people here in every walk of life. But in the main he was right.

'Were it not so, France would have better men as her national representatives. Combes and his colleagues are utterly despicable; but how much better would their opponents be if they came to power? A few may be honest, but how many more would turn out, like Syveton, blackguards and men who had been playing the party game for their own advancement? No, I have always admired the English. They are often stupid, but at least they have the courage of their convictions and are tolerant and just. Since I can no longer be a Frenchman, I am willing to change my nationality and become one of them. Would that please you?'

'Oh, Armand, you know it would. You could give me no finer wedding present.'

'Then it shall be done. But the thing that perturbs me is the immediate future. When we discussed an annulment it was agreed that while waiting until we could get married we should live together in secret, anyhow for a good part of the time. Now, apparently, you intend to return to your parents, and I can hardly suppose that their English code of morality would condone your entering into a liaison—even with a lover who was waiting only for legal sanction to become your husband.'

'It certainly would not,' Angela agreed hurriedly. 'What is more, I do not mean to tell them anything about us until the annulment comes through, because it would distress them to know that while married I loved a man other than my husband.'

'What you tell me bears out my worst fears concerning your going to England. In any other country we could have stayed in small hotels and varied that from time to time with the fun of sharing a little apartment for a few weeks. But in London, where you have so many friends, the risk of our being found out would be too great; and, since your parents must be kept in the dark about your having a lover, you will find it damnably difficult to think of watertight excuses for slipping away from them to be with me, even for a few days now and then.'

Angela gave an unhappy shrug. 'All that is true, darling; and I am just as loath for us to be forced into starting a hole-in-the-corner affaire after all as you are. But you must see that, to begin with at all events, I've no option but to return to my parents. I have no intention of remaining with them permanently, though. A few years ago one of my aunts left me some money; so I am quite able to support myself, and given time I know I can persuade my parents that it would be much more satisfactory for me to have a small place of my own. When I am installed it will be comparatively easy for me to play truant once in a while and join you somewhere in secret.'

' "Comparatively easy", and "once in a while",' he repeated with a wry grimace. 'That doesn't sound very promising; and it is far from what I had hoped for. Remember, your annulment will take anything from two to three years to go through. It is a poor look-out if for all that time we are to have only a few nights together occasionally.'

'Armand, please be reasonable. When we first talked of this you agreed that for us to be able to marry instead of living for the rest of our lives as social outcasts would be worth the long wait. It was I who pointed out that we need not deny ourselves a foretaste of happiness while we waited, but I did say that we would have to be very, very careful. That applies to any country in which we live, just as much as to England. If it were found out that we were actually living together it would become the subject of a scandal which might later close quite a lot of doors to us in society; still worse, it might mean that I would not be given my annulment.'

'I know! I know!' he exclaimed, standing up. 'But I do feel that there must be a way in which we could do better for ourselves than this.'

For a minute or two he paced agitatedly up and down, then, suddenly coming to a halt in front of her, he asked abruptly:

'Tell me, beloved. Just how much does religion mean to you?'

Raising her big brown eyes to meet his gaze, she replied frankly:

'Not a great deal. I believe in Our Lord, of course, and the Divine Mercy; but I was brought up in the Church of England, and only became a Catholic just before I married Gabriel, because he wished it. When I go to church I say my private prayers, but I don't really bother much about the service, and I'm afraid I tell my confessor only the sort of things I think he would expect to hear, because I have never believed that one needs a middle-man to secure God's forgiveness.'

He nodded. 'Our views are near enough alike, as I gave up observing the ceremonies of the Church while I was stationed in Madagascar. Why then, shouldn't we leave the Church out of this? Instead of your applying for an annulment let's go to America. Each of the United States has its own laws, you know, and in some of the Western ones divorce is both quick and easy. You could file a petition as soon as you got there. Gabriel's relations with Clothilde would secure you a decree without the least difficulty, and six months from now, or less, we could be married by a civil ceremony.'

For a few moments she considered the matter, then she asked, 'If such divorces are really valid, why do not the majority of couples who wish to regain their freedom, and can afford a trip to the United States, take advantage of them?'

'God forbid that I should mislead you,' he replied. 'They are no more than a sort of half-way house. The rulings of these courts are not generally accepted outside the States in which they sit. I gather that even in New York the more straight-laced leaders of society refuse to receive Nevada divorcees who have married again. But such a decree does at least give a semblance of legality to a new union. It would enable a couple like ourselves to live openly as husband and wife. In fact it would give me the right to call out anyone who implied that you had no claim to call yourself the Comtesse de Quesnoy.'

Again she remained thoughtful for a few moments. Then she murmured, 'No, Armand, no. That would not do. If such people are not received into the best New York society, you can be certain they would not be into that of London. We would be neither fish, nor fowl, nor good red herring; and the very idea of your having to fight a series of duels to protect me from insult quite appals me.'

'You need not worry yourself on that score. I would refrain from challenging people if you wished it, unless they became openly offensive; and it is most unlikely that they would do that.'

'Even so, there would always be some degree of uncertainty about by whom we would be accepted; whereas an annulment would make our position unassailable. As we are both still under thirty, I'm sure it would pay us to wait until the official sanction of the Church places us beyond criticism for the rest of our lives.'

'Perhaps you are right,' he muttered a shade doubtfully.

Reaching out for his hand she drew him down beside her again, kissed him on the ear, and said, 'Dearest Armand, please don't look so miserable. I feel certain things will turn out better than you suppose. After I've spent a few weeks with my parents I'll say that as I am not used to the London winter I must have a change. Then we'll slip abroad and meet at some quiet spot on the Continent for a stolen honeymoon. Later, when I am living on my own, providing I don't do it too frequently, we can snatch other holidays abroad together, and so make our time of waiting pass quite quickly. I swear to you that from now on I am entirely yours, and at the right moment will deny you nothing.'

With such a sweet assurance ringing in his ears, de Quesnoy could only agree and, realizing that Angela was still in a state bordering on nervous exhaustion, he soon afterwards urged her to go straight to bed, then took his leave of her.

On his way home he felt at first only elation that she was at last firmly pledged to him; yet after a while it wore off a little. The thought of a stolen honeymoon with her, perhaps even before Christmas, was as heady as a draught of strong wine, but he could not help feeling dubious about the long period which must elapse before they could make a life permanently together.

Since she was so averse as yet to presenting him to her parents, it would prove most embarrassing for her if he ran into her with them at some social function. To avoid the possibility of such a contretemps meant that he must refrain from entering London society through such friends as would normally have introduced him into it if he went to live there. In consequence, except for occasional stolen holidays with Angela, it looked as if for two years or more he would be at a loose end, drifting for short spells from one place on the Continent to another, unable to settle to anything, and driven nearly mad by boredom.

It occurred to him that it would be better for his peace of mind to forgo these stolen holidays and spend the next two years in the army of one of the South American Republics. But to do that would be to deprive Angela of the stolen holidays too; so he decided that he must resign himself to this far from satisfactory state of affairs until the annulment at last came through.

For him Friday, Saturday and Sunday seemed to drag on for ever;

but at last Monday dawned and, as he had done on the previous Monday, he went disguised as a middle-aged asthmatic to the Chamber of Deputies.

All France was waiting to learn the result of the critical debate that was to take place; so although de Quesnoy had gone early he had difficulty in squeezing his way into the Public Gallery. As soon as the Chamber was opened a flood of Deputies streamed into it, pushing and shoving to obtain seats on the best benches. When Combes and André entered there were boos and catcalls from all parts of the Chamber.

André rose to make his defence. Old, ill-looking and evidently without hope that he might ride the storm, he stammered out a succession of feeble excuses for having made use of the Grand Orient, and platitudes about the necessity of converting the Army to Republican principles. He was constantly interrupted and eventually howled down. Even the Ministerial Republicans, the Radicals and the Socialist leader Millerand attacked him.

Once more Jules Jaurès sprang to his defence. He castigated the Army as the last stronghold of Monarchist and Catholic ideals; declared that the State would never be safe from a *coup d'état* by the Generals until the old aristocratic element had been eliminated from the commissioned ranks; and asserted that to reduce the Army to its proper status of an obedient and willing servant of the Government any and all measures were justifiable.

For once his magnificent oratory failed to sway the Chamber. The majority of its members were that day concerned with facts, not theories, and realized that André had exposed France to a swift defeat by Germany. Again came the cries of 'Traitor! Resign! Down with the Government! Vote them out! Vote them out! Vote them out!'

A division was called. The Deputies streamed towards the lobbies. Then Syveton left his place among the leading Deputies of the Right, crossed the floor of the Chamber, went up to André and slapped the old General a succession of violent blows with the flat of the hand across his face.

Silence suddenly descended on the Chamber. André was an aged, physically feeble man, Syveton still in the full vigour of robust middle age. Someone cried 'Shame!' then there came shouts of 'Bully! Apache! Canaille! Coward! Hit a man who can hit you back!'

A moment later it became clear that Syveton's brutal act had had a profound psychological effect on many of his fellow Deputies. At least a score of those who had been heading for the Opposition lobby turned away and, to show their sympathy for the humiliated General, gave their vote in his support. The result was that on the vote of confidence the Government, which would unquestionably have been defeated, secured a majority.

Almost sick with rage, de Quesnoy left the gallery and, having pocketed his spectacles and asthma pad, again went through the tiresome business of having a barber whom he had never before patronized shampoo the powder out of his beard and hair.

It was ten days now since he had provided the ammunition for what should have been a decisive attack upon his enemies; but the direction of it had been out of his hands. There was no more that he could do; so he resigned himself to the thought that, having brought the Combes régime into grievous difficulties and ensured that André would never again dare to use the Grand Orient as an intelligence service to further his iniquitous vendetta, he must rest content.

That night, lying in bed in his room at the Pension Smirnoff, he decided that next day he would get in touch with Van Ryn, and put in train the arrangements by which he could, the following day, be shipped in his crate to England. Angela would soon be arriving there. Even if they had to wait for a while longer before they could be formally united, at least he would be able to see her frequently; to enjoy once more freedom from fear of arrest; and to live again among pleasant people with the comforts that a considerable income could provide.

Next morning, at about nine o'clock, he left his room. As he came down the stairs he saw Madame Smirnoff in conversation with two men in the little square hall at the bottom of the flight. He was two-thirds of the way down when one of the men looked up. Next moment the man pulled a revolver from his pocket and shouted:

'Stay where you are! Monsieur le Comte de Quesnoy, I hold a warrant for your arrest.'

CHAPTER XXIV

ON THE RUN

TAKING the rules of roulette as a fair guide to the laws of chance, de Quesnoy had been lucky. On average in the game, Zero comes up only once in thirty-seven spins, and he had been wanted by the police in Paris for eighty-six days without once having been challenged. When, too, Zero does turn up, those players who have put their money on even chances still have half a chance. Their bets remain on the table until the next spin of the wheel decides whether they lose their money or get it back.

Even now that Vasili Petrovitch had been identified as Colonel the Comte de Quesnoy, if he could keep his freedom for the next ten minutes there was still half a chance that he might keep it long enough to get out of France. But the wheel had been rigged against him. A yard away a loaded revolver was pointed at his chest.

Now that de Vendôme had secured evidence that would clear the Count of a charge of murder, arrest, at worst, could mean no more for him personally than a prison sentence; but it could do immense harm to the cause which he had served so selflessly.

His arrest would mean headlines in the Press and front-page articles digging up all that was known, or could plausibly be invented, about the de Vendôme conspiracy. It would provide the journals of the Left and Centre with a heaven-sent chance to prate of the dangers of a Monarchist *coup d'état*, and to urge the necessity of Republicanizing the Army as a safeguard against it. The scandal of the *fiches* had roused public indignation to fever pitch, but the only chance now remaining that the Government would fall was that the pressure of public opinion on individual Deputies should be maintained. The resurrection of the de Vendôme affair could cause it to cease overnight, and thus secure the Government a new lease of life.

Knowing that, de Quesnoy decided in an instant to gamble his life.

He staked it against the half-chance that he would not only get the better of the two detectives but also escape from Paris before he could be arrested. Instead of turning and attempting flight he took one more step down the stairs. His left foot shot out. It caught the wrist of the man who menaced him a sharp crack. The revolver flew from the detective's hand, described a parabola in mid-air, and landed on the hall table behind him with a resounding crash.

Grabbing at his injured wrist with his unhurt hand the man gave a yelp of pain. Madame Smirnoff screamed. The other detective swore and pulled out his revolver. As he cocked it de Quesnoy spun round and dashed up the stairs. On the top step he tripped. It saved his life. As he came down on his hands and knees a bullet sang over his head. Jerking himself up, he swerved sideways, crossed the landing in two uneven strides and dived into the side passage. A second bullet thudded into the wall just behind him. Madame Smirnoff screamed again. Next moment he had reached the door of his room; but, as was his custom, on leaving he had locked it.

Turning slightly, he flung himself sideways against it. The lock snapped, the door flew open and he was precipitated into the room. As he recovered his balance the pounding footsteps of the men who were after him came thundering across the landing. Only by gaining half a minute could he possibly hope to get away. Slamming the door shut, he grabbed at the painted deal washstand. As he jerked it forward, the water he had used to wash in slopped over his hands and forearms. Another heave and he threw it over behind the door. The china basin shot out of its circular slot in the wooden top. With the dishes for soap and sponge, and the tooth glass, it shattered against the wall. But the overturned washstand was just weighty enough to keep the door from being forced open for the all-important half-minute. Leaping on to the bed, he jumped down on its far side, flung open the window and scrambled out on to the ledge.

Now he had cause to thank his gods that, when in May Madame Smirnoff had offered him a choice of three vacant rooms he had, as a precaution against having to get out in a hurry, chosen this room at the back on the first floor rather than a bigger and better furnished one on the second. As he hung by his hands from the window-sill his toes dangled eight feet from the ground. A drop from that height could easily result in a broken ankle, and below him, menacingly, were the hard

flags of a small paved yard. Praying for a safe landing, he released his hold on the sill.

The second his feet hit the stone he let his knees go. They doubled under him, jerking savagely at the muscles round the knee-caps; then he was pitched violently forward and struck his forehead a frightful blow against the wall of the house. Stars and circles flamed in the pall of blackness that suddenly shut off his vision. For several precious seconds he was to all intents and purposes knocked out. But, like a punch-drunk yet still game boxer who manages to regain his feet after a count of eight, he staggered up, turned and reeled towards the entrance of the yard.

Shouts now came from above, for the two detectives had reached the window. But fate threw up another Zero. Two lines of washing were hanging out across the yard. When he had blundered through the nearest he was temporarily hidden by a wide expanse of sheets. The man with the revolver could only guess at his position, and once again he escaped being shot in the back. A moment later his sight had cleared sufficiently for him to see where he was going. Ducking beneath a pair of frilly drawers, he made a dash for the yard gate, wrenched it open and staggered through it.

It gave on to a long, narrow alley between brick walls. Turning right, he sped with flying feet down the seventy yards to its exit. There he pulled up, breathless, still half dazed, and with his leg muscles hurting atrociously. At a swift walk he emerged into the street. On one side it had a row of mean shops, on the other the railway tracks behind the Gare Montparnasse. Hurrying through the crowd of shoppers, he turned into the Rue du Maine, continued along it for a quarter of a mile and, now satisfied that he was safe from pursuit, entered the Montparnasse Cemetery. After following one of the narrower paths for a few minutes, he found a secluded spot among a group of large old family mausoleums and there sat down to recover his wind and wits.

His head ached intolerably, which made clear thinking difficult, and he could form no theory to account for the police having run him to earth. It was ten days since he had bought the *fiches* from Bidegain, and during that time he had on several occasions put in an appearance at both the headquarters of the Grand Orient and the billiards saloon which was the favourite haunt of the Masons who lived in

Montparnasse. At neither had any of them shown the least suspicion that he might be connected with the affair.

It was, of course, possible that on Bidegain's arrival in Brussels he might have been indiscreet about the source of his new wealth and that Masons there, learning of it, had passed the information on to their breathren in Paris. Yet Bidegain knew him only as Petrovitch, and while the Masons might have brought a charge against him for complicity in the theft of their papers, that could not account for the detective's having called on him to surrender himself as de Quesnoy. Besides, it seemed much more probable that, instead of taking such a step, they would have hired an Apache to exact a private vengeance.

It could be that the secret agents of the *Bloc des Gauches* were keeping the leaders of the Right under observation; that de Villeneuve had been shadowed to the Café Nichol, and de Quesnoy recognized when they had met there. But that meeting, too, had been ten days ago; so if he had been identified and followed back to the Pension Smirnoff, why had the police waited until now to take action?

The most plausible theory seemed to be that someone who knew him well had spotted him the day before in the Public Gallery of the Chamber, tracked him to his hide-out, and then informed the police; although it seemed difficult to believe that anyone could have penetrated such an elaborate disguise as he had been wearing at the time.

Whatever the truth of the matter, the salient fact was that the police again knew for certain that he was in Paris, and by now would be organizing all their resources to spread a net for him.

The thought was a disturbing one, but it did not cause him any great perturbation, because he had already taken precautions against just such an emergency. At least an hour must elapse before they could inform any considerable number of their men that they had him on the run and, unless he was exceptionally unlucky, well before the net was spread he could be safely hidden in his packing case. After dark he would come out and telephone Van Ryn or Plimsol, using only the simple code phrase they had agreed on, "Please send off the parcel". That night he would sleep in his crate, and the following afternoon should see it landed at Dover. He had just reached this highly satisfactory conclusion to his programme when he was suddenly struck by an awful thought. The key to the coach-house in which the crate was hidden was still under the loose board in his bedroom at the Pension.

To go back for it was out of the question. As a matter of routine the police would post a man to keep watch there, just in case he was tempted to return in the hope of collecting money, or papers, that he had had to leave behind. In any case, by now they would be ransacking the room. Experienced searchers could not fail to find the loose board beneath the bed, and below it his reserve of cash and the key.

Fortunately the key had no label or other indication of the whereabouts of the lock it had been made to fit; so it would not provide a clue to his intentions, or lead to the discovery of the packing case. But the awful thing was that to him it was irretrievably lost. That meant that until he could secure a duplicate of it he would be in the gravest danger.

As soon as the Sûreté sent out a general call to keep a look-out for him, it would be known to thousands of policemen that he had been living under the name of Petrovitch. Among the police there were many Masons. Some of them would be certain to flash the news to Grand Orient headquarters that the recently initiated Brother Petrovitch had turned out to be the Royalist conspirator de Quesnoy. There his acquaintance with Bidegain was known; so they would realize at once that it was he who had persuaded Bidegain to betray them and had enabled de Villeneuve to denounce André. Thirsting for revenge, they would lose not a moment in putting the word out to every Mason in Paris to keep his eyes skinned for the fugitive.

The result must be that, from mid-day, not only the whole police force of the capital, but civilians in almost every street, would be peering into the faces of every likely passer-by in the hope of identifying him. Had he been able to go to earth in his crate before the hunt was properly under way, they would have looked for him in vain. Now, he had many hours of daylight before him and no place in which to hide.

There was only one place in Paris where he could lie low with little risk during the daytime. That was the pavilion in the Syvetons' garden. But even if he could cross Paris and reach it without being caught, he would be no nearer getting into the crate on which he had been counting as his magic carpet to safety.

Van Ryn had the other key to the coach-house; so that when he had the word that de Quesnoy was going to earth in the crate he could have it collected the following morning. The only course now was to

347

get him to have another key cut. But, as the police knew the Van Ryn-Dupont connection, now that they were in full cry after the Count it was certain that they would have Van Ryn watched. De Quesnoy felt that even to explain what had happened over the telephone might result in his plan for escaping from France leaking out, and that for Van Ryn and himself to meet, so that he could receive the new key when it had been cut, would be extremely likely to lead to his arrest.

After some moments of most anxious thought, he decided that he must have a go-between, and that it would be much less risky to ask Angela to fulfil this role than either Laveriac or de Villeneuve. It might have been through one of the latter that he had been traced, but since his return to Paris no third person could ever have been aware of his meetings with the Syvetons. Without anyone's having the least suspicion that she was acting for him, Angela could walk into Van Ryn's office, ask him to have a duplicate key cut at once, and arrange for it to be delivered to her later in the day.

To pursue such a plan he must let Angela know his desperate plight and what he wished her to do for him; but he must run no risk of anyone's learning that he was in communication with her. Again the thought of the pavilion came to him, If he could reach it he could both see her in secret and lie doggo there all day, thus killing two birds with one stone.

Standing up, he left the cemetery at a quick walk, acutely aware that by now police telephones all over Paris must be buzzing with his name; so that every moment would increase his danger. Yet the morning's events had put one new card into his hand. Now that it was no longer necessary for him to maintain his contact with the Masons, and having been chased from the Pension Smirnoff, he was no longer compelled to retain the appearance of Dupont-Petrovitch.

The skin on his forehead was broken and a large bump had already risen there; so, entering the first pharmacy he came to, he said that he had just fallen downstairs, and had his head bound up. In the next street he went into a barber's and had his beard shaved off, but kept his moustache and had it waxed into points that turned up slightly. A quarter of a mile farther on, he purchased in a second-hand clothes shop a workman's blue blouse, a pair of trousers, a battered slouch hat and a straw basket of the kind in which carpenters carry their tools.

Walking on until he came to a back-lot, he slipped behind a fence and set about making himself less easily recognized by changing into the old clothes he had bought, and also altering the arrangement of the bandage so that it should come down almost over one eye. Having hidden his own clothes among some broken masonry, he collected a few short pieces of wood and rusty iron to bulge out his tool basket, then emerged again into the street.

While changing, he had been wondering how he could let Angela know that he wanted to see her urgently. He could not go to the house in daylight without having to face at least one of the servants and, although his workman's garb would be cover for him to send a bogus message in to her to the effect that he was the carpenter she had sent for to mend something in the pavilion, there was always the risk that whoever took the message would penetrate his disguise and, recalling the big reward that had been offered for his capture, betray him.

The problem was solved on his noticing a small Post Office. Going in, he sent Angela a *petit bleu*, which read:

Accept your invitation to lunch with pleasure will bring designs for alterations to garden-house mid-day, de Jvanets.

She, but no one else, would realize that a telegram signed with the name of the house in which they had first met must be from him, and, although the message might appear obscure at first sight, it could hardly mean anything else than that he wanted to see her in the pavilion at mid-day.

All this time he had instinctively been moving farther from the Boulevard Montparnasse, through the mean streets that lay to the south of it; and now an idea occurred to him for reaching the Parc Monceau without crossing central Paris. He was no distance from the outer Boulevards and the Ceinture Railway which ran right round the capital. By taking a westbound train from the Gare de Mont-rouge, he could reach the Gare de Courcelles in about forty-five minutes, and would then be within ten minutes' walk of his destination.

Outside the station, the placards displayed round a newspaper kiosk caught his eye and he bought three papers of varying shades of political opinion. Reading them in the train served the double purpose of hiding his face from his fellow passengers and cheering him up considerably. All three were filled with accounts of the previous day's scene in the Chamber and speculations about its future. Even

Clemenceau, in the Socialist *Aurore*, denounced André as a disgrace to any Ministry and the Masons as no better than lay Jesuits. It was clear that the General was finished and the Combes government on its last legs.

He accomplished the journey round the western outskirts of Paris without incident and, on his way down from Courcelles to the Parc Monceau, stopped to fill his straw basket further with purchases of bread, fruit, and meat from a charcuterie; but, even so, he arrived more than half-an-hour before mid-day.

On trying the door in the garden wall, he found it locked. As he had no key he could not let himself in and in daylight he dared not climb the wall. Angela would, he felt sure, have the sense to realize that and unlock the door for him. But when?

The *petit bleu* service was excellent, and they were usually delivered in an hour or less, but the trouble was that she might be out and—awful thought—perhaps out for the day. To sit on a bench in the Parc for a while presented no particular danger, but it was now two and a half hours since he had escaped from the police; so by this time the whole force would have been alerted to watch for him. If he had to hang about in the Parc for several hours it was quite on the cards that the curiosity of the patrolling gendarme at the sight of a workman idle for so long would result in his coming up and asking awkward questions.

Sitting down on a bench, he slowly munched a roll that he had stuffed with ham and tried to occupy his mind with guessing, by the different styles of goffered linen caps, black bows and frilled aprons worn by the passing nursemaids, from which provinces they came. Every now and again he cast a glance at the door to see if it had been opened a crack and twice, getting up, he strolled past it to test it with a surreptitious push, but it remained fast shut.

Mid-day chimed from a nearby church steeple, and by ten past he had been sitting there for three-quarters of an hour. Assuming now that Angela was out but might come home for lunch, he began to wonder if it would not be wisest for him to leave the Parc and not return to try the door again until half-past one. Five minutes later he decided to do so but, as he passed the door on his way to the gates of the Parc, he pushed it once more. It gave under the pressure. With infinite relief, after a swift look round to see that he was not observed, he slipped inside.

Up in the main room of the pavilion he found Angela waiting for him. She had thought it probable that, before leaving for England, he would again come by night to say good-bye to her, but he had promised to take no unnecessary risk; so his *petit bleu*, telling her to expect him at mid-day, had already caused her to fear that he was in trouble. For a moment the sight of his shaven chin, bandaged head and workman's clothes gave her hope that he had felt it safe enough to cross Paris in this new disguise, but in a few swift sentences he disillusioned her and told her how he had been cut off from his escape route.

She at once agreed to go to Van Ryn and get him to have another key cut; then he asked her if there had been any new developments in the affaire of Syveton and Clothilde.

'No,' she replied, 'and he is hoping now that for Clothilde's sake her family will decide to refrain from prosecuting.'

'Angela!' he cried in swift alarm. 'Don't tell me this means that you may put off taking any action?'

'Armand; please don't press me to do so for the moment,' she pleaded. 'I gave you my promise to get an annulment, and I won't go back on that. But if the de Vaucloses don't sue him there may be no scandal. In that case I'd be deprived of the reason I had for . . .'

'But this is intolerable! Why should you continue to sacrifice yourself in order to save such a swine, just because he has got himself into a financial mess?'

'Please; you didn't hear me out. To start with, I very much doubt if the de Vaucloses will be able to hush the matter up, even if they want to. The reason for Clothilde's leaving Henri is almost certain to leak out. I doubt, too, if Gabriel will be able to save himself from bankruptcy anyway. It is simply that I feel that I must conceal the fact that I mean to leave him for these few weeks when public knowledge of it might precipitate his downfall. And he is in worse trouble than ever now. He had a writ served on him this morning.'

'For debt?'

'No; for having assaulted General André in the Chamber yesterday.'

'And serve him right! But for him the Government would have been voted out. The fool ruined everything.'

'Only temporarily. De Villeneuve, Laveriac, the Marquis de Morés and the Vicomte de Camargue were all here last night. Gabriel excused his act to them by saying that for some weeks he had been ill and overwrought; so had lost his head. They were of the opinion, though, that it might do more good than harm. It was known then that the Government meant to prosecute him. They feel that a trial will give them an opportunity to wash much more of Combes's dirty linen than they could otherwise have done, and so ruin him beyond all hope of recovery. This morning, too, Gabriel has received scores of letters; some of abuse, it is true, but the great majority acclaiming him as a hero.'

'Then why do you count this writ as making his position still worse?'

'Well, it is he who is to be brought to trial. Others may make political capital out of it; but Combes still controls the judges, and you know how venal are the men he has appointed. In the teeth of public opinion they may still give their verdict against Gabriel and have him sent to prison. That is a further reason why I must stand by him for a little longer.'

De Quesnoy sighed. 'My love, you are a paragon among women, and to have you for my wife is more than I deserve. I will endeavour to be patient, then, until you know definitely if Syveton is fated to sink or swim.'

'Bless you, my darling!' She gave him a swift kiss and added, 'But the one thing that matters now is to get you safely out of France. Every moment is precious, and we have already talked too long. I must fly now. If Channock has left his office I'll probably find him lunching at the Scribe with Fiona and her mama. It is bound to take several hours to get the key cut; so I doubt if I shall receive it till this evening. As soon as it reaches me I will bring it over to you. Or, better still, as you must stay here until it is dark anyhow, we will have supper here together. Clothilde left a cupboard full of tinned things in the kitchen, and instead of bread we can make do with biscuits.'

When she had gone de Quesnoy unbandaged his head and bathed it. During the morning his headache had worn off, and although there was a large bump where he had banged himself, the skin was only slightly broken; so he did not replace the bandage. He felt very tired, though, so, after eating some more of the picnic lunch with which he had provided himself, he lay down on the bed and went to sleep.

He woke late in the afternoon and whiled away the time as best he could by thumbing over some magazines that Clothilde had left in one of the cupboards. But his mind was still far from at ease. Even given the key to the coach-house, the journey he meant to make was no light undertaking. A variety of unforeseen and highly unpleasant things might occur to prevent his stepping out of his crate a free man in England. And, greatly as he admired Angela's loyalty to her husband, that she should yet again postpone taking steps to put an end to her marriage was extremely depressing. They had suffered so many disappointments that it almost seemed as if there was a hoodoo on their love, and that Fate had decreed that they should never be permitted to enjoy it to the full by living together in peace and happiness.

Time drifted on. By eight o'clock he was hoping that at any moment she would appear. He laid the table for supper, opened tins of sardines, tongue and pineapple and chose the wine from the small selection in the cellarette; but it was nearly nine before she joined him.

The moment she was through the door she set his mind at rest about the key, and that Van Ryn would have the crate collected in the morning. He had said that he would not see the job done himself or have Harry Plimsol do so, in case they were being watched by the police, but would have it collected and despatched under the supervision of a thoroughly reliable member of his staff at the bank, and that to get it on the mid-day train might mean a van coming for it as early as eight o'clock; so de Quesnoy should be in it and lying silent in his bunk well before that hour.

As she fished the precious new key out of her bag and gave it to him, she went on to explain why she was so late. The key had not arrived until half-past seven, and just as she had been about to leave the house Laveriac had emerged from Syveton's study. It was evident that they had had a serious quarrel, as the General was still uttering threats before he stamped out through the hall. Instead of seeing him out, Syveton had remained leaning up against the doorway to his study, looking as if at any moment he was about to collapse.

Naturally she had taken him by the arm and led him back to his chair; but when she had asked him what they had quarrelled about he would only say that the General was being very hard on him.

'Perhaps,' suggested de Quesnoy, 'Laveriac has learned about the Clothilde business, and came to tell him that the Committee cannot possibly continue to associate with a moral delinquent; so he must resign from it.'

'No, it wasn't that. I heard enough to gather that it was something

353

to do with money. All the same, there has been a new development in the de Vauclose affaire. I got Gabriel a drink and spent about twenty minutes trying to put a little heart into him; then I told him that I must leave him because I was going out. I didn't tell him, though, that you were here, and that it was to you that I was going. I had hardly said that I must go, otherwise I would be late for my appointment, when Octave came in and announced that two gentlemen had called to see him.'

Angela sighed. 'Poor wretch, I think he must have known what was coming when he saw the names of his visitors on their cards as Octave held the salver out to him. He went as white as a sheet, remained silent for a moment, then asked me if I would wait in the conservatory while he saw them; and told Octave to show them in. I couldn't possibly refuse; so I went through the glass door, shut it behind me and sat down to wait out of sight round the corner. Another twenty minutes or so went by, then I felt that I really could not delay coming out to you any longer; so I tiptoed back and peeped round the corner of the plant stand. The room was empty except for Gabriel, and he was sitting at his desk with his head buried in his hands. When I went in he roused up and told me what had happened. Clothilde's father returned to Paris this morning and has challenged him to a duel; the two visitors were M. de Vauclose's seconds.'

De Quesnoy gave a grim smile. 'It ill becomes one to rejoice over another man's misfortune; but I can hardly say that I am sorry. This means the fact that he seduced Clothilde must come out, and the resulting scandal will give you the warrant you require to announce your intention of leaving him.'

'I doubt if things will work out that way.' Angela shook her head dubiously. 'Naturally Monsieur de Vauclose would wish both to prevent his daughter's name from being dragged through the mire and to punish Gabriel. I think that is what lies behind this challenge. He hopes to put a bullet into him instead of getting damages in a law court. Anyhow, so far Clothilde's name has been kept out of it. Her father has demanded satisfaction of Gabriel on the pretext that by his behaviour in the Chamber yesterday he disgraced the Monarchist party.'

'And so he did,' muttered the Count. 'What happened next?'

'Gabriel was terribly upset. He has never fought a duel in his life; so it is hardly surprising that he should not regard the prospect with the same detachment as would a man like yourself. I tried to persuade him to go up to bed and have a tray with a light supper brought up to him; then to take a strong sedative so that he could get some sleep. But he wouldn't. He insisted that he must spend several hours working on figures. It seems that General Laveriac's visit has upset all his calculations and that if he is to save himself he must find some new way out of his difficulties.'

As Angela finished speaking she produced a letter from her bag, and added, 'Mr. Van Ryn gave me this for you. It had just come in from Spain, and is addressed in François' writing. Do tell me what news there is of him.'

Taking de Vendôme's letter de Quesnoy opened it and read it out to her. It said:

'*My dear Count,*

It gives me especial pleasure to write to you on this occasion, as it is to tell you that yesterday I had the happiness of being able to repay a small part of the great debt I owe you.

Recently a stall in the Most Noble Order of the Golden Fleece has fallen vacant, and His Majesty the King, my cousin, signified to me his pleasure that I should occupy it. He has, of course, long since heard the story of the heroic way in which you sacrificed yourself for me, and saved me from an ordeal so terrible that I might well not have survived it. I recalled that to His Majesty's mind and humbly requested him to bestow the chain of this most illustrious Knighthood upon you instead of on myself.

At first he was reluctant to do so, on the grounds that in modern times the gift of the Fleece has been reserved almost exclusively for persons of royal blood. I pointed out that in giving it to you he would break no precedent, as your ancestor, the Marshal Duke de Richleau, had been a Knight of the Order; that the Order was founded for the purpose of rewarding chivalrous deeds, that no deed could have been more chivalrous than yours and that it had been performed in the service of a member of his own family.

His Majesty was graciously pleased to accept my submissions. Yesterday he commanded me to inform you that when you can come to Spain a Chapter of the Order will be convened to instal you; and I shall then ask you to accept a Chain and Fleece that I have instructed my jewellers to make for you.

355

Coming now to a more personal note, King Alfonso, whom you will find the most charming of men, has asked me to say that when you come to Spain he greatly looks forward to counting you among his friends, and we both hope that a visit from you will not be long delayed.

Here, we are all thrilled by the news from France. How I wish that I had been able to witness the scene in the Chamber when de Villeneuve denounced that villain André. In the despatch in which our Ambassador describes it, he adds that he is fully convinced that after that terrible indictment the Combes government cannot survive for long. What a triumph its fall will be for good over evil. And for the glorious Army of France; since one cannot doubt that those most promising officers who have been retired or had their promotion stopped, on account of their religious convictions, will shortly be reinstated, or given important appointments.[1]

I do not know where this letter will find you; but if, as you informed me in your last letter, you have carried out your intention of returning in secret to Paris, please convey my very kindest thoughts to Angela Syveton.

I pray daily that God will bless you and have you in His holy keeping.

> *With true affection,*
> *Always your devoted friend,*
> *François de Vendôme.'*

As de Quesnoy ceased reading Angela exclaimed, 'The Golden Fleece! Why, to receive that, or the Garter, is the greatest honour in the whole world. Oh, how glad I am for you!' And with shining eyes she threw her arms round his neck.

When he had returned her kiss, he murmured, 'I am quite overwhelmed; and so will be my Father. I fear that I am a far from satisfactory son; but this great honour that has been done me will make amends to him for many of my shortcomings. I think, too, that by behaving with such generosity François has proved himself a true Prince. Although, really, he owes his escape nearly as much to you as to myself.'

---

[1] *Historical Note.*—The Combes government did fall, ten weeks later, on January 24th, 1905, and among the officers reinstated were Lyautey, Fayolle, Joffre, Petain and Foche—the only five Generals who were made Marshals of France in the 1914–18 war. D.W.

'Surely I told you,' she laughed. 'He sent me a miniature of himself set in brilliants, and a *parure* of diamonds worth a small fortune, soon after he arrived safely in Spain. But that is ten months ago now, and since your return there have been so many other things to talk of on the few occasions we've been together.'

'That was good of him, but no more than you deserved. His letter gives me an idea, though. Why should we not go to Spain and combine my investiture with the Fleece and our stolen honeymoon?'

'How could we? For the investiture you would have to go to court under your own name.'

'Of course; and you would go there under yours too. As you played so prominent a part in François's escape, what could be more natural than that you should be invited to attend the ceremony at which I am to receive a reward for my part in it?'

'But we could not possibly outrage convention by sharing a suite at an hotel; so it would be a poor sort of honeymoon.'

'On the contrary,' he laughed. 'We'd observe the conventions by day while being shown all the sights under the aegis of royalty, and spend our nights in one another's arms.'

'Darling, you're joking, We couldn't have it both ways.'

'We could. Don't you realize that François is one of the few people we could trust with our secret, and that he would do anything for us. I should write to him in advance. Like most of the rich nobles in Madrid, he must own several *petites maisons* staffed with discreet servants. He could easily arrange for you to occupy one of them while I stayed officially with him; but spend all the time we were not being entertained, and my nights, with you.'

While they got out some tinned things for their picnic supper, and sat down to it, they gaily discussed this delightful plan. But after a while their gaiety ebbed from them owing to the intrusion of worrying thoughts about the present. Angela could no longer keep her mind free of the crisis facing the husband whom she despised yet pitied, while de Quesnoy became increasingly conscious of the incredibly harassing situation in which he must leave her, and the knowledge that the plan they had been making was indeed a "Castle in Spain"; for he had no idea how long it would be before he even saw her again.

It was towards the end of their meal that she remarked, 'Oh, telling you about Gabriel's having received a challenge from de Vauclose and

357

the letter from François made me forget to give you a message from Channock. He asked me to tell you not to worry, but he thought you ought to know that the draft that was due on Friday to repay the loan he made you has not yet reached his bank.'

De Quesnoy sat back and stared at her. His brain was working quickly, and after a moment he asked, 'Can you remember the exact words Laveriac used to Syveton this evening—when he threatened him, I mean?'

'It was to do with the *Ligue*,' Angela replied, knitting her brows. 'Yes, he snapped out something like this: "It is over a week since I asked you for an explanation. There were ample funds at the *Ligue's* disposal and this payment should have been made from them. The Committee has a right to know why you refused it. You will produce your accounts for us within forty-eight hours or we shall force you to by legal action"—or words to that effect.'

'So that is it;' the Count raised an eyebrow quizzically. 'This charming husband of yours does not stop at much, does he? Unless I am greatly mistaken he has let me in for the tidy sum of forty thousand francs.'

'How has he done that?' Angela asked with a frown.

'You will remember that I bought the *fiches* from Bidegain for that figure, but I don't think I told you where the money came from. Naturally I expected the *Ligue* to finance the deal; so I asked Syveton for the money. He said that the *Ligue* could not find such an amount in less than a week, and suggested that, as the matter was urgent, I might raise it from Van Ryn. I did, and Syveton promised that the loan should be repaid on Friday, November 1st. Today is Tuesday 5th and the money has not yet come in. Can you guess why?'

'It looks as if Gabriel has been doing something crooked.'

'Yes, and this is what must have happened. When I handed over the *fiches* to Laveriac and de Villeneuve I mentioned that I had found the money to pay for them because Syveton could not let me have it right away. Evidently if the *Ligue's* affairs had been in order he should have been able to do so; and the fact that he hadn't struck Laveriac as curious. A day or two later the General evidently tackled him about it, but did not receive a satisfactory explanation. Apparently Laveriac then reported it to the Committee, and probably one of them has heard a rumour that Syveton is in low water. Anyhow, they sent the General to Syveton tonight with an ultimatum. And, of course, the reason why he could not pay me, or explain matters to the General, is because, as Treasurer of the *Ligue de la Patrie Française*, he has been embezzling its funds.'

'You mean that he has been putting them to his own use?'

'Exactly!' The Count finished his last spoonful of pineapple and stood up. There was a dangerous gleam in his grey, yellow-flecked eyes as he said tersely, "And now I am going across to the house to make him pay up or take the consequences.'

CHAPTER XXV

"THERE IS MANY A SLIP . . ."

A S de Quesnoy rose from the table, Angela gave an anxious glance at his grim face, then she too stood up.

'Must you, Armand?' she asked a shade hesitantly. 'I know it is a terrible thing to have done; but today Gabriel has had as much as he can bear—the writ for assaulting General André, a challenge to a duel and this visit from Laveriac—which I realize now must be worrying him more than all else.'

'My dear, forty thousand francs is a lot of money. It is considerably more than my annual income. Fortunately, I am rich enough to repay Van Ryn out of my own resources, but I see no reason why I should allow this miserable swindler to rob me of it with impunity.'

'Darling, I understand how you feel; but in England we have a thing about not hitting a man when he is down, and Gabriel . . .'

'In France we are not altogether ignorant of the rules of chivalry,' he cut her short with unaccustomed sharpness, 'and it is not I who has laid him low. Were it possible, to please you, I would give him a few days' grace; but as I hope to leave Paris for good tomorrow, it is not. By confronting him now there is a chance that I might get from him bills for the amount spread over a period, which I could sell in London at a big discount. "Half a loaf," as they say, "is better than no bread;" but if I lose this opportunity I doubt if I will ever see back a single sou.'

Reluctantly, Angela accompanied him downstairs and across the garden to the house. Outside the conservatory they halted, and she said: 'God knows, I hold no brief for Gabriel, but I much prefer not to witness his humiliation; so I shall go straight up to my room. As we have said all we can for the time being about the future, I think we had better say good-bye here.'

He was loath to let her go; but he could not help feeling that, by carrying her loyalty to her husband to such quixotic lengths, she was being unfair to him, and that his resolve to confront Syveton in his present harassed state had driven a further wedge between them; so that if they met again in the pavilion later he had no hope of persuading her to give him a definite date when she would come to him.

In consequence, after a moment's thought, he agreed. They embraced and kissed, but without fervour on either side. She said that all her thoughts and prayers would be with him on his journey, and that should the Clothilde affaire become an open scandal, or Syveton be forced into bankruptcy, she would not delay a single day longer in seeing her lawyers about an annulment. Then they went into the conservatory.

She tiptoed straight through it and out by the far door. He waited until she had disappeared, then emerged from behind the pot plants and stepped up to the glass side door that gave on to Syveton's study. The Deputy was seated at his desk poring over a mass of papers.

As de Quesnoy pushed open the door and entered the room he sprang to his feet; his mouth fell open, his face went white and he cried:

'Merciful God! You!'

His instant reaction of fear and surprise caused something to click in the Count's brain. Like a curtain being drawn swiftly aside to reveal a lighted room, he saw now the complete answer to the riddle over which he had puzzled so fruitlessly that morning in the Montparnasse Cemetery.

'Yes,' he replied with sinister quietness. 'You did not expect to see me again, did you?'

'I . . . I thought you had been arrested,' Syveton stammered.

'You mean, you hoped that I had,' the Count corrected him.

'No, no! But I heard . . . I was told . . .'

'You were told nothing. Otherwise you would have known that I escaped. But you expected me to be arrested, because it was you who laid an information with the police that I was living under the name of Vasili Petrovitch at the Pension Smirnoff.'

'I deny it!' Syveton cried desperately. 'You must be mad! Why should I betray you?'

'That is easy to answer. You did so in the hope of saving yourself from being sued by me for the forty thousand francs that you have failed to pay into my account at Van Ryn's bank.'

'There has been a hitch. The investments took longer to sell than

I anticipated. You shall have the money next week. I swear to you. I swear . . .'

'I will spare you that trouble. I require your cheque for the full amount here and now.'

Syveton's hands trembled, and he gasped, 'I cannot give it to you! It would be useless. The bank would not honour it.'

De Quesnoy laughed, but his laugh was not a pleasant one. 'No, I don't suppose they would. You are at the end of your tether, aren't you? Having run through your own money, you embezzled the funds of the *Ligue*. That is why you could not produce the forty thousand francs from the Fighting Fund to pay for the *fiches*.'

'How . . . how do you know that?'

'Never mind. I take it that you have been fumbling round this evening in a last attempt to raise enough to square the accounts of the *Ligue*. But you knew that you could not put them right and also repay me; so you decided to get me out of the way. That is the truth of the matter; isn't it?' De Quesnoy's hypnotic stare held Syveton as that of a snake holds a bird, forcing confession from him.

'Yes,' he faltered, tears starting to his eyes. 'Yes; I had to have time . . . time to get straight. So that I could continue to . . .'

'Continue to enjoy life while I rotted in prison,' the Count cut in acidly.

'No, no; you wrong me there! With the fall of the Government I would have had the power to get you out.'

'After I had been convicted of conspiracy against the Republic? I don't believe it.'

'I could have arranged a pardon. I would have . . .'

'It is you who will soon need one; but you'll not get it. You are finished. Combes has not gone under yet. He'll see to it that you get a prison sentence for having assaulted André. Monsieur de Vauclose is after your blood, and good luck to him. If you fail to square the accounts of the *Ligue* they'll be after you too. It will be the end of you with the Committee, and they'll throw you out of the party for the dirty swindler that you are.'

Syveton groaned. 'It was to save myself with them that I . . . that I was tempted to sacrifice you.'

'So that if Combes falls France might have at least one crook in her new Ministry, eh?'

'You have a right to be bitter, but not unjust. I sought nothing for myself.'

'Liar!' cried de Quesnoy. 'During your whole life you have thought of no one but yourself.'

'That is not true!' the Deputy shouted back; and, his eyes glittering with fanaticism, he suddenly launched out into a tirade of self-justification.

'Today I am a ruined man; but why? Because I neglected my inheritance to work for the cause. My time, my money, everything, I gave to fight socialism and atheism. I could have remained rich and idle but I flung myself into the struggle, speaking, writing, organizing; so that right might triumph over wickedness and corruption. No one in the Party works as hard as I do, and no one understands its ramifications so well. That is why I had to save myself at whatever cost to my conscience and to you. The Party cannot afford to lose me. We are now within an ace of the victory for which I have striven for so long. But to achieve it we must still fight on. For me to allow myself to be dismissed from the councils of the Party because I lacked a miserable few thousand francs would have been the basest treachery to it. I have placed patriotism before honour.'

'So that is how you see yourself.' De Quesnoy's words came as cold and cutting as ice. 'It is then time that the mask of hypocrisy was torn from your mind, and I will tell you how others will see you in a week's time.

'Not patriotism but ambition has been the lodestar of your life. And it was a personal ambition that had in it no urge to serve the State. What you craved was to exchange the bourgeois circle into which you were born for one in which you could fool yourself that you were the equal of people of good breeding—however shallow or stupid many of those people might be. You were born both gifted and vicious. Your good brain earned you a professorial chair, the ability to lecture fluently and to write convincingly. I doubt if you have any genuine political convictions, but you were quick to realize that if you placed your talents at the service of the Monarchist party they might bring you into touch with men of title. Of your vices we will speak in a moment. When you inherited your fortune there was no question of continuing to live in modest comfort and devoting a great part of it to the Monarchist Fighting Fund. Oh no; you took a big house and used it as a ladder to climb into society. That is where your money went; in that and in ruining a whole succession of young girls. Snobbery and the moral corruption of the innocent have been your governing impulses. So morally debased are you that you could not even keep in check your lust for your son's wife.'

'I . . . I deny it,' Syveton protested feebly.

'To do so is useless. But I am not concerned with Clothilde. It is of Angela that I still have something to say. In purchasing her from her parents, which is virtually what you did, you served both your secret passions at one stroke. She was at the same time a stepping-stone to an exclusive circle that you had not then penetrated and a new victim on which to slake your sexual obsession. When I think of what she suffered at your hands I could kill you with as little compunction as I would kill a rat.'

Syveton's eyes lit with new hope, and he muttered thickly, 'You have always wanted her. Take her then! Take her away with you and provided you make no more trouble for me I'll do everything I can to help her secure the annulment she desires.'

'I would,' snapped the Count. 'But out of quixotic loyalty she will not go. I must therefore be content with that for which I came— my money. Sit down now and write a cheque payable to me for forty thousand francs.'

'I have already told you that it would not be met.'

'No matter; write it all the same. If you refuse I shall do two things. First, send an account to the Committee of how you have swindled me; secondly, send an account to the Public Prosecutor of how I found you in the pavilion with Clothilde in a negligée, and accuse you of immoral relations with her.'

'You . . . you mean to ruin me anyway.'

When de Quesnoy had come there, he had had no idea of going to such lengths; but on learning how Syveton had betrayed him to the police he had felt fully justified in taking the gloves off. With Syveton ruined Angela would, he knew, keep her promise and be in England within a week. Untroubled now by the least scruple, he nodded and said:

'Yes. That is my intention.'

'*Nom de diable!* You shall not,' the Deputy cried. 'You forget that you, too, are walking on a razor's edge.'

As he spoke he wrenched open a drawer in his desk, snatched a revolver from it, and pointed it at the Count.

'Now!' he snarled. 'We will see who is to be ruined first; you or I!' Then, side-stepping cautiously, he fumbled with his left hand until it found the handle of the china bell-pull by the chimney-piece. Grasping it, he jerked it down once, twice, thrice.

De Quesnoy was some feet away from him, and he was clearly desperate. His eyes gleamed with an unnatural light which showed the overwrought state of his mind. To have rushed him would have been to court death or, at that close range, nothing less than a serious wound. Furious with himself for not having foreseen the possibility of some such move, the Count could only remain where he was, speculating wildly on how Syveton meant to make use of his advantage.

He was not left long in doubt. It was not yet half-past ten; so Octave was still on duty. In answer to the imperative summons of the bell, the butler's quick footsteps sounded in the corridor. A moment later he entered the room. With a startled glance, he took in the situation. Syveton, still keeping his eyes on the Count, spat out the words:

'In spite of his workman's clothes, you may remember this . . . this gentleman.'

Octave stared at the ill-clad figure on the far side of the desk, then exclaimed, 'Why yes, Monsieur. It is Monsieur le Comte de Quesnoy.'

'Good evening, Octave,' said the Count quietly. 'I hope you are keeping well. But I fear your master is far from being his normal self.'

Before Octave could reply, Syveton retorted in a now carefully controlled voice, 'I am at least in my own house and in my right clothes; which is more than you are.' Then he added, to the butler, 'Monsieur le Comte has broken in here and has been threatening me. He is already wanted by the police. Get your police whistle, Octave. Go out into the street and summon a gendarme. Bring him here as quickly as you can.'

After another perturbed glance at each of them in turn, Octave muttered, 'Yes, Monsieur; yes,' and hurried away.

While Syveton had been giving his instructions he had shifted his position a little. Before, the revolver had been partly in shadow; now, full light showed up the details of the weapon clearly. De Quesnoy had been trying to catch the Deputy's eyes, with the faint hope that he might

365

be able to hold them long enough to hypnotize him swiftly. Failing in that, his glance fell for a moment on to the revolver. Instantly now, he saw that the chambers exposed to view were empty. That being so, the odds were that there was no bullet in the chamber opposite the barrel. Next second he flung himself at Syveton.

The Deputy gave a warning shout and raised the weapon a trifle; but before he could do more de Quesnoy was upon him. Grabbing Syveton's right hand with his left, he forced the revolver down and outward. It did not go off. With his clenched right fist he hit him hard beneath the chin. Syveton's head went back and he staggered. Using every ounce of his strength, the Count hit him again. His knees buckled under him, and he crashed unconscious to the floor behind his desk.

In a stride de Quesnoy reached the glass door to the conservatory. Another minute and he was out in the garden. Running hard, he crossed it ; but when he arrived at the gate in the wall he pulled up short. He had left both his carpenter's tool bag and his hat in the pavilion, expecting to return there. They were part of his disguise and without head covering of some kind he would be a much more conspicuous figure. Turning, he ran round the pavilion and upstairs. When he got there he was breathless from his exertions, so he perched on the arm of an easy chair for a moment to get his wind back.

While he sat panting there, it suddenly occurred to him that his wisest course would be to stay where he was. By now Syveton was probably coming round. At any moment Octave would return with a gendarme. It would then need only a telephone call and special patrols would be sent out. The police of the whole district would be buzzing like a swarm of bees. Now that his new disguise was known, and the streets were practically deserted, only with the greatest luck could he hope to get through unchallenged. Whereas the idea that he had had the audacity to remain within a hundred yards of the room in which he had assaulted Syveton was unlikely to occur to them. And by early morning they would have concluded that he had succeeded in getting clear away, so have relaxed their vigilance.

As he considered this new plan, he realized that it had an additional advantage. To remain confined in the crate for twelve hours at least would be strain enough. Why prolong his self-imprisonment in such close quarters by attempting to get into them tonight, when instead he could sleep between silk sheets in the airy comfort of the pavilion?

366

Coming to his feet, he quickly turned down the oil lamps that he and Angela had left burning, then drew back the curtains and began to keep an anxious watch on the house. There were lights in Syveton's study and in Angela's bedroom. For three-quarters of an hour he kept up his vigil, but neither of them went out. On the other hand, there had been no sign of police activity and no one came out from the house into the garden.

Deciding that if anyone intended to search the pavilion for him they would have done so by now, he re-drew the curtains, went into the bedroom and, having made sure that the window overlooking the Parc was properly screened, lit the lamp there. He rarely slept for more than six hours and it was only half-past eleven; so he had no fear that he would oversleep in the morning, but to make quite certain of waking early he meant to pull the curtains right back as soon as he had put out the light.

He was only half undressed when a faint sound caught his ear. Stiffening into immobility, he listened intently. Next moment he knew for certain that someone was coming up the stairs, Seizing his workman's blouse, he hastily pulled it on again. Swiftly he turned out the lamp. Tiptoeing to the window, he raised its lower sash so that he could drop down into the Parc. Footfalls now came from the living-room; but their lightness puzzled him. They could not possibly be those of several men come to make a search. Stealing back across the room, he eased the door open a crack and peered through. It was Angela.

She was bending over one of the oil lamps, which she had just lit. Beside her was a fair-sized valise that she had evidently put down, and she was wearing travelling tweeds, a flat hat and a veil that was tied beneath her chin.

Throwing the door open, he ran to her. She started back, and gasped: 'Armand! I thought that by now you were miles from here!' Before she could say more he had her in his arms.

A few moments later, she was saying, 'It was Octave. Instead of going for the police he came upstairs to me. He said that when passing through the hall he had heard Gabriel having a violent quarrel with someone; then the bell of the study rang for him. He found you there dressed as a workman, but apparently quite calm, while Gabriel seemed on the verge of madness and screamed at him to fetch the police. He could not believe that Gabriel really meant to disgrace our house by having an old friend like yourself arrested in it; so he came up to ask me what he should do.'

'Bless the old boy,' murmured de Quesnoy. 'He shall have a pension for this. What happened then?'

'We went downstairs together. You had fled, and I naturally supposed were making for your crate. Gabriel was groaning on the floor. I left Octave to bring him round and returned to my room. That he should have attempted to betray you—in fact would have done so if it had not been for Octave—filled me with horror. I regard treachery as the one crime that is beyond forgiveness. Then when I thought how for months past I had been fool enough to postpone your happiness and my own out of loyalty to him, and that just because of a quarrel about money he would have sent you to prison if he could, and so robbed me of you, I decided that it was the end.'

'Thank God for that! You couldn't have known though, that in the hope of escaping having to pay up those forty thousand francs, he had already betrayed me. It was he who laid an information with the police that I was Vasili Petrovitch. He admitted that when I charged him with it.'

Sadly she shook her head. 'Such vileness is hardly credible. Yet it makes me all the more contented in the resolution that I took. I vowed then and there that I would never spend another night under his roof. That is why I came here. I packed my jewels and toilet things and changed into travelling clothes. When I leave here tomorrow morning I am going straight to the Gare du Nord, and I mean to take the train that your crate is to be put upon to England.'

'My darling!' he cried. 'How wonderful. And you will apply for an annulment as soon as you get there?'

'Yes; I'll not lose a minute.' She smiled at him. 'Armand, please give me a drink.'

Because they had left the supper table so abruptly, a second bottle of champagne that he had opened still stood there untouched. He filled both their goblets. She drank half the contents of hers straight off, then set it down with a happy sigh and said:

'You have no idea what this decision has done for me. I must have been mad to stay with Gabriel for so long. At this moment I am experiencing what a prisoner must feel like when he has suddenly had his chains struck off.'

He smiled back at her. 'You will feel still better on the night that we arrive in Madrid. How I wish that we could set off here and now. But before I can even write to François asking him to make special arrangements for us, we have to get through this business of your establishing yourself with your parents as a model daughter.'

'I know, and I'm afraid that is going to take two or three months at least.'

'I was hoping that you might be able to get away by Christmas.'

'No; I'll have to spend Christmas in the bosom of my family. There is no way in which I could wriggle out of that.' She took another long drink of wine, then added more cheerfully. 'Still, now we really belong to one another I don't see why we should be so hard on ourselves. I mean, while I still feel that to start a hole-in-the-corner affair would be terribly unsatisfactory, and anyhow much too dangerous while we are in London, three months is an awfully long time to wait for our first real fling. That is, unless you feel that a few nights spent together before our proper honeymoon might spoil it.'

His eyes lit up. 'Of course it wouldn't! The sooner I can make you my very own the happier I'll be. But when, darling, when? How soon could you manage that?'

'How impatient you've suddenly become,' she laughed. 'But I love you for it. Can you bear to wait a fortnight. I think by then I could safely tell my parents that I was going to stay for a long week-end with some friends of mine that they have never met; and we'd spent it at some little hotel in the country.'

'My sweet! You open a vision of Heaven to me. I'll be counting the days, the hours, even the minutes.'

Finishing her wine, she stood up, untied her veil and threw her hat on a chair; then she said. 'I'll be counting minutes too, now we've agreed that we needn't wait until we get to Madrid. As that is settled then, and I'm tired, I think I'll go to bed. I'm sorry to deprive you of it; but as a soldier I expect you will manage to get quite a good sleep on the sofa.'

'Yes,' he agreed, 'I'll do well enough there.'

'Will you?' Her eyes began to dance. 'That is a poor compliment, with me lying counting the minutes until you come to me next door.'

'Angela! But . . . but you said that you were tired.'

'Tired!' she cried, throwing back her lovely head. 'You dear stupid;

I have never felt less tired in my life. I am free! Free! Free! And you've just said that the sooner you can make me your own the happier you'll be. The thought of it makes my blood sing like wine in my veins. God knows, we have waited ten years for this. But at last I am yours; now and for ever, to do what you will with.'

*   *   *   *   *

During the five hours that followed, neither of them came nearer sleep than occasionally to slip into a sweet half-consciousness in which each was still joyously aware of the presence of the other.

As the bell in the nearby church steeple chimed five, de Quesnoy raised himself on his elbow, kissed Angela into full consciousness and made love to her again; then he said, 'My sweet, it is time for us to be stirring.'

In the faint light of the lamp that they had left burning low, she smiled up at him and murmured, 'Yes, for poor you. But I can be a happy sluggard and lie abed for hours yet, and wish you with me still.'

He shook his head. 'No. There is one thing you must do; and before the servants in the house are up. You must write a note for Syveton to tell him that you have left him.'

'Why?' she pouted. 'He will know it soon enough.'

'He had no reason to suppose that you meant to last night. When he learns that you did not sleep in your room he will think that after leaving Octave to revive him you went out again and that some accident has befallen you; then he'll ring up the hospitals and the police. As he is a Deputy it is certain that the police will busy themselves in the matter. They may spot you at the Gare du Nord, and telephone him that you are about to leave by the train for England. A French husband's rights are considerable. He could instruct them to detain you and prevent you from leaving the country. Whereas if you let him know yourself that you have left him, and add that if he makes trouble for you he can expect the Public Prosecutor to be informed of his affaire with Clothilde, he will take no action.'

Reluctantly, Angela agreed to the soundness of her lover's argument; but as he made a move to get out of bed she threw an arm round his neck, pulled him back, then leaning right over him looked down into his eyes and said with sudden seriousness:

'Armand, I've known for years that lovemaking would be wonderful with you but, until this night we've just spent together, I'd never dreamed that two people could reach such heights of bliss. It has been playing with fire, though. I feel now like a tigress who has tasted blood. I know it was I who suggested an annulment and begged you to be patient until we could be married—just making do in the meantime with living together in secret for a week or two from time to time. But now two years, perhaps three, of that sort of thing would be more than I could bear. Between whiles I'd be driven crazy with longing for you.'

His voice was a little husky as he replied, 'I have feared all along that would prove the case. Anyhow, I knew it would be with me once you had given yourself to me. But what alternative is there to doing as we planned?'

'Let's go away together, just as you wanted me to before I persuaded you that it would be better to apply for an annulment. I have been thinking about it for the past hour, and I'm quite willing now to throw my shoes over the moon. After all, why should I not put your happiness and mine before that of my parents. They have had their lives, whereas we still have the best part of ours before us.'

'No, Angela; no! I can't let you do that. When I really thought about it I realized what an impossible situation it would place you in. To expose you to a constant risk of insult would be torture to me; and people like ourselves could never be happy buried away somewhere leading the lives of *petits bourgeois*.'

'Very well, then. Let's take the middle course that you suggested. We'll go to America and I'll get one of those divorces which would anyhow enable me to bear your name. My parents' feelings cannot be helped. Faced with a *fait accompli* they would probably come round after a while and accept the situation.'

He was sorely tempted to agree, but steeled himself to make another protest. 'It is not only your parents, dearest. There are quite a lot of people of our class who would refuse to receive you as my wife if they knew that your divorce was legal only in a remote American State.'

'What does that matter? It would apply only to the old and stuffy ones. Besides, we needn't live in Europe. Why shouldn't we make our home in Honolulu, or somewhere in the South Seas? Think how lovely I could make myself for you after bathing in the surf, with hibiscus in my hair and my body tanned all over to a beautiful golden brown.'

371

He had one arm about her bare shoulders, and as she lay upon him, pressing him down, her tumbled curls fell on each side of her glowing face, her eyes were wide with excitement and her mouth was a little open, showing her perfect teeth. Gazing up at her he murmured:

'You could never be more lovely than you are at this moment. But what you suggest is madness. After a while you would tire of lotus eating and become homesick for your country and friends, We had far better resign ourselves to making the best of a stolen week or two together every few months, until we can marry and face the whole world without shame or fear.'

'I won't resign myself! I couldn't now,' she cried, tears starting to her eyes. 'Armand, I beg you not to make me. Think of the long months of separation, when we'll be craving for one another night after night. As you said yourself, the next few years will be the best in our lives. We mustn't throw the greater part of them away. There's another thing. If we try to cheat our passion after this I know what will happen. Each time we meet in secret we'll want to be together more and more. We'll give way to that temptation and enter on a continuous intrigue. After a while we'll become careless and be found out. Then everything will be ruined, and we'll have suffered endless tribulation for nothing.'

For a long moment he lay silent, then he said, 'There is a lot in what you have just said. So be it then. But on one condition.'

'Name it, darling. I'll agree to anything you like so long as it allows us to live together permanently.'

'It is that you should go to England and spend a month with your parents. Put in your plea for an annulment. There is just a chance that you might still get it; although I think that very doubtful if we enter into a civil marriage after a Nevada divorce. Don't hurry things, but in due course tell your parents everything. How Gabriel mistreated you but you refrained from making a scandal by leaving him although you have been in love with me for many years; then how this affaire of Clothilde has brought things to a head and exactly what we mean to do. They may prove much more sympathetic than you give them credit for. Anyhow, it is worth trying; and if it comes off I will pay a formal call on your father before we leave England for America to become united for good.'

She nodded. 'Very well, darling. It will mean some horrid scenes, as I'm sure they will take it badly; anyway to begin with. But you are right to make me do it, because being honest with them now may make all the difference to their attitude towards me in the future.'

After a long lingering kiss they both got up, washed and dressed themselves. Then she used a sheet of the notepaper that had been left by Clothilde to write her farewell to Syveton.

When she had stuck down the envelope, she said, 'I won't be long. I will leave it on the desk in his study. He is bound to see it there as soon as he comes downstairs; and I'll come straight back.'

With a tender glance de Quesnoy watched her leave the living-room, then he set about making his final preparations for departure.

While he was making them his thoughts were in a turmoil. Less than twelve hours ago Angela was only promised to him in some nebulous future; since, she had suddenly and unexpectedly become his absolutely, and for good. Moreover, during their night together they had achieved a perfection of ecstasy rarely granted even to the most passionate lovers. So he knew that he ought to be feeling on top of the world.

But he was not. Instead his mind seethed with doubts and forebodings. The pros and cons of annulment—elopement, annulment—elopement, continued to shuttle back and forth in it at a furious tempo. He was still convinced that an annulment would bring them greater happiness in the long run, yet he knew that if Angela persisted in her new determination there was little hope of her being granted one. It was largely in the hope that reflection and the sobering influence of her parents might, perhaps, cause her again to change her mind that had led him to stipulate that she should spend a month with them. But he greatly doubted if it would. When she had said that she felt like a tigress who had tasted blood, she had put the situation in a nut-shell. And he was not slow to recognize that, as far as she was concerned, he too had become a man-eater overnight.

Strive as he would to prevent it, disturbing visions of their life together flitted through his thoughts. To preserve the conventions as long as possible he would insist on their sailing for America in separate ships; but once the divorce was through there could be no turning back. Owing to his title and the notoriety resulting from his part in the de Vendôme conspiracy, there could be no hope of keeping their civil marriage quiet. The news of it would be flashed round the world, and

373

the more scurrilous section of the Press would not scruple to inform its readers that Nevada divorces were the last resort of couples who were unable to secure legality for their unions in any accepted way. That would be noted by the entire official world, and bar them for good from every Embassy, Government reception and party at which even minor Royalties were to be present.

It would be three or four years at least before they would be able to live that down sufficiently to show their faces again in Europe. And what sort of life could they live in the meantime? They could go for a while to Honolulu or Tahiti, as Angela had suggested, and visit other outposts of civilization, such as those in the East Indies. But on every ship in which they sailed there would be some unpleasantness owing to righteous matrons showing that they regarded Angela as a "scarlet woman". And the only companionship they could hope for in the places where they stayed would be that of couples with dubious morals, adventurers, remittance men, and third-rate social climbers who would overcome any scruples for the sake of being seen with a Countess and a Count.

He was still harrowed by such thoughts when Angela returned. She had not been away for more than six minutes, but the moment she re-entered the room he saw that something had gone radically wrong. Her big brown eyes were wide with fright, the pink flush had faded from her cheeks and in her hand, now crumpled, she still held the letter.

'What's happened?' he asked in swift alarm.

'Gabriel!' The word seemed to rasp in her throat. 'He . . . he's killed himself.'

'*Mort de Dieu!* How?'

'With that long steel paper knife that he always kept on his desk. He must have held the point to his heart, then deliberately fallen on it. He had rolled over on his back and the thick bone handle was sticking up out of his chest.'

De Quesnoy gave a slight shrug. 'Neither of us is a hypocrite so we need make no pretence of grief. Anyway, he is out of all his troubles now.'

'But we are not! Oh, Armand, how I wish that you had listened to me last night, and not gone to him.'

'Why? Do you suggest that I drove him to it?'

374

'No, no; not that! He had so many troubles, and he was half out of his mind already. The thought of the duel, prison, bankruptcy, disgrace, would have continued to prey upon it. Since he has taken this way out, you may be sure that he would have done so as soon as some other crisis arose that he felt he could not surmount.'

De Quesnoy frowned. 'At least I am responsible for having administered to him the *coup de grâce*.'

'Yes; I suppose that's true. And both of us must pay a heavy penalty for it.'

'My love, you have nothing to reproach yourself with, and I—well, it weighs little on my conscience. After all, had I not gone in to him, neither of us would have come back here later, and, for one reason or another, many more months might have elapsed before you felt free for us to start a new life together.

'Armand! Armand! Where are your wits?' Her cry was one of despair. 'Do you not see that his dead body now lies between us?'

'I don't understand. Surely you don't . . . you can't mean that you'll have no more to do with me because it was my threats that caused him to take his life?'

'No, my dear; no.' She flung wide her hands and her words poured out in a torrent. 'But do you not see what will happen if I now go to England? In an hour or so someone will find his body. The police will be called in and will question all the servants. Octave, good man that he is, saved you last night by coming to me; but you cannot expect him to withhold from the police the fact that you were in the house and that you had a violent quarrel with Gabriel. My maid, Lucille, knows that too, because she was with me when Octave came up to my room. Once the police have heard their stories it is certain they will jump to the conclusion that Gabriel's death was not suicide, but murder.[1] That, having threatened him, you left the house, but returned later and killed him.'

'*Mon Dieu!*' de Quesnoy gasped. 'I believe you're right.'

[1] *Historical Note.*—It was asserted by the Monarchists that Syveton had been murdered by the Socialists in order to prevent further exposures at his trial of Prime Minister Combes's unscrupulous abuse of power. But his impending bankruptcy, his embezzlement of the funds of the *Ligue* and the scandal that was about to break on account of his immoral relations with his son's wife, formed such a strong combination of reasons for suicide that it can hardly be doubted that he took his own life.—D. W.

375

'I'm sure of it. And their least doubt would be swept aside by the fact that I have disappeared. Lucille knows that I have been in love with you for years. She is a loyal girl, but under cross-examination she may break down. Anyhow, Gabriel's death and my flight to London are bound to be connected. They are certain to assume that you killed him to get me and that I agreed to run away with you. Then your situation will be just as it was before François de Vendôme cleared you of shooting the police at Versailles. They will get a warrant of extradition. Wherever we go we shall be hunted. We would never dare to settle down anywhere from fear that one day a hand would be laid on your shoulder, and that you would be dragged back here to the guillotine.'

The Count clenched his fists and shook them. 'But this is terrible—terrible! Are we so utterly cursed that we must resign ourselves to separation for ever?'

'Oh, God forbid! But we must give up all the plans we've made if there is to be any hope at all of our making a happy life together sometime in the future.'

'That can never be, as long as I have this new charge of murder hanging over me. Since I am innocent it would be better that I should stay and face it, even if that does mean my receiving a prison sentence on account of the other business.'

'No, darling, no. Do you not see that by staying I can prevent a charge of murder ever being brought against you. If I go to bed in my room before the servants are up, no one will ever know that I spent the night here. They will come up to tell me of Gabriel's death as soon as his body is found, and I shall be on the scene when the police arrive. My presence will eliminate the principal motive for murder. No one can suggest that you killed Gabriel during your quarrel with him, because both Octave and I saw him alive after you had left the house. I shall tell the police of Gabriel's money difficulties, about his embezzling the funds of the *Ligue*, about his impending duel and about his illicit relations with Clothilde. No one else can do that before they can even form a theory about his death. But I can. And when I have done they will have no reason to suspect that it is anything but a clear case of suicide. That is why I *must* remain here.'

Breathless, she paused for a second, then, fighting back her tears, she added, 'But if I am to save you I must go at once. And so must you. If we are ever to live down the curse that seems to have been put upon our love, neither of us dare waste another moment.'

As she turned away, he caught her by the arm and cried, 'Wait! We can snatch one! My apparent danger has blinded us to the thing that concerns us above all else. Gabriel is dead, darling. Dead! Do you realize what that means? Handle the police as you suggest and we'll have nothing to fear. Within a month their inquiry will be closed and you'll be free to come to London. We have no need to talk of annulments or elopements any longer. After a decent interval we can be married with wedding bells and live happily ever after.'

This book
designed by William B. Taylor
is a production of
Heron Books, London

Printed in England by
Hazell Watson and Viney Limited
Aylesbury, Bucks